# SAN FRANCISCO NOIR 2

# SAN FRANCISCO NOIR 2

## THE CLASSICS

EDITED BY PETER MARAVELIS

AKASHIC BOOKS
NEW YORK

This collection is comprised of works of fiction. All names, characters, places, and incidents are the product of the authors' imaginations. Any resemblance to real events or persons, living or dead, is entirely coincidental.

Published by Akashic Books | ©2009 Akashic Books
Series concept by Tim McLoughlin and Johnny Temple
San Francisco map by Sohrab Habibion

ISBN: 978-1-933354-65-1
Library of Congress Control Number: 2008925933
All rights reserved | First printing

Akashic Books | PO Box 1456 | New York, NY 10009
info@akashicbooks.com | www.akashicbooks.com

Grateful acknowledgment is made for permission to reprint the stories in this anthology. "A Watcher by the Dead" by Ambrose Bierce was originally published in the *San Francisco Examiner* (December 29, 1889); "The Third Circle" by Frank Norris was originally published in the *San Francisco Wave* (August 28, 1897); "The Black Hole of San Francisco" by Mark Twain was originally published in the *Virginia City* (Nevada) *Territorial Enterprise* (December 29, 1865); "South of the Slot" by Jack London was originally published in the *Saturday Evening Post* (May 22, 1909); "The Scorched Face" by Dashiell Hammett was originally published in *Black Mask* (May 1925), licensed here from *The Big Knockover* by Dashiell Hammett, copyright © 1962, 1965, 1966 by Lillian Hellman, copyright © 1925, 1926, 1927, 1929 by Pro-Distributors Company, Inc., copyright renewed 1952, 1953, 1954, 1956 by Popular Publications, Inc., assigned to Lillian Hellman as successor to Dashiell Hammett, used by permission of Random House, Inc.; "The Collector Comes After Payday" by Fletcher Flora was originally published in *Manhunt* (August 1953), © 1953 by Fletcher Flora; "Souls Burning" by Bill Pronzini was originally published in *Dark Crimes* (New York: Carroll & Graf, 1991), © 1991 by Bill Pronzini; "The Second Coming" by Joe Gores was originally published in *Adam* (August 1966), © 1966 by Joe Gores; "Knives in the Dark" by Don Herron was originally published in *Measures of Poison* (Tucson, Arizona: Dennis McMillan Publications, 2002), © 2002 by Don Herron; "Christ Walked down Market Street" was originally published in *Callaloo* (Fall 2005), licensed here from *Mozart and Leadbelly: Stories and Essays* by Ernest J. Gaines, edited by Marcia Gaudet & Reggie Young, copyright © 2005 by Ernest J. Gaines, used by permission of Alfred A. Knopf, a division of Random House, Inc.; "Invisible Time" by Janet Dawson was originally published in *Once Upon a Crime: Fairy Tales for Mystery Lovers* (New York: Berkley Prime Crime, 1998), © 1998 by Janet Dawson; "The King Butcher of Bristol Bay" by Oscar Peñaranda was originally published in *Seasons by the Bay* (San Francisco: T'Boli Publishing, 2004), © 2004 by Oscar Peñaranda; "Deceptions" by Marcia Muller was originally published in *A Matter of Crime* (New York: Harcourt Brace Jovanovich, 1987), © 1987 by Marcia Muller; "Street Court" (excerpt) by Seth Morgan was originally published in *Homeboy* (New York: Random House, 1990), © 1990 by Seth Morgan; "The Numbers Game" by Craig Clevenger is printed by permission of Craig Clevenger; "The Woman Who Laughed" by William T. Vollman was originally published in *The Rainbow Stories* (New York: Atheneum, 1989), © 1989 by William T. Vollman; "Ash" by John Shirley was originally published in *Dead End: City Limits* (New York: St. Martin's Press, 1991), © 1991 by John Shirley.

## Also in the Akashic Noir Series:

*Baltimore Noir*, edited by Laura Lippman
*Bronx Noir*, edited by S.J. Rozan
*Brooklyn Noir*, edited by Tim McLoughlin
*Brooklyn Noir 2: The Classics*, edited by Tim McLoughlin
*Brooklyn Noir 3: Nothing but the Truth*
edited by Tim McLoughlin & Thomas Adcock
*Chicago Noir*, edited by Neal Pollack
*D.C. Noir*, edited by George Pelecanos
*D.C. Noir 2: The Classics*, edited by George Pelecanos
*Detroit Noir*, edited by E.J. Olsen & John C. Hocking
*Dublin Noir* (Ireland), edited by Ken Bruen
*Havana Noir* (Cuba), edited by Achy Obejas
*Las Vegas Noir*, edited by Jarret Keene & Todd James Pierce
*London Noir* (England), edited by Cathi Unsworth
*Los Angeles Noir*, edited by Denise Hamilton
*Manhattan Noir*, edited by Lawrence Block
*Manhattan Noir 2: The Classics*, edited by Lawrence Block
*Miami Noir*, edited by Les Standiford
*New Orleans Noir*, edited by Julie Smith
*Queens Noir*, edited by Robert Knightly
*San Francisco Noir*, edited by Peter Maravelis
*Toronto Noir*, edited by Janine Armin & Nathaniel G. Moore
*Trinidad Noir*, Lisa Allen-Agostini & Jeanne Mason
*Twin Cities Noir*, edited by Julie Schaper & Steven Horwitz
*Wall Street Noir*, edited by Peter Spiegelman

## Forthcoming:

*Barcelona Noir* (Spain), edited by Adriana Lopez & Carmen Ospina
*Delhi Noir* (India), edited by Hirsh Sawhney
*Istanbul Noir* (Turkey), edited by Mustafa Ziyalan & Amy Spangler
*Lagos Noir* (Nigeria), edited by Chris Abani
*Lone Star Noir*, edited by Bobby Byrd & John Byrd
*Mexico City Noir* (Mexico), edited by Paco I. Taibo II
*Moscow Noir* (Russia), edited by Natalia Smirnova & Julia Goumen
*Paris Noir* (France), edited by Aurélien Masson
*Phoenix Noir*, edited by Patrick Millikin
*Portland Noir*, edited by Kevin Sampsell
*Richmond Noir*, edited by Andrew Blossom,
Brian Castleberry & Tom De Haven
*Rome Noir* (Italy), edited by Chiara Stangalino & Maxim Jakubowski
*Seattle Noir*, edited by Curt Colbert

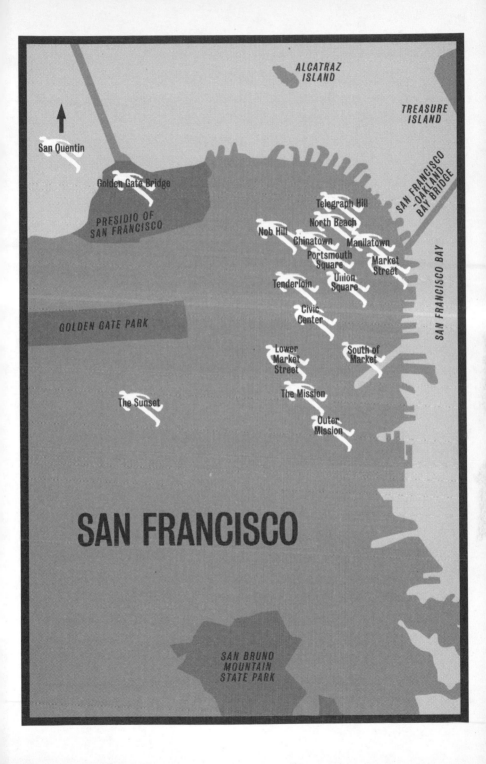

## ACKNOWLEDGMENTS

The editor extends a warm thanks to the following for their advice and support: Robert Mailer Anderson, Willis Barnstone, Karl Marx Bauer, Amy Beasom at Elsewhere Books, Andy Bellows, Chiam Bertman, Steven Black, Mary Bonds, Donna Joy Brodman, Carl at the Ha Ra, David Corbett, Elizabeth Gand, Geoffrey Green, Elaine Katzenberger, Ed Kaufman and the gang at "M" is for Mystery, Kevin Killian, Diane Kudisch at the SF Mystery Bookstore, Johanna Ingalls, John Law, Stacey Lewis, Julie Lindow, Mr. Lucky, Eddie Muller, Jim Nisbet, Ingrid Nystrom, Aaron Petrovich, Peter Plate, Richard Poccia, Erika Schmidt, Laura Sheppard, Mark Andre Singer, Faye Snowden, Rebecca Solnit, Domenic Stansberry, Gent Sturgeon, Lisa Sutcliffe, Johnny Temple, Paul Yamazaki, Frederick Young, and as always, Chris and Alex.

*Careful now. We're dealing here with a myth. This city is a point upon a map of fog; Lemuria in a city unkown. Like us, it doesn't quite exist.*

—Ambrose Bierce

# TABLE OF CONTENTS

15      *Introduction*

## PART I: BARBAROUS COAST

23      **AMBROSE BIERCE**                    North Beach
        *A Watcher By the Dead*                      1889

37      **FRANK NORRIS**                        Chinatown
        *The Third Circle*                           1897

47      **MARK TWAIN**                 Portsmouth Square
        *The Black Hole of San Francisco*            1865

50      **JACK LONDON**                   South of Market
        *South of the Slot*                          1909

## PART II: SHADOWS IN THE FOG

73      **DASHIELL HAMMETT**              Telegraph Hill
        *The Scorched Face*                          1925

120     **FLETCHER FLORA**          Lower Market Street
        *The Collector Comes After Payday*           1953

142     **BILL PRONZINI**                  Civic Center
        *Souls Burning*                              1991

152     **JOE GORES**                      San Quentin
        *The Second Coming*                          1966

165     **DON HERRON**                        Nob Hill
        *Knives in the Dark*                         2002

## PART III: ISLE OF BROKEN DREAMS

189    **ERNEST J. GAINES**    Market Street
*Christ Walked Down Market Street*    2005

200    **MARCIA MULLER**    Golden Gate Bridge
*Deceptions*    1987

227    **OSCAR PEÑARANDA**    Manilatown
*The King Butcher of Bristol Bay*    2004

247    **JANET DAWSON**    Union Square
*Invisible Time*    1998

## PART IV: DESOLATION ANGELS

271    **SETH MORGAN**    Outer Mission
*Street Court*    1990

289    **CRAIG CLEVENGER**    The Sunset
*The Numbers Game*    2009

307    **WILLIAM T. VOLLMANN**    Tenderloin
*The Woman Who Laughed*    1989

312    **JOHN SHIRLEY**    The Mission
*Ash*    1991

332    **About the Contributors**

# INTRODUCTION
CHASING SHADOWS

S an Francisco is a town made for noir. Long before
Hammett's muse seduced him with fog and mist to pen
*The Maltese Falcon*, European explorers and Christian
missionaries had already laid the groundwork for the genre.
Just ask the Ohlone indigenous peoples. The city's history is a
shadowy one. It is founded upon the spilling of blood.

From its origins as a frontier boomtown to its ascent as an
imperial financial giant, the city of Saint Francis has served as
an inviting home to all manner of transgression and villainy.
Drawn to the romantic landscape by the lure of possibility,
millions have flocked here to cast their stakes in the hope for
prosperity, pleasure, and a personal freedom seldom dreamed
of elsewhere. Following the imperatives of manifest destiny,
the city's pioneers engaged in fraud, larceny, kidnapping, and
murder. The prospect of gold led many to their demise while
establishing a terrain ruled by the human passions. Frank Norris so beautifully captured this in his classic novel *McTeague*,
later transformed into the epic film *Greed*, by legendary director Erich von Stroheim. It is a classic tale of dreams gone awry.
The avaricious appetites of the story's characters lead them
into a spiral of destruction where the possibility of redemption
is completely vanquished. By the tale's end, our antiheroes
are left with only two possible options: jail or the grave. What
could better illustrate a noir sensibility?

With the release four years ago of the first volume of *San
Francisco Noir*, we brought together a team of seasoned writ-

ers to compose original works that gave the reader a sinister sense of the city. The success of that volume was encouraging and we have returned with a new task at hand: to present a collection of classic reprints, some hitherto buried by the passage of time, which depict a town riddled by inequity from its very beginnings.

While tracing San Francisco's extensive noir canon, one essentially creates a bridge between past and present. The literary meets the historic in a lyrical weaving of narratives. Sociopolitical landscapes intersect with personal and collective histories, bringing to light forgotten fragments of the past. Noir serves as an oracle, a looking glass with which we reconnect with the vast continuum of events that have shaped the city's topography and the character of its citizens.

Noir is the language of politics without ideology.

The flowering of tragedy has taken many forms over the course of a century. Let us follow a timeline to better observe the recurring themes and significant patterns that emerge. Issues concerning race, class politics, identity, human rights, and the effects of industrialization correspond to the ebb and flow of San Francisco's history. Writers have explored the infernal underbelly of city since the California Gold Rush. Samuel Adams Drake, in his novel *The Young Vigilantes*, painted a picture of the harsh conditions of Barbary Coast living during the 1800s. In the shadow of the Civil War, shanghaiing flourished in the city and brought into existence an underworld culture of "crimps," "boatmen," and "vigilantes." This traffic in human flesh was to set the stage for modern noir fiction. Mark Twain, meanwhile, offered a satirical yet hellish portrait of the San Francisco criminal justice system in his short piece included here titled "The Black Hole of San Francisco." The birth of "noir journalism" was born, paving the way for future classics such as Norman Mailer's *The Executioner's Song*. It is interesting to note the use of Twain's language in this piece. As strongly anti-imperialist and progressively minded as he was, he too was touched by the way racism was embedded within the vernacular. A prison house of language made it possible to deny agency to persons of color and hence view them as something less than human. This problem is reflected in a few of the other stories in our collection as well. Even critical thinkers of the time could succumb to the prevailing prejudices.

It is significant to note that the post–Civil War era noir writers share similar threads of thinking in regards to the human condition. A dialectic between free will and determinism roams throughout their narrative structures. The persistent question arises: Do humans have any say in their own fate? The great satirist and storyteller Ambrose Bierce was a master at cultivating moody atmospherics that threatened to overtake his protagonists. In his short story "Beyond the Wall," he describes a desolate, foggy, and mysterious geography bordering on the supernatural. A man in a carriage struggles against the elements to reach his destination, only to realize upon arrival that the ailing friend he has come to visit has gone mad. In the Bierce story we've chosen for this volume, "A Watcher by the Dead," he experiments with claustrophobia, pitting human endurance against the morbidity of an enclosed space. Protagonists are seen gambling against the sanity of a fellow human. Bierce's macabre sensibility reveals a psychopathology rooted as much in naturalism as in the supernatural.

As noir entered the twentieth century, the engines of industrialism provided the backdrop for the themes of identity crisis and class division. Jack London's "South of the Slot" shines brightly as it prognosticates noir's interest in doppelgängers, split personalities, and the rough and tumble of the streets. First published in the *Saturday Evening Post* in 1909 and reprinted here, it also uncannily foreshadowed the General Strike of 1934, where suppressed class tensions led to battles in the streets of San Francisco between workers and the state apparatus. By the time Dashiell Hammett was busy producing work, noir was finding itself driven by the quickening of life. The post–world war era ushered in elements of anxiety and despair that cut deep into the fabric of culture. Works we have selected by Fletcher Flora and Joe Gores illustrate the destruction of the social contract. With the advent of the cold war, all bets placed during the New Deal were off. The militarization of the homeland led to the systematization of censorship, the beginning of the prison-industrial complex, Hollywood blacklisting, and the repression of individual liberties. Noir mirrored the damage.

By the time of the information explosion, a newer generation of writers arrived to herald the appearance of a wholly plutocratic era. Bill Prozini and Ernest J. Gaines's stories explore the ferocity with which urban living has ravaged those forced to the margins. Oscar Peñaranda's writings meditate upon the dashed hopes and dreams of immigrants living in the diaspora and how they manage to survive. His portrayal of life in San Francisco's Manilatown offers insight into a complex community that once thrived on the edge of Chinatown and North Beach. Janet Dawson looks at the fracturing of the nuclear family in her modern take on Hansel and Gretel called "Invisible Time." She asks if it is possible for innocence to exist in the face of brutality. William T. Vollmann has sought to find beauty in what most people would consider the grotesque. Prostitutes, serial killers, multiple personality types, and the marginalized populate his tales. (Through an alchemy of heart, his charcoal drawings of Tenderloin prostitutes have offered a rare view of the humanity to be found in the unlikeliest of places.) John Shirley takes an infernal ride and follows the doomed, and the newly doomed, upon their journey into the furnace of the inner city; reality warps as sanity and madness merge to form their own twisted logic. Craig Clevenger traverses the wastelands of suburbia with a razor tongue, cryptically decoding the lives of his characters with a vengeance. He has created an "algebra of noir," an urban "book of the dead," that navigates the twilight realm where lost souls, both living and dead, await their final dissolution.

We see San Francisco reflected in these tales. A city haunted by the specters of its past—a past that is quickly fleeting, leaving little trace as it disappears into oblivion. Perhaps the final vestiges of this town will someday be found in this handy little volume of pulp. Enjoy it while you can, before it, too, returns to dust.

*Peter Maravelis*
*San Francisco, CA*
*November 2008*

# PART I

*Barbarous Coast*

# A WATCHER BY THE DEAD

BY AMBROSE BIERCE

*North Beach*

(Originally published in 1889)

## I

In an upper room of an unoccupied dwelling in that part of San Francisco known as North Beach lay the body of a man, under a sheet. The hour was near nine in the evening; the room was dimly lighted by a single candle. Although the weather was warm, the two windows, contrary to the custom which gives the dead plenty of air, were closed and the blinds drawn down. The furniture of the room consisted of but three pieces—an armchair, a small reading stand supporting the candle, and a long kitchen table supporting the body of the man. All these, as also the corpse, seemed to have been recently brought in, for an observer, had there been one, would have seen that all were free from dust, whereas everything else in the room was pretty thickly coated with it, and there were cobwebs in the angles of the walls.

Under the sheet the outlines of the body could be traced, even the features, these having that unnaturally sharp definition which seems to belong to faces of the dead, but is really characteristic of those only that have been wasted by disease. From the silence of the room one would rightly have inferred that it was not in the front of the house, facing a street. It really faced nothing but a high breast of rock, the rear of the building being set into a hill.

As a neighboring church clock was striking nine with an indolence which seemed to imply such an indifference to the flight of time that one could hardly help wondering why it took the trouble to strike at all, the single door of the room was opened and a man entered, advancing toward the body. As he did so the door closed, apparently of its own volition; there was a grating, as of a key turned with difficulty, and the snap of the lock bolt as it shot into its socket. A sound of retiring footsteps in the passage outside ensued, and the man was to all appearance a prisoner. Advancing to the table, he stood a moment looking down at the body; then with a slight shrug of the shoulders walked over to one of the windows and hoisted the blind. The darkness outside was absolute, the panes were covered with dust, but by wiping this away he could see that the window was fortified with strong iron bars crossing it within a few inches of the glass and imbedded in the masonry on each side. He examined the other window. It was the same. He manifested no great curiosity in the matter, did not even so much as raise the sash. If he was a prisoner he was apparently a tractable one. Having completed his examination of the room, he seated himself in the armchair, took a book from his pocket, drew the stand with its candle alongside and began to read.

The man was young—not more than thirty—dark in complexion, smooth-shaven, with brown hair. His face was thin and high-nosed, with a broad forehead and a "firmness" of the chin and jaw which is said by those having it to denote resolution. The eyes were gray and steadfast, not moving except with definitive purpose. They were now for the greater part of the time fixed upon his book, but he occasionally withdrew them and turned them to the body on the table, not, apparently, from any dismal fascination which under such circumstances it might be supposed to exercise upon even a courageous person, nor with a conscious rebellion against the opposite influence which might dominate a timid one. He looked at it as if in his reading he had come upon something recalling him to a sense of his surroundings. Clearly this watcher by the dead was discharging his trust with intelligence and composure, as became him.

After reading for perhaps a half-hour he seemed to come to the end of a chapter and quietly laid away the book. He then rose and taking the reading stand from the floor carried it into a corner of the room near one of the windows, lifted the candle from it and returned to the empty fireplace before which he had been sitting.

A moment later he walked over to the body on the table, lifted the sheet, and turned it back from the head, exposing a mass of dark hair and a thin face cloth, beneath which the features showed with even sharper definition than before. Shading his eyes by interposing his free hand between them and the candle, he stood looking at his motionless companion with a serious and tranquil regard. Satisfied with his inspection, he pulled the sheet over the face again and returning to his chair, took some matches off the candlestick, put them in the side pocket of his sack coat, and sat down. He then lifted the candle from its socket and looked at it critically, as if calculating how long it would last. It was barely two inches long; in another hour he would be in darkness. He replaced it in the candlestick and blew it out.

## II

In a physician's office in Kearny Street three men sat about a table, drinking punch and smoking. It was late in the evening, almost midnight, indeed, and there had been no lack of punch. The gravest of the three, Dr. Helberson, was the host—it was in his rooms they sat. He was about thirty years of age; the others were even younger; all were physicians.

"The superstitious awe with which the living regard the dead," said Dr. Helberson, "is hereditary and incurable. One need no more be ashamed of it than of the fact that he inherits, for example, an incapacity for mathematics, or a tendency to lie."

The others laughed. "Oughtn't a man to be ashamed to lie?" asked the youngest of the three, who was in fact a medical student not yet graduated.

"My dear Harper, I said nothing about that. The tendency to lie is one thing; lying is another."

"But do you think," said the third man, "that this superstitious feeling, this fear of the dead, reasonless as we know it to be, is universal? I am myself not conscious of it."

"Oh, but it is 'in your system' for all that," replied Helberson; "it needs only the right conditions—what Shakespeare calls the 'confederate season'—to manifest itself in some very disagreeable way that will open your eyes. Physicians and soldiers are of course more nearly free from it than others."

"Physicians and soldiers! Why don't you add hangmen and headsmen? Let us have in all the assassin classes."

"No, my dear Mancher; the juries will not let the public executioners acquire sufficient familiarity with death to be altogether unmoved by it."

Young Harper, who had been helping himself to a fresh cigar at the sideboard, resumed his seat. "What would you consider conditions under which any man of woman born would become insupportably conscious of his share of our common weakness in this regard?" he asked, rather verbosely.

"Well, I should say that if a man were locked up all night

with a corpse—alone—in a dark room—of a vacant house—with no bed covers to pull over his head—and lived through it without going altogether mad, he might justly boast himself not of woman born, nor yet, like Macduff, a product of Caesarean section."

"I thought you never would finish piling up conditions," said Harper, "but I know a man who is neither a physician nor a soldier who will accept them all, for any stake you like to name."

"Who is he?"

"His name is Jarette—a stranger here; comes from my town in New York. I have no money to back him, but he will back himself with loads of it."

"How do you know that?"

"He would rather bet than eat. As for fear—I daresay he thinks it some cutaneous disorder, or possibly a particular kind of religious heresy."

"What does he look like?" Helberson was evidently becoming interested.

"Like Mancher, here—might be his twin brother."

"I accept the challenge," said Helberson, promptly.

"Awfully obliged to you for the compliment, I'm sure," drawled Mancher, who was growing sleepy. "Can't I get into this?"

"Not against me," Helberson said. "I don't want *your* money."

"All right," said Mancher; "I'll be the corpse."

The others laughed.

The outcome of this crazy conversation we have seen.

### III

In extinguishing his meager allowance of candle Mr. Jarette's object was to preserve it against some unforeseen need. He may have thought, too, or half thought, that the darkness would be no worse at one time than another, and if the situation became insupportable it would be better to have a means of relief, or even release. At any rate it was wise to have a little reserve of light, even if only to enable him to look at his watch.

No sooner had he blown out the candle and set it on the floor at his side than he settled himself comfortably in the armchair, leaned back and closed his eyes, hoping and expecting to sleep. In this he was disappointed; he had never in his life felt less sleepy, and in a few minutes he gave up the attempt. But what could he do? He could not go groping about in the absolute darkness at the risk of bruising himself—at the risk, too, of blundering against the table and rudely disturbing the dead. We all recognize their right to lie at rest, with immunity from all that is harsh and violent. Jarette almost succeeded in making himself believe that considerations of that kind restrained him from risking the collision and fixed him to the chair.

While thinking of this matter he fancied that he heard a faint sound in the direction of the table—what kind of sound he could hardly have explained. He did not turn his head. Why should he—in the darkness? But he listened—why should he not? And listening he grew giddy and grasped the arms of the chair for support. There was a strange ringing in his ears; his head seemed bursting; his chest was oppressed by the constriction of his clothing. He wondered why it was so, and whether these were symptoms of fear. Then, with a long and strong expiration, his chest appeared to collapse, and with the great gasp with which he refilled his exhausted lungs the vertigo left him and he knew that so intently had he listened that he had held his breath almost to suffocation. The revelation was vexatious; he arose, pushed away the chair with his foot, and strode to the center of the room. But one does not stride far in darkness; he began to grope and finding the wall followed it to an angle, turned, followed it past the two windows and there in another corner came into violent contact with the reading stand, overturning it. It made a clatter that startled him. He was annoyed. "How the devil could I have forgotten where it was?" he muttered, and groped his way along the third wall to the fireplace. "I must put things to rights," said he, feeling the floor for the candle.

Having recovered that, he lighted it and instantly turned his eyes to the table, where, naturally, nothing had undergone any change. The reading stand lay unobserved upon the floor; he had forgotten to "put it to rights." He looked all about the room, dispersing the deeper shadows by movements of the candle in his hand, and crossing over to the door tested it by turning and pulling the knob with all his strength. It did not yield and this seemed to afford him a certain satisfaction; indeed, he secured it more firmly by a bolt which he had not before observed. Returning to his chair, he looked at his watch; it was half-past nine. With a start of surprise he held the watch at his ear. It had not stopped. The candle was now visibly shorter. He again extinguished it, placing it on the floor at his side as before.

Mr. Jarette was not at his ease; he was distinctly dissatisfied with his surroundings, and with himself for being so. "What have I to fear?" he thought. "This is ridiculous and disgraceful; I will not be so great a fool." But courage does not come of saying, "I will be courageous," nor of recognizing its appropriateness to the occasion. The more Jarette condemned himself, the more reason he gave himself for condemnation;

the greater the number of variations which he played upon the simple theme of the harmlessness of the dead, the more insupportable grew the discord of his emotions. "What!" he cried aloud in the anguish of his spirit. "What! Shall I, who have not a shade of superstition in my nature—I, who have no belief in immortality—I, who know (and never more clearly than now) that the afterlife is the dream of a desire—shall I lose at once my bet, my honor, and my self-respect, perhaps my reason, because certain savage ancestors dwelling in caves and burrows conceived the monstrous notion that the dead walk by night—that—" Distinctly, unmistakably, Mr. Jarette heard behind him a light, soft sound of footfalls, deliberate, regular, successively nearer!

## IV

Just before daybreak the next morning Dr. Helberson and his young friend Harper were driving slowly through the streets of North Beach in the doctor's coupé.

"Have you still the confidence of youth in the courage or stolidity of your friend?" said the elder man. "Do you believe that I have lost this wager?"

"I *know* you have," replied the other, with enfeebling emphasis.

"Well, upon my soul, I hope so."

It was spoken earnestly, almost solemnly. There was a silence for a few moments.

"Harper," the doctor resumed, looking very serious in the shifting half-lights that entered the carriage as they passed the street lamps, "I don't feel altogether comfortable about this business. If your friend had not irritated me by the contemptuous manner in which he treated my doubt of his endurance—purely physical quality—and by the cool incivility of his suggestion that the corpse be that of a physician, I would not have gone on with it. If anything should happen we are ruined, as I fear we deserve to be."

"What can happen? Even if the matter should be taking a serious turn, of which I am not at all afraid, Mancher has only to 'resurrect' himself and explain matters. With a genuine 'subject' from the dissecting room, or one of your late patients, it might be different."

Dr. Mancher, then, had been as good as his promise; he was the "corpse."

Dr. Helberson was silent for a long time, as the carriage, at a snail's pace, crept along the same street it had traveled two or three times already. Presently he spoke: "Well, let us hope that Mancher, if he has had to rise from the dead, has been discreet about it. A mistake in that might make matters worse instead of better."

"Yes," said Harper. "Jarette would kill him. But, Doctor"—looking at his watch as the carriage passed a gas lamp—"it is nearly four o'clock at last."

A moment later the two had quitted the vehicle and were walking briskly toward the long-unoccupied house belonging to the doctor in which they had immured Mr. Jarette in accordance with the terms of the mad wager. As they neared it they met a man running. "Can you tell me," he cried, suddenly checking his speed, "where I can find a doctor?"

"What's the matter?" Helberson asked, noncommittal.

"Go and see for yourself," said the man, resuming his running.

They hastened on. Arrived at the house, they saw several persons entering in haste and excitement. In some of the dwellings nearby and across the way the chamber windows were thrown up, showing a protrusion of heads. All heads were asking questions, none heeding the questions of the others. A few of the windows with closed blinds were illuminated; the inmates of those rooms were dressing to come down. Exactly opposite the door of the house that they sought a street lamp threw a yellow, insufficient light upon the scene, seeming to say that it could disclose a good deal more if it wished. Harper paused at the door and laid a hand upon his companion's arm. "It is all up with us, Doctor," he said in extreme agitation, which contrasted strangely with his free-and-easy words: "The game has gone against us all. Let's not go in there; I'm for lying low."

"I'm a physician," said Dr. Helberson, calmly; "there may be need of one."

They mounted the doorsteps and were about to enter. The door was open; the street lamp opposite lighted the passage into which it opened. It was full of men. Some had ascended the stairs at the farther end, and, denied admittance above, waited for better fortune. All were talking, none listening. Suddenly, on the upper landing there was a great commotion; a man had sprung out of a door and was breaking away from those endeavoring to detain him. Down through the mass of affrighted idlers he came, pushing them aside, flattening them against the wall on one side, or compelling them to cling by the rail on the other, clutching them by the throat, striking them savagely, thrusting them back down the stairs and walking over the fallen. His clothing was in disorder, he was without a hat. His eyes, wild and restless, had in them something more terrifying than his apparently superhuman strength. His face, smooth-shaven, was bloodless, his hair frost-white.

As the crowd at the foot of the stairs, having more freedom, fell away to let him pass, Harper sprang forward. "Jarette! Jarette!" he cried.

Dr. Helberson seized Harper by the collar and dragged him back. The man looked into their faces without seeming to see them and sprang through the door, down the steps, into the street, and away. A stout policeman, who had had inferior success in conquering his way down the stairway, followed a moment later and started in pursuit, all the heads in the windows—those of women and children now—screaming in guidance.

The stairway being now partly cleared, most of the crowd having rushed down to the street to observe the flight and pursuit, Dr. Helberson mounted to the landing, followed by Harper. At a door in the upper passage an officer denied them admittance. "We are physicians," said the doctor, and they passed in. The room was full of men, dimly seen, crowded about a table. The newcomers edged their way forward and looked over the shoulders of those in the front rank. Upon the table, the lower limbs covered with a sheet, lay the body of a man, brilliantly iluminated by the beam of a bull's-eye lantern held by a policeman standing at the feet. The others, excepting those near the head—the officer himself—all were in darkness. The face of the body showed yellow, repulsive, horrible! The eyes were partly open and upturned and the jaw fallen; traces of froth defiled the lips, the chin, the cheeks. A tall man, evidently a doctor, bent over the body with his hand thrust under the shirt front. He withdrew it and placed two fingers in the open mouth. "This man has been about six hours dead," said he. "It is a case for the coroner."

He drew a card from his pocket, handed it to the officer, and made his way toward the door.

"Clear the room—out, all!" said the officer, sharply, and the body disappeared as if it had been snatched away, as shifting the lantern he flashed its beam of light here and there against the faces of the crowd. The effect was amazing! The men, blinded, confused, almost terrified, made a tumultuous rush for the door, pushing, crowding, and tumbling over one another as they fled, like the hosts of Night before the shafts of Apollo. Upon the struggling, trampling mass the officer poured his light without pity and without cessation. Caught in the current, Helberson and Harper were swept out of the room and cascaded down the stairs into the street.

"Good God, Doctor! Did I not tell you that Jarette would kill him?" said Harper, as soon as they were clear of the crowd.

"I believe you did," replied the other, without apparent emotion.

They walked on in silence, block after block. Against the graying east the dwellings of the hill tribes showed in silhouette. The familiar milk wagon was already astir in the streets; the baker's man would soon come upon the scene; the newspaper carrier was abroad in the land.

"It strikes me, youngster," said Helberson, "that you and I have been having too much of the morning air lately. It is unwholesome; we need a change. What do you say to a tour in Europe?"

"When?"

"I'm not particular. I should suppose that four o'clock this afternoon would be early enough."

"I'll meet you at the boat," said Harper.

## V

Seven years afterward these two men sat upon a bench in Madison Square, New York, in familiar conversation. Another man, who had been observing them for some time, himself unobserved, approached and, courteously lifting his hat from locks as white as frost, said: "I beg your pardon, gentlemen, but when you have killed a man by coming to life, it is best to change clothes with him, and at the first opportunity make a break for liberty."

Helberson and Harper exchanged significant glances. They were obviously amused. The former then looked the stranger kindly in the eye and replied:

"That has always been my plan. I entirely agree with you as to its advant—"

He stopped suddenly, rose, and went white. He stared at the man, open-mouthed; he trembled visibly.

"Ah!" said the stranger. "I see that you are indisposed, Doctor. If you cannot treat yourself, Dr. Harper can do something for you, I am sure."

"Who the devil are you?" said Harper, bluntly.

The stranger came nearer and, bending toward them, said in a whisper: "I call myself Jarette sometimes, but I don't mind telling you, for old friendship, that I am Dr. William Mancher."

The revelation brought Harper to his feet. "Mancher!" he cried; and Helberson added: "It is true, by God!"

"Yes," said the stranger, smiling vaguely, "it is true enough, no doubt."

He hesitated and seemed to be trying to recall something, then began humming a popular air. He had apparently forgotten their presence.

"Look here, Mancher," said the elder of the two, "tell us just what occurred that night—to Jarette, you know."

"Oh yes, about Jarette," said the other. "It's odd I should have neglected to tell you—I tell it so often. You see, I knew, by overhearing him talking to himself, that he was pretty badly frightened. So I couldn't resist the temptation to come to life and have a bit of fun out of him—I couldn't really. That was all right, though certainly I did not think he would take it so seriously; I did not, truly. And afterward—well, it was a tough job changing places with him, and then—damn you! You didn't let me out!"

Nothing could exceed the ferocity with which these last words were delivered. Both men stepped back in alarm.

"We? Why—why," Helberson stammered, losing his self-possession utterly, "we had nothing to do with it."

"Didn't I say you were Drs. Hell-born and Sharper?" inquired the man, laughing.

"My name is Helberson, yes; and this gentleman is Mr. Harper," replied the former, reassured by the laugh. "But we are not physicians now; we are—well, hang it, old man, we are gamblers."

And that was the truth.

"A very good profession—very good, indeed; and, by the way, I hope Sharper here paid over Jarette's money like an honest stakeholder. A very good and honorable profession," he repeated, thoughtfully, moving carelessly away; "but I stick to the old one. I am High Supreme Medical Officer of the Bloomingdale Asylum; it is my duty to cure the superintendent."

# THE THIRD CIRCLE

BY FRANK NORRIS

*Chinatown*

(Originally published in 1897)

There are more things in San Francisco's Chinatown than are dreamed of in Heaven and earth. In reality there are three parts of Chinatown—the part the guides show you, the part the guides don't show you, and the part that no one ever hears of. It is with the latter part that this story has to do. There are a good many stories that might be written about this third circle of Chinatown, but believe me, they never will be written—at any rate not until the "town" has been, as it were, drained off from the city, as one might drain a noisome swamp, and we shall be able to see the strange, dreadful life that wallows down there in the lowest ooze of the place—wallows and grovels there in the mud and in the dark. If you don't think this is true, ask some of the Chinese detectives (the regular squad are not to be relied on), ask them to tell you the story of the Lee On Ting affair, or ask them what was done to old Wong Sam, who thought he could break up the trade in slave girls, or why Mr. Clarence Lowney (he was a clergyman from Minnesota who believed in direct methods) is now a "dangerous" inmate of the State Asylum—ask them to tell you why Matsokura, the Japanese dentist, went back to his home lacking a face—ask them to tell you why the murderers of Little Pete will never be found, and ask them to tell you about the little slave girl,

Sing Yee, or—no, on the second thought, don't ask for that story.

The tale I am to tell you now began some twenty years ago in a See Yup restaurant on Waverly Place—long since torn down—where it will end I do not know. I think it is still going on. It began when young Hillegas and Miss Ten Eyck (they were from the East, and engaged to be married) found their way into the restaurant of the Seventy Moons, late in the evening of a day in March. (It was the year after the downfall of Kearney and the discomfiture of the sandlotters.)

"What a dear, quaint, curious old place!" exclaimed Miss Ten Eyck.

She sat down on an ebony stool with its marble seat, and let her gloved hands fall into her lap, looking about her at the huge hanging lanterns, the gilded carven screens, the lacquer work, the inlay work, the colored glass, the dwarf oak trees growing in satsuma pots, the marquetry, the painted matting, the incense jars of brass, high as a man's head, and all the grotesque gimcrackery of the Orient. The restaurant was deserted at that hour. Young Hillegas pulled up a stool opposite her and leaned his elbows on the table, pushing back his hat and fumbling for a cigarette.

"Might just as well be in China itself," he commented.

"Might?" she retorted; "we are in China, Tom—a little bit of China dug out and transplanted here. Fancy all America and the Nineteenth Century just around the corner! Look! You can even see the Palace Hotel from the window. See out yonder, over the roof of that temple—the Ming Yen, isn't it?— and I can actually make out Aunt Hattie's rooms."

"I say, Harry (Miss Ten Eyck's first name was Harriett), let's have some tea."

"Tom, you're a genius! Won't it be fun! Of course we must

have some tea. What a lark! And you can smoke if you want to."

"This is the way one ought to see places," said Hillegas, as he lit a cigarette; "just nose around by yourself and discover things. Now, the guides never brought us here."

"No, they never did. I wonder why. Why, we just found it out by ourselves. It's ours, isn't it, Tom, dear, by right of discovery?"

At that moment Hillegas was sure that Miss Ten Eyck was quite the most beautiful girl he ever remembered to have seen. There was a daintiness about her—a certain chic trimness in her smart tailor-made gown, and the least perceptible tilt of her crisp hat that gave her the last charm. Pretty she certainly was—the fresh, vigorous, healthful prettiness only seen in certain types of unmixed American stock. All at once Hillegas reached across the table, and, taking her hand, kissed the little crumpled round of flesh that showed where her glove buttoned.

The China boy appeared to take their order, and while waiting for their tea, dried almonds, candied fruit and watermelon rinds, the pair wandered out upon the overhanging balcony and looked down into the darkening streets.

There's that fortune-teller again," observed Hillegas presently. "See—down there on the steps of the joss house?"

"Where? Oh, yes, I see."

"Let's have him up. Shall we? We'll have him tell our fortunes while we're waiting."

Hillegas called and beckoned, and at last got the fellow up into the restaurant.

"Hoh! You're no Chinaman," said he, as the fortune-teller came into the circle of the lantern light. The other showed his brown teeth.

"Part Chinaman, part Kanaka."

"Kanaka?"

"All same Honolulu. Sabe? Mother Kanaka lady—washum clothes for sailor peoples down Kaui way," and he laughed as though it were a huge joke.

"Well, say, Jim," said Hillegas; "we want you to tell our fortunes. You sabe? Tell the lady's fortune. Who she going to marry, for instance."

"No fortune—tattoo."

"Tattoo?"

"Um. All same tattoo—three, four, seven, plenty lil birds on lady's arm. Hey? You want tattoo?"

He drew a tattooing needle from his sleeve and motioned towards Miss Ten Eyck's arm.

"Tattoo my arm? What an idea! But wouldn't it be funny, Tom? Aunt Hattie's sister came back from Honolulu with the prettiest little butterfly tattooed on her finger. I've half a mind to try. And it would be so awfully queer and original."

"Let him do it on your finger, then. You never could wear evening dress if it was on your arm."

"Of course. He can tattoo something as though it was a ring, and my marquise can hide it."

The Kanaka-Chinaman drew a tiny fantastic-looking butterfly on a bit of paper with a blue pencil, licked the drawing a couple of times, and wrapped it about Miss Ten Eyck's little finger—the little finger of her left hand. The removal of the wet paper left an imprint of the drawing. Then he mixed his ink in a small sea shell, dipped his needle, and in ten minutes had finished the tattooing of a grotesque little insect, as much butterfly as anything else.

"There," said Hillegas, when the work was done and the fortune-teller gone his way; "there you are, and it will never come out. It won't do for you now to plan a little burglary, or forge a little check, or slay a little baby for the coral round its neck, 'cause you can always be identified by that butterfly upon the little finger of your left hand."

"I'm almost sorry now I had it done. Won't it ever come out? Pshaw! Anyhow I think it's very chic," said Harriett Ten Eyck.

"I say, though!" exclaimed Hillegas, jumping up; "where's our tea and cakes and things? It's getting late. We can't wait here all evening. I'll go out and jolly that chap along."

The Chinaman to whom he had given the order was not to be found on that floor of the restaurant. Hillegas descended the stairs to the kitchen. The place seemed empty of life. On the ground floor, however, where tea and raw silk were sold, Hillegas found a Chinaman figuring up accounts by means of little balls that slid to and fro upon rods. The Chinaman was a very gorgeous-looking chap in round horn spectacles and a costume that looked like a man's nightgown, of quilted blue satin.

"I say, John," said Hillegas to this one, "I want some tea. You sabe?—upstairs—restaurant. Give China boy order—he no come. Get plenty much move on. Hey?"

The merchant turned and looked at Hillegas over his spectacles.

"Ah," he said calmly, "I regret that you have been detained. You will, no doubt, be attended to presently. You are a stranger in Chinatown?"

"Ahem!—well, yes—I—we are."

"Without doubt—without doubt!" murmured the other.

"I suppose you are the proprietor?" ventured Hillegas.

"I? Oh, no! My agents have a silk house here. I believe they sublet the upper floors to the See Yups. By the way, we have just received a consignment of India silk shawls you may be pleased to see."

He spread a pile upon the counter, and selected one that was particularly beautiful.

"Permit me," he remarked gravely, "to offer you this as a present to your good lady."

Hillegas's interest in this extraordinary Oriental was aroused. Here was a side of the Chinese life he had not seen, nor even suspected. He stayed for some little while talking to this man, whose bearing might have been that of Cicero before the Senate assembled, and left him with the understanding to call upon him the next day at the Consulate. He returned to the restaurant to find Miss Ten Eyck gone. He never saw her again. No white man ever did.

There is a certain friend of mine in San Francisco who calls himself Manning. He is a Plaza bum—that is, he sleeps all day in the old Plaza (that shoal where so much human jetsam has been stranded), and during the night follows his own devices in Chinatown, one block above. Manning was at one time a deep-sea pearl diver in Oahu, and, having burst his ear drums in the business, can now blow smoke out of either ear. This accomplishment first endeared him to me, and latterly I found out that he knew more of Chinatown than is meet and right for a man to know. The other day I found Manning in the shade of the Stevenson ship, just rousing from the effects of a jag on undiluted gin, and told him, or rather recalled to him the story of Harriett Ten Eyck.

"I remember," he said, resting on an elbow and chewing grass. "It made a big noise at the time, but nothing ever came of it—nothing except a long row and the cutting down of one of Mr. Hillegas's Chinese detectives in Gambler's Alley. The See Yups brought a chap over from Peking just to do the business."

"Hachet man?" said I.

"No," answered Manning, spitting green; "he was a two-knife Kai Gingh."

"As how?"

"Two knives—one in each hand—cross your arms and then draw 'em together, right and left, scissor-fashion—damn near slashed his man in two. He got five thousand for it. After that the detectives said they couldn't find much of a clue."

"And Miss Ten Eyck was not so much as heard from again?"

"No," answered Manning, biting his fingernails. "They took her to China, I guess, or may be up to Oregon. That sort of thing was new twenty years ago, and that's why they raised such a row, I suppose. But there are plenty of women living with Chinamen now, and nobody thinks anything about it, and they are Canton Chinamen, too—lowest kind of coolies. There's one of them up in St. Louis Place, just back of the Chinese theater, and she's a Sheeny. There's a queer team for you—the Hebrew and the Mongolian—and they've got a kid with red, crinkly hair, who's a rubber in a Hammam bath. Yes, it's a queer team, and there's three more white women in a slave-girl joint under Ah Yee's tan room. There's where I get my opium. They can talk a little English even yet. Funny thing—one of 'em's dumb, but if you get her drunk enough she'll talk a little English to you. It's a fact! I've seen 'em do it with her often—actually get her so drunk that she can talk. Tell you what," added Manning, struggling to his feet, "I'm going up there now to get some dope. You can come along, and we'll get Sadie (Sadie's her name), we'll get Sadie full, and ask her if she ever heard about Miss Ten Eyck. They do a big business," said Manning, as we went along. "There's Ah Yee and these three women and a policeman named Yank. They get all the yen shee—that's the cleanings of the opium pipes, you know—and make it into pills and smuggle it into the cons over at San Quentin prison by means of the trusties. Why, they'll make five dollars' worth of dope sell for thirty by the time it gets into the yard over at the Pen. When I was over there, I saw a chap knifed behind a jute mill for a pill as big as a pea. Ah Yee gets the stuff, the three women roll it into pills, and the policeman, Yank, gets it over to the trusties somehow. Ah Yee is independent rich by now, and the policeman's got a bank account."

"And the women?"

"Lord! they're slaves—Ah Yee's slaves! They get the swift kick most generally."

Manning and I found Sadie and her two companions four floors underneath the tan room, sitting cross-legged in a room about as big as a big trunk. I was sure they were Chinese women at first, until my eyes got accustomed to the darkness of the place. They were dressed in Chinese fashion, but I noted soon that their hair was brown and the bridges of each one's nose was high. They were rolling pills from a jar of yen shee that stood in the middle of the floor, their fingers twinkling with a rapidity that was somehow horrible to see.

Manning spoke to them briefly in Chinese while he lit a pipe, and two of them answered with the true Canton singsong—all vowels and no consonants.

"That one's Sadie," said Manning, pointing to the third one, who remained silent the while. I turned to her. She was smoking a cigar, and from time to time spat through her teeth man-fashion. She was a dreadful-looking beast of a woman, wrinkled like a shriveled apple, her teeth quite black from nicotine, her hands bony and prehensile, like a hawk's claws—but a white woman beyond all doubt. At first Sadie refused to drink, but the smell of Manning's can of gin removed her objections, and in half an hour she was hopelessly loquacious. What effect the alcohol had upon the paralyzed organs of her speech I cannot say. Sober, she was tongue-tied—drunk, she could emit a series of faint birdlike twitterings that sounded like a voice heard from the bottom of a well.

"Sadie," said Manning, blowing smoke out of his ears, "what makes you live with Chinamen? You're a white girl. You got people somewhere. Why don't you get back to them?"

Sadie shook her head.

"Like um China boy better," she said, in a voice so faint we had to stoop to listen. "Ah Yee's pretty good to us—plenty to eat, plenty to smoke, and as much yen shee as we can stand. Oh, I don't complain."

"You know you can get out of this whenever you want. Why don't you make a run for it someday when you're out? Cut for the Mission House on Sacramento Street—they'll be good to you there."

"Oh!" said Sadie listlessly, rolling a pill between her stained palms, "I been here so long I guess I'm kind of used to it. I've about got out of white people's ways by now. They wouldn't let me have my yen shee and my cigar, and that's about all I want nowadays. You can't eat yen shee long and care for much else, you know. Pass that gin along, will you? I'm going to faint in a minute."

"Wait a minute," said I, my hand on Manning's arm. "How long have you been living with Chinamen, Sadie?"

"Oh, I don't know. All my life, I guess. I can't remember back very far—only spots here and there. Where's that gin you promised me?"

"Only in spots?" said I; "here a little and there a little—is that it? Can you remember how you came to take up with this kind of life?"

"Sometimes I can and sometimes I can't," answered Sadie. Suddenly her head rolled upon her shoulder, her eyes closing. Manning shook her roughly.

"Let be! let be!" she exclaimed, rousing up; "I'm dead sleepy. Can't you see?"

"Wake up, and keep awake, if you can," said Manning; "this gentleman wants to ask you something."

"Ah Yee bought her from a sailor on a junk in the Pei Ho River," put in one of the other women.

"How about that, Sadie?" I asked. "Were you ever on a junk in a China river? Hey? Try and think."

"I don't know," she said. "Sometimes I think I was. There's lots of things I can't explain, but it's because I can't remember far enough back."

"Did you ever hear of a girl named Ten Eyck—Harriett Ten Eyck—who was stolen by Chinamen here in San Francisco a long time ago?"

There was a long silence. Sadie looked straight before her, wide-eyed; the other women rolled pills industriously; Manning looked over my shoulder at the scene, still blowing smoke through his ears; then Sadie's eyes began to close and her head to loll sideways.

"My cigar's gone out," she muttered. "You said you'd have gin for me. Ten Eyck! Ten Eyck! No, I don't remember anybody named that." Her voice failed her suddenly, then she whispered:

"Say, how did I get that on me?"

She thrust out her left hand, and I saw a butterfly tattooed on the little finger.

# THE BLACK HOLE
# OF SAN FRANCISCO

BY MARK TWAIN

*Portsmouth Square*

(Originally published in 1865)

I f I were Police Judge here, I would hold my court in the city prison and sentence my convicts to imprisonment in the present Police Court room. That would be capital punishment—it would be the Spartan doom of death for all crimes, whether important or insignificant. The Police Court room, with its deadly miasma, killed Judge Shepheard and Dick Robinson, the old reporter, and will kill Judge Rix, and Fitz Smythe also. The papers are just now abusing the police room—a thing which they do in concert every month. This time, however, they are more than usually exercised, because somebody has gone and built a house right before the only window the room had, and so it is midnight there during every hour of the twenty-four, and gas has to be burned while all other people are burning daylight.

That Police Court room is *not* a nice place. It is the infernalest smelling den on earth, perhaps. A deserted slaughterhouse, festering in the sun, is bearable, because it only has one smell, albeit it is a lively one; a soap-factory has its disagreeable features, but the soap-factory has but one smell, also; to stand to leeward of a sweating negro is rough, but even a sweating negro has but one smell; the salute of the playful polecat has its little drawbacks, but even the playful polecat has but one smell, and you can bury yourself to the chin in damp sand and get rid of the odor eventually. Once enter the Police Court though—once get yourself saturated with the fearful combination of miraculous stenches that infect its atmosphere, and neither sand nor salvation can ever purify you any more! You will smell like a polecat, like a slaughter-house, like a soap-factory, like a sweating negro, like a graveyard after an earthquake—for all time to come—and you will have a breath like a buzzard. You enter the door of the Police Court, and your nostrils are saluted with an awful stench; you think it emanates from Mr. Hess, the officer in charge of the door; you say to yourself, "Some animal has crawled down this poor man's throat and died"; you step further in, and you smell the same smell, with another, still more villainous, added to it; you remark to yourself, "This is wrong—very wrong; these spectators ought to have been buried days ago." You go a step further and you smell the same two smells, and another more ghastly than both put together; you think it comes from the spectators on the right. You go further and a fourth, still more powerful, is added to your three horrible smells; and you say to yourself, "These lawyers are too far gone—chloride of lime would be of no benefit here." One more step, and you smell the Judge; you reel, and gasp; you stagger to the right and smell the Prosecuting Attorney—worse and worse; you stagger fainting to the left, and your doom is sealed; you enter the fatal blue mist where ten reporters sit and stink from morning until night—and down you go! You are carried out on a shutter, and you cannot stay in the same room with yourself five minutes at a time for weeks.

You cannot imagine what a horrible hole that Police Court is. The cholera itself couldn't stand it there. The room is about 24 x 40 feet in size, I suppose, and is blocked in on all sides by massive brick walls; it has three or four doors, but they are never opened—and if they were they only open into airless courts and closets anyhow; it has but one window, and now that is blocked up, as I was telling you; there is not a solitary air-hole as big as your nostril about the whole place. Very well; down two sides of the room, drunken filthy loafers, thieves, prostitutes, China chicken-stealers, witnesses, and slimy gutter-snipes who come to see, and belch and issue deadly smells, are banked and packed, four ranks deep—a solid mass of rotting, steaming corruption. In the centre of the room are Dan Murphy, Zabriskie, the Citizen Sam Platt, Prosecuting Attorney Louderback, and other lawyers, either of whom would do for a censer to swing before the high altar of hell. Then, near the Judge are a crowd of reporters—a kind of cattle that did never smell good in any land. The house is full—so full that you have to actually squirm and shoulder your way from one part of it to another—and not a single crack or crevice in the walls to let in one poor breath of God's pure air! The dead, exhausted, poisoned atmosphere looks absolutely blue and filmy, sometimes—did when they had a little daylight. Now they have only gas-light and the added heat it brings. Another Judge will die shortly if this thing goes on.

# SOUTH OF THE SLOT

BY JACK LONDON

*South of Market*

(Originally published in 1909)

O ld San Francisco, which is the San Francisco of only the other day, the day before the Earthquake, was divided midway by the Slot. The Slot was an iron crack that ran along the center of Market Street, and from the Slot arose the burr of the ceaseless, endless cable that was hitched at will to the cars it dragged up and down. In truth, there were two slots, but in the quick grammar of the West time was saved by calling them, and much more that they stood for, "The Slot." North of the Slot were the theaters, hotels, and shopping district, the banks and the staid, respectable business houses. South of the Slot were the factories, slums, laundries, machine-shops, boiler works, and the abodes of the working class.

The Slot was the metaphor that expressed the class cleavage of Society, and no man crossed this metaphor, back and forth, more successfully than Freddie Drummond. He made a practice of living in both worlds, and in both worlds he lived signally well. Freddie Drummond was a professor in the Sociology Department of the University of California, and it was as a professor of sociology that he first crossed over the Slot, lived for six months in the great labor-ghetto, and wrote "The Unskilled Laborer"—a book that was hailed everywhere as an able contribution to the literature of progress, and as a splendid reply to the literature of discontent. Politically and economically it was nothing if not orthodox. Presidents of great railway systems bought whole editions of it to give to their employees. The Manufacturers' Association alone distributed fifty thousand copies of it. In a way, it was almost as immoral as the far-famed and notorious "Message to Garcia," while in its pernicious preachment of thrift and content it ran "Mrs. Wiggs of the Cabbage Patch" a close second.

At first, Freddie Drummond found it monstrously difficult to get along among the working people. He was not used to their ways, and they certainly were not used to his. They were suspicious. He had no antecedents. He could talk of no previous jobs. His hands were soft. His extraordinary politeness was ominous. His first idea of the role he would play was that of a free and independent American who chose to work with his hands and no explanations given. But it wouldn't do, as he quickly discovered. At the beginning they accepted him, very provisionally, as a freak. A little later, as he began to know his way about better, he insensibly drifted into the role that would work—namely, he was a man who had seen better days, very much better days, but who was down in his luck, though, to be sure, only temporarily.

He learned many things, and generalized much and often erroneously, all of which can be found in the pages of "The Unskilled Laborer." He saved himself, however, after the sane and conservative manner of his kind, by labeling his generalizations as "tentative." One of his first experiences was in the great Wilmax Cannery, where he was put on piece-work making small packing cases. A box factory supplied the parts, and all Freddie Drummond had to do was to fit the parts into a form and drive in the wire nails with a light hammer.

It was not skilled labor, but it was piece-work. The ordinary laborers in the cannery got a dollar and a half per day. Freddie Drummond found the other men on the same job with him jogging along and earning a dollar and seventy-five cents a day. By the third day he was able to earn the same. But he was ambitious. He did not care to jog along and, being unusually able and fit, on the fourth day earned two dollars. The next day, having keyed himself up to an exhausting high-tension, he earned two dollars and a half. His fellow workers favored him with scowls and black looks, and made remarks, slangily witty and which he did not understand, about sucking up to the boss and pace-making and holding her down when the rains set in. He was astonished at their malingering on piece-work, generalized about the inherent laziness of the un-skilled laborer, and proceeded next day to hammer out three dollars' worth of boxes.

And that night, coming out of the cannery, he was inter-viewed by his fellow workmen, who were very angry and inco-herently slangy. He failed to comprehend the motive behind their action. The action itself was strenuous. When he refused to ease down his pace and bleated about freedom of contract, independent Americanism, and the dignity of toil, they pro-ceeded to spoil his pace-making ability. It was a fierce battle, for Drummond was a large man and an athlete, but the crowd finally jumped on his ribs, walked on his face, and stamped on his fingers, so that it was only after lying in bed for a week that he was able to get up and look for another job. All of which is duly narrated in that first book of his, in the chapter entitled "The Tyranny of Labor."

A little later, in another department of the Wilmax Can-nery, lumping as a fruit-distributor among the women, he es-sayed to carry two boxes of fruit at a time, and was promptly reproached by the other fruit-lumpers. It was palpable malingering; but he was there, he decided, not to change conditions, but to observe. So he lumped one box thereafter, and so well did he study the art of shirking that he wrote a special chapter on it, with the last several paragraphs devoted to tentative generalizations.

In those six months he worked at many jobs and developed into a very good imitation of a genuine worker. He was a natural linguist, and he kept notebooks, making a scientific study of the workers' slang or argot, until he could talk quite intelligibly. This language also enabled him more intimately to follow their mental processes, and thereby to gather much data for a projected chapter in some future book which he planned to entitle "Synthesis of Working-Class Psychology."

Before he arose to the surface from that first plunge into the underworld he discovered that he was a good actor and demonstrated the plasticity of his nature. He was himself astonished at his own fluidity. Once having mastered the language and conquered numerous fastidious qualms, he found that he could flow into any nook of working-class life and fit it so snugly as to feel comfortably at home. As he said, in the preface to his second book, "The Toiler," he endeavored really to know the working people, and the only possible way to achieve this was to work beside them, eat their food, sleep in their beds, be amused with their amusements, think their thoughts, and feel their feelings.

He was not a deep thinker. He had no faith in new theories. All his norms and criteria were conventional. His Thesis, on the French Revolution, was noteworthy in college annals, not merely for its painstaking and voluminous accuracy, but for the fact that it was the dryest, deadest, most formal, and most orthodox screed ever written on the subject. He was a very reserved man, and his natural inhibition was large in quantity and steel-like in quality. He had but few friends. He was too undemonstrative, too frigid. He had no vices, nor had anyone ever discovered any temptations. Tobacco he detested, beer he abhorred, and he was never known to drink anything stronger than an occasional light wine at dinner.

When a freshman he had been baptized "Ice-Box" by his warmer-blooded fellows. As a member of the faculty he was known as "Cold-Storage." He had but one grief, and that was "Freddie." He had earned it when he played full-back on the 'Varsity eleven, and his formal soul had never succeeded in living it down. "Freddie" he would ever be, except officially, and through nightmare vistas he looked into a future when his world would speak of him as "Old Freddie."

For he was very young to be a Doctor of Sociology, only twenty-seven, and he looked younger. In appearance and atmosphere he was a strapping big college man, smooth-faced and easy-mannered, clean and simple and wholesome, with a known record of being a splendid athlete and an implied vast possession of cold culture of the inhibited sort. He never talked shop out of class and committee rooms, except later on, when his books showered him with distasteful public notice and he yielded to the extent of reading occasional papers before certain literary and economic societies.

He did everything right—too right; and in dress and comportment was inevitably correct. Not that he was a dandy. Far from it. He was a college man, in dress and carriage as like as a pea to the type that of late years is being so generously turned out of our institutions of higher learning. His handshake was satisfyingly strong and stiff. His blue eyes were coldly blue and convincingly sincere. His voice, firm and masculine, clean and crisp of enunciation, was pleasant to the ear. The one drawback to Freddie Drummond was his inhibition.

He never unbent. In his football days, the higher the tension of the game, the cooler he grew. He was noted as a boxer, but he was regarded as an automaton, with the inhuman precision of a machine judging distance and timing blows, guarding, blocking, and stalling. He was rarely punished himself, while he rarely punished an opponent. He was too clever and too controlled to permit himself to put a pound more weight into a punch than he intended. With him it was a matter of exercise. It kept him fit.

As time went by, Freddie Drummond found himself more frequently crossing the Slot and losing himself in South of Market. His summer and winter holidays were spent there, and, whether it was a week or a week-end, he found the time spent there to be valuable and enjoyable. And there was so much material to be gathered. His third book, "Mass and Master," became a text-book in the American universities; and almost before he knew it, he was at work on a fourth one, "The Fallacy of the Inefficient."

Somewhere in his make-up there was a strange twist or quirk. Perhaps it was a recoil from his environment and training, or from the tempered seed of his ancestors, who had been bookmen generation preceding generation; but at any rate, he found enjoyment in being down in the working-class world. In his own world he was "Cold-Storage," but down below he was "Big" Bill Totts, who could drink and smoke, and slang and fight, and be an all-around favorite. Everybody liked Bill, and more than one working girl made love to him. At first he had been merely a good actor, but as time went on, simulation became second nature. He no longer played a part, and he loved sausages, sausages and bacon, than which, in his own proper sphere, there was nothing more loathsome in the way of food.

From doing the thing for the need's sake, he came to doing the thing for the thing's sake. He found himself regretting as the time drew near for him to go back to his lecture-room and his inhibition. And he often found himself waiting with anticipation for the dreamy time to pass when he could cross the Slot and cut loose and play the devil. He was not wicked, but as "Big" Bill Totts he did a myriad things that Freddie Drummond would never have been permitted to do. Moreover, Freddie Drummond never would have wanted to do them. That was the strangest part of his discovery. Freddie Drummond and Bill Totts were two totally different creatures. The desires and tastes and impulses of each ran counter to the other's. Bill Totts could shirk at a job with clear conscience, while Freddie Drummond condemned shirking as vicious, criminal, and un-American, and devoted whole chapters to condemnation of the vice. Freddie Drummond did not care for dancing, but Bill Totts never missed the nights at the various dancing clubs, such as The Magnolia, The Western Star, and The Elite; while he won a massive silver cup, standing thirty inches high, for being the best-sustained character at the Butchers and Meat Workers' annual grand masked ball. And Bill Totts liked the girls and the girls liked him, while Freddie Drummond enjoyed playing the ascetic in this particular, was open in his opposition to equal suffrage, and cynically bitter in his secret condemnation of coeducation.

Freddie Drummond changed his manners with his dress, and without effort. When he entered the obscure little room used for his transformation scenes, he carried himself just a bit too stiffly. He was too erect, his shoulders were an inch too far back, while his face was grave, almost harsh, and practically expressionless. But when he emerged in Bill Totts' clothes he was another creature. Bill Totts did not slouch, but somehow his whole form limbered up and became graceful. The very sound of the voice was changed, and the laugh was loud and hearty, while loose speech and an occasional oath were as a matter of course on his lips. Also, Bill Totts was a trifle inclined to later hours, and at times, in saloons, to be good-naturedly bellicose with other workmen. Then, too, at Sunday picnics or when coming home from the show, either arm betrayed a practiced familiarity in stealing around girls' waists, while he displayed a wit keen and delightful in the flirtatious badinage that was expected of a good fellow in his class.

So thoroughly was Bill Totts himself, so thoroughly a workman, a genuine denizen of South of the Slot, that he was as class-conscious as the average of his kind, and his hatred for a scab even exceeded that of the average loyal union man. During the Water Front Strike, Freddie Drummond was somehow able to stand apart from the unique combination, and coldly critical, watch Bill Totts hilariously slug scab longshoremen. For Bill Totts was a dues-paying member of the Longshoremen Union and had a right to be indignant with the usurpers of his job. "Big" Bill Totts was so very big, and so very able, that it was "Big" Bill to the front when trouble was brewing. From acting outraged feelings, Freddie Drummond, in the role of his other self, came to experience genuine outrage, and it was only when he returned to the classic atmosphere of the university that he was able, sanely and conservatively, to generalize upon his underworld experiences and put them down on paper as a trained sociologist should. That Bill Totts lacked the perspective to raise him above class-consciousness, Freddie Drummond clearly saw. But Bill Totts could not see it. When he saw a scab taking his job away, he saw red at the same time, and little else did he see. It was Freddie Drummond, irreproachably clothed and comported, seated at his study desk or facing his class in "Sociology 17," who saw Bill Totts, and all around Bill Totts, and all around the whole scab and union-labor problem and its relation to the economic welfare of the United States in the struggle for the world market. Bill Totts really wasn't able to see beyond the next meal and the prize-fight the following night at the Gaiety Athletic Club.

It was while gathering material for "Women and Work" that Freddie received his first warning of the danger he was in. He was too successful at living in both worlds. This strange dualism he had developed was after all very unstable, and, as he sat in his study and meditated, he saw that it could not endure. It was really a transition stage, and if he persisted he saw that he would inevitably have to drop one world or the other. He could not continue in both. And as he looked at the row of volumes that graced the upper shelf of his revolving book-case, his volumes, beginning with his Thesis and ending with "Women and Work," he decided that that was the world he would hold to and stick by. Bill Totts had served his purpose, but he had become a too dangerous accomplice. Bill Totts would have to cease.

Freddie Drummond's fright was due to Mary Condon, President of the International Glove Workers' Union No. 974. He had seen her, first, from the spectators' gallery, at the annual convention of the Northwest Federation of Labor, and he had seen her through Bill Totts' eyes, and that individual had been most favorably impressed by her. She was not Freddie Drummond's sort at all. What if she were a royal-bodied woman, graceful and sinewy as a panther, with amazing black eyes that could fill with fire or laughter-love, as the mood might dictate? He detested women with a too exuberant vitality and a lack of . . . well, of inhibition. Freddie Drummond accepted the doctrine of evolution because it was quite universally accepted by college men, and he flatly believed that Man had climbed up the ladder of life out of the weltering muck and mess of lower and monstrous organic things. But he was a trifle ashamed of this genealogy, and preferred not to think of it. Wherefore, probably, he practiced his iron inhibition and preached it to others, and preferred women of his own type, who could shake free of this bestial and regrettable ancestral line and by discipline and control emphasize the wideness of the gulf that separated them from what their dim forbears had been.

Bill Totts had none of these considerations. He had liked Mary Condon from the moment his eyes first rested on her in the convention hall, and he had made it a point, then and there, to find out who she was. The next time he met her, and quite by accident, was when he was driving an express wagon for Pat Morrissey. It was in a lodging house in Mission Street, where he had been called to take a trunk into storage. The landlady's daughter had called him and led him to the little bedroom, the occupant of which, a glove-maker, had just been removed to hospital. But Bill did not know this. He stooped, up-ended the trunk, which was a large one, got it on his shoulder, and struggled to his feet with his back toward the open door. At that moment he heard a woman's voice.

"Belong to the union?" was the question asked.

"Aw, what's it to you?" he retorted. "Run along now, an' git outa my way. I wanta turn round."

The next he knew, big as he was, he was whirled half around and sent reeling backward, the trunk overbalancing him, till he fetched up with a crash against the wall. He started to swear, but at the same instant found himself looking into Mary Condon's flashing, angry eyes.

"Of course I b'long to the union," he said. "I was only kiddin' you."

"Where's your card?" she demanded in business-like tones.

"In my pocket. But I can't git it out now. This trunk's too damn heavy. Come on down to the wagon an' I'll show it to you."

"Put that trunk down," was the command.

"What for? I got a card, I'm tellin' you."

"Put it down, that's all. No scab's going to handle that trunk. You ought to be ashamed of yourself, you big coward, scabbing on honest men. Why don't you join the union and be a man?"

Mary Condon's color had left her face, and it was apparent that she was in a rage.

"To think of a big man like you turning traitor to his class. I suppose you're aching to join the militia for a chance to shoot down union drivers the next strike. You may belong to the militia already, for that matter. You're the sort—"

"Hold on, now, that's too much!" Bill dropped the trunk to the floor with a bang, straightened up, and thrust his hand into his inside coat pocket. "I told you I was only kiddin'. There, look at that."

It was a union card properly enough.

"All right, take it along," Mary Condon said. "And the next time don't kid."

Her face relaxed as she noticed the ease with which he got the big trunk to his shoulder, and her eyes glowed as they glanced over the graceful massiveness of the man. But Bill did not see that. He was too busy with the trunk.

The next time he saw Mary Condon was during the Laundry Strike. The Laundry Workers, but recently organized,

were green at the business, and had petitioned Mary Condon
to engineer the strike. Freddie Drummond had had an inkling
of what was coming, and had sent Bill Totts to join the union
and investigate. Bill's job was in the wash-room, and the men
had been called out first, that morning, in order to stiffen the
courage of the girls; and Bill chanced to be near the door to
the mangle-room when Mary Condon started to enter. The
superintendent, who was both large and stout, barred her way.
He wasn't going to have his girls called out, and he'd teach
her a lesson to mind her own business. And as Mary tried to
squeeze past him he thrust her back with a fat hand on her
shoulder. She glanced around and saw Bill.

"Here you, Mr. Totts," she called. "Lend a hand. I want
to get in."

Bill experienced a startle of warm surprise. She had remembered his name from his union card. The next moment
the superintendent had been plucked from the doorway raving about rights under the law, and the girls were deserting
their machines. During the rest of that short and successful
strike, Bill constituted himself Mary Condon's henchman and
messenger, and when it was over returned to the University
to be Freddie Drummond and to wonder what Bill Totts could
see in such a woman.

Freddie Drummond was entirely safe, but Bill had fallen in
love. There was no getting away from the fact of it, and it was
this fact that had given Freddie Drummond his warning. Well,
he had done his work, and his adventures could cease. There
was no need for him to cross the Slot again. All but the last
three chapters of his latest, "Labor Tactics and Strategy," was
finished, and he had sufficient material on hand adequately to
supply those chapters.

Another conclusion he arrived at, was that in order to

sheet-anchor himself as Freddie Drummond, closer ties and relations in his own social nook were necessary. It was time that he was married, anyway, and he was fully aware that if Freddie Drummond didn't get married, Bill Totts assuredly would, and the complications were too awful to contemplate. And so, enters Catherine Van Vorst. She was a college woman herself, and her father, the one wealthy member of the faculty, was the head of the Philosophy Department as well. It would be a wise marriage from every standpoint, Freddie Drummond concluded when the engagement was consummated and announced. In appearance cold and reserved, aristocratic and wholesomely conservative, Catherine Van Vorst, though warm in her way, possessed an inhibition equal to Drummond's.

All seemed well with him, but Freddie Drummond could not quite shake off the call of the underworld, the lure of the free and open, of the unhampered, irresponsible life South of the Slot. As the time of his marriage approached, he felt that he had indeed sowed wild oats, and he felt, moreover, what a good thing it would be if he could have but one wild fling more, play the good fellow and the wastrel one last time, ere he settled down to gray lecture-rooms and sober matrimony. And, further to tempt him, the very last chapter of "Labor Tactics and Strategy" remained unwritten for lack of a trifle more of essential data which he had neglected to gather.

So Freddie Drummond went down for the last time as Bill Totts, got his data, and, unfortunately, encountered Mary Condon. Once more installed in his study, it was not a pleasant thing to look back upon. It made his warning doubly imperative. Bill Totts had behaved abominably. Not only had he met Mary Condon at the Central Labor Council, but he had stopped in at a chop-house with her, on the way home, and treated her to oysters. And before they parted at her door, his arms had been about her, and he had kissed her on the lips and kissed her repeatedly. And her last words in his ear, words uttered softly with a catchy sob in the throat that was nothing more nor less than a love cry, were "Bill . . . dear, dear Bill."

Freddie Drummond shuddered at the recollection. He saw the pit yawning for him. He was not by nature a polygamist, and he was appalled at the possibilities of the situation. It would have to be put an end to, and it would end in one only of two ways: either he must become wholly Bill Totts and be married to Mary Condon, or he must remain wholly Freddie Drummond and be married to Catherine Van Vorst. Otherwise, his conduct would be beneath contempt and horrible.

In the several months that followed, San Francisco was torn with labor strife. The unions and the employers' associations had locked horns with a determination that looked as if they intended to settle the matter, one way or the other, for all time. But Freddie Drummond corrected proofs, lectured classes, and did not budge. He devoted himself to Catherine Van Vorst, and day by day found more to respect and admire in her—nay, even to love in her. The Street Car Strike tempted him, but not so severely as he would have expected; and the great Meat Strike came on and left him cold. The ghost of Bill Totts had been successfully laid, and Freddie Drummond with rejuvenescent zeal tackled a brochure, long-planned, on the topic of "diminishing returns."

The wedding was two weeks off, when, one afternoon, in San Francisco, Catherine Van Vorst picked him up and whisked him away to see a Boys' Club, recently instituted by the settlement workers with whom she was interested. It was her brother's machine, but they were alone with the exception of the chauffeur. At the junction with Kearny Street, Market and Geary Streets intersect like the sides of a sharp-angled letter "V." They, in the auto, were coming down Market with the intention of negotiating the sharp apex and going up Geary. But they did not know what was coming down Geary, timed by fate to meet them at the apex. While aware from the papers that the Meat Strike was on and that it was an exceedingly bitter one, all thought of it at that moment was farthest from Freddie Drummond's mind. Was he not seated beside Catherine? And, besides, he was carefully expositing to her his views on settlement work—views that Bill Totts' adventures had played a part in formulating.

Coming down Geary Street were six meat wagons. Beside each scab driver sat a policeman. Front and rear, and along each side of this procession, marched a protecting escort of one hundred police. Behind the police rear guard, at a respectful distance, was an orderly but vociferous mob, several blocks in length, that congested the street from sidewalk to sidewalk. The Beef Trust was making an effort to supply the hotels, and, incidentally, to begin the breaking of the strike. The St. Francis had already been supplied, at a cost of many broken windows and broken heads, and the expedition was marching to the relief of the Palace Hotel.

All unwitting, Drummond sat beside Catherine, talking settlement work, as the auto, honking methodically and dodging traffic, swung in a wide curve to get around the apex. A big coal wagon, loaded with lump coal and drawn by four huge horses, just debouching from Kearny Street as though to turn down Market, blocked their way. The driver of the wagon seemed undecided, and the chauffeur, running slow but disregarding some shouted warning from the crossing policemen, swerved the auto to the left, violating the traffic rules, in order to pass in front of the wagon.

At that moment Freddie Drummond discontinued his

conversation. Nor did he resume it again, for the situation was developing with the rapidity of a transformation scene. He heard the roar of the mob at the rear, and caught a glimpse of the helmeted police and the lurching meat wagons. At the same moment, laying on his whip and standing up to his task, the coal driver rushed horses and wagon squarely in front of the advancing procession, pulled the horses up sharply, and put on the big brake. Then he made his lines fast to the brake-handle and sat down with the air of one who had stopped to stay. The auto had been brought to a stop, too, by his big panting leaders which had jammed against it.

Before the chauffeur could back clear, an old Irishman, driving a rickety express wagon and lashing his one horse to a gallop, had locked wheels with the auto. Drummond recognized both horse and wagon, for he had driven them often himself. The Irishman was Pat Morrissey. On the other side a brewery wagon was locking with the coal wagon, and an east-bound Kearny Street car, wildly clanging its gong, the motorman shouting defiance at the crossing policeman, was dashing forward to complete the blockade. And wagon after wagon was locking and blocking and adding to the confusion. The meat wagons halted. The police were trapped. The roar at the rear increased as the mob came on to the attack, while the vanguard of the police charged the obstructing wagons.

"We're in for it," Drummond remarked coolly to Catherine.

"Yes," she nodded, with equal coolness. "What savages they are."

His admiration for her doubled on itself. She was indeed his sort. He would have been satisfied with her even if she had screamed and clung to him, but this—this was magnificent. She sat in that storm center as calmly as if it had been no more than a block of carriages at the opera.

The police were struggling to clear a passage. The driver of the coal wagon, a big man in shirt sleeves, lighted a pipe and sat smoking. He glanced down complacently at a captain of police who was raving and cursing at him, and his only acknowledgment was a shrug of the shoulders. From the rear arose the rat-tat-tat of clubs on heads and a pandemonium of cursing, yelling, and shouting. A violent accession of noise proclaimed that the mob had broken through and was dragging a scab from a wagon. The police captain reinforced from his vanguard, and the mob at the rear was repelled. Meanwhile, window after window in the high office building on the right had been opened, and the class-conscious clerks were raining a shower of office furniture down on the heads of police and scabs. Waste-baskets, ink-bottles, paper-weights, typewriters—anything and everything that came to hand was filling the air.

A policeman, under orders from his captain, clambered to the lofty seat of the coal wagon to arrest the driver. And the driver, rising leisurely and peacefully to meet him, suddenly crumpled him in his arms and threw him down on top of the captain. The driver was a young giant, and when he climbed on top his load and poised a lump of coal in both hands, a policeman, who was just scaling the wagon from the side, let go and dropped back to earth. The captain ordered half a dozen of his men to take the wagon. The teamster, scrambling over the load from side to side, beat them down with huge lumps of coal.

The crowd on the sidewalks and the teamsters on the locked wagons roared encouragement and their own delight. The motorman, smashing helmets with his controller bar, was beaten into insensibility and dragged from his platform. The captain of police, beside himself at the repulse of his men, led the next assault on the coal wagon. A score of police were swarming up the tall-sided fortress. But the teamster multiplied himself. At times there were six or eight policemen rolling on the pavement and under the wagon. Engaged in repulsing an attack on the rear end of his fortress, the teamster turned about to see the captain just in the act of stepping on to the seat from the front end. He was still in the air and in most unstable equilibrium, when the teamster hurled a thirty-pound lump of coal. It caught the captain fairly on the chest, and he went over backward, striking on a wheeler's back, tumbling on to the ground, and jamming against the rear wheel of the auto.

Catherine thought he was dead, but he picked himself up and charged back. She reached out her gloved hand and patted the flank of the snorting, quivering horse. But Drummond did not notice the action. He had eyes for nothing save the battle of the coal wagon, while somewhere in his complicated psychology, one Bill Totts was heaving and straining in an effort to come to life. Drummond believed in law and order and the maintenance of the established, but this riotous savage within him would have none of it. Then, if ever, did Freddie Drummond call upon his iron inhibition to save him. But it is written that the house divided against itself must fall. And Freddie Drummond found that he had divided all the will and force of him with Bill Totts, and between them the entity that constituted the pair of them was being wrenched in twain.

Freddie Drummond sat in the auto, quite composed, alongside Catherine Van Vorst; but looking out of Freddie Drummond's eyes was Bill Totts, and somewhere behind those eyes, battling for the control of their mutual body, were Freddie Drummond, the sane and conservative sociologist, and Bill Totts, the class-conscious and bellicose union working-man. It was Bill Totts, looking out of those eyes, who saw the inevitable end of the battle on the coal wagon. He saw a policeman gain the top of the load, a second, and a third. They lurched clumsily on the loose footing, but their long riot-clubs were out and winging. One blow caught the teamster on the head. A second he dodged, receiving it on the shoulder. For him the game was plainly up. He dashed in suddenly, clutched two policemen in his arms, and hurled himself a prisoner to the pavement, his hold never relaxing on his two captors.

Catherine Van Vorst was sick and faint at sight of the blood and brutal fighting. But her qualms were vanquished by the sensational and most unexpected happening that followed. The man beside her emitted an unearthly and uncultured yell and rose to his feet. She saw him spring over the front seat, leap to the broad rump of the wheeler, and from there gain the wagon. His onslaught was like a whirlwind. Before the bewildered officer on top the load could guess the errand of this conventionally clad but excited-seeming gentleman, he was the recipient of a punch that arched him back through the air to the pavement. A kick in the face led an ascending policeman to follow his example. A rush of three more gained the top and locked with Bill Totts in a gigantic clinch, during which his scalp was opened up by a club, and coat, vest, and half his starched shirt were torn from him. But the three policemen were flung wide and far, and Bill Totts, raining down lumps of coal, held the fort.

The captain led gallantly to the attack, but was bowled over by a chunk of coal that burst on his head in black baptism. The need of the police was to break the blockade in front before the mob could break in at the rear, and Bill Totts' need was to hold the wagon till the mob did break through. So the battle of the coal went on.

The crowd had recognized its champion. "Big" Bill, as usual, had come to the front, and Catherine Van Vorst was bewildered by the cries of "Bill! O you Bill!" that arose on every hand. Pat Morrissey, on his wagon seat, was jumping and screaming in an ecstasy, "Eat 'em, Bill! Eat 'em! Eat 'em alive!" From the sidewalk she heard a woman's voice cry out, "Look out, Bill—front end!" Bill took the warning and with well-directed coal cleaned the front end of the wagon of assailants. Catherine Van Vorst turned her head and saw on the curb of the sidewalk a woman with vivid coloring and flashing black eyes who was staring with all her soul at the man who had been Freddie Drummond a few minutes before.

The windows of the office building became vociferous with applause. A fresh shower of office chairs and filing cabinets descended. The mob had broken through on one side the line of wagons, and was advancing, each segregated policeman the center of a fighting group. The scabs were torn from their seats, the traces of the horses cut, and the frightened animals put in flight. Many policemen crawled under the coal wagon for safety, while the loose horses, with here and there a policeman on their backs or struggling at their heads to hold them, surged across the sidewalk opposite the jam and broke into Market Street.

Catherine Van Vorst heard the woman's voice calling in warning. She was back on the curb again, and crying out:

"Beat it, Bill! Now's your time! Beat it!"

The police for the moment had been swept away. Bill Totts leaped to the pavement and made his way to the woman on the sidewalk. Catherine Van Vorst saw her throw her arms around him and kiss him on the lips; and Catherine Van Vorst watched him curiously as he went on down the sidewalk, one arm around the woman, both talking and laughing, and he with a volubility and abandon she could never have dreamed possible.

The police were back again and clearing the jam while waiting for reinforcements and new drivers and horses. The mob had done its work and was scattering, and Catherine Van Vorst, still watching, could see the man she had known as Freddie Drummond. He towered a head above the crowd. His arm was still about the woman. And she in the motorcar, watching, saw the pair cross Market Street, cross the Slot, and disappear down Third Street into the labor ghetto.

In the years that followed no more lectures were given in the University of California by one Freddie Drummond, and no more books on economics and the labor question appeared over the name of Frederick A. Drummond. On the other hand there arose a new labor leader, William Totts by name. He it was who married Mary Condon, President of the International Glove Workers' Union No. 974; and he it was who called the notorious Cooks and Waiters' Strike, which, before its successful termination, brought out with it scores of other unions, among which, of the more remotely allied, were the Chicken Pickers and the Undertakers.

# PART II

SHADOWS IN THE FOG

# THE SCORCHED FACE

BY DASHIELL HAMMETT
*Telegraph Hill*
(Originally published in 1925)

"We expected them home yesterday," Alfred Banbrock ended his story. "When they had not come by this morning, my wife telephoned Mrs. Walden. Mrs. Walden said they had not been down there—had not been expected, in fact."

"On the face of it, then," I suggested, "it seems that your daughters went away of their own accord, and are staying away on their own accord?"

Banbrock nodded gravely. Tired muscles sagged in his fleshy face.

"It would seem so," he agreed. "That is why I came to your agency for help instead of going to the police."

"Have they ever disappeared before?"

"No. If you read the papers and magazines, you've no doubt seen hints that the younger generation is given to irregularity. My daughters came and went pretty much as they pleased. But, though I can't say I ever knew what they were up to, we always knew where they were in a ge neral way."

"Can you think of any reason for their going away like this?"

He shook his weary head.

"Any recent quarrels?" I probed.

"N—" He changed it to: "Yes—although I didn't attach

any importance to it, and wouldn't have recalled it if you hadn't jogged my memory. It was Thursday evening—the evening before they went away."

"And it was about—?"

"Money, of course. We never disagreed over anything else. I gave each of my daughters an adequate allowance—perhaps a very liberal one. Nor did I keep them strictly within it. There were few months in which they didn't exceed it. Thursday evening they asked for an amount of money even more than usual in excess of what two girls should need. I wouldn't give it to them, though I finally did give them a somewhat smaller amount. We didn't exactly quarrel—not in the strict sense of the word—but there was a certain lack of friendliness between us."

"And it was after this disagreement that they said they were going down to Mrs. Walden's, in Monterey, for the weekend?"

"Possibly. I'm not sure of that point. I don't think I heard of it until the next morning, but they may have told my wife before that."

"And you know of no other possible reason for their running away?"

"None. I can't think that our dispute over money—by no means an unusual one—had anything to do with it."

"What does their mother think?"

"Their mother is dead," Banbrock corrected me. "My wife is their stepmother. She is only two years older than Myra, my older daughter. She is as much at sea as I."

"Did your daughters and their stepmother get along all right together?"

"Yes! Yes! Excellently! If there was a division in the family, I usually found them standing together against me."

"Your daughters left Friday afternoon?"

"At noon, or a few minutes after. They were going to drive down."

"The car, of course, is still missing?"

"Naturally."

"What was it?"

"A Locomobile, with a special cabriolet body. Black."

"You can give me the license and engine numbers?"

"I think so."

He turned in his chair to the big roll-top desk that hid a quarter of one office wall, fumbled with papers in a compartment, and read the numbers over his shoulder to me. I put them on the back of an envelope.

"I'm going to have this car put on the police department list of stolen machines," I told him. "It can be done without mentioning your daughters. The police bulletin might find the car for us. That would help us find your daughters."

"Very well," he agreed, "if it can be done without disagreeable publicity. As I told you at first, I don't want any more advertising than is absolutely necessary—unless it becomes likely that harm has come to the girls."

I nodded understanding, and got up.

"I want to go out and talk to your wife," I said. "Is she home now?"

"Yes, I think so. I'll phone her and tell her you are coming."

In a big limestone fortress on top of a hill in Sea Cliff, looking down on ocean and bay, I had my talk with Mrs. Banbrock. She was a tall dark girl of not more than twenty-two years, inclined to plumpness.

She couldn't tell me anything her husband hadn't at least mentioned, but she could give me finer details.

I got descriptions of the two girls:

Myra—20 years old; 5 feet 8 inches; 150 pounds; athletic; brisk, almost masculine manner and carriage; bobbed brown hair; brown eyes; medium complexion; square face, with large chin and short nose; scar over left ear, concealed by hair; fond of horses and all outdoor sports. When she left the house she wore a blue and green wool dress, small blue hat, short black seal coat, and black slippers.

Ruth—18 years; 5 feet 4 inches; 105 pounds; brown eyes; brown bobbed hair; medium complexion; small oval face; quiet, timid, inclined to lean on her more forceful sister. When last seen she had worn a tobacco-brown coat trimmed with brown fur over a gray silk dress, and a wide brown hat.

I got two photographs of each girl, and an additional snapshot of Myra standing in front of the cabriolet. I got a list of the things they had taken with them—such things as would naturally be taken on a weekend visit. What I valued most of what I got was a list of their friends, relatives, and other acquaintances, so far as Mrs. Banbrock knew them.

"Did they mention Mrs. Walden's invitation before their quarrel with Mr. Banbrock?" I asked, when I had my lists stowed away.

"I don't think so," Mrs. Banbrock said thoughtfully. "I didn't connect the two things at all. They didn't really quarrel with their father, you know. It wasn't harsh enough to be called a quarrel."

"Did you see them when they left?"

"Assuredly! They left about half-past twelve Friday afternoon. They kissed me as usual when they went, and there was certainly nothing in their manner to suggest anything out of the ordinary."

"You've no idea at all where they might have gone?"

"None."

"Can't even make a guess?"

"I can't. Among the names and addresses I have given you are some of friends and relatives of the girls in other cities. They may have gone to one of those. Do you think we should—?"

"I'll take care of that," I promised. "Could you pick out one or two of them as the most likely places for the girls to have gone?"

She wouldn't try it. "No," she said positively, "I could not."

From this interview I went back to the Agency, and put the Agency machinery in motion: arranging to have operatives from some of the Continental's other branches call on the out-of-town names on my list, having the missing Locomobile put on the police department list, turning one photograph of each girl over to a photographer to be copied.

That done, I set out to talk to the persons on the list Mrs. Banbrock had given me. My first call was on a Constance Delee, in an apartment building on Post Street. I saw a maid. The maid said Miss Delee was out of town. She wouldn't tell me where her mistress was, or when she would be back.

From there I went up on Van Ness Avenue and found a Wayne Ferris in an automobile salesroom: a sleek-haired young man whose very nice manners and clothes completely hid anything else—brains for instance—he might have had. He was very willing to help me, and he knew nothing. It took him a long time to tell me so. A nice boy.

Another blank: "Mrs. Scott is in Honolulu."

In a real estate office on Montgomery Street I found my next one—another sleek, stylish, smooth-haired young man with nice manners and nice clothes. His name was Raymond Elwood. I would have thought him a no more distant relative of Ferris than cousin if I hadn't known that the world—

especially the dancing, teaing world—was full of their sort. I learned nothing from him.

Then I drew some more blanks: "Out of town," "Shopping," "I don't know where you can find him."

I found one more of the Banbrock girls' friends before I called it a day. Her name was Mrs. Stewart Correll. She lived in Presidio Terrace, not far from the Banbrocks. She was a small woman, or girl, of about Mrs. Banbrock's age. A little fluffy blonde person with wide eyes of that particular blue which always looks honest and candid no matter what is going on behind it.

"I haven't seen either Ruth or Myra for two weeks or more," she said in answer to my question.

"At that time—the last time you saw them—did either say anything about going away?"

"No."

Her eyes were wide and frank. A little muscle twitched in her upper lip. "And you've no idea where they might have gone?"

"No."

Her fingers were rolling her lace handkerchief into a little ball.

"Have you heard from them since you last saw them?"

"No."

She moistened her mouth before she said it.

"Will you give me the names and addresses of all the people you know who were also known by the Banbrock girls?"

"Why—? Is there—?"

"There's a chance that some of them may have seen them more recently than you," I explained. "Or may even have seen them since Friday."

Without enthusiasm, she gave me a dozen names. All were

already on my list. Twice she hesitated as if about to speak a name she did not want to speak. Her eyes stayed on mine, wide and honest. Her fingers, no longer balling the handkerchief, picked at the cloth of her skirt.

I didn't pretend to believe her. But my feet weren't solidly enough on the ground for me to put her on the grill. I gave her a promise before I left, one that she could get a threat out of if she liked.

"Thanks, very much," I said. "I know it's hard to remember things exactly. If I run across anything that will help your memory, I'll be back to let you know about it."

"Wha—? Yes, do!" she said.

Walking away from the house, I turned my head to look back just before I passed out of sight. A curtain swung into place at a second-floor window. The street lights weren't bright enough for me to be sure the curtain had swung in front of a blonde head.

My watch told me it was nine-thirty: too late to line up any more of the girls' friends. I went home, wrote my report for the day, and turned in, thinking more about Mrs. Correll than about the girls.

She seemed worth an investigation.

Some telegraphic reports were in when I got to the office the next morning. None was of any value. Investigation of the names and addresses in other cities had revealed nothing. An investigation in Monterey had established reasonably—which is about as well as anything is ever established in the detecting business—that the girls had not been there recently, that the Locomobile had not been there.

The early editions of the afternoon papers were on the street when I went out to get some breakfast before taking up the grind where I had dropped it the previous night.

I bought a paper to prop behind my grapefruit. It spoiled my breakfast for me:

## BANKER'S WIFE SUICIDE

*Mrs. Stewart Correll, wife of the vice-president of the Golden Gate Trust Company, was found dead early this morning by her maid in her bedroom, in her home in Presidio Terrace. A bottle believed to have contained poison was on the floor beside the bed.*

*The dead woman's husband could give no reason for his wife's suicide. He said she had not seemed depressed or . . .*

At the Correll residence I had to do a lot of talking before I could get to Correll. He was a tall, slim man of less than thirty-five, with a sallow, nervous face and blue eyes that fidgeted.

"I'm sorry to disturb you at a time like this," I apologized when I had finally insisted my way into his presence. "I won't take up more of your time than necessary. I am an operative of the Continental Detective Agency. I have been trying to find Ruth and Myra Banbrock, who disappeared several days ago. You know them, I think."

"Yes," he said without interest. "I know them."

"You knew they had disappeared?"

"No." His eyes switched from a chair to a rug. "Why should I?"

"Have you seen either of them recently?" I asked, ignoring his question.

"Last week—Wednesday, I think. They were just leaving—standing at the door talking to my wife—when I came home from the bank."

"Didn't your wife say anything to you about their vanishing?"

"No. Really, I can't tell you anything about the Misses Banbrock. If you'll excuse me—"

"Just a moment longer," I said. "I wouldn't have bothered you if it hadn't been necessary. I was here last night to question Mrs. Correll. She seemed nervous. My impression was that some of her answers to my questions were—uh—evasive. I want—"

He was up out of his chair. His face was red in front of mine.

"You!" he cried. "I can thank you for—"

"Now, Mr. Correll," I tried to quiet him, "there's no use—"

But he had himself all worked up.

"You drove my wife to her death," he accused me. "You killed her with your damned prying—with your bulldozing threats, with your—"

That was silly. I felt sorry for this young man whose wife had killed herself. Apart from that, I had work to do. I tightened the screws.

"We won't argue, Correll," I told him. "The point is that I came here to see if your wife could tell me anything about the Banbrocks. She told me less than the truth. Later, she committed suicide. I want to know why. Come through for me, and I'll do what I can to keep the papers and the public from linking her death with the girls' disappearance."

"Linking her death with their disappearance?" he exclaimed. "That's absurd!"

"Maybe—but the connection is there!" I hammered away at him. I felt sorry for him, but I had work to do. "It's there. If you'll give it to me, maybe it won't have to be advertised. I'm going to get it, though. You give it to me—or I'll go after it out in the open."

For a moment I thought he was going to take a poke at me. I wouldn't have blamed him. His body stiffened—then sagged, and he dropped back into his chair. His eyes fidgeted away from mine. "There's nothing I can tell," he mumbled. "When her maid went to her room to call her this morning, she was dead. There was no message, no reason, nothing."

"Did you see her last night?"

"No. I was not home for dinner. I came in late and went straight to my own room, not wanting to disturb her. I hadn't seen her since I left the house that morning."

"Did she seem disturbed or worried then?"

"No."

"Why do you think she did it?"

"My God, man, I don't know! I've thought and thought, but I don't know!"

"Health?"

"She seemed well. She was never ill, never complained."

"Any recent quarrels?"

"We never quarreled—never in the year and a half we have been married!"

"Financial trouble?"

He shook his head without speaking or looking up from the floor.

"Any other worry?"

He shook his head again.

"Did the maid notice anything peculiar in her behavior last night?"

"Nothing."

"Have you looked through her things—for papers, letters?"

"Yes—and found nothing." He raised his head to look at me. "The only thing"—he spoke very slowly—"there was a little pile of ashes in the grate in her room, as if she had burned papers, or letters."

Correll held nothing more for me—nothing I could get out of him, anyway.

The girl at the front gate in Alfred Banbrock's Shoreman's Building suite told me he was *in conference*. I sent my name in. He came out of conference to take me into his private office. His tired face was full of questions.

I didn't keep him waiting for the answers. He was a grown man. I didn't edge around the bad news.

"Things have taken a bad break," I said as soon as we were locked in together. "I think we'll have to go to the police and newspapers for help. A Mrs. Correll, a friend of your daughters, lied to me when I questioned her yesterday. Last night she committed suicide."

"Irma Correll? Suicide?"

"You knew her?"

"Yes! Intimately! She was—that is, she was a close friend of my wife and daughters. She killed herself?"

"Yes. Poison. Last night. Where does she fit in with your daughters' disappearance?"

"Where?" he repeated. "I don't know. Must she fit in?"

"I think she must. She told me she hadn't seen your daughters for a couple of weeks. Her husband told me just now that they were talking to her when he came home from the bank last Wednesday afternoon. She seemed nervous when I questioned her. She killed herself shortly afterward. There's hardly a doubt that she fits in somewhere."

"And that means—?"

"That means," I finished for him, "that your daughters may be perfectly safe, but that we can't afford to gamble on that possibility."

"You think harm has come to them?"

"I don't think anything," I evaded, "except that with a death tied up closely with their going, we can't afford to play around."

Banbrock got his attorney on the phone—a pink-faced, white-haired old boy named Norwall, who had the reputation of knowing more about corporations than all the Morgans, but who hadn't the least idea as to what police procedure was all about—and told him to meet us at the Hall of Justice.

We spent an hour and a half there, getting the police turned loose on the affair, and giving the newspapers what we wanted them to have. That was plenty of dope on the girls, plenty of photographs and so forth, but nothing about the connection between them and Mrs. Correll. Of course we let the police in on that angle.

After Banbrock and his attorney had gone away together, I went back to the detectives' assembly room to chew over the job with Pat Reddy, the police sleuth assigned to it.

Pat was the youngest member of the detective bureau—a big blond Irishman who went in for the spectacular in his lazy way.

A couple of years ago he was a new copper, pounding his feet in harness on a hillside beat. One night he tagged an automobile that was parked in front of a fireplug. The owner came out just then and gave him an argument. She was Althea Wallach, only and spoiled daughter of the owner of the Wallach Coffee Company—a slim, reckless youngster with hot eyes. She must have told Pat plenty. He took her over to the station and dumped her in a cell.

Old Wallach, so the story goes, showed up the next morning with a full head of steam and half the lawyers in San Francisco. But Pat made his charge stick, and the girl was fined.

Old Wallach did everything but take a punch at Pat in the corridor afterward. Pat grinned his sleepy grin at the coffee importer, and drawled, "You better lay off me—or I'll stop drinking your coffee."

That crack got into most of the newspapers in the country, and even into a Broadway show.

But Pat didn't stop with the snappy comeback. Three days later he and Althea Wallach went over to Alameda and got themselves married. I was in on that part. I happened to be on the ferry they took and they dragged me along to see the deed done.

Old Wallach immediately disowned his daughter, but that didn't seem to worry anybody else. Pat went on pounding his beat, but, now that he was conspicuous, it wasn't long before his qualities were noticed. He was boosted into the detective bureau.

Old Wallach relented before he died, and left Althea his millions.

Pat took the afternoon off to go to the funeral, and went back to work that night, catching a wagonload of gunmen. He kept on working. I don't know what his wife did with her money, but Pat didn't even improve the quality of his cigars—though he should have. He lived now in the Wallach mansion, true enough, and now and then on rainy mornings he would be driven down to the Hall in a Hispano-Suiza brougham; but there was no difference in him beyond that.

That was the big blond Irishman who sat across a desk from me in the assembly room and fumigated me with something shaped like a cigar.

He took the cigar-like thing out of his mouth presently, and spoke through the fumes. "This Correll woman you think's tied up with the Banbrocks—she was stuck-up a couple of months back and nicked for eight hundred dollars. Know that?"

I hadn't known it. "Lose anything besides cash?" I asked.

"No."

"You believe it?"

He grinned. "That's the point," he said. "We didn't catch the bird who did it. With women who lose things that way—especially money—it's always a question whether it's a hold-up or a hold-out."

He teased some more poison-gas out of the cigar-thing, and added, "The hold-up might have been on the level, though. What are you figuring on doing now?"

"Let's go up to the Agency and see if anything new has turned up. Then I'd like to talk to Mrs. Banbrock again. Maybe she can tell us something about the Correll woman."

At the office I found that reports had come in on the rest of the out-of-town names and addresses. Apparently none of these people knew anything about the girls' whereabouts. Reddy and I went on up to Sea Cliff to the Banbrock home.

Banbrock had telephoned the news of Mrs. Correll's death to his wife, and she had read the papers. She told us she could think of no reason for the suicide. She could imagine no possible connection between the suicide and her stepdaughters' vanishing.

"Mrs. Correll seemed as nearly contented and happy as usual the last time I saw her, two or three weeks ago," Mrs. Banbrock said. "Of course she was by nature inclined to be dissatisfied with things, but not to the extent of doing a thing like this."

"Do you know of any trouble between her and her husband?"

"No. So far as I know, they were happy, though—"

She broke off. Hesitancy, embarrassment showed in her dark eyes.

"Though?" I repeated.

"If I don't tell you now, you'll think I am hiding something," she said, flushing, and laughing a little laugh that held more nervousness than amusement. "It hasn't any bearing, but I was always just a little jealous of Irma. She and my husband were—well, everyone thought they would marry. That was a little before he and I married. I never let it show, and I dare say it was a foolish idea, but I always had a suspicion that Irma married Stewart more in pique than for any other reason, and that she was still fond of Alfred—Mr. Banbrock."

"Was there anything definite to make you think that?"

"No, nothing—really! I never thoroughly believed it. It was just a sort of vague feeling. Cattiness, no doubt, more than anything else."

It was getting along toward evening when Pat and I left the Banbrock house. Before we knocked off for the day, I called up the Old Man—the Continental's San Francisco branch manager, and therefore my boss—and asked him to sic an operative on Irma Correll's past.

I took a look at the morning papers—thanks to their custom of appearing almost as soon as the sun is out of sight—before I went to bed. They had given our job a good spread. All the facts except those having to do with the Correll angle were there, plus photographs, and the usual assortment of guesses and similar garbage.

The following morning I went after the friends of the missing girls to whom I had not yet talked. I found some of them and got nothing of value from them. Late in the morning I telephoned the office to see if anything new had turned up. It had.

"We've just had a call from the sheriff's office at Martinez," the Old Man told me. "An Italian grape-grower near Knob Valley picked up a charred photograph a couple of days ago, and recognized it as Ruth Banbrock when he saw her picture in this morning's paper. Will you get up there? A deputy sheriff and the Italian are waiting for you in the Knob Valley marshal's office."

"I'm on my way," I said.

At the ferry building I used the four minutes before my boat left trying to get Pat Reddy on the phone, with no success.

Knob Valley is a town of less than a thousand people, a dreary, dirty town in Contra Costa County. A San Francisco–Sacramento local set me down there while the afternoon was still young.

I knew the marshal slightly—Tom Orth. I found two men in the office with him. Orth introduced us. Abner Paget, a gawky man of forty-something, with a slack chin, scrawny face, and pale intelligent eyes, was the deputy sheriff. Gio Cereghino, the Italian grape-grower, was a small, nut-brown man with strong yellow teeth that showed in an everlasting smile under his black mustache, and soft brown eyes.

Paget showed me the photograph. A scorched piece of paper the size of a half-dollar, apparently all that had not been burned of the original picture. It was Ruth Banbrock's face. There was little room for doubting that. She had a peculiarly excited—almost drunken—look, and her eyes were larger than in the other pictures of her I had seen. But it was her face.

"He says he found it day 'fore yesterday," Paget explained dryly, nodding at the Italian. "The wind blew it against his foot when he was walkin' up a piece of road near his place. He picked it up an' stuck it in his pocket, he says, for no special reason, I guess." He paused to regard the Italian meditatively. The Italian nodded his head in vigorous affirmation.

"Anyways," the deputy sheriff went on, "he was in town this mornin', an' seen the pictures in the papers from Frisco. So he come in here an' told Tom about it. Tom an' me decided the best thing was to phone your agency—since the papers said you was workin' on it."

I looked at the Italian. Paget, reading my mind, explained, "Cereghino lives over in the hills. Got a grape ranch there. Been around here five or six years, an' ain't killed nobody that I know of."

"Remember the place where you found the picture?" I asked the Italian.

His grin broadened under his mustache, and his head went up and down. "For sure, I remember that place."

"Let's go there," I suggested to Paget.

"Right. Comin' along, Tom?"

The marshal said he couldn't. He had something to do in town. Cereghino, Paget and I went out and got into a dusty Ford that the deputy sheriff drove.

We rode for nearly an hour, along a county road that bent up the slope of Mount Diablo. After a while, at a word from the Italian, we left the county road for a dustier and ruttier one. A mile of this one.

"This place," Cereghino said.

Paget stopped the Ford. We got out in a clearing. The trees and bushes that had crowded the road retreated here for twenty feet or so on either side, leaving a little dusty circle in the woods.

"About this place," the Italian was saying. "I think by this stump. But between that bend ahead and that one behind, I know for sure."

Paget was a countryman. I am not. I waited for him to move.

He looked around the clearing, slowly, standing still between the Italian and me. His pale eyes lighted presently. He went around the Ford to the far side of the clearing. Cereghino and I followed.

Near the fringe of brush at the edge of the clearing, the scrawny deputy stopped to grunt at the ground. The wheelmarks of an automobile were there. A car had turned around here.

Paget went on into the woods. The Italian kept close to his heels. I brought up the rear. Paget was following some sort of track. I couldn't see it, either because he and the Italian blotted it out ahead of me, or because I'm a shine Indian. We went back quite a way.

Paget stopped. The Italian stopped.

Paget said, "Uh-huh," as if he had found an expected thing.

The Italian said something with the name of God in it. I trampled a bush, coming beside them to see what they saw. I saw it.

At the base of a tree, on her side, her knees drawn up close to her body, a girl was dead. She wasn't nice to see. Birds had been at her.

A tobacco-brown coat was half on, half off her shoulders. I knew she was Ruth Banbrock before I turned her over to look at the side of her face the ground had saved from the birds.

Cereghino stood watching me while I examined the girl. His face was mournful in a calm way. The deputy sheriff paid little attention to the body. He was off in the brush, moving around, looking at the ground. He came back as I finished my examination.

"Shot," I told him, "once in the right temple. Before that, I think, there was a fight. There are marks on the arm that was under her body. There's nothing on her—no jewelry, money—nothing."

"That goes," Paget said. "Two women got out of the car back in the clearin', an' came here. Could've been three women—if the others carried this one. Can't make out how many went back. One of 'em was larger than this one. There was a scuffle here. Find the gun?"

"No," I said.

"Neither did I. It went away in the car, then. There's what's left of a fire over there." He ducked his head to the left. "Paper an' rags burnt. Not enough left to do us any good. I reckon the photo Cereghino found blew away from the fire. Late Friday, I'd put it, or maybe Saturday mornin' . . . No nearer than that."

I took the deputy sheriff's word for it. He seemed to know his stuff.

"Come here. I'll show you somethin'," he said, and led me over to a little black pile of ashes.

He hadn't anything to show me. He wanted to talk to me away from the Italian's ears.

"I think the Italian's all right," he said, "but I reckon I'd best hold him a while to make sure. This is some way from his place, an' he stuttered a little bit too much tellin' me how he happened to be passin' here. Course, that don't mean nothin' much. All these Italians peddle *vino*, an' I guess that's what brought him out this way. I'll hold him a day or two, anyways."

"Good," I agreed. "This is your country, and you know the people. Can you visit around and see what you can pick up? Whether anybody saw anything? Saw a Locomobile cabriolet? Or anything else? You can get more than I could."

"I'll do that," he promised.

"All right. Then I'll go back to San Francisco now. I suppose you'll want to camp here with the body?"

"Yeah. You drive the Ford back to Knob Valley, an' tell Tom what's what. He'll come or send out. I'll keep the Italian here with me."

Waiting for the next westbound train out of Knob Valley, I got the office on the telephone. The Old Man was out. I told my story to one of the office men and asked him to get the news to the Old Man as soon as he could.

Everybody was in the office when I got back to San Francisco. Alfred Banbrock, his face a pink-gray that was deader than solid gray could have been. His pink and white old lawyer. Pat Reddy, sprawled on his spine with his feet on another chair. The Old Man, with his gentle eyes behind gold spectacles and his mild smile, hiding the fact that fifty years of sleuthing had left him without any feelings at all on any subject.

Nobody said anything when I came in. I said my say as briefly as possible.

"Then the other woman—the woman who killed Ruth was—?"

Banbrock didn't finish his question. Nobody answered it.

"We don't know what happened," I said after a while. "Your daughter and someone we don't know may have gone there. Your daughter may have been dead before she was taken there. She may have—"

"But Myra!" Banbrock was pulling at his collar with a finger inside. "Where is Myra?"

I couldn't answer that, nor could any of the others.

"You are going up to Knob Valley now?" I asked him.

"Yes, at once. You will come with me?"

I wasn't sorry I could not. "No. There are things to be

done here. I'll give you a note to the marshal. I want you to look carefully at the piece of your daughter's photograph the Italian found—to see if you remember it."

Banbrock and the lawyer left.

Reddy lit one of his awful cigars.

"We found the car," the Old Man said.

"Where was it?"

"In Sacramento. It was left in a garage there either late Friday night or early Saturday. Foley has gone up to investigate it. And Reddy has uncovered a new angle."

Pat nodded through his smoke.

"A hockshop dealer came in this morning," Pat said, "and told us that Myra Banbrock and another girl came to his joint last week and hocked a lot of stuff. They gave him phony names, but he swears one of them was Myra. He recognized her picture as soon as he saw it in the paper. Her companion wasn't Ruth. It was a little blonde."

"Mrs. Correll?"

"Uh-huh. The shark can't swear to that, but I think that's the answer. Some of the jewelry was Myra's, some Ruth's, and some we don't know. I mean we can't prove it belonged to Mrs. Correll—though we will."

"When did all this happen?"

"They soaked the stuff Monday before they went away."

"Have you seen Correll?"

"Uh-huh. I did a lot of talking to him, but the answers weren't worth much. He says he don't know whether any of her jewelry is gone or not, and doesn't care. It was hers, he says, and she could do anything she wanted with it. He was kind of disagreeable. I got along a little better with one of the maids. She says some of Mrs. Correll's pretties disappeared last week. Mrs. Correll said she had lent them to a friend. I'm going to show the stuff the hockshop has to the maid tomorrow to see if she can identify it. She didn't know anything else—except that Mrs. Correll was out of the picture for a while on Friday—the day the Banbrock girls went away."

"What do you mean, out of the picture?" I asked.

"She went out late in the morning and didn't show up until somewhere around three the next morning. She and Correll had a row over it, but she wouldn't tell him where she had been."

I liked that. It could mean something.

"And," Pat went on, "Correll has just remembered that his wife had an uncle who went crazy in Pittsburgh in 1902, and that she had a morbid fear of going crazy herself, and that she had often said she would kill herself if she thought she was going crazy. Wasn't it nice of him to remember those things at last? To account for her death?"

"It was," I agreed, "but it doesn't get us anywhere. It doesn't even prove that he knows anything. Now my guess is—"

"To hell with your guess," Pat said, getting up and pushing his hat in place. "Your guesses all sound like a lot of static to me. I'm going home, eat my dinner, read my Bible, and go to bed."

I suppose he did. Anyway, he left us.

We all might as well have spent the next three days in bed for all the profit that came out of our running around. No place we visited, nobody we questioned, added to our knowledge. We were in a blind alley.

We learned that the Locomobile was left in Sacramento by Myra Banbrock, and not by anyone else, but we didn't learn where she went afterward. We learned that some of the jewelry in the pawnshop was Mrs. Correll's. The Locomobile was brought back from Sacramento. Mrs. Correll was buried. Ruth Banbrock was buried. The newspapers found other mysteries. Reddy and I dug and dug, and all we brought up was dirt.

The following Monday brought me close to the end of my rope. There seemed nothing more to do but sit back and hope that the circulars with which we had plastered North America would bring results. Reddy had already been called off and put to running out fresher trails. I hung on because Banbrock wanted me to keep at it so long as there was the shadow of anything to keep at. But by Monday I had worked myself out.

Before going to Banbrock's office to tell him I was licked, I dropped in at the Hall of Justice to hold a wake over the job with Pat Reddy. He was crouched over his desk, writing a report on some other job.

"Hello!" he greeted me, pushing his report away and smearing it with ashes from his cigar. "How go the Banbrock doings?"

"They don't," I admitted. "It doesn't seem possible, with the stack-up what it is, that we should have come to a dead stop! It's there for us, if we can find it. The need of money before both the Banbrock and Correll calamities, Mrs. Correll's suicide after I had questioned her about the girls, her burning things before she died and the burning of things immediately before or after Ruth Banbrock's death."

"Maybe the trouble is," Pat suggested, "that you're not such a good sleuth."

"Maybe."

We smoked in silence for a minute or two after that insult.

"You understand," Pat said presently, "there doesn't have to be any connection between the Banbrock death and disappearance and the Correll death."

"Maybe not. But there has to be a connection between the Banbrock death and the Banbrock disappearance. There was a connection—in a pawnshop—between the Banbrock and Correll actions before these things. If there is that connection, then—" I broke off, all full of ideas.

"What's the matter?" Pat asked. "Swallow your gum?"

"Listen!" I let myself get almost enthusiastic. "We've got what happened to three women hooked up together. If we could tie up some more in the same string—I want the names and addresses of all the women and girls in San Francisco who have committed suicide, been murdered, or have disappeared within the past year."

"You think this is a wholesale deal?"

"I think the more we can tie up together, the more lines we'll have to run out. And they can't all lead nowhere. Let's get our list, Pat!"

We spent all the afternoon and most of the night getting it. Its size would have embarrassed the Chamber of Commerce. It looked like a hunk of the telephone book. Things happened in a city in a year. The section devoted to strayed wives and daughters was the largest; suicides next; and even the smallest division—murders—wasn't any too short.

We could check off most of the names against what the police department had already learned of them and their motives, weeding out those positively accounted for in a manner nowise connected with our present interest. The remainder we split into two classes: those of unlikely connection, and those of more possible connection. Even then, the second list was longer than I had expected, or hoped.

There were six suicides in it, three murders, and twenty-one disappearances.

Reddy had other work to do. I put the list in my pocket and went calling.

For four days I ground at the list. I hunted, found, questioned, and investigated friends and relatives of the women and girls on my list. My questions all hit in the same direction. Had she been acquainted with Myra Banbrock? Ruth? Mrs. Correll? Had she been in need of money before her death or disappearance? Had she destroyed anything before her death or disappearance? Had she known any of the other women on my list?

Three times I drew yesses.

Sylvia Varney, a girl of twenty, who had killed herself on November 5th, had drawn six hundred dollars from the bank the week before her death. No one in her family could say what she had done with the money. A friend of Sylvia Varney's—Ada Youngman, a married woman of twenty-five or -six—had disappeared on December 2nd, and was still gone. The Varney girl had been at Mrs. Youngman's home an hour before she—the Varney girl—killed herself.

Mrs. Dorothy Sawdon, a young widow, had shot herself on the night of January 13th. No trace was found of either the money her husband had left her or the funds of a club whose treasurer she was. A bulky letter her maid remembered having given her that afternoon was never found.

These three women's connection with the Banbrock-Correll affair was sketchy enough. None of them had done anything that isn't done by nine out of ten women who kill themselves or run away. But the troubles of all three had come to a head within the past few months—and all three were women of about the same financial and social position as Mrs. Correll and the Banbrocks.

Finishing my list with no fresh leads, I came back to these three.

I had the names and addresses of sixty-two friends of the Banbrock girls. I set about getting the same sort of catalogue on the three women I was trying to bring into the game. I didn't have to do all the digging myself. Fortunately, there were two or three operatives in the office with nothing else to do just then.

We got something.

Mrs. Sawdon had known Raymond Elwood. Sylvia Varney had known Raymond Elwood. There was nothing to show Mrs. Youngman had known him, but it was likely she had. She and the Varney girl had been thick.

I had already interviewed this Raymond Elwood in connection with the Banbrock girls, but had paid no especial attention to him. I had considered him just one of the sleek-headed, high-polished young men of whom there were quite a few listed.

I went back to him, all interest now. The results were promising.

He had, as I have said, a real estate office on Montgomery Street. We were unable to find a single client he had ever served, or any signs of one's existence. He had an apartment out in the Sunset District, where he lived alone. His local record seemed to go back no farther than ten months, though we couldn't find its definite starting point. Apparently he had no relatives in San Francisco. He belonged to a couple of fashionable clubs. He was vaguely supposed to be "well connected in the East." He spent money.

I couldn't shadow Elwood, having too recently interviewed him. Dick Foley did. Elwood was seldom in his office during the first three days Dick tailed him. He was seldom in the financial district. He visited his clubs, he danced and teaed and so forth, and each of those three days he visited a house on Telegraph Hill.

The first afternoon Dick had him, Elwood went to the Telegraph Hill house with a tall fair girl from Burlingame. The second day—in the evening—with a plump young woman who came out of a house out on Broadway. The third evening with a very young girl who seemed to live in the same building as he.

Usually Elwood and his companion spent from three to four hours in the house on Telegraph Hill. Other people—all apparently well-to-do—went in and out of the house while it was under Dick's eye.

I climbed Telegraph Hill to give the house the up-and-down. It was a large house—a big frame house painted egg-yellow. It hung dizzily on a shoulder of the hill, a shoulder that was sharp where rock had been quarried away. The house seemed about to go skiing down on the roofs far below.

It had no immediate neighbors. The approach was screened by bushes and trees.

I gave that section of the hill a good strong play, calling at all the houses within shooting distance of the yellow one. Nobody knew anything about it, or about its occupants. The folks on the Hill aren't a curious lot—perhaps because most of them have something to hide on their own account.

My climbing uphill and downhill got me nothing until I succeeded in learning who owned the yellow house. The owner was an estate whose affairs were in the hands of the West Coast Trust Company.

I took my investigations to the trust company, with some satisfaction. The house had been leased eight months ago by Raymond Elwood, acting for a client named T. F. Maxwell.

We couldn't find Maxwell. We couldn't find anybody who knew Maxwell. We couldn't find any evidence that Maxwell was anything but a name.

One of the operatives went up to the yellow house on the hill, and rang the bell for half an hour with no result. We didn't try that again, not wanting to stir things up at this stage.

I made another trip up the hill, house-hunting. I couldn't find a place as near the yellow house as I would have liked, but I succeeded in renting a three-room flat from which the approach to it could be watched.

Dick and I camped in the flat—with Pat Reddy, when he wasn't off on other duties—and watched machines turn into the screened path that led to the egg-tinted house. Afternoon and night there were machines. Most of them carried women. We saw no one we could place as a resident of the house. Elwood came daily, once alone, the other time with women whose faces we couldn't see from our window.

We shadowed some of the visitors away. They were without exception reasonably well off financially, and some were socially prominent. We didn't go up against any of them with talk. Even a carefully planned pretext is as likely as not to tip your mitt when you're up against a blind game.

Three days of this—and our break came.

It was early evening, just dark. Pat Reddy had phoned that he had been up on a job for two days and a night, and was going to sleep the clock around. Dick and I were sitting at the window of our flat, watching automobiles turn toward the yellow house, writing down their license numbers as they passed through the blue-white patch of light an arc-lamp put in the road just beyond our window.

A woman came climbing the hill, afoot. She was a tall woman, strongly built. A dark veil not thick enough to advertise the fact that she wore it to hide her features, nevertheless did hide them. Her way was up the hill, past our flat, on the other side of the roadway.

A night wind from the Pacific was creaking a grocer's sign down below, swaying the arc-light above. The wind caught the woman as she passed out of our building's sheltered area. Coat and skirts tangled. She put her back to the wind, a hand to her hat. Her veil whipped out straight from her face.

Her face was a face from a photograph—Myra Banbrock's face.

Dick made her with me. "Our baby!" he cried, bouncing to his feet.

"Wait," I said. "She's going into the joint on the edge of the hill. Let her go. We'll go after her when she's inside. That's our excuse for frisking the joint."

I went into the next room, where our telephone was, and called Pat Reddy's number.

"She didn't go in," Dick called from the window. "She went past the path."

"After her!" I ordered. "There's no sense to that! What's the matter with her?" I felt sort of indignant about it. "She's got to go in! Tail her. I'll find you after I get Pat."

Dick went.

Pat's wife answered the telephone. I told her who I was.

"Will you shake Pat out of the covers and send him up here? He knows where I am. Tell him I want him in a hurry."

"I will," she promised. "I'll have him there in ten minutes—wherever it is."

Outdoors, I went up the road, hunting for Dick and Myra Banbrock. Neither was in sight. Passing the bushes that masked the yellow house, I went on, circling down a stony path to the left. No sign of either.

I turned back in time to see Dick going into our flat. I followed.

"She's in," he said when I joined him. "She went up the

road, cut across through some bushes, came back to the edge of the cliff, and slid feet-first through a cellar window."

That was nice. The crazier the people you are sleuthing act, as a rule, the nearer you are to an ending of your troubles.

Reddy arrived within a minute or two of the time his wife had promised. He came in buttoning his clothes.

"What the hell did you tell Althea?" he growled at me. "She gave me an overcoat to put over my pajamas, dumped the rest of my clothes in the car, and I had to get in them on the way over."

"I'll cry with you after a while," I dismissed his troubles. "Myra Banbrock just went into the joint through a cellar window. Elwood has been there an hour. Let's knock it off."

Pat is deliberate.

"We ought to have papers, even at that," he stalled.

"Sure," I agreed, "but you can get them fixed up afterward. That's what you're here for. Contra Costa County wants her—maybe to try her for murder. That's all the excuse we need to get into the joint. We go there for her. If we happen to run into anything else—well and good."

Pat finished buttoning his vest.

"Oh, all right!" he said sourly. "Have it your way. But if you get me smashed for searching a house without authority, you'll have to give me a job with your law-breaking agency."

"I will." I turned to Foley. "You'll have to stay outside, Dick. Keep your eye on the gateway. Don't bother anybody else, but if the Banbrock girl gets out, stay behind her."

"I expected it," Dick howled. "Any time there's any fun I can count on being stuck off somewhere on a street corner!"

Pat Reddy and I went straight up the bush-hidden path to the yellow house's front door, and rang the bell.

A big black man in a red fez, red silk jacket over red-striped silk shirt, red zouave pants and red slippers opened the door. He filled the opening, framed in the black of the hall behind him.

"Is Mr. Maxwell home?" I asked.

The black man shook his head and said words in a language I don't know.

"Mr. Elwood, then?"

Another shaking of the head. More strange language.

"Let's see whoever is home then," I insisted.

Out of the jumble of words that meant nothing to me, I picked three in garbled English, which I thought were "master," "not," and "home."

The door began to close. I put a foot against it.

Pat flashed his buzzer.

Though the black man had poor English, he had knowledge of police badges.

One of his feet stamped on the floor behind him. A gong boomed deafeningly in the rear of the house.

The black man bent his weight to the door.

My weight on the foot that blocked the door, I leaned sidewise, swaying to the Negro.

Slamming from the hip, I put my fist in the middle of him.

Reddy hit the door and we went into the hall.

"'Fore God, Fat Shorty," the black man gasped in good Virginian, "you done hurt me!"

Reddy and I went by him, down the hall whose bounds were lost in darkness.

The bottom of a flight of steps stopped my feet.

A gun went off upstairs. It seemed to point at us. We didn't get the bullets.

A babble of voices—women screaming, men shouting—

came and went upstairs; came and went as if a door was being opened and shut.

"Up, my boy!" Reddy yelped in my ear.

We went up the stairs. We didn't find the man who had shot at us.

At the head of the stairs, a door was locked. Reddy's bulk forced it.

We came into a bluish light. A large room, all purple and gold. Confusion of overturned furniture and rumpled rugs. A gray slipper lay near a far door. A green silk gown was in the center of the floor. No person was there.

I raced Pat to the curtained door beyond the slipper. The door was not locked. Reddy yanked it wide.

A room with three girls and a man crouching in a corner, fear in their faces. Neither of them was Myra Banbrock, or Raymond Elwood, or anyone we knew.

Our glances went away from them after the first quick look.

The open door across the room grabbed our attention.

The door gave to a small room.

The room was chaos.

A small room, packed and tangled with bodies. Live bodies, seething, writhing. The room was a funnel into which men and women had been poured. They boiled noisily toward the one small window that was the funnel's outlet. Men and women, youths and girls, screaming, struggling, squirming, fighting. Some had no clothes.

"We'll get through and block the window!" Pat yelled in my ear.

"Like hell—" I began, but he was gone ahead into the confusion.

I went after him.

I didn't mean to block the window. I meant to save Pat from his foolishness. No five men could have fought through that boiling turmoil of maniacs. No ten men could have turned them from the window.

Pat—big as he is—was down when I got to him. A half-dressed girl—a child—was driving at his face with sharp high-heels. Hands, feet, were tearing him apart.

I cleared him with a play of gun-barrel on chins and wrists—dragged him back.

"Myra's not there!" I yelled into his ear as I helped him up. "Elwood's not there!"

I wasn't sure, but I hadn't seen them, and I doubted that they would be in this mess. These savages, boiling again to the window, with no attention for us, whoever they were, weren't insiders. They were the mob, and the principals shouldn't be among them.

"We'll try the other rooms," I yelled again. "We don't want these."

Pat rubbed the back of his hand across his torn face and laughed.

"It's a cinch I don't want 'em anymore," he said.

We went back to the head of the stairs the way we had come. We saw no one. The man and girls who had been in the next room were gone.

At the head of the stairs we paused. There was no noise behind us except the now fainter babble of the lunatics fighting for their exit.

A door shut sharply downstairs.

A body came out of nowhere, hit my back, flattened me to the landing.

The feel of silk was on my cheek. A brawny hand was fumbling at my throat.

I bent my wrist until my gun, upside down, lay against my cheek. Praying for my ear, I squeezed.

My cheek took fire. My head was a roaring thing, about to burst.

The silk slid away.

Pat hauled me upright.

We started down the stairs.

Swish!

A thing came past my face, stirring my bared hair.

A thousand pieces of glass, china, plaster, exploded upward at my left.

I tilted head and gun together.

A Negro's red-silk arms were still spread over the balustrade above.

I sent him two bullets. Pat sent him two.

The Negro teetered over the rail.

He came down on us, arms outflung—a deadman's swan-dive.

We scurried down the stairs from under him.

He shook the house when he landed, but we weren't watching him then.

The smooth sleek head of Raymond Elwood took our attention.

In the light from above, it showed for a furtive split second around the newel-post at the foot of the stairs. Showed and vanished.

Pat Reddy, closer to the rail than I, went over it in a one-hand vault down into the blackness below.

I made the foot of the stairs in two jumps, jerked myself around with a hand on the newel, and plunged into the suddenly noisy dark of the hall.

A wall I couldn't see hit me. Caroming off the opposite

wall, I spun into a room whose curtained grayness was the light of day after the hall.

Pat Reddy stood with one hand on a chair-back, holding his belly with the other. His face was mouse-colored under its blood. His eyes were glass agonies. He had the look of a man who had been kicked.

The grin he tried failed. He nodded toward the rear of the house. I went back.

In a little passageway I found Raymond Elwood.

He was sobbing and pulling frantically at a locked door. His face was the hard white of utter terror.

I measured the distance between us.

He turned as I jumped.

I put everything I had in the downswing of my gun-barrel—

A ton of meat and bone crashed into my back.

I went over against the wall, breathless, giddy, sick.

Red-silk arms that ended in brown hands locked around me.

I wondered if there was a whole regiment of these gaudy Negroes—or if I was colliding with the same one over and over.

This one didn't let me do much thinking.

He was big. He was strong. He didn't mean any good.

My gun-arm was flat at my side, straight down. I tried a shot at one of the Negro's feet. Missed. Tried again. He moved his feet. I wriggled around, half-facing him.

Elwood piled on my other side.

The Negro bent me backward, folding my spine on itself like an accordion.

I fought to hold my knees stiff. Too much weight was hanging on me. My knees sagged. My body curved back.

Pat Reddy, swaying in the doorway, shone over the Negro's shoulder like the Angel Gabriel.

Gray pain was in Pat's face, but his eyes were clear. High right hand held a gun. His left was getting a blackjack out of his hip pocket.

He swung the sap down on the Negro's shaven skull.

The black man wheeled away from me, shaking his head.

Pat hit him once more before the Negro closed with him—hit him full in the face, but couldn't beat him off.

Twisting my freed gun hand up, I drilled Elwood neatly through the chest, and let him slide down me to the floor.

The Negro had Pat against the wall, bothering him a lot. His broad red back was a target.

But I had used five of the six bullets in my gun. I had more in my pocket, but reloading takes time.

I stepped out of Elwood's feeble hands, and went to work with the flat of my gun on the Negro. There was a roll of fat where his skull and neck fit together. The third time I hit it, he flopped, taking Pat with him.

I rolled him off. The blond police detective—not very blond now—got up.

At the other end of the passageway an open door showed an empty kitchen.

Pat and I went to the door that Elwood had been playing with. It was a solid piece of carpentering, and neatly fastened.

Yoking ourselves together, we began to beat the door with our combined three hundred and seventy or eighty pounds.

It shook, but held. We hit again. Wood we couldn't see tore.

Again.

The door popped away from us. We went through—down

a flight of steps—rolling, snowballing down—until a cement floor stopped us.

Pat came back to life first.

"You're a hell of an acrobat," he said. "Get off my neck!"

I stood up. He stood up. We seemed to be dividing the evening between falling on the floor and getting up from the floor.

A light switch was at my shoulder. I turned it on.

If I looked anything like Pat, we were a fine pair of nightmares. He was all raw meat and dirt, with not enough clothes left to hide much of either.

I didn't like his looks, so I looked around the basement in which we stood. To the rear was a furnace, coalbins and a woodpile. To the front was a hallway and rooms, after the manner of the upstairs.

The first door we tried was locked, but not strongly. We smashed through it into a photographer's dark-room.

The second door was unlocked, and put us in a chemical laboratory; retorts, tubes, burners and a small still. There was a little round iron stove in the middle of the room. No one was there.

We went out into the hallway and to the third door, not so cheerfully. This cellar looked like a bloomer. We were wasting time here, when we should have stayed upstairs. I tried the door.

It was firm beyond trembling.

We smacked it with our weight, together, experimentally. It didn't shake.

"Wait."

Pat went to the woodpile in the rear and came back with an axe.

He swung the axe against the door, flaking out a hunk of

wood. Silvery points of light sparkled in the hole. The other side of the door was an iron or steel plate.

Pat put the axe down and leaned on the helve.

"You write the next prescription," he said.

I didn't have anything to suggest, except, "I'll camp here. You beat it upstairs, and see if any of your coppers have shown up. This is a God-forsaken hole, but somebody may have sent in an alarm. See if you can find another way into this room—a window, maybe—or manpower enough to get us in through this door."

Pat turned toward the steps.

A sound stopped him—the clicking of bolts on the other side of the iron-lined door.

A jump put Pat on one side of the frame. A step put me on the other.

Slowly the door moved in. Too slowly.

I kicked it open.

Pat and I went into the room on top of my kick.

His shoulder hit the woman. I managed to catch her before she fell.

Pat took her gun. I steadied her back on her feet.

Her face was a pale blank square.

She was Myra Banbrock, but she had none of the masculinity that had been in her photographs and description.

Steadying her with one arm—which also served to block her arms—I looked around the room.

A small cube of a room whose walls were brown-painted metal. On the floor lay a queer little dead man.

A little man in tight-fitting black velvet and silk. Black velvet blouse and breeches, black silk stockings and skull cap, black patent-leather pumps. His face was small and old and bony, but smooth as stone, without line or wrinkle.

A hole was in his blouse, where it fit high under his chin. The hole bled very slowly. The floor around him showed it had been bleeding faster a little while ago.

Beyond him, a safe was open. Papers were on the floor in front of it, as if the safe had been tilted to spill them out.

The girl moved against my arm.

"You killed him?" I asked.

"Yes," too faint to have been heard a yard away.

"Why?"

She shook her short brown hair out of her eyes with a tired jerk of her head.

"Does it make any difference?" she asked. "I did kill him."

"It might make a difference," I told her, taking my arm away, and going over to shut the door. People talk more freely in a room with a closed door. "I happen to be in your father's employ. Mr. Reddy is a police detective. Of course, neither of us can smash any laws, but if you'll tell us what's what, maybe we can help you."

"My father's employ?" she questioned.

"Yes. When you and your sister disappeared, he engaged me to find you. We found your sister, and—"

Life came into her face and eyes and voice.

"I didn't kill Ruth!" she cried. "The papers lied! I didn't kill her! I didn't know she had the revolver. I didn't know it! We were going away to hide from—from everything. We stopped in the woods to burn the—those things. That's the first time I knew she had the revolver. We had talked about suicide at first, but I had persuaded her—thought I had persuaded her—not to. I tried to take the revolver away from her, but I couldn't. She shot herself while I was trying to get it away. I tried to stop her. I didn't kill her!"

This was getting somewhere.

"And then?" I encouraged her.

"And then I went to Sacramento and left the car there, and came back to San Francisco. Ruth told me she had written Raymond Elwood a letter. She told me that before I persuaded her not to kill herself—the first time. I tried to get the letter from Raymond. She had written him she was going to kill herself. I tried to get the letter, but Raymond said he had given it to Hador.

"So I came here this evening to get it. I had just found it when there was a lot of noise upstairs. Then Hador came in and found me. He bolted the door. And—and I shot him with the revolver that was in the safe. I—I shot him when he turned around, before he could say anything. It had to be that way, or I couldn't."

"You mean you shot him without being threatened or attacked by him?" Pat asked.

"Yes. I was afraid of him, afraid to let him speak. I hated him! I couldn't help it. It had to be that way. If he had talked I couldn't have shot him. He—he wouldn't have let me!"

"Who was this Hador?" I asked.

She looked away from Pat and me, at the walls, at the ceiling, at the queer little dead man on the floor.

"He was a—" She cleared her throat, and started again, staring down at her feet. "Raymond Elwood brought us here the first time. We thought it was funny. But Hador was a devil. He told you things and you believed them. You couldn't help it. He told you *everything* and you believed it. Perhaps we were drugged. There was always a warm bluish wine. It must have been drugged. We couldn't have done those things if it hadn't. Nobody would. He called himself a priest—a priest of Alzoa. He taught a freeing of the spirit from the flesh by—"

Her voice broke huskily. She shuddered.

"It was horrible!" she went on presently in the silence Pat and I had left for her. "But you believed him. That is the whole thing. You can't understand it unless you understand that. The things he taught could not be so. But he said they were, and you *believed* they were. Or maybe—I don't know—maybe you pretended you believed them, because you were crazy and drugs were in your blood. We came back again and again, for weeks, months, before the disgust that had to come drove us away.

"We stopped coming, Ruth and I—and Irma. And then we found out what he was. He demanded money, more money than we had been paying while we believed—or pretended belief—in his cult. We couldn't give him the money he demanded. I told him we wouldn't. He sent us photographs—of us—taken during the—the times here. They were—*pictures*—*you—couldn't—explain*. And they were true! We knew them true! What could we do? He said he would send copies to our father, every friend, everyone we knew—unless we paid.

"What could we do—except pay? We got the money somehow. We gave him money—more—more—more. And then we had no more—could get no more. We didn't know what to do! There was nothing to do, except—Ruth and Irma wanted to kill themselves. I thought of that, too. But I persuaded Ruth not to. I said we'd go away. I'd take her away—keep her safe. And then—then—this!"

She stopped talking, went on staring at her feet.

I looked again at the little dead man on the floor, weird in his black cap and clothes. No more blood came from his throat.

It wasn't hard to put the pieces together. This dead Hador, self-ordained priest of something or other, staging orgies under the alias of religious ceremonies. Elwood, his confederate, bringing women of family and wealth to him. A room lighted for photography, with a concealed camera. Contributions from his converts so long as they were faithful to the cult. Blackmail—with the help of the photographs—afterward.

I looked from Hador to Pat Reddy. He was scowling at the dead man. No sound came from outside the room.

"You have the letter your sister wrote Elwood?" I asked the girl.

Her hand flashed to her bosom, and crinkled paper there.

"Yes."

"It says plainly she meant to kill herself?"

"Yes."

"That ought to square her with Contra Costa County," I said to Pat.

He nodded his battered head.

"It ought to," he agreed. "It's not likely that they could prove murder on her even without that letter. With it, they'll not take her into court. That's a safe bet. Another is that she won't have any trouble over this shooting. She'll come out of court free, and thanked in the bargain."

Myra Banbrock flinched away from Pat as if he had hit her in the face.

I was her father's hired man just now. I saw her side of the affair.

I lit a cigarette and studied what I could see of Pat's face through blood and grime. Pat is a right guy.

"Listen, Pat," I wheedled him, though with a voice that was as if I were not trying to wheedle him at all. "Miss Banbrock can go into court and come out free and thanked, as you say. But to do it, she's got to use everything she knows.

She's got to have all the evidence there is. She's got to use all those photographs Hador took—or all we can find of them.

"Some of those pictures have sent women to suicide, Pat—at least two that we know. If Miss Banbrock goes into court, we've got to make the photographs of God knows how many other women public property. We've got to advertise things that will put Miss Banbrock—and you can't say how many other women and girls—in a position that at least two women have killed themselves to escape."

Pat scowled at me and rubbed his dirty chin with a dirtier thumb.

I took a deep breath and made my play. "Pat, you and I came here to question Raymond Elwood, having traced him here. Maybe we suspected him of being tied up with the mob that knocked over the St. Louis bank last month. Maybe we suspected him of handling the stuff that was taken from the mail cars in that stick-up near Denver week before last. Anyway, we were after him, knowing that he had a lot of money that came from nowhere, and a real estate office that did no real estate business.

"We came here to question him in connection with one of these jobs I've mentioned. We were jumped by a couple of the Negroes upstairs when they found we were sleuths. The rest of it grew out of that. This religious cult business was just something we ran into, and didn't interest us especially. So far as we knew, all these folks jumped us just through friend-ship for the man we were trying to question. Hador was one of them, and, tussling with you, you shot him with his own gun, which, of course, is the one Miss Banbrock found in the safe."

Reddy didn't seem to like my suggestion at all. The eyes with which he regarded me were decidedly sour.

"You're goofy," he accused me. "What'll that get anybody? That won't keep Miss Banbrock out of it. She's here, isn't she, and the rest of it will come out like thread off a spool."

"But Miss Banbrock *wasn't* here," I explained. "Maybe the upstairs is full of coppers by now. Maybe not. Anyway, you're going to take Miss Banbrock out of here and turn her over to Dick Foley, who will take her home. She's got nothing to do with this party. Tomorrow she, and her father's lawyer, and I, will all go up to Martinez and make a deal with the prosecuting attorney of Contra Costa County. We'll show him how Ruth killed herself. If somebody happens to connect the Elwood who I hope is dead upstairs with the Elwood who knew the girls and Mrs. Correll, what of it? If we keep out of court—as we'll do by convincing the Contra Costa people they can't possibly convict her of her sister's murder—we'll keep out of the newspapers—and out of trouble."

Pat hung fire, thumb still to chin.

"Remember," I urged him, "it's not only Miss Banbrock we're doing this for. It's a couple of dead ones, and a flock of live ones, who certainly got mixed up with Hador of their own accords, but who don't stop being human beings on that account."

Pat shook his head stubbornly.

"I'm sorry," I told the girl with faked hopelessness. "I've done all I can, but it's a lot to ask of Reddy. I don't know that I blame him for being afraid to take a chance on—"

Pat is Irish. "Don't be so damned quick to fly off," he snapped at me, cutting short my hypocrisy. "But why do I have to be the one that shot this Hador? Why not you?"

I had him!

"Because," I explained, "you're a bull and I'm not. There'll be less chance of a slip-up if he was shot by a bona fide, star-wearing, flat-footed officer of the peace. I killed most of those birds upstairs. You ought to do something to show you were here."

That was only part of the truth. My idea was that if Pat took the credit, he couldn't very well ease himself out afterward, no matter what happened. Pat's a right guy, and I'd trust him anywhere—but you can trust a man just as easily if you have him sewed up.

Pat grumbled and shook his head, but, "I'm ruining myself, I don't doubt," he growled, "but I'll do it, this once."

"Attaboy!" I went over to pick up the girl's hat from the corner in which it lay. "I'll wait here until you come back from turning her over to Dick." I gave the girl her hat and orders together. "You go to your home with the man Reddy turns you over to. Stay there until I come, which will be as soon as I can make it. Don't tell anybody anything, except that I told you to keep quiet. That includes your father. Tell him I told you not to tell him even where you saw me. Got it?"

"Yes, and I—"

Gratitude is nice to think about afterward, but it takes time when there's work to be done.

"Get going, Pat!"

They went.

As soon as I was alone with the dead man I stepped over him and knelt in front of the safe, pushing letters and papers away, hunting for photographs. None was in sight. One compartment of the safe was locked.

I frisked the corpse. No key. The locked compartment wasn't very strong, but neither am I the best safe-burglar in the West. It took me a while to get into it.

What I wanted was there. A thick sheaf of negatives. A stack of prints—half a hundred of them.

I started to run through them, hunting for the Banbrock girls' pictures. I wanted to have them pocketed before Pat came back. I didn't know how much farther he would let me go.

Luck was against me—and the time I had wasted getting into the compartment. He was back before I had got past the sixth print in the stack. Those six had been—pretty bad.

"Well, that's done," Pat growled at me as he came into the room. "Dick's got her. Elwood is dead, and so is the only one of the Negroes I saw upstairs. Everybody else seems to have beat it. No bulls have shown—so I put in a call for a wagonful."

I stood up, holding the sheaf of negatives in one hand, the prints in the other.

"What's all that?" he asked.

I went after him again. "Photographs. You've just done me a big favor, Pat, and I'm not hoggish enough to ask another. But I'm going to put something in front of you, Pat. I'll give you the lay, and you can name it.

"These"—I waved the pictures at him—"are Hador's meal-tickets—the photos he was either collecting on or planning to collect on. They're photographs of people, Pat, mostly women and girls, and some of them are pretty rotten.

"If tomorrow's papers say that a flock of photos were found in this house after the fireworks, there's going to be a fat suicide-list in the next day's papers, and a fatter list of disappearances. If the papers say nothing about the photos, the lists may be a little smaller, but not much. Some of the people whose pictures are here know they are here. They will expect the police to come hunting for them. We know this much about the photographs—two women have killed themselves to get away from them. This is an armful of stuff that can dynamite a lot of people, Pat, and a lot of families—no matter which of those two ways the papers read.

"But, suppose, Pat, the papers say that just before you shot Hador he succeeded in burning a lot of pictures and papers, burning them beyond recognition. Isn't it likely, then, that there won't be any suicides? That some of the disappearances of recent months may clear themselves up? There she is, Pat—you name it."

Looking back, it seems to me I had come a lot nearer being eloquent than ever before in my life.

But Pat didn't applaud. He cursed me. He cursed me thoroughly, bitterly, and with an amount of feeling that told me I had won another point in my little game. He called me more things than I ever listened to before from a man who was built of meat and bone, and who therefore could be smacked.

When he was through, we carried the papers and photographs and a small book of addresses we found in the safe into the next room, and fed them to the little round iron stove there. The last of them was ash before we heard the police overhead.

"That's absolutely all!" Pat declared when we got up from our work. "Don't ever ask me to do anything else for you if you live to be a thousand."

"That's absolutely all," I echoed.

I like Pat. He is a right guy. The sixth photograph in the stack had been of his wife—the coffee importer's reckless, hot-eyed daughter.

# THE COLLECTOR COMES AFTER PAYDAY

BY FLETCHER FLORA

*Lower Market Street*

(Originally published in 1953)

Frankie looked through a lot of bars before he found the old man. He was sitting in a booth in a joint on lower Market Street with a dame Frankie didn't know. They were both sitting on the same side of the booth, and Frankie could see that their thighs were plastered together like a couple of strips of Scotch tape.

"Come on home, Pop," Frankie said. "You come on home."

The woman looked up at him, and her lips twisted in a scarlet sneer. The scarlet was smeared on the lips, as if she'd been doing a lot of kissing, and the lips had a kind of bruised and swollen look, as if the kisses had been pretty enthusiastic.

"Go to hell away, sonny," she said.

She lifted her martini glass by its thin stem and tilted it against her mouth. Frankie reached across the booth in front of the old man and slapped the glass out of her hand. It shivered with a thin, musical sound against the wall, and gin and vermouth splashed down between the full, alert breasts that were half out of her low-cut dress. The olive bounced on the table and rolled off.

The woman raised up as far as she could in the cramped booth, her eyes hot and smoky with gin and rage.

"You little son of a bitch," she said softly.

Frankie grabbed her by a wrist and twisted the skin around on the bone.

"Leave Pop alone," he said. "You quit acting like a tramp and leave him alone."

Then the old man hacked down on Frankie's arm with the horny edge of his hand. It was like getting hit with a dull hatchet. Frankie's fingers went numb, dropping away from the woman's wrist, and he swung sideways with his left hand at the old man's face. The old man caught the fist in a big palm and gave Frankie a hard shove backward.

"Blow, sonny," he said.

For a guy not young at all, he was plenty tough. His eyes were like two yellow agates, and his mouth was a thin, cruel trap under a bold nose. From the way his body behaved, it was obvious that he still had good muscular coordination. He was poised, balanced like a trained fighter.

Frankie saw everything in a kind of pink, billowing mist. He moved back up to the booth with his fists clenched, and in spite of everything he could do, tears of fury and frustration spilled out of his eyes and streaked his cheeks.

"You get the hell out of this," he said. "You ought to be ashamed, drinking and playing around this way."

The old man slipped out of the booth, quick as a snake, and chopped Frankie in the mouth with a short right that traveled straight as a piston. Frankie hit the floor and rolled over, spitting a tooth and blood. He was crazy. Getting up, he staggered back at the old man, cursing and sobbing and swinging like a girl. This time the old man set him up with a left jab and threw a bomb. Frankie went over backward like a post, his head smacking with a wet rotten sound.

No one bothered about him. Except to laugh, that is. Lying there on the floor, he could hear the laughter rise and diminish and rise again. It was the final and utter degradation of a guy who'd never had much dignity to start with. Rolling over and struggling up to his hands and knees, he was violently sick, his stomach contracting and expanding in harsh spasms. After a long time, he got the rest of the way to his feet in slow, agonizing stages. His chin and shirt front were foul with blood and spittle.

In the booth, ignoring him, the old man and the woman were in a hot clinch, their mouths adhering in mutual suction. The lecherous old man's right hand was busy, and Frankie saw through his private red fog the quivering reaction of the woman's straining body. Turning away, Frankie went out. The floor kept tilting up under his feet and then dropping suddenly away. All around him, he could hear the ribald laughter.

It was six blocks to the place where he'd parked his old Plymouth. He walked slowly along the littered, narrow street, hugging the dark buildings, the night air a knife in his lungs. Now and then he stopped to lean against solid brick until the erratic pavement leveled off and held still. Once, at the mouth of an alley, he was sick again, bringing up a thin, bitter fluid into his mouth.

It took him almost an hour to get back to the shabby walkup apartment that was the best a guy with no luck could manage. In the bathroom, he splashed cold water on his face, gasping with pain. The smoky mirror above the lavatory distorted his face, exaggerating the ugliness of smashed, swollen lips drawn back from bloody gums. He patted his face dry with a towel and poured himself a double shot in the living room. He tossed the whiskey far back into his mouth beyond his raw lips, gagging and choking from the sudden fiery wash in his throat.

Dropping into a chair, he began to think. Not with any conscious direction. His mind functioned, with everything coming now to a bad end, in a kind of numb and lucid detachment. Suddenly, he was strangely indifferent. Nothing had happened, after all, that couldn't have been anticipated by a guy with no luck whatever.

It was funny, the way he was no longer very concerned about anything. Sitting there in the drab living room in the dull immunity to shame that comes from the ultimate humiliation, he found his mind working itself back at random to the early days at home with the old man. Back to the days when his mother, a beaten nonentity, had been alive. Not a lovable character, the old man. Not easy on wife or kid. A harsh meter of stern discipline for all delinquencies but his own. A master of the deferred payment technique. In the old days, when Frankie was a kid at home, wrongdoing had never been met with swift and unconsidered punishment that would have been as quickly forgotten. The old man had remarked and remembered. Later, often after Frankie had completely forgotten the adolescent evil he'd committed, there was sure to be something that he wanted very much to do. Then the old man would look at him with skimmed milk eyes and say, "No. Have you forgotten the offense for which you haven't paid? For that, you cannot do this thing."

Wait till it really hurts. That had been the old man's way.

Remembering, Frankie laughed softly, air hissing with no inflection of humor through the hole where his lost tooth had been. No luck. Never any luck. He'd even been a loser in drawing an old man—a bastard with a memory like an elephant and a perverted set of values.

The laughter hurt Frankie's mangled lips, and he cut it off, sitting slumped in the chair with his eyes in a dead focus on the floor. It was really very strange, the way he felt. Not tired. Not sleepy. Not much of anything. Just sort of released and out of it, like a religious queer staring at his belly button.

He was still sitting there at three o'clock in the morning when the old man came in. He was sloppy drunk, and the lines of his face had blurred, letting his features run together in a kind of soft smear. His eyes were rheumy infections in the smear, and his mouth still wore enough of the cheap lipstick to give him the appearance of wearing a grotesque clown's mask. He stood, swaying, almost helpless, with his legs spread wide and his hands on his hips in a posture of defiance, and Frankie looked back at him from his chair. It made him sick to see the old man so ugly, satiety in his flaccid face and the nauseous perfume of juniper berries like a fog around him.

The old man spit and laughed hoarsely. The saliva landed on the toe of Frankie's shoe, a milky blob. Without moving, Frankie watched the old man weave into the bedroom with erratic manipulation of legs and hips.

Frankie kept on sitting in the chair for perhaps five minutes longer, then he sighed and got up and walked into the bedroom after the old man. The old man was standing in the middle of the room in his underwear. His legs were corded with swollen blue veins that bulged the fish-belly skin. On the right thigh there was an angry red spot that would probably blacken. When he saw Frankie watching him, his rheumy eyes went hot with scorn.

"My son," he said. "My precious son, Frankie."

Frankie didn't answer. As he moved toward the old man slowly, smiling faintly, the pain of the smile on his mangled lips was a pale reflection of the dull pain in his heart. He had almost closed the distance between them before the old man's gin-soaked brain understood that Frankie was going to kill him. And he was too drunk now to defend himself, even against Frankie. The scorn faded from his eyes and terror flooded in, cold and incredulous.

"No, Frankie," he whispered. "For God's sake, no."

Frankie still didn't say anything, and the old man tried to back away, but by that time it was too late, and Frankie's thumbs were buried in his throat. His tongue came out, his legs beat in a hellish threshing, and his fists battered wildly at Frankie's face. But it did no good, for Frankie was feeling very strong. He was feeling stronger than he had ever felt in his life before. And good, too. A powerful, surging sense of well-being. A wild, singing exhilaration that increased in ratio to the pressure of his grip.

The old man had been dead for minutes when Frankie finally let him go. He slipped down to the floor in a limp huddle of old flesh and fabric, and Frankie stood looking down at him, the narcotic-like pleasure draining out of him and leaving him again with that odd, incongruous feeling of detachment.

He realized, of course, that the end was his as much as the old man's. It was the end for both of them. Recalling the .38 revolver on a shelf in the closet, he considered for a moment the idea of suicide, but not very seriously. Not that he was repelled by the thought of death. It was just that he didn't quite have the guts.

He supposed that he should call the police, and he went so far as to turn away toward the living room and the telephone. Then he stopped, struck by an idea that captured his fancy. He saw himself walking into the precinct station with the old man's dead body in his arms. He heard himself saying quietly, "This is my father. I've just killed him." Drab little Frankie, no-luck Frankie, having in the end his moment of dramatic ascendancy. It was a prospect that fed an old and functional hunger of his soul, and he turned back, looking at the body on the floor. Smiling dreamily with his thick lips, he felt within himself a rebirth of that singing exhilaration.

At the last moment, he found in himself a sick horror that made it impossible for him to bear excessive contact with the dead flesh, so he dressed the body, struggling with uncooperative arms and legs. After that, it was so easy. It was so crazy easy. If he'd given a damn, if he'd really been trying to get away with it, he could never have pulled it off in a million years.

With the old man dead in his arms, he walked out of the apartment and down the stairs and across the walk to the Plymouth at the curb. He opened the front door and put him in the seat and closed the door again. Then, standing there beside the car, he looked around and saw that there was no one in sight. So far as he knew, not a soul had seen him.

It was then that the enormity of the thing struck him, and he began to laugh softly, hysteria threading the laughter. No-luck Frankie doing a thing like that. No-luck Frankie himself just walking out of an apartment house with a corpse in his arms and not a damned soul the wiser. You couldn't get life any crazier than that. He kept on laughing, clutching the handle of the car door with one hand, his body shaking and his lips cracking open again to let a thin red line trace its way down his chin.

After a while, he choked off the laughter on a series of throaty little gasps that tore painfully at his throat. Lighting a cigarette, he went around the car and got in beside the old man on the driver's side.

He drove at a moderate rate of speed, savoring morbidly the approach to his big scene. Now, in the process of execution, the drama of it gained even more in its appeal to him.

It gave him a kind of satisfaction he had never known.

He was driving east on Mason Street. The side streets on the south descended to their intersections on forty-five-degree grades. Possessing the right-of-way, he crossed the intersections without looking, absorbed in his thoughts. For that reason, he neither saw nor heard the transport van until it was too late. At the last instant, he heard the shrill screaming of rubber on concrete and looked up and right to see the tremendous steel monster roaring down upon him.

His own scream cut across the complaint of giant tires, and he hurled himself away reflexively, striking the door with a shoulder and clawing at the handle. The door burst open at the precise instant of impact, and he was catapulted through the air like a flapping doll. Striking the pavement, he rolled over and over, protecting his head with his arms instinctively. The overwhelming crash of the Plymouth crumpling under the van was modified in his ears by the fading of consciousness.

On his back, he lay quietly and was aware of smaller sounds—distant screams, pounding feet, horrified voices, and, after a bit, the far away whine of sirens growing steadily nearer and louder.

Someone knelt beside him, felt his pulse, said in manifest incredulity, "This guy's hardly scratched. It's a God-damned miracle."

A voice, more distant, rising on the threat of hysteria, "Christ! This one's hamburger. Nothing but hamburger."

And he continued to lie there in the screaming night with the laughter coming back and the wild wonder growing. What was it? What in God's name was it? A guy who'd started and ended with a sour bastard of an old man and never any luck between. A guy who'd had it all, and most of it bad. A guy like that getting, all of a sudden, two fantastic breaks you wouldn't have believed could happen. Walking out of a house with a body in his arms, scot-free and away. Surviving with no more than a few bruises a smash-up that should have smeared him for keeps. Maybe it was because he'd quit caring. Maybe the tide turns when you no longer give a damn.

Then, in a sudden comprehensive flash, the full significance of the situation struck him. Hamburger, someone had said. Nothing but hamburger. Thanks to the cock-eyed collaboration of the gods and a truck driver, *he had disposed of the old man in a manner above suspicion.* He lay on the pavement with the wonder of it still growing and growing, and his insides shook with delirious internal laughter.

In time, he rode a litter to an ambulance, and the ambulance to a hospital. He slept like a child in antiseptic cleanliness between cool sheets, and in the morning he had pictures taken of his head. Twenty-four hours later he was told that there was no concussion, and released. With the most sympathetic cooperation of officials, he collected the old man at the morgue and transferred him to a crematory.

When he left the crematory, he took the old man with him in an urn. In the apartment, he set the urn on a table in the living room and stood looking at it. He had developed for the old man, since the smash-up, a feeling of warm affection. In his heart there was no hard feeling, no lingering animosity. He found his parent in his present state, a handful of ashes, considerably more lovable than he had ever found him before. Besides, he had brought Frankie luck. In the end, in shame and violence and blood, he had brought him the luck he had never had.

Putting the old man away on a shelf in the closet, Frankie checked his finances and found that he could assemble forty dollars. He fingered the green stuff and considered possibilities. Eagerness to ride his luck had assumed the force of compulsion. In the saddle, he left the apartment and went over to Nick Loemke's bar on Market Street.

He found Nick in a lull, polishing glass behind the mahogany. Nick examined him sleepily and made a swipe at the bar with his towel.

"What's on your mind, Frankie?"

"Double shot of rye," Frankie said.

His lips and gums were still a little raw, so he took it easy with the rye, tossing it in short swallows on the back of his tongue.

"Where's Joe Tonty anchored this week?" he asked.

"What the hell do you care, Frankie? You can't afford to operate in that class."

"You never know. You never know until you try."

Frankie finished his rye and spun the glass off his fingertips across the bar. It hit the trough on the inside edge and hopped up into the air. Nick had to grab it in a hurry to keep it from going off onto the floor. He glared at Frankie and doused the glass in the antiseptic solution under the bar.

"What the hell's the matter with you, Frankie? You lost your marbles?"

"Okay, okay," Frankie said. "I ask for information and you give me lip. You going to tell me where Tonty's anchored, or aren't you?"

Nick shrugged. "All right, sucker. It's your lettuce. Over on Third Street. Upstairs over the old Bonfile garage."

Frankie dropped a skin on the bar and went out. Between Third and Fourth, he navigated a narrow, cluttered alley to the rear of the Bonfile garage and climbed a flight of iron, exterior stairs to a plank door that was locked. He pounded on the door with the meaty heel of his fist and got the response of a crack with an eye and a voice behind it.

The voice said, "Hello, Frankie. What the hell you doing here?"

"This where Tonty's anchored?"

"That's right."

"Then what the hell you think I'm doing here? You want me to spell it out for you?"

The crack widened to reveal a flat face split in a grin between thick ears. "My, my. We're riding high tonight, ain't we?"

"You want my money or not?"

The crack spread still wider, and the grinning gorilla shuffled back out of it. "Sure, Frankie, sure. Every little bit helps."

Frankie went in past the gorilla and down the long cement-floored room to the craps table. It was still early, and the big stuff wasn't moving yet. Just right for forty bucks. Or thirty-nine, deducting a double shot.

Frankie got his belly against the edge of the table and laid a fast side bet that the point would come.

It came.

He laid three more in a hurry, betting the accumulation and mixing them pro and con without thinking much about it.

The points came or not, just as Frankie bet them.

When the dice came around to him, he was fat, and he laid the bundle. He tossed a seven, made his point twice, and tossed another seven, letting the bundle grow. Then, playing a hunch without benefit of thought, he drew most of the bundle off the table.

He crapped out and passed the dice.

Across the table, Joe Tonty's face was a slab of gray rock. His eyes flicked over Frankie, and his shoulders twitched in a shrug.

"Your luck's running, Frankie. You better ride it."

"Sure," Frankie said. "I'll ride."

It kept running for two hours, and Frankie rode it all the way. When he finally had a sudden flat feeling, a kind of interior collapse, he pulled out. Not that he felt his luck had quit running for keeps. Just resting. Just taking a breather. He descended the iron steps into the alley and crossed over to Market for a nightcap at Nick's. A little later, in the living room of the apartment, he counted eight grand. It was hard to believe, little Frankie with eight big grand all at once and all his own. Not even any withholding tax.

He was shaken again by the silent delirium that was becoming an integral element of his chronic mood, and he went over to the closet and opened the door, looking up at the old man in his urn.

"Thanks, Pop," he said. "Thanks."

He slept soundly and got up about noon. After a hearty lunch, he went to the track with the eight grand in his pocket. He was in time for the second race, and he checked the entries. But he didn't feel anything, so he let it go.

Checking the entries in the third, he still didn't get any nudge. Something seemed to be getting in the way, coming between him and his luck. Maybe, he realized suddenly, it was the warm pressure of a long flank against his.

He turned, looking into brown eyes that were as warm and the touch of flank. Under the eyes there was a flash of white in a margin of red, and above them, a heavy sheen of pale yellow with streaks of off-white running through it. At first, Frankie thought she'd just been sloppy with a dye job, but then he saw that the two-toned effect was natural.

"Crowded, isn't it?" she said.

Frankie grinned. "I like crowds."

He was trying to think of what the hair reminded him of when he got the nudge. His eyes popped down to the program in his hands and back up to the dame. Inside, he'd gone breathless and tense, the way a guy does when he's on the verge of something big.

"What's your name, baby?"

The red and white smile flashed again. "Call me Taffy. Because of my hair, you see."

He saw, all right. He saw a hell of a lot more than she thought he did. He saw number four in the third, and the name was Taffy Candy. One would bring ten if Taffy won, and even Frankie, who was no mental giant, could add another cipher to eight thousand and read the result.

Don't give yourself time to think, that was the trick. If you start thinking, you start figuring odds and consequences, and you're a dead duck. He stood up and slapped the program against his leg.

"Hold a spot for me, baby. If I'm on the beam, it'll be a big day for you and me and a horse."

He hit the window just before closing time and laid the eight grand on Taffy's nose. At the rail of the track, he watched the horses run, and he wasn't surprised, not even excited, when Taffy came in by the nose that had his eight grand on it. It was astonishing how quickly he was becoming accustomed to good fortune. He was already anticipating the breaks as if he'd had them forever. As if they were a natural right.

Like that girl in the stands, for instance. The girl who called herself Taffy. Standing there by the rail, he thought with glan-

dular stirrings of the warm pressure of flank, the strangely al-
luring two-toned pastel hair, the brown eyes and scarlet smile.
A few days ago, he wouldn't have given himself a chance with
a dame like that. He'd have taken it out in thinking. But now
it was different. Luck and a few grand made a hell of a difference. The difference between thinking and acting.

With eight times ten in his pocket, he went back to the
stands. Climbing up to her level with his eyes full of nylon, he
grinned and said, "We all came in, baby, you and me and the
horse. Let's move out of here."

She strained a mocking look through incredible lashes.
"I've already got a date, honey. I'm supposed to meet a guy
here."

"To hell with him."

Her eyebrows arched their plucked backs, and a practiced
tease showed through the lashes. "What makes you think I'd
just walk off with you, mister?"

Frankie dug into his pocket for enough green to make
an impression. The bills were crisp. They made small ticking
sounds when he flipped them with a thumb nail.

"This, maybe," he said.

She eyed the persuasion and stood up. "That's good thinking, honey," she said.

A long time and a lot of places later, Frankie awoke to the gray
light that filtered into his shabby apartment. It was depressing,
he thought, to awake in a dump like this. It was something
that had to be changed.

"Look, baby," he said. "Today we shop for another place.
A big place uptown. Carpets up to your knees, foam rubber
stuff, the works. How about it, baby?"

Beside him, Taffy pressed closer, her lips moving against his naked shoulder with a sleepy animal purr of contentment.

So that day they rented the uptown place, and moved in, and a couple months later Frankie bought the Circle Club.

The club was a nice little spot tucked into a so-so block just outside the perimeter of the big-time glitter area. It was a good location for a brisk trade with the right guy handling it. The current owner was being pressed for the payment of debts by parties who didn't like waiting, and Frankie bought him out for a song.

It was a swell break. Just one more in a long line. Frankie shot a wad on fancy trimmings, and booked a combination that could really jump. With the combo there was a sleek canary who had something for the eyes as well as the ears. The food and the liquor were fair, which is all anyone expects in a night spot, and up to the time of Linda Lee, business was good.

After Linda Lee, business was more than good. It was booming. The word always goes out on a gal like Linda. The guys come in with their dames, and after they've had the quota of looking that the tariff buys, they go someplace and turn off the lights and pretend that the dames are Linda.

Linda Lee wasn't her real name, of course, but it suited her looks and her business. Ostensibly, the business was dancing. Actually, it was taking off her clothes. In Linda's case, that was sufficient. As for the looks, they were Linda's, and they were something. Dusky skin and eyes on the slant. Black hair with blue highlights, soft and shining, brushing her shoulders and slashing across her forehead in bangs above perfect unplucked brows. A lithe, vibrant body with an upswept effect that a guy couldn't believe from seeing and so had to keep coming back for another look to convince himself.

She sent Frankie. At first, the day she came into his office at the Circle Club looking for a job, he didn't see anything but a looker in a town that was littered with them. That was when she still had her clothes on.

He rocked back in his swivel and stared across his desk at her through the thin, lifting smoke from his cigarette.

"You a dancer, you say?"

"Yes."

"A good one."

"Not very."

That surprised Frankie. He took his cigarette out of his mouth and let his eyes make a brief tour of her points of interest.

"No? What else you got that a guy would pay to see?"

She showed him what she had. Frankie sat there watching her emerge slowly from her clothes, and the small office got steadily smaller, so hot that it was almost suffocating. Frankie's knitted tie was hemp instead of silk, and the knot was a hangman's knot, cutting deeply into his throat until he was breathing in labored gasps. The palms of his hands dripped salty water. His whole body was wet with sweat.

When he was able to speak, he said, "Who the hell's going to care about the dancing? Can you start tonight?"

She could and did. And so did Frankie. For a guy with a temperature as high as his, he played it pretty cool. He kept the pressure on her, all right, but he didn't force it. Not that he was too good for it. It just wasn't practical. The threat of being fired doesn't mean much to a gal with a dozen other places to go. By the time Frankie was desperate enough for threats, he was having to raise her pay every second week to hang on to her.

She liked him, though. He knew damned well she liked him. He could tell by the way the heat came up in her slanted eyes when she looked at him. He could tell by the way her hands sometimes reached out for him, touching him lightly, straying with brief abandon. But she was like mercury. He couldn't hold her when he reached back.

The night he decided to try mink, he came into the club late, just as Linda was moving onto the small circular floor in a blue spot. He stood for a minute against the wall, holding the long cardboard box under his arm, watching the emerging dusky body, his pulse matching the tropical tempo of drums in the darkness. Before the act was over, he moved on around the edge of the floor and back to the door of Linda's room.

Inside, he lay the box on the dressing table and sat down. Waiting, he could hear faintly the crescendo of drums and muted brass that indicated Linda's exit. The sound of her footsteps in the hall was lost in the surge of applause that continued long after she had left the floor.

She closed the door behind her and stood leaning against it, head back and eyes shining, her breasts rising and falling in deep, rhythmic breathing. Light and shadow stressed the convexities and hollows of her body.

"Hello, Frankie," she said. "Nice surprise."

He stood up, pulses hammering. "Nicer than you think, baby. I've brought you something."

She saw the box behind him on the dressing table and moved toward it, flat muscles rippling with silken smoothness beneath dusky skin. Her exclamation was like a delighted child's.

"Tell me what it is."

"Open it, baby."

Her fingers worked deftly at the knot of the cord, lifted the top of the box away. Without speaking, she shook out the luxurious fur coat, slipped into it and hugged it around her body. She stood entranced, her back to Frankie, looking at her reflection in the dim depths of the mirror.

Closing in behind her, he took her shoulders in his hands. Capturing the hands in hers, she pulled them around her body and under the coat. Her head fell back onto his shoulder. Her breath sighed through parted lips. He could feel in his hands the vibrations of her shivering flesh.

She said sleepily, "You're a sweet guy, Frankie. A lucky guy, too. You're going places. Too bad I can't go along."

"Why not, baby? Why not go along?"

Her head rolled on his shoulder, her lips burning his neck. "Look, Frankie. When I go for a ride, I go first-class. No cheap tourist accommodations for Linda."

"I don't get you, baby. You call mink cheap?"

"It's not the mink. It's being second. It's the idea of taking what's left over."

"You mean Taffy?"

She closed her eyes and said nothing, and Frankie laughed softly. "Taffy's expendable, baby. Strictly expendable."

"Just like that? Maybe she won't let go."

"How the hell can she help it?"

"She's legal. That always helps."

"Married? You think Taffy and I are married?" He laughed again, his shoulders shaking with it. "Taffy and I are temporary, baby. I never figure it any other way. Nothing on paper. All off the record. We last just as long as I want us to."

She twisted against him, her arms coming up around his neck. Her breath was in his mouth.

"How long, Frankie? How long do you want?"

His hand moved down the soft curve of her spine, drawing her in. He said hoarsely, "As far as Taffy's concerned, I quit wanting when I saw you. Tonight I'll make it official."

She put her mouth over his, and he felt the hot flicking of her tongue. Then she pushed away violently, staggering back against the dressing table. The mink hung open from her shoulders.

"Afterward, Frankie," she whispered. "Afterward."

He stood there blind, everything dissolved in shimmering waves of heat. At last, sight returning, he laughed shakily and moved to the door. Hand on the knob, he looked back at her.

"Like you say, baby—afterward."

He went out into the hall and through the rear door into the alley. There was a small area back there in which he kept his convertible Caddy tucked away. Long, sleek, ice-blue and glittering chrome. A long way from the old Plymouth.

Behind the wheel, sending the big machine singing through the streets, he felt the tremendous uplift that comes to a man who approaches a crisis with assurance of triumph. His emotional drive was in harmony with the leashed power of the Caddy's throbbing engine. Wearing his new personality, he could hardly remember the old Frankie. It was impossible to believe that he had once, not long ago, been driven by shame to a longing for death. Life was good. All it required was luck and guts. With luck and guts, a guy could do anything. A guy could live forever.

At the uptown apartment house, he ascended in the swift, whispering elevator and let himself into his living room with the key he carried. The living room itself was dark, but light sliced into the darkness from the partially open door of the bedroom. Silently, he crossed the carpet that wasn't actually quite up to his knees and pushed the bedroom door all the way open.

Taffy was reading in bed. Her sheer nylon gown kept nothing hidden, but what it showed was nothing Frankie hadn't seen before, and he was tired of it. He stood for a moment looking at her, wondering what would be the best way to do it. The direct way, he decided. The tough way. Get it over with, and to hell with it.

From the bed, Taffy said, "Hi, honey. You're early tonight."

Without answering, Frankie walked over to the closet and slammed back one of the sliding panels. He dragged a cowhide overnight bag off a shelf and carried it to the bed. Snapping the locks, he spread the bag open.

Taffy sat up straighter against her silk pillows, two small spots of color burning suddenly over her cheek bones. "What's up, Frankie? You going someplace?"

He went to a chest of drawers, returned with pajamas and a clean shirt. "That ought to be obvious. As a matter of fact, I'm going to a hotel."

"Why, Frankie? What's the idea?"

He looked down at her, feeling the strong emotional drive. "The idea is that we're through, baby. Finished. I'm moving out."

Her breath whistled in a sharp sucking inhalation, and she swung out of bed in a fragile nylon mist. Her hands clutched at him.

"No, Frankie! Not like this. Not after all the luck I've brought you."

He laughed brutally, remembering the old man. "It wasn't you who brought me luck, baby. It was someone else. That's something you'll never know anything about."

He turned, heading for the chest again, and she grabbed his arm, jerking. He spun with the force of the jerk, smashing his backhand across her mouth. She staggered off until the underside of her knees caught on the bed and held her steady. A bright drop of blood formed on her lower lip and dropped onto her chin. A whimper of pain crawled out of her throat.

"Why, Frankie? Just tell me why."

He shrugged. "A guy grows. A guy goes on to something better. That's just the way it is, baby."

"It's more than that. It's a lot bigger than that. You think I've been two-timing you, Frankie?"

He repeated his brutal laugh. "Two-timing me? I'll tell you something, baby. I wouldn't give a damn if you were sleeping with every punk in town. That's how much I care." He paused, savoring sadism, finding it pleasant. "You want it straight, baby? It's just that I'm sick of you. I'm sick to my guts with the sight of you. That clear enough?"

She came back to him, slowly, lifting her arms like a supplicant. He waited until she was close enough, then he hit her across the mouth again.

Turning his back, he returned to the chest and got the rest of the articles he needed. Just a few things. Enough for the night and tomorrow. In the morning he'd send someone around to clean things out.

At the bed, he tossed the stuff into the overnight bag and snapped it shut.

Over his shoulder, he said, "The rent's paid to the end of the month. After that, you better look for another place to live."

She didn't respond, and remembering his tooth brush, he went into the bathroom for it. When he came out, she was standing there with a .38 in her hand. It was the same .38 he'd once considered killing himself with. That had been the old Frankie, of course.

Not the new Frankie. Death was no consideration in the life of the new Frankie.

"You rotten son of a bitch," she said.

He laughed aloud and started for her, and he just couldn't believe it when the slug slammed into his shoulder.

He looked down in amazement at the place where the crimson began to seep, and his incredulous eyes raised just in time to receive the second slug squarely between them.

And, like the night the old man died, it was funny. In the last split second of sight, it wasn't Taffy standing there with the gun at all. It was the old man again.

The old man with a memory like an elephant.

The old man who always waited until it really hurt.

# SOULS BURNING

BY BILL PRONZINI

*Civic Center*

(Originally published in 1991)

H otel Majestic, Sixth Street, downtown San Francisco. A hell of an address—a hell of a place for an ex-con not long out of Folsom to set up housekeeping. Sixth Street, south of Market—South of the Slot, it used to be called—is the heart of the city's Skid Road and has been for more than half a century.

Eddie Quinlan. A name and a voice out of the past, neither of which I'd recognized when he called that morning. Close to seven years since I had seen or spoken to him, six years since I'd even thought of him. Eddie Quinlan. Edgewalker, shadowman with no real substance or purpose, drifting along the narrow catwalk that separates conventional society from the underworld. Information seller, gofer, small-time bagman, doer of any insignificant job, legitimate or otherwise, that would help keep him in food and shelter, liquor and cigarettes. The kind of man you looked at but never really saw: a modern-day Yehudi, the little man who wasn't there. Eddie Quinlan. Nobody, loser—fall guy. Drug bust in the Tenderloin one night six and a half years ago; one dealer setting up another, and Eddie Quinlan, smalltime bagman, caught in the middle; hard-assed judge, five years in Folsom, goodbye Eddie Quinlan. And the drug dealers? They walked, of course. Both of them.

And now Eddie was out, had been out for six months. And

after six months of freedom, he'd called me. Would I come to his room at the Hotel Majestic tonight around eight? He'd tell me why when he saw me. It was real important—would I come? All right, Eddie. But I couldn't figure it. I had bought information from him in the old days, bits and pieces for five or ten dollars; maybe he had something to sell now. Only I wasn't looking for anything and I hadn't put the word out, so why pick me to call?

If you're smart you don't park your car on the street at night, South of the Slot. I put mine in the Fifth and Mission Garage at 7:45 and walked over to Sixth. It had rained most of the day and the streets were still wet, but now the sky was cold and clear. The kind of night that is as hard as black glass, so that light seems to bounce off the dark instead of shining through it; lights and their colors so bright and sharp reflecting off the night and the wet surfaces that the glare is like splinters against your eyes.

Friday night, and Sixth Street was teeming. Sidewalks jammed—old men, young men, bag ladies, painted ladies, blacks, whites, Asians, addicts, pushers, muttering mental cases, drunks leaning against walls in tight little clusters while they shared paper-bagged bottles of sweet wine and cans of malt liquor; men and women in filthy rags, in smart new outfits topped off with sunglasses, carrying ghetto blasters and red-and-white canes, some of the canes in the hands of individuals who could see as well as I could, and a hidden array of guns and knives and other lethal instruments. Cheap hotels, greasy spoons, seedy taverns, and liquor stores complete with barred windows and cynical proprietors that stayed open well past midnight. Laughter, shouts, curses, threats; bickering and dickering. The stenches of urine and vomit and unwashed bodies and rotgut liquor, and over those like an umbrella, the subtle effluvium of despair. Predators and prey, half hidden in shadow, half revealed in the bright, sharp dazzle of fluorescent lights and bloody neon.

It was a mean street, Sixth, one of the meanest, and I walked it warily. I may be fifty-eight but I'm a big man and I walk hard too; and I look like what I am. Two winos tried to panhandle me and a fat hooker in an orange wig tried to sell me a piece of her tired body, but no one gave me any trouble.

The Majestic was five stories of old wood and plaster and dirty brick, just off Howard Street. In front of its narrow entrance, a crack dealer and one of his customers were haggling over the price of a baggie of rock cocaine; neither of them paid any attention to me as I moved past them. Drug deals go down in the open here, day and night. It's not that the cops don't care, or that they don't patrol Sixth regularly; it's just that the dealers outnumber them ten to one. On Skid Road any crime less severe than aggravated assault is strictly low priority.

Small, barren lobby: no furniture of any kind. The smell of ammonia hung in the air like swamp gas. Behind the cubbyhole desk was an old man with dead eyes that would never see anything they didn't want to see. I said, "Eddie Quinlan," and he said, "Two-oh-two," without moving his lips. There was an elevator but it had an Out of Order sign on it; dust speckled the sign. I went up the adjacent stairs.

The disinfectant smell permeated the second floor hallway as well. Room 202 was just off the stairs, fronting on Sixth; one of the metal 2s on the door had lost a screw and was hanging upside down. I used my knuckles just below it. Scraping noise inside, and a voice said, "Yeah?" I identified myself. A lock clicked, a chain rattled, the door wobbled open, and for the first time in nearly seven years I was looking at Eddie Quinlan.

He hadn't changed much. Little guy, about five-eight, and past forty now. Thin, nondescript features, pale eyes, hair the color of sand. The hair was thinner and the lines in his face were longer and deeper, almost like incisions where they bracketed his nose. Otherwise he was the same Eddie Quinlan.

"Hey," he said, "thanks for coming. I mean it, thanks."

"Sure, Eddie."

"Come on in."

The room made me think of a box—the inside of a huge rotting packing crate. Four bare walls with the scaly remnants of paper on them like psoriatic skin, bare uncarpeted floor, unshaded bulb hanging from the center of a bare ceiling. The bulb was dark; what light there was came from a low-wattage reading lamp and a wash of red-and-green neon from the hotel's sign that spilled in through a single window. Old iron-framed bed, unpainted nightstand, scarred dresser, straight-backed chair next to the bed and in front of the window, alcove with a sink and toilet and no door, closet that wouldn't be much larger than a coffin.

"Not much, is it," Eddie said.

I didn't say anything.

He shut the hall door, locked it. "Only place to sit is that chair there. Unless you want to sit on the bed? Sheets are clean. I try to keep things clean as I can."

"Chair's fine."

I went across to it; Eddie put himself on the bed. A room with a view, he'd said on the phone. Some view. Sitting here you could look down past Howard and up across Mission— almost two full blocks of the worst street in the city. It was so close you could hear the beat of its pulse, the ugly sounds of its living and its dying.

"So why did you ask me here, Eddie? If it's information for sale, I'm not buying right now."

"No, no, nothing like that. I ain't in the business any more."

"Is that right?"

"Prison taught me a lesson. I got rehabilitated." There was no sarcasm or irony in the words; he said them matter-of-factly.

"I'm glad to hear it."

"I been a good citizen ever since I got out. No lie. I haven't had a drink, ain't even been in a bar."

"What are you doing for money?"

"I got a job," he said. "Shipping department at a wholesale sporting goods outfit on Brannan. It don't pay much but it's honest work."

I nodded. "What is it you want, Eddie?"

"Somebody I can talk to, somebody who'll understand—that's all I want. You always treated me decent. Most of 'em, no matter who they were, they treated me like I wasn't even human. Like I was a turd or something."

"Understand what?"

"About what's happening down there."

"Where? Sixth Street?"

"Look at it," he said. He reached over and tapped the window; stared through it. "Look at the people . . . there, you see that guy in the wheelchair and the one pushing him? Across the street there?"

I leaned closer to the glass. The man in the wheelchair wore a military camouflage jacket, had a heavy wool blanket across his lap; the black man manipulating him along the crowded sidewalk was thick-bodied, with a shiny bald head. "I see them."

"White guy's name is Baxter," Eddie said. "Grenade blew up under him in 'Nam and now he's a paraplegic. Lives right here in the Majestic, on this floor down at the end. Deals crack and smack out of his room. Elroy, the black dude, is his bodyguard and roommate. Mean, both of 'em. Couple of months ago, Elroy killed a guy over on Minna that tried to stiff them. Busted his head with a brick. You believe it?"

"I believe it."

"And they ain't the worst on the street. Not the worst."

"I believe that too."

"Before I went to prison I lived and worked with people like that and I never saw what they were. I mean I just never saw it. Now I do, I see it clear—every day walking back and forth to work, every night from up here. It makes you sick after a while, the things you see when you see 'em clear."

"Why don't you move?"

"Where to? I can't afford no place better than this."

"No better room, maybe, but why not another neighborhood? You don't have to live on Sixth Street."

"Wouldn't be much better, any other neighborhood I could buy into. They're all over the city now, the ones like Baxter and Elroy. Used to be it was just Skid Road and the Tenderloin and the ghettos. Now they're everywhere, more and more every day. You know?"

"I know."

"Why? It don't have to be this way, does it?"

Hard times, bad times: alienation, poverty, corruption, too much government, not enough government, lack of social services, lack of caring, drugs like a cancer destroying society. Simplistic explanations that were no explanations at all and as dehumanizing as the ills they described. I was tired of hearing them and I didn't want to repeat them, to

Eddie Quinlan or anybody else. So I said nothing.

He shook his head. "Souls burning everywhere you go," he said, and it was as if the words hurt his mouth coming out.

Souls burning. "You find religion at Folsom, Eddie?"

"Religion? I don't know, maybe a little. Chaplain we had there, I talked to him sometimes. He used to say that about the hard-timers, that their souls were burning and there wasn't nothing he could do to put out the fire. They were doomed, he said, and they'd doom others to burn with 'em.'"

I had nothing to say to that either. In the small silence a voice from outside said distinctly, "Dirty bastard, what you doin' with my pipe?" It was cold in there, with the hard bright night pressing against the window. Next to the door was a rusty steam radiator but it was cold too; the heat would not be on more than a few hours a day, even in the dead of winter, in the Hotel Majestic.

"That's the way it is in the city," Eddie said. "Souls burning. All day long, all night long, souls on fire."

"Don't let it get to you."

"Don't it get to *you?*"

". . . Yes. Sometimes."

He bobbed his head up and down. "You want to do something, you know? You want to try to fix it somehow, put out the fires. There has to be a way."

"I can't tell you what it is," I said.

He said, "If we all just did *something*. It ain't too late. You don't think it's too late?"

"No."

"Me neither. There's still hope."

"Hope, faith, blind optimism—sure."

"You got to believe," he said, nodding. "That's all, you just got to believe."

Angry voices rose suddenly from outside; a woman screamed, thin and brittle. Eddie came off the bed, hauled up the window sash. Chill damp air and street noises came pouring in: shouts, cries, horns honking, cars whispering on the wet pavement, a Muni bus clattering along Mission; more shrieks. He leaned out, peering downward.

"Look," he said, "look."

I stretched forward and looked. On the sidewalk below, a hooker in a leopard-skin coat was running wildly toward Howard; she was the one doing the yelling. Chasing behind her, tight black skirt hiked up over the tops of net stockings and hairy thighs, was a hideously rouged transvestite waving a pocket knife. A group of winos began laughing and chanting "Rape! Rape!" as the hooker and the transvestite ran zig-zagging out of sight on Howard.

Eddie pulled his head back in. The flickery neon wash made his face seem surreal, like a hallucinogenic vision. "That's the way it is," he said sadly. "Night after night, day after day."

With the window open, the cold was intense; it penetrated my clothing and crawled on my skin. I'd had enough of it, and of this room and Eddie Quinlan and Sixth Street.

"Eddie, just what is it you want from me?"

"I already told you. Talk to somebody who understands how it is down there."

"Is that the only reason you asked me here?"

"Ain't it enough?"

"For you, maybe." I got to my feet. "I'll be going now."

He didn't argue. "Sure, you go ahead."

"Nothing else you want to say?"

"Nothing else." He walked to the door with me, unlocked it, and then put out his hand. "Thanks for coming. I appreciate it, I really do."

"Yeah. Good luck, Eddie."

"You too," he said. "Keep the faith."

I went out into the hall, and the door shut gently and the lock clicked behind me.

Downstairs, out of the Majestic, along the mean street and back to the garage where I'd left my car. And all the way I kept thinking: There's something else, something more he wanted from me . . . and I gave it to him by going there and listening to him. But what? What did he really want?

I found out later that night. It was all over the TV—special bulletins and then the eleven o'clock news.

Twenty minutes after I left him, Eddie Quinlan stood at the window of his room-with-a-view, and in less than a minute, using a high-powered semiautomatic rifle he'd taken from the sporting goods outfit where he worked, he shot down fourteen people on the street below. Nine dead, five wounded, one of the wounded in critical condition and not expected to live. Six of the victims were known drug dealers; all of the others also had arrest records, for crimes ranging from prostitution to burglary. Two of the dead were Baxter, the paraplegic ex–Vietnam vet, and his bodyguard, Elroy.

By the time the cops showed up, Sixth Street was empty except for the dead and the dying. No more targets. And up in his room, Eddie Quinlan had sat on the bed and put the rifle's muzzle in his mouth and used his big toe to pull the trigger.

My first reaction was to blame myself. But how could I have known or even guessed? Eddie Quinlan. Nobody, loser, shadow-man without substance or purpose. How could anyone have figured him for a thing like that?

*Somebody I can talk to, somebody who'll understand—that's all I want.*

No. What he'd wanted was somebody to help him justify to himself what he was about to do. Somebody to record his verbal suicide note. Somebody he could trust to pass it on afterward, tell it right and true to the world.

*You want to do something, you know? You want to try to fix it somehow, put out the fires. There has to be a way.*

Nine dead, five wounded, one of the wounded in critical condition and not expected to live. Not that way.

*Souls burning. All day long, all night long, souls on fire.*

The soul that had burned tonight was Eddie Quinlan's.

# THE SECOND COMING

BY JOE GORES

*San Quentin*

(Originally published in 1966)

> *But fix thy eyes upon the valley:*
> *for the river of blood draws nigh, in which boils*
> *every one who by violence injures other.*
> —Canto XII, 46–48, *The Inferno of Dante Alighieri*

I've thought about it a lot, man; like why Victor and I made that terrible scene out there at San Quentin, putting ourselves on that it was just for kicks. Victor was hung up on kicks; they were a thing with him. He was a sharp dark-haired cat with bright eyes, built lean and hard like a French skin-diver. His old man dug only money, so he'd always had plenty of bread. We got this idea out at his pad on Potrero Hill—a penthouse, of course—one afternoon when we were lying around on the sun-porch in swim trunks and drinking gin.

"You know, man," he said, "I have made about every scene in the world. I have balled all the chicks, red and yellow and black and white, and I have gotten high on muggles, bluejays, redbirds, and mescaline. I have even tried the white stuff a time or two. But—"

"You're a goddam tiger, dad."

"—but there is one kick I've never had, man."

When he didn't go on I rolled my head off the quart gin

bottle I was using for a pillow and looked at him. He was giving me a shot with those hot, wild eyes of his.

"So like what is it?"

"I've never watched an execution."

I thought about it a minute, drowsily. The sun was so hot
it was like nailing me right to the air mattress. Watching an
execution. Seeing a man go through the wall. A groovy idea
for an artist.

"Too much," I murmured. "I'm with you, dad."

The next day, of course, I was back at work on some ab-
stracts for my first one-man show and had forgotten all about
it; but that night Victor called me up.

"Did you write to the warden up at San Quentin today,
man? He has to contact the San Francisco police chief and
make sure you don't have a record and aren't a psycho and are
useful to the community."

So I went ahead and wrote the letter, because even sober
it still seemed a cool idea for some kicks; I knew they always
need twelve witnesses to make sure that the accused isn't
sneaked out the back door or something at the last minute
like an old Jimmy Cagney movie. Even so, I lay dead for two
months before the letter came. The star of our show would be
a stud who'd broken into a house trailer near Fort Ord to rape
this Army lieutenant's wife, only right in the middle of it she'd
started screaming so he'd put a pillow over her face to keep
her quiet until he could finish. But she'd quit breathing. There
were eight chicks on the jury and I think like three of them
got broken ankles in the rush to send him to the gas chamber.
Not that I cared. Kicks, man.

Victor picked me up at seven-thirty in the morning, an
hour before we were supposed to report to San Quentin. He
was wearing this really hip Italian import, and fifty-dollar

shoes, and a narrow-brim hat with a little feather in it, so all he needed was a briefcase to be Chairman of the Board. The top was down on the Mercedes, cold as it was, and when he saw my black suit and hand-knit tie he flashed this crazy white-toothed grin you'd never see in any Director's meeting.

"*Too much*, killer! If you'd like comb your hair you could pass for an undertaker coming after the body."

Since I am a very long, thin cat with black hair always hanging in my eyes, who fully dressed weighs as much as a medium-size collie, I guess he wasn't too far off. I put a pint of Jose Cuervo in the side pocket of the car and we split. We were both really turned on: I mean this senseless, breathless hilarity as if we'd just heard the world's funniest joke. Or were just going to.

It was one of those chilly California brights with blue sky and cold sunshine and here and there a cloud like Mr. Big was popping Himself a cap down beyond the horizon. I dug it all: the sail of a lone early yacht out in the Bay like a tossed-away paper cup; the whitecaps flipping around out by Angel Island like they were stoned out of their minds; the top down on the 300-SL so we could smell salt and feel the icy bite of the wind. But beyond the tunnel on U.S. 101, coming down towards Marin City, I felt a sudden sharp chill as if a cloud had passed between me and the sun, but none had; and then I dug for the first time what I was actually doing.

Victor felt it, too, for he turned to me and said, "Must maintain cool, dad."

"I'm with it."

San Quentin Prison, out on the end of its peninsula, looked like a sprawled ugly dragon sunning itself on a rock; we pulled up near the East Gate and there were not even any birds singing. Just a bunch of quiet cats in black, Quakers or

Mennonites or something, protesting capital punishment by their silent presence as they'd done ever since Chessman had gotten his out there. I felt dark frightened things move around inside me when I saw them.

"Let's fall out right here, dad," I said in a momentary sort of panic, "and catch the matinee next week."

But Victor was in kicksville, like desperate to put on all those squares in the black suits. When they looked over at us he jumped up on the back of the bucket seat and spread his arms wide like the Sermon on the Mount. With his tortoise-shell shades and his flashing teeth and that suit which had cost three yards, he looked like Christ on his way to Hollywood.

"Whatsoever ye do unto the least of these, my brethren, ye do unto me," he cried in this ringing apocalyptic voice.

I grabbed his arm and dragged him back down off the seat. "For Christ sake, man, cool it!"

But he went into high laughter and punched my arm with feverish exuberance, and then jerked a tiny American flag from his inside jacket pocket and began waving it around above the windshield. I could see the sweat on his forehead.

"It's worth it to live in this country!" he yelled at them.

He put the car in gear and we went on. I looked back and saw one of those cats crossing himself. It put things back in perspective: they were from nowhere. The Middle Ages. Not that I judged them: that was their scene, man. Unto every cat what he digs the most.

The guard on the gate directed us to a small wooden building set against the outside wall, where we found five other witnesses. Three of them were reporters, one was a fat cat smoking a .45-calibre stogy like a politician from Sacramento, and the last was an Army type in lieutenant's bars, his belt buckle and insignia looking as if he'd been up all night with a can of *Brasso*.

A guard came in and told us to surrender everything in our pockets and get a receipt for it. We had to remove our shoes, too; they were too heavy for the fluoroscope. Then they put us through this groovy little room one-by-one to x-ray us for cameras and so on; they don't want anyone making the Kodak scene while they're busy dropping the pellets. We ended up inside the prison with our shoes back on and with our noses full of that old prison detergent-disinfectant stink.

The politician type, who had these cold slitted eyes like a Sherman tank, started coming on with rank jokes: but everyone put him down, hard, even the reporters. I guess nobody but fuzz ever gets used to executions. The Army stud was at parade rest with a face so pale his freckles looked like a charge of shot. He had reddish hair.

After a while five guards came in to make up the twelve required witnesses. They looked rank, as fuzz always do, and got off in a corner in a little huddle, laughing and gassing together like a bunch of kids kicking a dog. Victor and I sidled over to hear what they were saying.

"Who's sniffing the eggs this morning?" asked one.

"I don't know, I haven't been reading the papers." He yawned when he answered.

"Don't you remember?" urged another, "it's the guy who smothered the woman in the house trailer. Down in the Valley by Salinas."

"Yeah. Soldier's wife; he was raping her and . . ."

Like dogs hearing the plate rattle, they turned in unison toward the Army lieutenant; but just then more fuzz came in to march us to the observation room. We went in a column of twos with a guard beside each one, everyone unconsciously in step as if following a cadence call. I caught myself listening for measured mournful drum rolls.

The observation room was built right around the gas chamber, with rising tiers of benches for extras in case business was brisk. The chamber itself was hexagonal; the three walls in our room were of plate glass with a waist-high brass rail around the outside like the rail in an old-time saloon. The other three walls were steel plate, with a heavy door, rivet-studded, in the center one, and a small observation window in each of the others.

Inside the chamber were just these two massive chairs, probably oak, facing the rear walls side-by-side; their backs were high enough to come to the nape of the neck of anyone sitting in them. Under each was like a bucket that I knew contained hydrochloric acid. At a signal the executioner would drop sodium cyanide pellets into a chute; the pellets would roll down into the bucket; hydrocyanic acid gas would form; and the cat in the chair would be wasted.

The politician type, who had this rich fruity baritone like Burl Ives, asked why they had two chairs.

"That's in case there's a double-header, dad," I said.

"You're kidding." But by his voice the idea pleased him. Then he wheezed plaintively: "I don't see why they turn the chairs away—we can't even watch his face while it's happening to him."

He was a true rank genuine creep, right out from under a rock with the slime barely dry on his scales; but I wouldn't have wanted his dreams. I think he was one of those guys who tastes the big draught many times before he swallows it.

We milled around like cattle around the chute, when they smell the blood from inside and know they're somehow involved; then we heard sounds and saw the door in the back of the chamber swing open. A uniformed guard appeared to stand at attention, followed by a priest dressed all in black like Zorro, with his face hanging down to his belly button. He must have been a new man, because he had trouble maintaining his cool: just standing there beside the guard he dropped his little black book on the floor like three times in a row.

The Army cat said to me, as if he'd wig out unless he broke the silence: "They . . . have it arranged like a stage play, don't they?"

"But no encores," said Victor hollowly.

Another guard showed up in the doorway and they walked in the condemned man. He was like sort of a shock. You expect a stud to *act* like a murderer: I mean, cringe at the sight of the chair because he knows this is it, there's finally no place to go, no appeal to make, or else bound in there full of cheap bravado and go-to-hell. But he just seemed mildly interested, nothing more.

He wore a white shirt with the sleeves rolled up, suntans that looked Army issue, and no tie. Under thirty, brown crew-cut hair—the terrible thing is that I cannot even remember the features on his face, man. The closest I could come to a description would be that he resembled the Army cat right there beside me with his nose to the glass.

The one thing I'll never forget is that stud's hands. He'd been on Death Row all these months, and here his hands were still red and chapped and knobby, as if he'd still been out picking turnips in the San Joaquin Valley. Then I realized: I was thinking of him in the past tense.

Two fuzz began strapping him down in the chair. A broad leather strap across the chest, narrower belts on the arms and legs. God they were careful about strapping him in. I mean they wanted to make sure he was comfortable. And all the time he was talking with them. Not that we could hear it, but I suppose it went *that's fine, fellows, no, that strap isn't too tight, gee, I hope I'm not making you late for lunch.*

That's what bugged me, he was so damned *apologetic!* While they were fastening him down over that little bucket of oblivion, that poor dead lonely son of a bitch twisted around to look over his shoulder at us, and he *smiled.* I mean if he'd had an arm free he might have *waved!* One of the fuzz, who had white hair and these sad gentle eyes like he was wearing a hair shirt, patted him on the head on the way out. No personal animosity, son, just doing my job.

After that the tempo increased, like your heart beat when you're on a black street at three a.m. and the echo of your own footsteps begins to sound like someone following you. The warden was at one observation window, the priest and the doctor at the other. The blackrobe made the sign of the cross, having a last go at the condemned, but he was digging only Ben Casey. Here was this M.D. cat who'd taken the Hippocratean Oath to preserve life, waving his arms around like a tv director to show that stud the easiest way to *die.*

*Hold your breath, then breathe deeply: you won't feel a thing. Of course hydrocyanic acid gas melts your guts into a red-hot soup and burns out every fibre in the lining of your lungs, but you won't be really feeling it as you jerk around: that'll just be raw nerve endings.*

Like they should have called *his* the Hypocritical Oath.

So there we were, three yards and half an inch of plate glass apart, with us staring at him and him by just turning his head able to stare right back: but there were a million light years between the two sides of the glass. He didn't turn. He was shrived and strapped in and briefed on how to die, and he was ready for the fumes. I found out afterwards that he had even willed his body to medical research.

I did a quick take around.

Victor was sweating profusely, his eyes glued to the window.

The politician was pop-eyed, nose pressed flat and belly indented by the brass rail, pudgy fingers like plump garlic sausages smearing the glass on either side of his head. A look on his face, already, like that of a stud making it with a chick.

The reporters seemed ashamed, as if someone had caught them peeking over the transom into the ladies' john.

The Army cat just looked sick.

Only the fuzz were unchanged, expending no more emotion on this than on their targets after rapid-fire exercises at the range.

On no face was there hatred.

Suddenly, for the first time in my life, I was part of it. I wanted to yell out *STOP!* We were about to gas this stud and *none of us wanted him to die!* We've created this society and we're all responsible for what it does, but none of us as individuals is willing to take that responsibility. We're like that Nazi cat at Nuremberg who said that everything would have been all right if they'd only given him more ovens.

The warden signalled. I heard gas whoosh up around the chair.

The condemned man didn't move. He was following doctor's orders. Then he took the huge gulping breath the M.D. had pantomimed. All of a sudden he threw this tremendous convulsion, his body straining up against the straps, his head slewed around so I could see his eyes were tight shut and his lips were pulled back from his teeth. Then he started panting like a baby in an oxygen tent, swiftly and shallowly. Only it wasn't oxygen his lungs were trying to work on.

The lieutenant stepped back smartly from the window, blinked, and puked on the glass. His vomit hung there for an instant like a phosphorus bomb burst in a bunker; then two fuzz were supporting him from the room and we were all jerking back from the mess. All except the politician. He hadn't even noticed: he was in Henry Millerville, getting his sex kicks the easy way.

I guess the stud in there had never dug that he was supposed to be gone in two seconds without pain, because his body was still arched up in that terrible bow, and his hands were still claws. I could see the muscles standing out along the sides of his jaws like marbles. Finally he flopped back and just hung there in his straps like a machine-gunned paratrooper.

But that wasn't the end. He took another huge gasp, so I could see his ribs pressing out against his white shirt. After that one, twenty seconds. We decided that he had cut out.

Then another gasp. Then nothing. Half a minute nothing.

Another of those final terrible shuddering racking gasps. At last: all through. All used up. Making it with the angels.

But then he did it *again*. Every fibre of that dead wasted comic thrown-away body strained for air on this one. No air: only hydrocyanic acid gas. Just nerves, like the fish twitching after you whack it on the skull with the back edge of the skinning knife. Except that it wasn't a fish we were seeing die.

His head flopped sideways and his tongue came out slyly like the tongue of a dead deer. Then this gunk ran out of his mouth. It was just saliva—they said it couldn't be anything else—but it reminded me of the residue after light-line resistors have been melted in an electrical fire. That kind of black. That kind of scorched.

Very softly, almost to himself, Victor murmured: "Later, dad."

*That was it. Dig you in the hereafter, dad. Ten little minutes and you're through the wall. Mistah Kurtz, he dead. Mistah Kurtz, he very very god-damn dead.*

I believed it. Looking at what was left of that cat was like looking at a chick who's gotten herself bombed on the heavy, so when you hold a match in front of her eyes the pupils don't react and there's no one home, man. No one. Nowhere. End of the lineville.

We split.

But on the way out I kept thinking of that Army stud, and wondering what had made him sick. Was it because the cat in the chair had been the last to enter, no matter how violently, the body of his beloved, and now even that febrile connection had been severed? Whatever the reason, his body had known what perhaps his mind had refused to accept: this ending was no new beginning, this death would not restore his dead chick to him. This death, no matter how just in his eyes, had generated only nausea.

Victor and I sat in the Mercedes for a long time with the top down, looking out over that bright beautiful empty peninsula, not named, as you might think, after a saint, but after some poor dumb Indian they had hanged there a hundred years or so before. Trees and clouds and blue water, and still no birds making the scene. Even the cats in the black suits had vanished, but now I understood why they'd been there. In their silent censure, they had been sounding the right gong, man. We were the ones from the Middle Ages.

Victor took a deep shuddering breath as if he could never get enough air. Then he said in a barely audible voice: "How did you dig that action, man?"

I gave a little shrug and, being myself, said the only thing I could say. "It was a gas, dad."

"I dig, man. I'm hip. A gas."

Something was wrong with the way he said it, but I broke the seal on the tequila and we killed it in fifteen minutes,

JOE GORES // 163

without even a lime to suck in between. Then he started the car and we cut out, and I realized what was wrong. Watching that cat in the gas chamber, Victor had realized for the very first time that life is far, far more than just kicks. We were both partially responsible for what had happened in there, and we had been ineluctably diminished by it.

On U.S. 101 he coked the Mercedes up to 104 m.p.h. through the traffic, and held it there. It was wild: it was the end: but I didn't sound. I was alone without my Guide by the boiling river of blood. When the Highway Patrol finally got us stopped, Victor was coming on so strong and I was coming on so mild that they surrounded us with their holsters flaps unbuckled, and checked our veins for needle marks.

I didn't say a word to them, man, not one. Not even my name. Like they had to look in my wallet to see who I was. And while they were doing that, Victor blew his cool entirely. You know, biting, foaming at the mouth, the whole bit—he gave a very good show until they hit him on the back of the head with a gun butt. I just watched.

They lifted his license for a year, nothing else, because his old man spent a lot of bread on a shrinker who testified that Victor had temporarily wigged out, and who had him put away in the zoo for a time. He's back now, but he still sees that wig picker, three times a week at forty clams a shot.

He needs it. A few days ago I saw him on Upper Grant, stalking lithely through a grey raw February day with the fog in, wearing just a t-shirt and jeans—and no shoes. He seemed agitated, pressed, confined within his own concerns, but I stopped him for a minute.

"Ah . . . how you making it, man? Like, ah, what's the gig?"

He shook his head cautiously. "They will not let us get

away with it, you know. Like to them, man, just living is a crime."

"Why no strollers, dad?"

"I cannot wear shoes." He moved closer and glanced up and down the street, and said with tragic earnestness: "I can hear only with the soles of my feet, man."

Then he nodded and padded away through the crowds on silent naked soles like a puzzled panther, drifting through the fruiters and drunken teen-agers and fuzz trying to bust some cat for possession who have inherited North Beach from the true swingers. I guess all Victor wants to listen to now is Mother Earth: all he wants to hear is the comforting sound of the worms, chewing away.

Chewing away, and waiting for Victor; and maybe for the Second Coming.

# KNIVES IN THE DARK

BY DON HERRON

*Nob Hill*

(Originally published in 2002)


## I.

The hunt began when Blackjack Jerome swaggered into the office, looking for talk. A lusty pirate, .45 tucked into the pants belt under his jacket as usual, the man was slicing out his pieces of the pie on the rougher edges of the San Francisco business scene and signing cheques on a lot of billable hours for the agency. My first assignment when I transferred in from Chi after the war involved a little head-busting he needed done down on the docks, so we had some history. If Blackjack wanted talk, he'd get talk.

I pulled my hat off the rack and caught the eye of the office girl on the way out the door. Five other operatives lounged around reading and playing cards, waiting for assignment, so I could be spared to keep a good customer contented. We took the rear exit and I stepped toward John's in 57 Ellis, when Blackjack yanked my sleeve.

"Naw. I just ate there last night."

"Okay by me. I don't much care where I put the meat on my bones."

We walked toward Market Street along the row of restaurants and pulled up chairs in Hartman and Maloney's. While Blackjack unburdened what passed for his soul of his recent doings, I dug into a plate of Hangtown Fry, a meal that keeps you going for a few hours. You couldn't know when some action was going to pop and hold you away from the table, and I never liked going hungry.

As I listened to the new tales of navigating his business around our city officials and police force, I thought as I usually did that Blackjack might step across the line someday and become fresh quarry I might be sent out to find, haul in and put behind bars. With his temperament, he could even commit a hanging offense. He'd make a fine trophy, a great shaggy head to put on the wall, but I enjoyed his company, so maybe instead he'd live to be an old man, ripe from his privateering. Unlikely as it seemed, seated listening to him, death in bed was a possibility. If it came to that, a man was long out of the game.

When my turn to bend ears came I was prepared, and said, "I saw The Fin last week."

"No kidding? He out of jail or—"

"Walking the streets like a white man."

The Fin was a local boy no one could find a use for until Blackjack came along with an angle, sending the kid armed with folding money into the waterfront speaks. Gin flowed until a sizeable crew sailed under all sheets, then some tougher members on Blackjack's payroll would appear, load them into trucks and drive boldly through the strike lines on the docks. The shanghais could unload cargo all day to pay off their binge and be driven back out come nightfall, or walk away right then across the lines of maddened union men armed with clubs and shivs. The arithmetic was simple enough.

If I heard the kid tell it once, though, I heard it a hundred times, how when he was in short pants growing up out in the Mission, his family marched to the top of Bernal Hill with a picnic basket day after day and watched San Francisco burn in the distance. The whole downtown was brand spanking new, a land of opportunity, that's all The Fin ever talked about. You'd think someone with one grand idea like that might have others, but that was as far as the kid's intellect wandered. At the height of his success recruiting for Blackjack one morning he walked into an Italian grocer's with a rod and boosted the till for close to an even fin. When he returned to that very same store in the early evening to buy tobacco, of course the old coot recognized him and managed to pull out a shotgun. The grocer held him arms high for the police instead of blasting him, which was a break, but that's where The Fin picked up his moniker, which he hated. The kid could never see the humor in the situation.

The wheels were turning in Blackjack's head, figuring out some new purpose for The Fin when he found him. To Jerome the kid was like a box of matches, waiting to be slipped opened and burnt a stick at a time until the fire was all gone. The box must not be empty yet, with The Fin still walking around and breathing.

"Say," Blackjack said, reminded of old times, "do you remember those guys horsing around in the blood?"

"Sure."

Dawn was just breaking on East Street when we had come across a group of our strike-breakers, squatting around in a circle. Blackjack and I had strolled over to see what the action might be. On the pavement gleamed a fresh splash of blood, and a couple of the crew used sticks to play Tic Tac Toe in it while the others gambled on the outcome.

"It helps," I added, "to have some boys working for you who know how to keep themselves entertained."

Blackjack laughed in agreement. He loved that particular

strike, because he came out on top, with lots of stories everyone liked to hear.

Scraping back our chairs, we tossed some coins on the table for the luncheon and stepped out the door. As we hit the sidewalk I saw a face float by in the crowd that rang some kind of bell for me. Why was this mug sticking in my mind? Yeah. I had it. Oak Park.

"Catch you later, Jack. I just spotted a bird whose feathers may need picking."

I fell into step with Riordan, a shadow two dozen paces back, intent on hanging at his heels until I determined what he was up to in my burg. I wasn't sure if Danny Riordan's rep had traveled to the coast, but his face once decorated the Chicago papers for a couple of weeks when I worked out of that branch. A banker over in Oak Park had hired a rival agency to guard jewels and other presents bought for his daughter's wedding, but the operative working the perimeter had been run down and killed. At least he'd gotten a couple of rounds snapped out of his gun before they plowed him over. Riordan was the inside man for Burns, and he was found with a lump on his noggin, his unsmoked pistol in a side holster. The jewels were gone and I had never heard of a recovery.

The whole set-up sounded hinkey, but the DA couldn't convince himself to charge Riordan with a crime. After a brief stir he was clear, though the Burns management allowed him to take his services elsewhere. It was a black mark for Burns, the sort of affair that made all of us in the business look bad.

Riordan reached the Powell Street corner just as a cable car was pulling forward, heading north toward the hill. He swung easily onto the front running panel and the gripman allowed the cable to heave the machine ahead. I had to swing out my beefy legs double time to overtake the rear steps and grab the railing, hoping I looked like nothing more sinister than the short fat man I am, anxious to make the train.

As far as I knew, Riordan and I had never crossed paths, so I had an advantage. His photograph was in a thousand newspaper morgues. I'd managed to hold my picture out of the papers by keeping my killings legal.

## II.

I dropped off the cable car a block after Riordan left it, and had to hustle to pull him back into sight. He'd looked around for tails when he put foot to the pavement, and checked again as he crossed Powell and hoofed west on Clay. I was beginning to feel good about all this exercise. If he thought his movements were worth watching, then maybe he was involved in something I needed to know more about—or he may have been holding on to some basic caution, which you learn as a detective. He didn't impress me as being someone you could just sap across the head without a single pill fired. I was confident that whoever had insured the banker's gifts could be talked into picking up the bill on this job.

Riordan went into an apartment house on Clay off Mason. It was barely noon. Odds were good that he wouldn't come back out instantly, the same odds that told me that if he had gone crooked, chances were he was living off a woman. Most crooks don't work steadily enough to make rent or even buy smokes, and need that female with a job to baby them along. If he had honest labor, these daylight hours should see him on the stick.

I figured I had some time, and hiked to a phone in the Fairmont and told the operator to ring the agency.

"I need someone to take over on a shadow job. Who've you got handy?"

"Everyone else went out on a robbery, but Arney just walked in."

"He'll do. Have him meet me in front of the Fairmont. Tell him to hire a taxi and get here quick. And tell him to leave every bullet in his arsenal behind."

I liked the Arney kid, and was putting in a hand training him. Enthusiastic as hell, he looked on jobs as Wild West Shows, carrying twin .45s and enough extra clips and ammo boxes so that he walked around bowlegged, like he was trying to ride a hog in a trench. You had to explain things to him a few times to make sure he understood—it wasn't until the war was nearly over that finally he'd changed his name from Von Arnim, tired of taking the ribbing. A new all-American, from his mother's mouth he was fluent in Yiddish, a common language of the underworld. If we got him trained properly, he'd be good to ship east and work from those offices, a fresh face to send out against crime.

I was lighting another Fatima when he piled out of the taxi.

"Young Wilhelm!" I greeted him.

"Cut it out. My name is Bill now."

"Sure it is. Come with me, youngster."

I guided him to a stakeout a few doors down from the building Riordan had entered and pointed it out to him.

"How will I spot him?"

"A Mick, County Cork sort. Sandy-red hair. Six footer. He had on a teal two-piece with yellow pinstriped vest when I tailed him here. Brown hat, yellow ribbon."

Arney stood there, absorbing this information.

"Stay behind him. See where he goes, who he meets." Looking upon the youth, I couldn't resist saying, "Oh, yeah. He's only got one arm."

Arney looked startled, and then asked, "Which one?"

I grinned at him. "I'm kidding about the arm. He used to be a detective, Burns out of Chicago. When he steps out the door, he'll look left and right and he'll check again quickly. Same at every intersection. Just trail along slowly in his wake, do us proud."

I climbed back to the Fairmont and grabbed a hack down to the office, where the lazy atmosphere of the morning had given way to some real bustle. The secretaries were working the phones and typing reports based on the field notes operatives were handing in. More bodies had been pulled into the fray, going in and out the doors. The only note of calm was Vincent Emery, a thin agent of a couple years standing, fast asleep in the waiting room. They must have hauled him out of bed before his proper rest was finished up.

"Who got robbed?" I asked the first secretary I came to who looked less than fully occupied.

"An old money family, South of the Slot. Jewelry, looted from a safe, valued at—" she consulted the notes, "—hmm, extent of loss not yet determined. Their butler was killed, but the family members were all someplace else at the time."

Little Foley strolled easily into the din and told me, "Patrick Helland had some caper cooking."

"Said who?"

"A source."

"Reliable?"

"Sometimes."

"And who is Paddy working with these days?"

"Shaky Squires. Plus some yegg out from Hackensack."

I filed this information away for subsequent chewing and strolled across the room to where Emery sawed away at his dreams. Kicking his foot, I said, "Wake up. Don't you know that we never sleep?"

While the operative struggled toward consciousness, I instructed him to wire Chicago, and have the boys there do some backtracking on the old Riordan case. Talk with the banker. Phone the insurance agency and give them hope that funds might be returning to the coffers.

I sat around smoking, offering advice when asked on the new robbery down in the Rincon Hill mansion. Two hours passed in this fashion. Then Arney rang in from the trenches.

"He went to the Warrington in Post Street," he reported, "walked all the way. Like you said, he kept his eyes roving."

"You find out why he likes that building?"

"The doorman told me he's been coming around for a couple of weeks, seeing this woman and a man who just moved in there."

"A couple?"

"They're keeping separate suites. The woman is pure dynamite."

I took that observation with a pound of salt. Young Wild West thought that everything with a minimum of two legs covered in a skirt rolled off the line in a TNT factory.

"What about the man?"

"About the same build as Riordan, brown suit, black applejack. He's really mean-looking."

Another useless observation, in all likelihood. How few people who'd gladly kill you bear some mark of Cain?

"Where are you now, kid?"

"The theatre lobby on Geary. They went to eat across the street."

"All three?"

"Yes. It looks as if the men are both interested in the woman. She's a knockout. Beautiful silver eyes."

"Silver? You mean gray or bl— Did you make eye contact with the dame? I told you never to make eye contact."

"Well, no, I—"

The youngster had looked in her eyes. Bad procedure. It would have been worse if he'd exchanged a look with either of the men, because they were no doubt more dangerous. But still, the skirt might see him later and remember his face, and tip the fellows with stronger arms.

"I'm pulling you off. I'll have a couple of other operatives there in five minutes to relieve you. Once they get on the tail, you back out."

"I can handle it, I'm sure I can," Arney pleaded. A good lad.

"If you had more hours logged on the chase, maybe. But you don't know what you're facing and you don't have your rods with you, because their weight in your clothes would have sang out to Riordan. You back off. Go home. Get some rest. We'll take it from hence forward."

I figured that was the best play. The child might not be safe out on the streets, without his brace of pistols to blow many mighty holes through Frisco.

### III.

Reports from the Chicago branch would be awhile coming, so I left the office by the front entrance and cut like a cat across the streetcar tracks on Market to the Pacific Building. I wanted dinner in the States Restaurant before returning to the Clay Street apartment house. Fortified with bratwurst, potato pancakes, and black coffee, my plan was to relieve Riordan's new shadow and catch up on my prey's doings until something more stimulating happened.

Neither of the men I'd sent out to double for young Arney was in evidence, so I took a position in a doorway and set fire to a Fatima. The light changed rapidly, as a bank of clouds to seaward blotted up the setting sun. The only activity in the block was the appearance of a couple of Flips, dressed to the nines, moving east down the hill toward Manilatown off Portsmouth Square. If they were lucky, they'd see some kind of action tonight. Knives could get yanked out and wetted under the very shadow of the Hall of Justice, and if their skin didn't get pricked, they'd come home happy.

I smoked and contemplated the merry pursuits of the species, when I heard the roar of an engine pushed to sudden agonized life.

A gunshot boomed. Another. Where? Up the hill. I dropped the fag and ran against the grade toward Mason Street just as a black coupé came skidding on screaming tyres into Clay, driven by a dead man.

The corpse took his machine smack into a flivver parked in the gutter, pushing it up on the kerb and spraying glass shards around. I glanced at the carnage. No question about the driver being dead, because Paddy Helland had the bone handle of a throwing knife lodged in his left eye socket, with the gleaming point of the blade showing above his right ear.

I made the corner with caution, leaving my own gun pocketed so I might appear as just another excitable citizen until circumstances dictated otherwise. A figure went pounding across the weeded lot west of Mason. Fast. I'd never catch up.

From what I'd seen, I figured Helland for the shooter, yanking his roscoe and firing off a couple of shots as he tried to make a getaway. Whoever tossed the blade was good with it, some farm boy with years of no other gags or a city kid who'd gotten inspired reading Fenimore Cooper. I almost turned back to investigate Paddy's pockets and check the smell of his gun, when I saw a slight movement in a doorway up Mason.

Walking over, I found The Fin crouched back in the vestibule with fear printed bold on his face like a headline. If he hadn't risked a look, I might have missed him. I guess his experience of the rough and tumble stopped with head-busting, so he was having trouble adjusting to homicide.

"Well, well. The kid himself," I greeted him.

He stared at me with a blank look, but stuck his head out of the doorway again for another gander. Then he said, "Where'd you come from?" The kid didn't quite recognize me.

"Your mother sent me out to find you before the city burns down again. She's made sandwiches."

Comprehension came to him. "What are *you* doing here?"

"Blackjack Jerome is looking for you. He asked me to reel you in." One statement of fact and one lie. The shakes were starting work in The Fin's hands. "But maybe you're in on a better business these days. Is it good? Anything in it for me?"

The Fin didn't know what to say, so I took his arm and led him toward the Fairmont, away from the wreckage and the attention that could not be much longer in arriving. It took him three entire blocks before he started to calm down.

"San Francisco is a city of opportunity, you know," he blurted out.

"Yeah, I've heard that."

"We're in a new century now," he looked searchingly into my face. "The *twentieth* century."

"Fin, I know what year it is. How about we do this? Allow me to take you to your new partners in opportunity. If there's something in it for me, swell. If not, I'll go tell Blackjack that he's lost a good man to a better deal."

What few brains the kid had were shaken up enough so that he agreed to the proposition, though no doubt he had little native objection to having someone along with thick forearms. The way The Fin's intellect worked, though, it probably had not yet occurred to him that it didn't look likely that he'd live out this night.

We flagged a taxi and dropped off Nob Hill to the Palace Hotel. In the ornate lobby, parked at an angle good for observing the bank of elevators, I saw one of the agents I'd sent to relieve young Arney. Lagging a step behind The Fin, I gave my fellow op the sign for first up, meaning he was to take the first shadow assigned, Riordan, if this dance broke apart suddenly.

The Palace was the largest hotel in town, a city within a city. Definitely a good place to hide yourself for a time if that was what interested you. The Fin took us to a room on the seventh floor.

Riordan came to the door and let us in. Another man came out of the bath, pulling on a freshly laundered shirt. The woman sat on a couch near the windows. Our youthful operative had been correct enough—she was a tightly wrapped little package and the fuse was lit.

The man in the shirt asked, "Who've you got with you, Elisha?"

The kid said, "This is Mr. Hunt."

The Fin had never known my real name, nor much else. He figured me for just another skull-breaker, because that's the way Blackjack and I thought that card should be played.

I stepped forward with my palm out, grinning, and pretended to correct his memory, "Make that Hunter." It or a variant thereof was a favorite alias.

"You can call me Mac," the man said, ignoring my hand. He pointed a thumb at Riordan. "That's Johnson." He glanced toward the couch. "And she's Irene."

It was going to be a fun little party.

"So," he said, finishing his last button and tucking the shirttails in, "what do you want?"

I decided to try fitting some pieces of the puzzle together. "Okay, it's like this. I'm guessing you might need some local muscle for your operation. Now that Helland is out of the picture."

"You know Helland?"

"Sure. When he used to be alive."

Riordan froze like a statue and I didn't hear any oxygen passing through The Fin. The man who called himself Mac gazed upon me more closely, and I saw where young Arney got the impression he wasn't the convivial sort. But it was the woman who spoke, spitting out the words, "Just kill that fat little fuck."

Well, change my name from Michael to Dennis! I didn't know exactly who this dame was, but she was going to get someone else boxed up, and fast, if she had her way.

"I guess I'm not your brand of medicine," I said, taking a quick look into those pale icy blue eyes. I glanced at her companions. "You like to keep long lean monkeys on your leash."

Figuring he was used to it, I tugged my rod out of a pocket and stepped quickly to the left, bringing it smashing into the side of Riordan's head and tumbling him to the carpet. Three steps back enabled me to catch The Fin around the throat with an elbow and hold him in front of me, gun arm stretched across his shoulder. Mac had a knife in his hand by this time, but I cautioned him against unnecessary movements by thumbing back the hammer on my .38 Special. I wasn't some sitting duck in a coupé for him to practice tricks on.

Silvery eyes ablaze, the woman sat forward on the edge of the couch, breathing hard, legs parted, taking every detail in. I admit it was all very thrilling, but I've seen more excitement in my time.

I pulled The Fin's head tight against my cheek, forcing a strangled gasp out of his pipes. With his ear at my lips and my face hidden by his, I whispered, "You want out?"

"Tell Blackjack," he said hoarsely, "I'm busy," but then I caught the ghostly words *Second and Howard* before he gave out with a cough. I took him rearward with me to the door, found the handle and slipped out, shoving him back inside the suite.

## IV.

The Fin was taking more of a risk than I'd have thought prudent, but he had his cover story about Blackjack to lurk behind. And he was just dumb enough to believe he might be able to come out of this business in sole possession of the latest cache of stolen jewels. Maybe he dreamed of taking that beautiful woman along, too, eloping from this city of plenty, wealthy at last. A hopeful sap.

The clue he'd piped out was clear enough, though. One of the places we gathered before heading to the docks was a warehouse Blackjack rented near Second and Howard, only a couple of blocks from the Palace. If the kid still had a key or knew a way in, that would be a dandy hideout for the loot. Nothing at hand to pin the crime on them if the cops got wise, and safe as safe until they chose to grab the bundle and flee the town.

I knew this turf well enough, and wanted to insure recovery on the stolen property. A fiasco like Oak Park wouldn't do on my watch. The Fin might or might not be able to tell us where the stash was, but The Fin might be knifed already. If I got spotted following any of them on the street, the game would play out longer, perhaps a lot longer, so I bounded out of the stairwell into the lobby with a freshly baked plan.

"Come here, you," I said to the first bellhop I saw, grabbing him by an arm and slipping a silver dollar into his mitt. "Use your key to get me over to the gin mill. And make speed."

Clutching his prize in a tight fist, he plunged ahead of me to the basement, then through the connecting tunnel that led from the Palace to the neighborhood still. Frank Dorr's restaurant did business upstairs in 35 New Montgomery, right across the street from the main lobby entrance, but the gin operation downstairs was the big moneymaker. They vented the fumes into the parking garage in back of the eatery, but anyone who knew anything had it marked as the place in that part of town for a thirsty man to buy a pint. Demand from the hotel denizens was met via shipping bellboys to and fro underneath the street.

The bellhop unlocked the gate that connected the walkway from the Palace and pulled to a stop before the bootleggers' solid door. He started to make the two-three knock at the latched eyehole to attract their attention, but I nixed him. "No hooch tonight, sonny. You can scurry back to work."

My destination lay over a block south and another east through passages that honeycombed this part of town below the sidewalks. I knew of another set of tunnels around Eighth and Folsom, and had heard that they connected to this network. I was going to have to check into that someday, because obviously the knowledge might come in handy.

The tunnels had been dug years ago as storage depots for unloading supplies into the various buildings, but now provided a greased pipeline for moving gin about in quantities large or small. For that reason, I didn't expect any of the massive fire doors I might encounter to be locked. The keys the bellboys used were merely a formality, part of their racket.

Occasional bulbs of light dangled from ceilings, and dim rays filtered through grates up at street level, brighter when the headlamps on machines swung past. I stopped under a cone of illumination and took out my gun, thumbing the cylinder open. I usually carried five slugs loaded and left one chamber empty beneath the hammer, but dug out a folded piece of waxed paper from an inner jacket pocket, where I toted extra pills. Four were wrapped in the paper. I took one out and put it into service. Looking over, I saw a couple of Chinese labourers sitting on their haunches in the shadows, watching my movements with unflinching black eyes. I snapped the cylinder back into place and put the gun away as I moved off into the dark.

These tunnels were wide and high, but this march nonetheless reminded me of the war and running at night along the trenches. Since then dark narrow holes had little appeal for me. For a moment I almost heard the rattle of the Huns' machine-guns, but maybe it was only a truck rumbling by overhead on Howard.

I eased a thick firewall aside on its slides and stepped through into a section I calculated must belong to Blackjack. More lights burned here, and crates were piled all over. The Fin ambled out of a door, entering from a basement.

"What the—!" he yelled when he saw me.

"Softly, Fin. You gave me an opportunity, and I took it. So, are the jewels from today's robbery here?"

"Wha—, what—?"

"And stop stuttering. Yeah, I may want a piece. Include

me and you can bump the two men out of the play and be a whole share ahead. Then you can figure out for yourself what to do with the dame." I looked into his eyes and said confidentially, "I don't think she goes for me."

The youngster took on an odd expression as another grand conception forced its way into his thoughts. "Yeah. *Yeah*. Irene's *that* kind of woman. She can give you *anything* you want."

"You mean she can cook?" I asked.

He stared at me in puzzlement, as I brought a fist to the point of his jaw and dropped him. I grabbed his shirtfront with the other hand and eased The Fin to the cement floor. Then I dragged his body by an arm and stuffed him behind some boxes. If Blackjack wanted the kid, I'd give him a fair chance. Maybe the cops wouldn't tumble, in which case justice could be served by The Fin encountering whatever perils Jerome set before him. If you asked me for an honest opinion, however, I suspected this one would make a better tool if he got honed by a few more years behind bars.

I knew I was going to have company soon. No way in this world would Mac or even some fall-guy like Riordan have sent The Fin out to retrieve the loot on his own, no matter how they instructed him. The lights cut out before I emerged from behind the packing crates. I didn't hear the knife coming, only the *thunk* and *hum* of the blade when it bit into some wood close by.

Hunkering down, I felt my way backward along the tunnel, treading lightly on my gumshoes, fingers running over the rims of the stacks. I noticed the luminous dial on my wristwatch and quickly slipped it off and stuffed it into my pants. I pulled my coat close and buttoned it over my white shirt, and removed my hat and held it at an angle in front of my face, almost as pallid a target as the shirtfront in this murk.

The .38 felt good in my other paw. Give me a few yards and some kind of light drifting down from a grate, and I had more than an even chance. The Fin was right about one thing. It was a new century, and in these modern times efficient killing utilized bullets.

Illumination of some kind, narrow like a penlight, appeared behind some crates. I figured it must be Mac, by himself—I'd tried to give Riordan a concussion that would last for a while and was confident I had succeeded. But why ruin his night vision by snapping on the torch? Maybe he needed that thrown knife. My odds were getting better every moment.

The light moving among the stacks snapped out. Most people feared a blade pointed their way more than a gun, but I've been cut and shot enough times to know better. I started to advance, to take advantage of the moments it would take for his eyes to adjust, when I heard the distant *rat-tat-rat-tat* of machine-guns approaching and sensed more than saw a halo of diffused light appear behind me as a truck bounced along the cobblestone street overhead.

I swung to one side and felt the knife whiz by my ear. The next one caught the hat in my outstretched hand, nailing it to my flesh. *Goddam!* This bastard was like lightning. I flung the ruined fedora away from me and must have heard the blade clatter on the floor, but my ears strained to gauge that machine-gun rattle as it receded in the distance beyond my enemy. He'd had a second or two. Now I had my turn.

Down the tunnel spectral light drifted in from a grate as the truck rumbled past. A silhouette shaped like a man seemed to appear. In the war, when you'd catch impressions of the Germans tossing themselves over mounded earth in the flashes made by exploding shells, you'd shoot fast for the heart. I did that.

The powder flash from my rod blinded me and the report in this tunnel was like the thunder of big artillery. Keeping my hand as steady as I could, I fired another round unseeing, then hurled myself to the side against a wall of crates.

I couldn't see or hear, but then neither could Mac. The hand hit by the knife was numb and dripping blood. I waited.

Minutes passed. Out of the darkness, I thought I heard moaning. Maybe I'd plugged him. Or maybe he was just trying to lure me into range. He must have had a last knife, for hand-to-hand, and might have had another to toss. I had four pills left, without risking reloading in the dark.

As the ringing in my ears lessened, the moaning grew clear. I couldn't sit here all night and drip to death. I pushed my .38 into my pants belt and dug around one-handed in pockets until I felt a book of matches I'd picked up in the States Restaurant. I thumbed one to life and pushed it in among its brothers, then flung the blazing packet toward the sound.

In the fitful illumination from the flaring matchbook, I saw my target leaning back against an uneven stack of wooden boxes, like he was tacked there. A dark patch marked the shirt below his throat. He moved his head slightly. Hard to tell if the wound was fatal.

I moved clear of the boxes, raised my gun and shot him dead center.

## V.

Later, I regretted killing Dewey Mains. While behind the crates, he'd pulled a blade across The Fin's throat and ended all Blackjack's ambitions for that dull tool. Paddy Helland he'd eliminated already, and we found the corpses of Shaky Squires and B. P. Indick, the safecracker Helland had imported from Hackensack, in a cheap flop in Eddy Street the next day. They liked to tidy up as they went along, this little gang.

Which left us with only Daniel Riordan and Mabel Stearns. The wires soon were humming with messages from the Chicago office, where the banker Hobart Stearns was frantic to find his missing offspring. She'd disappeared within weeks of the robbery, which had inconvenienced her big sister on the brink of her wedding. Stearns had hired our rivals, once again, to work this wandering daughter job, but we were the ones who had her.

As pieces of the puzzle fell together, Stearns and his attorneys looked upon it as a case where Riordan had abducted young Mabel against her will. From what I had seen, I felt it was just as likely that young Mabel had conceived the plan herself and pulled that Irish fool in on it. We assembled other glimpses of their life as they spent the money from the fenced jewels, living in a fashion more in the style of a rich man's daughter than a fellow who was only an agency detective at the height of his ambition. Another heist may have been theirs before they met Mains, but two or three more could be wiped off the books after that. Still, the lawyers made the argument that she had been nothing more than a white slave, with one of the men always on guard. Stearns could afford to settle with the wronged parties, to remove them from the contest.

If we'd had The Fin or Dewey Mains or someone else to pit against Riordan, maybe we'd have gotten somewhere in breaking that story. As it was, all we had was my word against hers and her father's money. Riordan wouldn't give her up, and stood by that fairy tale all the way to the gallows, where they hanged him.

Well, he wasn't the first man to take the drop because of his taste in women.

Mabel returned with Daddy to the Oak Park mansion, to life as she used to live it, although I suspect family gatherings may be more rowdy than old man Stearns would admit publicly, with that wild one sat down among the lambs at the dinner table. I have hopes that her taste for the more exciting existence some of us live may bring her back into my sphere someday, where I can have a shot at putting that fine head on the wall.

I think about that trophy more than some others because when they sewed up my hand they missed the point of the knife, which had broken off in the heel of my thumb. I can see it now, buried deep. Cold and gray. Like her eyes.

# PART III

*Isle of Broken Dreams*

# CHRIST WALKED DOWN MARKET STREET

BY ERNEST J. GAINES

*Market Street*

(Originally published in 2005)

You remember how it used to be when a bum was a bum—just a bum? No flower child, no hippie, Beatle, punker—nothing but a plain bum—you remember? You would have to go back twenty-five, thirty years—the late fifties, the early sixties, say. Back before Jack Kennedy was assassinated there in Dallas. Before Alioto had all these high-rises built here in San Francisco. About the time the Giants came to the city and had to play at the old Seal Stadium at 16th and Bryant. God almighty, I wish they were still playing at Seal Stadium and not in the goddamn icebox they call Candlestick Park. It makes me shiver just to think of that place . . .

Well, now, thank you for the drink, sir, thank you for the drink. May all your days be sunny and bright, and your nights spent in the arms of some luscious babe. Only the best for a gentleman, sir, and I can tell by your attire that you are a true gentleman.

Sir, please do not take me for a drunk or a cynic. Maybe in some ways I am both—but I have not always been this way. As you see me, sir, in the past I have been as sober and sensitive, as compassionate, as loving, as giving and caring as the next man. Yes, sir, in the past I have possessed all these noble qualities. Yes, sir, I have. Yes, sir, I have.

Sir, I know the streets of San Francisco like very few men do. I am seventy-one now, and I have lived here most of my life. Oh, I have traveled this country many, many times—a job here, a job there—looking for something—I know not what— but I've always returned to the city of Saint Francis. Whored this town, drank this town from bar to bar, and walked this town from one end to the other. I've seen it all in this town, sir. Yes, sir, you're looking at a man who has seen it all.

To your health, sir. To your health. Yes, sir, I can see you're a true gentleman. Thanks for the drink.

Now, you take bums, sir. To be a true bum, it takes real talent, a genius. He knows man better than the psychologist. More clever than the novelist, or your poet. Knows more of man than your social scientist will ever know. (Shakespeare was right. Make your fool wise . . . Oh, what Mr. William knew.) I respect the bum for that innate knowledge of man. Yes, sir, I do . . .

Sir, are you one of the chosen? Ah, I see by your expression you don't know what I mean by one of the chosen. Then I'll explain. The chosen is the one that the bum uses . . .

Let me explain, let me explain. Because if you're not a chosen, then you think bums bum off everyone alike. Well, you're right in a way, but only half right. The bum will alike beg off man, woman, or child, but unless you're one of the chosen he'll go so far and give up. But now with the chosen, he never gives up. He will hound and hound the chosen long as he can find him. He feels that the chosen owes him, and for some reason deep inside himself the chosen feels the same way.

Now, I know I'm getting a little philosophical. But that is true, sir, as night follows day and—et al. There are people—

chosens; a word I thought of some thirty years ago—whom the bum will haunt when all others turn him down. For example, sir, you are looking at a hundred percent genuine chosen right now in the person of me. I am more of a chosen than your average chosen is. By that I mean I hunt for bums to give handouts; they don't have to hunt for me. Or I should say I did it in the past . . .

Bend an ear, sir; bend an ear—as that master of English drama, Mr. William, would say. I shall say one more thing about the habits of bums, then I shall get down to the nitty-gritty, as the saying goes today. But again to your health, sir. Sunny days; nights of wine and love.

Take a bum now, sir. A bum can spot one of the chosens in a crowd of a thousand people. I've been at football games among eighty thousand people; baseball games where there were fifty thousand or more; crowded airports, bus stations, crowded streets. On the other hand I've been on empty buses, just me and the driver. Driver picks up the bum at a bus stop—and guess what the bum does? Go on and guess; go ahead and guess. Give up? Then I'll tell you. He comes and plops down right beside me. Fifty, sixty empty seats—does he sit in one of them? Nosiree, bob. Plops down right beside me with his hand out.

Another example. Two o'clock in the morning. Twenty, twenty-five people on the bus. Hispanics, Asians, blacks, whites—name the races here in San Francisco, and they're on that bus. Bus stops; bum gets on. Passes the Mexican, passes the Chinaman, the black, the Italian, the Russian, everybody; then plops next to me, his hand out, already.

Take a good look at me, sir. Am I so different from other men—even, say, yourself? Maybe I need a shave, can stand a shower; a change of clothes I can use, a haircut, too, I suppose. But these are minor things. The major thing—do I look different from other men? And the answer is no. No. Still, I am. Because I'm one of the chosens.

Now, to get to my story, sir. And it is a very short story . . . But first, well, before I get started, the old throat gets a little dry after so much talking . . . Well, now, thank you, sir. Thank you. And may all your days be sunny and—well, you know all the rest . . .

I am a walker, sir. Walked most of the major seaport cities of this country. Longshoreman being my work, I've been to Seattle, Portland, New Orleans, Boston, New York. You name them, and I've walked them all. But my favorite has always and will be the city of Saint Francis, San Francisco.

To walk around Stow Lake in Golden Gate Park at seven o'clock on a cool, windy morning, with that fog rolling in from the ocean, to smell the eucalyptus and the pine, not even your best wine is more intoxicant. Take Kennedy Drive to the Great Highway, stroll along Ocean Beach from the Cliff House to the Zoo and back—that is a blessing for any man who loves land, wind, and sea. There are so many wonderful places to walk here in this great city, should I stand here all day I could not name half of them.

But bend an ear, sir, as Mr. William would say. My story does not take place in the park or on the beach. Neither does it take place in one of the more romantic settings in the city— the Mission, Chinatown, Fisherman's Wharf, Twin Peaks— no, sir. Market Street. Of all places—Market Street. Between Fifth and Sixth on Market Street.

It is raining; it's windy and cold. Twelve-thirty, maybe one o'clock in the afternoon. Umbrellas all over the place, but doing little good against the wind. Must be fifty, sixty people on the block, all in a hurry to get out of the weather. Myself, I had been to the post office at Seventh and Mission to cash a money order, and now I was on my way down to Roos Atkins to get a jacket that they had on sale.

I saw him maybe a hundred feet away. But I'm sure he had seen me long before then. There were probably a dozen people between us, so he didn't have too much trouble picking me out. And you have never seen a more pathetic figure in your life. Barefooted. Half his denim shirt inside his black trousers, the other half hanging out. No belt, no zipper—holding up his trousers with one hand. They were much too big for him, much too long, and even holding them up as high as he could, and as tight as he could, they still dragged in mud on the sidewalk. From the moment I saw him, I told myself that I was not going to give him a single dime. I had already given a quarter to one who stood out in the rain in front of the post office.

As we came closer, I saw him passing the other people like they weren't even there. And they were doing the same to him, avoiding him like they didn't even see him. I could see from twenty-five, thirty feet away that he was angling straight toward me. I moved far to the right of the sidewalk as if I might go into one of the stores, but he knew I wasn't, and He moved over, too, and kept coming toward me. Then about a distance of about six feet away He reached out his hand in slow motion. The palm of his hand was black with grime; his fingers were long and skeletal. I went by him without looking into his face. I made two more steps then I jerked around. Because I had seen something in the palm of that hand that looked like an ugly sunken scar.

But as God be my witness He was not there. He was not there, sir, He was not there. No one was within ten or fifteen feet of where He should have been. No, sir, I had not made more than two or three steps before I turned around. And I should have seen Him as clearly as I'm seeing you now—but He was not there. Just this empty space between me and all the other people. Just empty space.

I stood there searching for Him. I looked all the way to the end of the block. I looked across the street. He could not have entered one of the stores that quickly. But nothing, nothing. Only the people rushing toward me or rushing by. I couldn't possibly tell anyone what I had seen. They would have thought certainly I was mad.

I was, terrified. And with all the traffic noise round me, I could still hear my heart beating—beating too fast, too loud. I forgot about the jacket; I went back home. I sat in my kitchen drinking a brandy, trying to calm myself. But I couldn't rest, and I came back to Market Street. It was raining harder, it was colder, but I had to come back. I walked that one block between Fifth and Sixth a half dozen times. Late that afternoon, never mentioning it to anybody, I went back home.

I was a longshoreman then, working off Pier 50 in the China Basin. Each evening when I got off I'd walk down Market Street. On days when I didn't get work, I would walk down Market Street. I wouldn't dare tell anyone what I had seen, afraid they would think I was crazy. But if I saw Him again I would tell the world and I wouldn't care what they thought.

Market Street became a second home to me. For a couple of years, day or night, I would walk down Market Street. When I didn't see Him again I got the idea that maybe He would not come back in that same form. Maybe He had already returned in a different form and I hadn't recognized Him. Maybe He was one of my neighbors.

Though I continued to look for Him as I had seen Him that first time now I searched the faces of anyone and everyone I passed. I also looked closely at the palm of all hands I came in contact with, whether it was the hand of one of the dock workers, black or white; whether it was the left or right hand of a store clerk, a bus driver when I got my transfer, or the butcher when he gave me my change—I looked at all their hands.

And I have searched thousands of faces. I have been insulted, threatened with violence for looking too closely in the face of man, woman, or child. You have no idea, sir, what names you're called for looking people in the face. And for Christ's sake, don't speak to a stranger. You speak to a strange woman, you're a possible rapist; to a man, you're labeled a faggot; to a child, you're suspected of molestation. You're not supposed to speak to your fellow man anymore. Not anymore. At least a half dozen times the last thirty years I've been arrested for soliciting. And do you know what that means, sir, soliciting? It means looking closely into someone's eyes, hoping that he's Christ. Soliciting.

The people down at the Hall of Justice got so used to seeing me that they would hurry up and process me and kick me out on the street again as if I was some kind of San Francisco nut. Not nutty enough for the loony ward or even a halfway house—but just a benign nut as though I was a certain kind of San Francisco character. So with a word of warning to not do it anymore—that is, look people in the face or speak to them—they would boot me back out on the street. And soon as they did, I would walk up Sixth to Market Street and begin all over again to search faces and hands, hoping that one of them would be His.

I began to think He might return in the form of the trinity—Father, Son, and Holy Ghost. So I started concentrating on threes. Whenever I saw three men walking together

I paid them very close attention. They could be white, black, Asian, or a mixture of the three. There could be three Jews or three Muslims; I would look them over. He's in all of us, so we didn't have to come back as any one race. I got so hung up on threes, one day I followed three Filipinos up Kearney Street. You see, by now I was looking for Him everywhere—not only on Market Street alone—but any place I happened to be. Of course these little fellows I was following were much smaller than the figure I had seen that day on Market Street—but who is to say in what form He'll come back? Anyway I caught up with them—and was sorry that I did. Two wore sports jackets and the third one wore a seersucker suit and a bow tie, and he had the greatest command of the filthiest language you have ever heard. He called me every kind of faggot he could think of. He even said some things about my mother no man should say to another man no matter how he looks at him. I tried to explain to him why I had followed them and why I had looked closely at them, but he told me that all us Frisco faggots were alike—only our approach was different. Again I apologized to him and his friends, and I was lucky to get out of there with my balls, because those little fellows can sure use knives.

I was in Golden Gate Park one day, walking down Kennedy Drive, near the flower conservatory. Twelve Japanese were outside taking pictures of flowers. Now there could have been more than twelve—maybe fifteen; and there could have been less than twelve—nine or ten. But to me they seemed like twelve, and since that was the number of His disciples I thought maybe He could be among them. I came up to them and started looking into faces. Not satisfied, I asked them to let me see the palms of their hands. They were very cooperative; you know the Japanese—all manners—bowing, smiling, showing me their hands. I had gotten to number eight when

I was suddenly grabbed from behind and thrown into a police van. The people at the Hall of Justice remembered me and didn't keep me in jail. They just told me to stay out of Golden Gate Park. I told them that I would—but I could no more stay away from that park than could a priest from his church. I've walked in that park at least twice a week since the thirties. Especially on Sunday morning. That is my church. I'm closer to God there than in any church building I've ever been in. When it's cold I wear my old army field jacket, and I put peanuts in the right pocket for the squirrels, and bread in the left pocket to feed the ducks and the geese. And I spend an hour out there with them, every Sunday. And I feel so close to God there, with the squirrels and the ducks and geese, and the eucalyptus and pines swaying in the wind, and the fog coming in from the ocean and floating over the lake like smoke—that is my church.

Not to say I didn't go to any other churches; I went to many of them in search of Him. To the black churches in the Fillmore, to the upper crust in Pacific Heights, to churches in the Mission. For thirty years I've searched for that figure I'd seen that day. I've been arrested, beaten, robbed, knives held to my throat—all because I've looked too closely in faces and hands.

Sometimes on Sunday, when I came from the park, I would turn on my little black-and-white television set and watch the church services. I would watch any denomination and everyone that I could find. But not once. Not once have I seen Him in the audience. Some of these hippies around here dress up like Him every now and then—but you can tell a phony when you see one.

Well, sir, that is my story. What do you think of it? Do you think it's fair to show up once and never again? Tell me what you think of that.

"You down there," I heard the bartender saying.

"You speaking to me?"

"Finish that drink and get out of here."

"I beg your pardon?"

"I said finish that drink and get out of here," the bartender said. "You've been playing with that one drink long enough. You'll give the place a bad name."

"My friend bought this drink for me, and I'll take as long as I want to finish it."

"You've never had a friend in your life," the bartender said. "Finish that drink and get out of here."

"I do have a friend," I told him. "The gentleman who was in here a moment ago."

"What gentleman?" the bartender said. "You've been playing 'round with that one drink the past hour."

"You're crazy," I said.

"What did you say, you bum?" the bartender said, coming toward me.

"There was a gentleman standing right here talking to me," I said. "He wore a pinstripe suit and a trench coat. He had on a striped shirt and a red tie. He bought me three drinks, and you served it out of that bottle there."

The bartender glared at the bottle on the shelf. He started to look back at me, then he jerked his head around to look at the bottle again, staring at it for several seconds.

"Finish that damned drink and get out of here," he said to me. "Ain't nobody been in here but you."

"You're crazy or you're—"

"I'm what, you lousy bum?"

"Nothing. Nothing. But tell me once more. Tell me true. You honestly didn't see him?"

"You've been the only one standing there the last hour,"

the bartender said. "I just bet you have a friend with a pin-striped suit."

"Why did you look at that bottle so long?" I asked him. "I'll tell you why. You got three less drinks in that bottle now."

"I can't remember the amount of liquor in every bottle in this bar," the bartender said. "Now, finish that drink and get out of here, or I'll throw you out."

"Just one more time," I said to him. "Please. One more time, you didn't see him?"

"You've been the only person standing there the last hour," the bartender said. "Your clothes probably scared all my other customers away."

"Then I shall finish my drink and leave, sir. But before I go, let me tell you something, you're one of the unluckiest men in the world. You don't have to worry about being a chosen one."

"Just get out of here," the bartender said.

"I'm on my way, sir. If I hurry, maybe I'll see Him again!"

# DECEPTIONS

BY MARCIA MULLER

*Golden Gate Bridge*

(Originally published in 1987)

S an Francisco's Golden Gate Bridge is deceptively fragile-looking, especially when fog swirls across its high span. But from where I was standing, almost underneath it at the south end, even the mist couldn't disguise the massiveness of its concrete piers and the taut strength of its cables. I tipped my head back and looked up the tower to where it disappeared into the drifting grayness, thinking about the other ways the bridge is deceptive.

For one thing, the color isn't gold, but rust red, reminiscent of dried blood. And though the bridge is a marvel of engineering, it is also plagued by maintenance problems that keep the Bridge District in constant danger of financial collapse. For a reputedly romantic structure, it has seen more than its fair share of tragedy: Some eight hundred–odd lost souls have jumped to their deaths from its deck.

Today I was there to try to find out if that figure should be raised by one. So far I'd met with little success.

I was standing next to my car in the parking lot of Fort Point, a historic fortification at the mouth of San Francisco Bay. Where the pavement stopped, the land fell away to jagged black rocks; waves smashed against them, sending up geysers of salty spray. Beyond the rocks the water was choppy, and Angel Island and Alcatraz were mere humpbacked shapes in the mist. I shivered, wishing I'd worn something heavier than my poplin jacket, and started toward the fort.

This was the last stop on a journey that had taken me from the toll booths and Bridge District offices to Vista Point at the Marin County end of the span, and back to the National Parks Services headquarters down the road from the fort. None of the Parks Service or bridge personnel—including a group of maintenance workers near the north tower—had seen the slender dark-haired woman in the picture I'd shown them, walking south on the pedestrian sidewalk at about four yesterday afternoon. None of them had seen her jump.

It was for that reason—plus the facts that her parents had revealed about twenty-two-year-old Vanessa DiCesare—that I tended to doubt she actually had committed suicide, in spite of the note she'd left taped to the dashboard of the Honda she'd abandoned at Vista Point. Surely at four o'clock on a Monday afternoon *someone* would have noticed her. Still, I had to follow up every possibility, and the people at the Parks Service station had suggested I check with the rangers at Fort Point.

I entered the dark-brick structure through a long, low tunnel—called a sally port, the sign said—which was flanked at either end by massive wooden doors with iron studding. Years before I'd visited the fort, and now I recalled that it was more or less typical of harbor fortifications built in the Civil War era: a ground floor topped by two tiers of working and living quarters, encircling a central courtyard.

I emerged into the court and looked up at the west side; the tiers were a series of brick archways, their openings as black as empty eyesockets, each roped off by a narrow strip of yellow plastic strung across it at waist level. There was construction gear in the courtyard; the entire west side was under renovation and probably off limits to the public.

As I stood there trying to remember the layout of the place and wondering which way to go, I became aware of a hollow metallic clanking that echoed in the circular enclosure. The noise drew my eyes upward to the wooden watchtower atop the west tiers, and then to the red arch of the bridge's girders directly above it. The clanking seemed to have something to do with cars passing over the roadbed, and it was underlaid by a constant grumbling rush of tires on pavement. The sounds, coupled with the soaring height of the fog-laced girders, made me feel very small and insignificant. I shivered again and turned to my left, looking for one of the rangers.

The man who came out of a nearby doorway startled me, more because of his costume than the suddenness of his appearance. Instead of the Parks Service uniform I remembered the rangers wearing on my previous visit, he was clad in what looked like an old Union Army uniform: a dark blue frock coat, lighter blue trousers, and a wide-brimmed hat with a red plume. The long saber in a scabbard that was strapped to his waist made him look thoroughly authentic.

He smiled at my obvious surprise and came over to me, bushy eyebrows lifted inquiringly. "Can I help you, ma'am?"

I reached into my bag and took out my private investigator's license and showed it to him. "I'm Sharon McCone, from All Souls Legal Cooperative. Do you have a minute to answer some questions?"

He frowned, the way people often do when confronted by a private detective, probably trying to remember whether he'd done anything lately that would warrant investigation. Then he said, "Sure," and motioned for me to step into the shelter of the sally port.

"I'm investigating a disappearance, a possible suicide from

the bridge," I said. "It would have happened about four yesterday afternoon. Were you on duty then?"

He shook his head. "Monday's my day off."

"Is there anyone else here who might have been working
then?"

"You could check with Lee—Lee Gottschalk, the other
ranger on this shift."

"Where can I find him?"

He moved back into the courtyard and looked around.
"I saw him start taking a couple of tourists around just a few
minutes ago. People are crazy; they'll come out in any kind of
weather."

"Can you tell me which way he went?"

The ranger gestured to our right. "Along this side. When
he's done down here, he'll take them up that iron stairway to
the first tier, but I can't say how far he's gotten yet."

I thanked him and started off in the direction he'd indicated.

There were open doors in the cement wall between the
sally port and the iron staircase. I glanced through the first
and saw no one. The second led into a narrow dark hallway;
when I was halfway down it, I saw that this was the fort's jail.
One cell was set up as a display, complete with a manne-
quin prisoner; the other, beyond an archway that was not
much taller than my own five-foot-six, was unrestored. Its
waterstained walls were covered with graffiti, and a metal
railing protected a two-foot-square iron grid on the floor
in one corner. A sign said that it was a cistern with a forty-
thousand-gallon capacity.

Well, I thought, that's interesting, but playing tourist isn't
helping me catch up with Lee Gottschalk. Quickly I left the
jail and hurried up the iron staircase the first ranger had indi-

cated. At its top, I turned to my left and bumped into a chain link fence that blocked access to the area under renovation. Warning myself to watch where I was going, I went the other way, toward the east tier. The archways there were fenced off with similar chain link so no one could fall, and doors opened off the gallery into what I supposed had been the soldiers' living quarters. I pushed through the first one and stepped into a small museum.

The room was high-ceilinged, with tall, narrow windows in the outside wall. No ranger or tourists were in sight. I looked toward an interior door that led to the next room and saw a series of mirror images: one door within another leading off into the distance, each diminishing in size until the last seemed very tiny. I had the unpleasant sensation that if I walked along there, I would become progressively smaller and eventually disappear.

From somewhere down there came the sound of voices. I followed it, passing through more museum displays until I came to a room containing an old-fashioned bedstead and footlocker. A ranger, dressed the same as the man downstairs except that he was bearded and wore granny glasses, stood beyond the bedstead lecturing to a man and a woman who were bundled to their chins in bulky sweaters.

"You'll notice that the fireplaces are very small," he was saying, motioning to the one on the wall next to the bed, "and you can imagine how cold it could get for the soldiers garrisoned here. They didn't have a heated employees' lounge like we do." Smiling at his own little joke, he glanced at me. "Do you want to join the tour?"

I shook my head and stepped over by the footlocker. "Are you Lee Gottschalk?"

"Yes." He spoke the word a shade warily.

"I have a few questions I'd like to ask you. How long will the rest of the tour take?"

"At least half an hour. These folks want to see the unrestored rooms on the third floor."

I didn't want to wait around that long, so I said, "Could you take a couple of minutes and talk with me now?"

He moved his head so the light from the windows caught his granny glasses and I couldn't see the expression in his eyes, but his mouth tightened in a way that might have been annoyance. After a moment he said, "Well, the rest of the tour on this floor is pretty much self-guided." To the tourists, he added, "Why don't you go on ahead and I'll catch up after I talk with this lady."

They nodded agreeably and moved on into the next room. Lee Gottschalk folded his arms across his chest and leaned against the small fireplace. "Now what can I do for you?"

I introduced myself and showed him my license. His mouth twitched briefly in surprise, but he didn't comment. I said, "At about four yesterday afternoon, a young woman left her car at Vista Point with a suicide note in it. I'm trying to locate a witness who saw her jump." I took out the photograph I'd been showing to people and handed it to him. By now I had Vanessa DiCesare's features memorized: high forehead, straight nose, full lips, glossy wings of dark-brown hair curling inward at the jawbone. It was a strong face, not beautiful but striking—and a face I'd recognize anywhere.

Gottschalk studied the photo, then handed it back to me. "I read about her in the morning paper. Why are you trying to find a witness?"

"Her parents have hired me to look into it."

"The paper said her father is some big politician here in the city."

I didn't see any harm in discussing what had already appeared in print. "Yes, Ernest DiCesare—he's on the Board of Supes and likely to be our next mayor."

"And she was a law student, engaged to some hotshot lawyer who ran her father's last political campaign."

"Right again."

He shook his head, lips pushing out in bewilderment. "Sounds like she had a lot going for her. Why would she kill herself? Did that note taped inside her car explain it?"

I'd seen the note, but its contents were confidential. "No. Did you happen to see anything unusual yesterday afternoon?"

"No. But if I'd seen anyone jump, I'd have reported it to the Coast Guard station so they could try to recover the body before the current carried it out to sea."

"What about someone standing by the bridge railing, acting strangely, perhaps?"

"If I'd noticed anyone like that, I'd have reported it to the bridge offices so they could send out a suicide prevention team." He stared almost combatively at me, as if I'd accused him of some kind of wrongdoing, then he seemed to relent a little. "Come outside," he said, "and I'll show you something."

We went through the door to the gallery, and he guided me to the chain link barrier in the archway and pointed up. "Look at the angle of the bridge, and the distance we are from it. You couldn't spot anyone standing at the rail from here, at least not well enough to tell if they were acting upset. And a jumper would have to hurl herself way out before she'd be noticeable."

"And there's nowhere else in the fort from where a jumper would be clearly visible?"

"Maybe from one of the watchtowers or the extreme west side. But they're off limits to the public, and we only give them one routine check at closing."

Satisfied now, I said, "Well, that about does it. I appreciate your taking the time."

He nodded and we started along the gallery. When we reached the other end, where an enclosed staircase spiraled up and down, I thanked him again and we parted company.

The way the facts looked to me now, Vanessa DiCesare had faked this suicide and just walked away—away from her wealthy old-line Italian family, from her up-and-coming liberal lawyer, from a life that either had become too much or just hadn't been enough. Vanessa was over twenty-one; she had a legal right to disappear if she wanted to. But her parents and her fiancé loved her, and they also had a right to know she was alive and well. If I could locate her and reassure them without ruining whatever new life she planned to create for herself, I would feel I'd performed the job I'd been hired to do. But right now I was weary, chilled to the bone, and out of leads. I decided to go back to All Souls and consider my next moves in warmth and comfort.

All Souls Legal Cooperative is housed in a ramshackle Victorian on one of the steeply sloping side streets of Bernal Heights, a working-class district in the southern part of the city. The co-op caters mainly to clients who live in the area: people with low to middle incomes who don't have much extra money for expensive lawyers. The sliding fee scale allows them to obtain quality legal assistance at reasonable prices—a concept that is probably outdated in the self-centered 1980s, but is kept alive by the people who staff All Souls. It's a place where the lawyers care about their clients, and a good place to work.

I left my MG at the curb and hurried up the front steps through the blowing fog. The warmth inside was almost a shock after the chilliness at Fort Point; I unbuttoned my jacket and went down the long deserted hallway to the big country kitchen at the rear. There I found my boss, Hank Zahn, stirring up a mug of the Navy grog he often concocts on cold November nights like this one.

He looked at me, pointed to the rum bottle, and said, "Shall I make you one?" When I nodded, he reached for another mug.

I went to the round oak table under the windows, moved a pile of newspapers from one of the chairs, and sat down. Hank added lemon juice, hot water, and sugar syrup to the rum; dusted it artistically with nutmeg; and set it in front of me with a flourish. I sampled it as he sat down across from me, then nodded my approval.

He said, "How's it going with the DiCesare investigation?"

Hank had a personal interest in the case; Vanessa's fiancé, Gary Stornetta, was a long-time friend of his, which was why I, rather than one of the large investigative firms her father normally favored, had been asked to look into it. I said, "Everything I've come up with points to it being a disappearance, not a suicide."

"Just as Gary and her parents suspected."

"Yes. I've covered the entire area around the bridge. There are absolutely no witnesses, except for the tour bus driver who saw her park her car at four and got suspicious when it was still there at seven and reported it. But even he didn't see her walk off toward the bridge." I drank some more grog, felt its warmth, and began to relax.

Behind his thick horn-rimmed glasses, Hank's eyes became concerned. "Did the DiCesares or Gary give you any idea why she would have done such a thing?"

"When I talked with Ernest and Sylvia this morning, they said Vanessa had changed her mind about marrying Gary. He's not admitting to that, but he doesn't speak of Vanessa the way a happy husband-to-be would. And it seems like an unlikely match to me—he's close to twenty years older than she."

"More like fifteen," Hank said. "Gary's father was Ernest's best friend, and after Ron Stornetta died, Ernest more or less took him on as a protégé. Ernest was delighted that their families were finally going to be joined."

"Oh, he was delighted all right. He admitted to me that he'd practically arranged the marriage. 'Girl didn't know what was good for her,' he said. 'Needed a strong older man to guide her.'" I snorted.

Hank smiled faintly. He's a feminist, but over the years his sense of outrage has mellowed; mine still has a hair trigger.

"Anyway," I said, "when Vanessa first announced she was backing out of the engagement, Ernest told her he would cut off her funds for law school if she didn't go through with the wedding."

"Jesus, I had no idea he was capable of such . . . Neanderthal tactics."

"Well, he is. After that Vanessa went ahead and set the wedding date. But Sylvia said she suspected she wouldn't go through with it. Vanessa talked of quitting law school and moving out of their home. And she'd been seeing other men; she and her father had a bad quarrel about it just last week. Anyway, all of that, plus the fact that one of her suitcases and some clothing are missing, made them highly suspicious of the suicide."

Hank reached for my mug and went to get us more grog. I

began thumbing through the copy of the morning paper that I'd moved off the chair, looking for the story on Vanessa. I found it on page three.

*The daughter of Supervisor Ernest DiCesare apparently committed suicide by jumping from the Golden Gate Bridge late yesterday afternoon.*

*Vanessa DiCesare, 22, abandoned her 1985 Honda Civic at Vista Point at approximately four p.m., police said. There were no witnesses to her jump, and the body has not been recovered. The contents of a suicide note found in her car have not been disclosed.*

*Ms. DiCesare, a first-year student at Hastings College of Law, is the only child of the supervisor and his wife, Sylvia. She planned to be married next month to San Francisco attorney Gary R. Stornetta, a political associate of her father . . .*

Strange how routine it all sounded when reduced to journalistic language. And yet how mysterious—the "undisclosed contents" of the suicide note, for instance.

"You know," I said as Hank came back to the table and set down the fresh mugs of grog, "that note is another factor that makes me believe she staged this whole thing. It was so formal and controlled. If they had samples of suicide notes in etiquette books, I'd say she looked one up and copied it."

He ran his fingers through his wiry brown hair. "What I don't understand is why she didn't just break off the engagement and move out of the house. So what if her father cut off her money? There are lots worse things than working your way through law school."

"Oh, but this way she gets back at everyone, and has the

advantage of actually being alive to gloat over it. Imagine her parents' and Gary's grief and guilt—it's the ultimate way of getting even."

"She must be a very angry young woman."

"Yes. After I talked with Ernest and Sylvia and Gary, I spoke briefly with Vanessa's best friend, a law student named Kathy Graves. Kathy told me that Vanessa was furious with her father for making her go through with the marriage. And she'd come to hate Gary because she'd decided he was only marrying her for her family's money and political power."

"Oh, come on. Gary's ambitious, sure. But you can't tell me he doesn't genuinely care for Vanessa."

"I'm only giving you her side of the story."

"So now what do you plan to do?"

"Talk with Gary and the DiCesares again. See if I can't come up with some bit of information that will help me find her."

"And then?"

"Then it's up to them to work it out."

The DiCesare home was mock-Tudor, brick and half-timber, set on a corner knoll in the exclusive area of St. Francis Wood. When I'd first come there that morning, I'd been slightly awed; now the house had lost its power to impress me. After delving into the lives of the family who lived there, I knew that it was merely a pile of brick and mortar and wood that contained more than the usual amount of misery.

The DiCesares and Gary Stornetta were waiting for me in the living room, a strangely formal place with several group-ings of furniture and expensive-looking knickknacks laid out in precise patterns on the tables. Vanessa's parents and fiancé—like the house—seemed diminished since my previous visit: Sylvia huddled in an armchair by the fireplace, her gray-blonde hair straggling from its elegant coiffure; Ernest stood behind her, haggard-faced, one hand protectively on her shoulder. Gary paced, smoking and clawing at his hair with his other hand. Occasionally he dropped ashes on the thick wall-to-wall carpeting, but no one called it to his attention.

They listened to what I had to report without interruption. When I finished, there was a long silence. Then Sylvia put a hand over her eyes and said, "How she must hate us to do a thing like this!"

Ernest tightened his grip on his wife's shoulder. His face was a conflict of anger, bewilderment, and sorrow.

There was no question of which emotion had hold of Gary; he smashed out his cigarette in an ashtray, lit another, and resumed pacing. But while his movements before had merely been nervous, now his tall, lean body was rigid with thinly controlled fury. "Damn her!" he said. "Damn her anyway!"

"Gary." There was a warning note in Ernest's voice.

Gary glanced at him, then at Sylvia. "Sorry."

I said, "The question now is, do you want me to continue looking for her?"

In shocked tones, Sylvia said, "Of course we do!" Then she tipped her head back and looked at her husband.

Ernest was silent, his fingers pressing hard against the black wool of her dress.

"Ernest?" Now Sylvia's voice held a note of panic.

"Of course we do," he said. But the words somehow lacked conviction.

I took out my notebook and pencil, glancing at Gary. He had stopped pacing and was watching the DiCesares. His craggy face was still mottled with anger, and I sensed he shared Ernest's uncertainty.

Opening the notebook, I said, "I need more details about Vanessa, what her life was like the past month or so. Perhaps something will occur to one of you that didn't this morning."

"Ms. McCone," Ernest said, "I don't think Sylvia's up to this right now. Why don't you and Gary talk, and then if there's anything else, I'll be glad to help you."

"Fine." Gary was the one I was primarily interested in questioning, anyway. I waited until Ernest and Sylvia had left the room, then turned to him.

When the door shut behind them, he hurled his cigarette into the empty fireplace. "Goddamn little bitch!" he said.

I said, "Why don't you sit down."

He looked at me for a few seconds, obviously wanting to keep on pacing, but then he flopped into the chair Sylvia had vacated. When I'd first met with Gary this morning, he'd been controlled and immaculately groomed, and he had seemed more solicitous of the DiCesares than concerned with his own feelings. Now his clothing was disheveled, his graying hair tousled, and he looked to be on the brink of a rage that would flatten anyone in its path.

Unfortunately, what I had to ask him would probably fan that rage. I braced myself and said, "Now tell me about Vanessa. And not all the stuff about her being a lovely young woman and a brilliant student. I heard all that this morning—but now we both know it isn't the whole truth, don't we?"

Surprisingly he reached for a cigarette and lit it slowly, using the time to calm himself. When he spoke, his voice was as level as my own. "All right, it's not the whole truth." Vanessa *is* lovely and brilliant. She'll make a top-notch lawyer. There's a hardness in her; she gets it from Ernest. It took guts to fake this suicide . . ."

"What do you think she hopes to gain from it?"

"Freedom. From me. From Ernest's domination. She's probably taken off somewhere for a good time. When she's ready she'll come back and make her demands."

"And what will they be?"

"Enough money to move into a place of her own and finish law school. And she'll get it, too. She's all her parents have."

"You don't think she's set out to make a new life for herself?"

"Hell, no. That would mean giving up all this." The sweep of his arm encompassed the house and all of the DiCesares' privileged world.

But there was one factor that made me doubt his assessment. I said, "What about the other men in her life?"

He tried to look surprised, but an angry muscle twitched in his jaw.

"Come on, Gary," I said, "you know there were other men. Even Ernest and Sylvia were aware of that."

"Ah, Christ!" He popped out of the chair and began pacing again. "All right, there were other men. It started a few months ago. I didn't understand it; things had been good with us; they still *were* good physically. But I thought, okay, she's young; this is only natural. So I decided to give her some rope, let her get it out of her system. She didn't throw it in my face, didn't embarrass me in front of my friends. Why shouldn't she have a last fling?"

"And then?"

"She began making noises about breaking off the engagement. And Ernest started that shit about not footing the bill for law school. Like a fool I went along with it, and she seemed to cave in from the pressure. But a few weeks later, it all started up again—only this time it was purposeful, cruel."

"In what way?"

"She'd know I was meeting political associates for lunch or dinner, and she'd show up at the restaurant with a date. Later she'd claim he was just a friend, but you couldn't prove it from the way they acted. We'd go to a party and she'd flirt with every man there. She got sly and secretive about where she'd been, what she'd been doing."

I had pictured Vanessa as a very angry young woman; now I realized she was not a particularly nice one, either.

Gary was saying, ". . . the last straw was on Halloween. We went to a costume party given by one of her friends from Hastings. I didn't want to go—costumes, a young crowd, not my kind of thing—and so she was angry with me to begin with. Anyway, she walked out with another man, some jerk in a soldier outfit. They were dancing . . ."

I sat up straighter. "Describe the costume."

"An old-fashioned soldier outfit. Wide-brimmed hat with a plume, frock coat, sword."

"What did the man look like?"

"Youngish. He had a full beard and wore granny glasses."

Lee Gottschalk.

The address I got from the phone directory for Lee Gottschalk was on California Street not far from Twenty-fifth Avenue and only a couple of miles from where I'd first met the ranger at Fort Point. When I arrived there and parked at the opposite curb, I didn't need to check the mailboxes to see which apartment was his; the corner windows on the second floor were ablaze with light, and inside I could see Gottschalk, sitting in an armchair in what appeared to be his living room. He seemed to be alone but expecting company, because frequently he looked up from the book he was reading and checked his watch.

In case the company was Vanessa DiCesare, I didn't want to go barging in there. Gottschalk might find a way to warn her off, or simply not answer the door when she arrived. Besides, I didn't yet have a definite connection between the two of them; the "jerk in a soldier outfit" *could* have been someone else, someone in a rented costume that just happened to resemble the working uniform at the fort. But my suspicions were strong enough to keep me watching Gottschalk for well over an hour. The ranger *had* lied to me that afternoon.

The lies had been casual and convincing, except for two mistakes—such small mistakes that I hadn't caught them even when I'd read the newspaper account of Vanessa's purported suicide later. But now I recognized them for what they were: The paper had called Gary Stornetta a "political associate" of Vanessa's father, rather than his former campaign manager, as Lee had termed him. And while the paper mentioned the suicide note, it had not said it was *taped* inside the car. While Gottschalk conceivably could know about Gary managing Ernest's campaign for the Board of Supes from other newspaper accounts, there was no way he could have known how the note was secured—except from Vanessa herself.

Because of those mistakes, I continued watching Gottschalk, straining my eyes as the mist grew heavier, hoping Vanessa would show up or that he'd eventually lead me to her. The ranger appeared to be nervous: He got up a couple of times and turned on a TV, flipped through the channels, and turned it off again. For about ten minutes he paced back and forth. Finally, around twelve-thirty, he checked his watch again, then got up and drew the draperies shut. The lights went out behind them.

I tensed, staring through the blowing mist at the door of the apartment building. Somehow Gottschalk hadn't looked like a man who was going to bed. And my impression was correct: In a few minutes he came through the door onto the sidewalk carrying a suitcase—pale leather like the one of Vanessa's Sylvia had described to me—and got into a dark-colored Mustang parked on his side of the street. The car started up and he made a U-turn, then went right on Twenty-fifth Avenue. I followed. After a few minutes, it became apparent that he was heading for Fort Point.

When Gottschalk turned into the road to the fort, I kept going until I could pull over on the shoulder. The brake lights of the Mustang flared, and then Gottschalk got out and unlocked the low iron bar that blocked the road from sunset to sunrise; after he'd driven through he closed it again, and the car's lights disappeared down the road.

Had Vanessa been hiding at drafty, cold Fort Point? It seemed a strange choice of place, since she could have used a motel or Gottschalk's apartment. But perhaps she'd been afraid someone would recognize her in a public place, or connect her with Gottschalk and come looking, as I had. And while the fort would be a miserable place to hide during the hours it was open to the public—she'd have had to keep to one of the off-limits areas, such as the west side—at night she could probably avail herself of the heated employees' lounge.

Now I could reconstruct most of the scenario of what had gone on: Vanessa meets Lee; they talk about his work; she decides he is the person to help her fake her suicide. Maybe there's a romantic entanglement, maybe not; but for whatever reason, he agrees to go along with the plan. She leaves her car at Vista Point, walks across the bridge, and later he drives over there and picks up the suitcase . . .

But then why hadn't he delivered it to her at the fort? And to go after the suitcase after she'd abandoned the car was too much of a risk; he might have been seen, or the people at the fort might have noticed him leaving for too long a break. Also, if she'd walked across the bridge, surely at least one of the people I'd talked with would have seen her—the mainte-nance crew near the north tower, for instance.

There was no point in speculating on it now, I decided. The thing to do was to follow Gottschalk down there and confront Vanessa before she disappeared again. For a moment I debated taking my gun out of the glovebox, but then decided against it. I don't like to carry it unless I'm going into a dan-gerous situation, and neither Gottschalk nor Vanessa posed any particular threat to me. I was merely here to deliver a message from Vanessa's parents asking her to come home. If she didn't care to respond to it, that was not my business—or my problem.

I got out of my car and locked it, then hurried across the road and down the narrow lane to the gate, ducking under it and continuing along toward the ranger station. On either side of me were tall, thick groves of eucalyptus; I could smell their acrid fragrance and hear the fog-laden wind rustle their brittle leaves. Their shadows turned the lane into a black winding alley, and the only sound besides distant traffic noises was my tennis shoes slapping on the broken pavement. The ranger station was dark, but ahead I could see Gottschalk's car parked next to the fort. The area was illuminated only by small security lights set at intervals on the walls of the struc-ture. Above it the bridge arched, washed in fog-muted yellow-ish light; as I drew closer I became aware of the grumble and clank of traffic up there.

I ran across the parking area and checked Gottschalk's car. It was empty, but the suitcase rested on the passenger seat. I turned and started toward the sally port, noticing that its heavily studded door stood open a few inches. The low tunnel was completely dark. I felt my way along it toward the courtyard, one hand on its icy stone wall.

The doors to the courtyard also stood open. I peered through them into the gloom beyond. What light there was came from the bridge and more security beacons high up on the wooden watchtowers; I could barely make out the shapes of the construction equipment that stood near the west side. The clanking from the bridge was oppressive and eerie in the still night.

As I was about to step into the courtyard, there was a movement to my right. I drew back into the sally port as Lee Gottschalk came out of one of the ground-floor doorways. My first impulse was to confront him, but then I decided against it. He might shout, warn Vanessa, and she might escape before I could deliver her parents' message.

After a few seconds I looked out again, meaning to follow Gottschalk, but he was nowhere in sight. A faint shaft of light fell through the door from which he had emerged and rippled over the cobblestone floor. I went that way, through the door and along a narrow corridor to where an archway was illuminated. Then, realizing the archway led to the unrestored cell of the jail I'd seen earlier, I paused. Surely Vanessa wasn't hiding in there . . .

I crept forward and looked through the arch. The light came from a heavy-duty flashlight that sat on the floor. It threw macabre shadows on the waterstained walls, showing their streaked and painted graffiti. My gaze followed its beams upward and then down, to where the grating of the cistern lay out of place on the floor beside the hole. Then I moved over to the railing, leaned across it, and trained the flashlight down into the well.

I saw, with a rush of shock and horror, the dark hair and once-handsome features of Vanessa DiCesare.

She had been hacked to death. Stabbed and slashed, as if in a frenzy. Her clothing was ripped; there were gashes on her face and hands; she was covered with dark smears of blood. Her eyes were open, staring with that horrible flatness of death.

I came back on my heels, clutching the railing for support. A wave of dizziness swept over me, followed by an icy cold-ness. I thought: He killed her. And then I pictured Gottschalk in his Union Army uniform, the saber hanging from his belt, and I knew what the weapon had been.

"God!" I said aloud.

*Why* had he murdered her? I had no way of knowing yet. But the answer to why he'd thrown her into the cistern, in-stead of just putting her into the bay, was clear: She was sup-posed to have committed suicide; and while bodies that fall from the Golden Gate Bridge sustain a great many injuries, slash and stab wounds aren't among them. Gottschalk could not count on the body being swept out to sea on the current; if she washed up somewhere along the coast, it would be obvi-ous she had been murdered—and eventually an investigation might have led back to him. To him and his soldier's saber.

It also seemed clear that he'd come to the fort tonight to move the body. But why not last night, why leave her in the cistern all day? Probably he'd needed to plan, to secure keys to the gate and the fort, to check the schedule of the night patrols for the best time to remove her. Whatever his reason, I realized now that I'd walked into a very dangerous situation. Walked right in without bringing my gun. I turned quickly to get out of there . . .

And came face-to-face with Lee Gottschalk.

His eyes were wide, his mouth drawn back in a snarl of

surprise. In one hand he held a bundle of heavy canvas. "You!" he said. "What the hell are you doing here?"

I jerked back from him, bumped into the railing, and dropped the flashlight. It clattered on the floor and began rolling toward the mouth of the cistern. Gottschalk lunged toward me, and as I dodged, the light fell into the hole and the cell went dark. I managed to push past him and ran down the hallway to the courtyard.

Stumbling on the cobblestones, I ran blindly for the sally port. Its doors were shut now—he'd probably taken that precaution when he'd returned from getting the tarp to wrap her body in. I grabbed the iron hasp and tugged, but couldn't get it open. Gottschalk's footsteps were coming through the courtyard after me now. I let go of the hasp and ran again.

When I came to the enclosed staircase at the other end of the court, I started up. The steps were wide at the outside, narrow at the inside. My toes banged into the risers of the steps; a couple of times I teetered and almost fell backwards. At the first tier I paused, then kept going. Gottschalk had said something about unrestored rooms on the second tier; they'd be a better place to hide than in the museum.

Down below I could hear him climbing after me. The sound of his feet—clattering and stumbling—echoed in the close space. I could hear him grunt and mumble: low, ugly sounds that I knew were curses.

I had absolutely no doubt that if he caught me, he would kill me. Maybe do to me what he had done to Vanessa . . .

I rounded the spiral once again and came out on the top floor gallery, my heart beating wildly, my breath coming in pants. To my left were archways, black outlines filled with dark-gray sky. To my right was blackness. I went that way, hands out, feeling my way.

My hands touched the rough wood of a door. I pushed, and it opened. As I passed through it, my shoulder bag caught on something; I yanked it loose and kept going. Beyond the door I heard Gottschalk curse loudly, the sound filled with surprise and pain; he must have fallen on the stairway. And that gave me a little more time.

The tug at my shoulder bag had reminded me of the small flashlight I keep there. Flattening myself against the wall next to the door, I rummaged through the bag and brought out the flash. Its beam showed high walls and arching ceilings, plaster and lath pulled away to expose dark brick. I saw cubicles and cubbyholes opening into dead ends, but to my right was an arch. I made a small involuntary sound of relief, then thought *Quiet!* Gottschalk's footsteps started up the stairway again as I moved through the archway.

The crumbling plaster walls beyond the archway were set at odd angles—an interlocking funhouse maze connected by small doors. I slipped through one and found myself in an ir-regularly shaped room heaped with debris. There didn't seem to be an exit, so I ducked back into the first room and moved toward the outside wall, where gray outlines indicated small high-placed windows. I couldn't hear Gottschalk anymore—couldn't hear anything but the roar and clank from the bridge directly overhead.

The front wall was brick and stone, and the windows had wide waist-high sills. I leaned across one, looked through the salt-caked glass, and saw the open sea. I was at the front of the fort, the part that faced beyond the Golden Gate; to my immediate right would be the unrestored portion. If I could slip over into that area, I might be able to hide until the other rangers came to work in the morning.

But Gottschalk could be anywhere. I couldn't hear his

footsteps above the infernal noise from the bridge. He could be right here in the room with me, pinpointing me by the beam of my flashlight . . .

Fighting down panic, I switched the light off and continued along the wall, my hands recoiling from its clammy stone surface. It was icy cold in the vast, echoing space, but my own flesh felt colder still. The air had a salt tang, underlaid by odors of rot and mildew. For a couple of minutes the darkness was unalleviated, but then I saw a lighter rectangular shape ahead of me.

When I reached it I found it was some sort of embrasure, about four feet tall, but only a little over a foot wide. Beyond it I could see the edge of the gallery where it curved and stopped at the chain link fence that barred entrance to the other side of the fort. The fence wasn't very high—only five feet or so. If I could get through this narrow opening, I could climb it and find refuge . . .

The sudden noise behind me was like a firecracker popping. I whirled, and saw a tall figure silhouetted against one of the seaward windows. He lurched forward, tripping over whatever he'd stepped on. Forcing back a cry, I hoisted myself up and began squeezing through the embrasure.

Its sides were rough brick. They scraped my flesh clear through my clothing. Behind me I heard the slap of Gottschalk's shoes on the wooden floor.

My hips wouldn't fit through the opening. I gasped, grunted, pulling with my arms on the outside wall. Then I turned on my side, sucking in my stomach. My bag caught again, and I let go of the wall long enough to rip its strap off my elbow. As my hips squeezed through the embrasure, I felt Gottschalk grab at my feet. I kicked out frantically, breaking his hold, and fell off the sill to the floor of the gallery.

Fighting for breath, I pushed off the floor, threw myself at the fence, and began climbing. The metal bit into my fingers, rattled and clashed with my weight. At the top, the leg of my jeans got hung up on the spiky wires. I tore it loose and jumped down the other side.

The door to the gallery burst open and Gottschalk came through it. I got up from a crouch and ran into the darkness ahead of me. The fence began to rattle as he started up it. I raced, half-stumbling, along the gallery, the open archways to my right. To my left was probably a warren of rooms similar to those on the east side. I could lose him in there . . .

Only I couldn't. The door I tried was locked. I ran to the next one and hurled my body against its wooden panels. It didn't give. I heard myself sob in fear and frustration.

Gottschalk was over the fence now, coming toward me, limping. His breath came in erratic gasps, loud enough to hear over the noise from the bridge. I twisted around, looking for shelter, and saw a pile of lumber lying across one of the open archways.

I dashed toward it and slipped behind, wedged between it and the pillar of the arch. The courtyard lay two dizzying stories below me. I grasped the end of the top two-by-four. It moved easily, as if on a fulcrum.

Gottschalk had seen me. He came on steadily, his right leg dragging behind him. When he reached the pile of lumber and started over it toward me, I yanked on the two-by-four. The other end moved and struck him on the knee.

He screamed and stumbled back. Then he came forward again, hands outstretched toward me. I pulled back further against the pillar. His clutching hands missed me, and when they did he lost his balance and toppled onto the pile of lumber. And then the boards began to slide toward the open archway.

He grabbed at the boards, yelling and flailing his arms. I tried to reach for him, but the lumber was moving like an avalanche now, pitching over the side and crashing down into the courtyard two stories below. It carried Gottschalk's thrashing body with it, and his screams echoed in its wake. For an awful few seconds the boards continued to crash down on him, and then everything was terribly still. Even the thrumming of the bridge traffic seemed muted.

I straightened slowly and looked down into the courtyard. Gottschalk lay unmoving among the scattered pieces of lumber. For a moment I breathed deeply to control my vertigo; then I ran back to the chain link fence, climbed it, and rushed down the spiral staircase to the courtyard.

When I got to the ranger's body, I could hear him moaning. I said, "Lie still. I'll call an ambulance."

He moaned louder as I ran across the courtyard and found a phone in the gift shop, but by the time I returned, he was silent. His breathing was so shallow that I thought he'd passed out, but then I heard mumbled words coming from his lips. I bent closer to listen.

"Vanessa," he said. "Wouldn't take me with her . . ."

I said, "Take you where?"

"Going away together. Left my car . . . over there so she could drive across the bridge. But when she . . . brought it here she said she was going alone . . ."

So you argued, I thought. And you lost your head and slashed her to death.

"Vanessa," he said again. "Never planned to take me . . . tricked me . . ."

I started to put a hand on his arm, but found I couldn't touch him. "Don't talk anymore. The ambulance'll be here soon."

"Vanessa," he said. "Oh God, what did you do to me?"

I looked up at the bridge, rust red through the darkness and the mist. In the distance, I could hear the wail of a siren.

Deceptions, I thought.

Deceptions . . .

# THE KING BUTCHER OF BRISTOL BAY

BY OSCAR PEÑARANDA

*Manilatown*

(Originally published in 2004)

W ho knows?
*Some say he escaped from a jail in California. The "captain," a small, weather-beaten, battered, mousy old man, said that the guy was wanted by the law somewhere. That was one thing about the cannery community and life in general in the small villages along the Naknek River in Bristol Bay, Alaska: Talk traveled fast. He may have looked like a man who was running away from something, yet to others he looked more like one gathering resources to get back to something. But who was going to ask? For the man in question was the King Butcher himself, the man who handled the biggest blade in the cannery.*

*From the outside window, two young onlookers disappeared in the flash that the glint the sun and blade had made when Kip Benito, the King Butcher, slashed the big king salmon's guts, the conveyer belt still moving, cleaning the enormous fish with one swift, smooth stroke upward; and then, after flipping it over, a downward stroke to scrape and cut the rest of the clinging entrails. And he would tap the fish and the table each time he completed a fish, as people from all around the cannery, including the two young spectators, would shove each other, edging to get a better look at Kip working his magic with the terrifyingly beautiful King Butcher knife.*

*The foreman now walked past the docks outside, framed by*

*that same window that held the onlookers. "That," he told the two boys, for they were college students, "you won't find in the books. Guaranteed," he said. "Heh, heh. Guaranteed."*

At dusk sometimes, a veil of mist lingers in the twilight over the city. Coming home from the Golden Gate Fields racetracks in the winds of March, a loser in many more ways than just playing the horses, driving over the Bay Bridge, Kip Benito, an American citizen for two years now, mused over that delicate gauze curtain clinging over the jagged gray skyline of San Francisco. On the hills behind and beyond, a penciled, wispy line of cloud pointed at rows of houses and buildings baring their teeth. Windows goldened in the fading twilight, streaks of pink and magenta glowing in the darkening sky.

He was on his way to Blanco's to down a few beers and bullshit a bit with Rudy the bartender. He was worried about Nena's pregnancy and their planned elopement this Saturday. He was going to borrow money from Rudy. A lot of money.

He was down two thousand: He had lost his cousin Mando's fifteen hundred dollars that he needed for Nena's "going away" money, for she was starting to show.

But he couldn't lose, he had said to himself. He couldn't lose. Hard-luck stories he only liked in books, not in real life. He'd lost so many times before. "Just this once, God, let me win," he pleaded in Cebuano. "And after this, you can let loose on me as much as you want." He did not know whether he was bargaining with God or the devil.

Just yesterday, less than twenty-four hours ago, his wallet was comfortably padded with eighteen hundred-dollar bills that he had accumulated from various winnings here and there. Will, discipline, nerve, stamina, and smarts were ingredients for winning in that crucible of poker, dice, and horses that helped him get by in those past few months. But it still had not been enough. If he paid back Mando the fifteen hundred, that would only leave three hundred for him and Nena and Seattle and Alaska and a new life—maybe. That was their original plan.

Preparing himself to be satisfied with winning two or three hundred, he had instead lost it all, all of the eighteen hundred-dollar bills. He had borrowed five hundred more from friends at the tracks and lost that too. That day, everything fell through. And that was when he decided to go to Blanco's and see Rudy.

Nena had been going to stewardess school and had decided that upon finishing she would head to the main office in Denver where there were more opportunities. But when she missed her period, she started to worry and told Kip about it—and *he* began to worry.

This money situation really started some time back when Mando was talking to him in a small Pinoy hangout on Kearny Street called the Palate of Fine Arts—right beside Mike's Pool Hall across from Ramona's Café, and beside the Bataan Restaurant in Manilatown. Mando was talking about money. He had tried to persuade Kip to join up with him. He would be a perfect collector, Mando urged him.

"Collector?" Kip had laughed. "Mando, I hate those guys! The blood of champions runs in my veins—and yours too," he told his cousin in Filipino.

"Is that why you accepted three thousand dollars to marry?" Mando answered curtly in English, before softly adding: "C'mon, Kip. Everybody is stained. We're just people."

Shortly after the conversation, Kip accepted a loan of fifteen hundred dollars from Mando.

*I can't lose now,* he had said to himself as he crossed the Bay

Bridge to go into the Golden Gate Fields racetrack that morning and remembered the feeling. Everyone else had already lost. His friends had all lost, his relatives, his sometime opponents in the ring, everyone had already lost. He approached the ticket window to put in his first bets on Comes the Dawn and The Seventh Sun. "Box it," he told the man at the window, and handed him a hundred dollars.

Well, Comes the Dawn came in around midnight and The Seventh Sun, a seven-to-one shot, came in seventh. Everyone had already lost; he couldn't lose now. But he did.

And he was down two thousand dollars when he took the Broadway exit at the end of the bridge to head for Blanco's. It was a good bar and a good location—two blocks down from Broadway, the tourists' Sin City attraction, and nestled cozily between Chinatown on one side and North Beach, the Italian section, on the other. Though Kip Benito was not a regular at the bar, he understood the feeling of the place, a little corner of the world with your seat and your place and yourself. It was a refuge, he admitted—a haven, yet a battlefield. Once in a great while, when he's had too much to drink, he felt this. Kip tried to express it in words many times, in both English or Filipino, but he just couldn't do it. Only Nena understood the unspoken inside of him. If blades or fists were words, he would be a poet. He thought Rudy the bartender might be a poet in his own way. He did not falter with words, and Kip envied and admired that.

When Kip sat down at one end of the counter, several stools beside him empty, Rudy was already explaining something to several tourists complaining about the hills.

"But the city *is* hills," he said. "That's just another part of her sex appeal. See, you can't *drive* in this town, no. You gotta *ride it*, up and down, in and out of alleyways, hard and soft turns, and then up and down again. All the time up and down, you see . . . ?" Without looking down, Rudy pulled a towel from under the counter and wiped his forehead and neck quickly but gracefully, not skipping a beat, then stuck it right back under and continued: "Hills are nothing but mounds and curves . . ." Hidden behind the towel rack was a *bolo*, a long blade similar to the Mexican machete, a souvenir that he had bought from a pawnshop in Reno. It hung terrifyingly beautiful against the back panel under the counter.

Kip didn't know exactly what the hell Rudy was telling the tourists this time, but it sounded like another one of his dirty jokes. Kip was getting drunk and horny.

"She'll dictate the rhythm," Rudy said carefully, "by which you must get to your destination." And he dropped a fist firmly on the counter just as Kip downed his fourth beer. Rudy quickly turned to Kip all the way on the other end and said, "Be right with you, champ," and continued regaling his audience of five or six tourists. "You see, Coit Tower, for those of you who don't know, is supposed—or *was* supposed—to have been the phallic symbol of San Francisco. Some rich old lady named Coit, what a name, built it because she had a thing for firemen, see."

"Firemen?" one of the tourists said.

"Yeah, the hose, you see. The nozzle, you know?" And his right hand dove under the counter, swept his brown mustached face with the towel, and disappeared again under the bar. From the jukebox, Sam Cooke was wailing *". . . It's been a long, a long time comin', but I know, a change gonna come, oh yes it will . . ."*

Kip looked at Rudy from the other end of the counter.

"Sure," Rudy said, sniffing and touching his nose as he looked around, "I live by there, below and behind. And in front of it is the bay, with its vessels of ferries and ships and tankers and tugboats and sailboats and cruise liners. On light windy days like this, it's like a big parade out there." Rudy was getting carried away with his descriptions again.

"Right, Rudy, hey?" Kip laughed from the other end of the counter.

"You're chuckling over your glass again. You're getting drunk, my man," Rudy said, walking toward Kip, and as he got closer, whispered in his ear, "C'mon inside, man. I gotta show you something. Harry!" Rudy called, and a man approached the bar. "Harry, I know you're the wrong man to put behind a bar, but what the hell. I got no choice. You got seniority." And the men sitting at the table where Harry came from exploded in laughter and derision. "Take over for a few minutes, will you?" Rudy said.

Kip got up quickly, too quickly, but, graceful to the end, he managed to keep his balance by bending his knees slightly. He lifted the split board at the end of the counter and followed Rudy to a narrow hallway and into a small room. Rudy switched the light on.

"What is it?" Kip asked the bartender.

"Nothing," Rudy said. "I just wanted to get you outta there. What's up, my man? What's eating you, champ?"

"Rudy," he said, "I need some money."

"I knew I asked a stupid question."

"I gotta borrow some money, Rudy. You gotta help me out."

"How much do you need? I'm afraid to ask."

"Two thousand."

"Dollars?"

"No, pesos. Of course, dollars!"

"Jesus Christ, who'd you kill? Two thousand dollars, Jesus Christ!" After a moment, a change came over the bartender's face. "It's that bad, huh?"

"It's bad, Rudy. You know me. I never asked you for nothing . . ."

"I know. I know that, champ. Maybe I can come up with some of it, but . . ."

"Whatever you can, Rudy . . ." And he told the bartender about Nena and himself and the racetracks that afternoon.

Kip, the son of a blacksmith in the Philippines, had arrived about seven years ago. Rudy had put him up for a while to help him get started because, as he said, "I believed in the kid. He had potential."

Some years back, Kip had doffed his blades of burning steel for a pair of leather gloves and became the champion of four divisions of boxing in the Philippines. Now only in his thirties, he had whirlpooled into calamity after calamity, disaster upon disaster, bad luck upon bad luck.

"Sometimes I feel I have degenerated into something untouchable. In my prime, Rudy. In my prime!" he told the bartender in Filipino. Rudy spoke no Filipino, but he understood enough of it.

Rudy's cousin, who visited the Philippines frequently, had told him that he had seen Kip fight. According to him, Kip would sing and cry after winning each championship title. The Crooning Champion from Cebu, they called him. He was a sight to behold. Blood streaming from cuts on his face and sweat glistening, he would belt out a mushy love song from his heart . . . and weep right there in the ring. He was the only fighter in the history of Philippine boxing who had held four titles simultaneously. He had lost them all, of course, one by one. Bad management, age, and time, the most corrupt of all handlers, drove and sucked him into the nightlife of fast women, drinking, and gambling, and those were not really in his nature. When he came to Rudy five years ago, he was sleeping by the benches and sidewalks and enclaves of Howard Street and the Tenderloin district. After Rudy got him the job as a cab driver two years ago, Kip became pretty stable. During this time he married a woman from a prominent family from the Philippines, for papers only. Her people had given him some money.

And then he met Nena. That is, he met Nena again. They'd met in the Philippines before, in Cebu City, at some party. But she was very young then. She was nineteen and he, the multidivision champion, was twenty-three. Her older sisters and their friends had thrown Kip Benito a party; Nena was just a tagalong. They hardly noticed each other. That was years ago. Kip was still the champion then, and Nena, who knew nothing of boxing, could not have cared less about his athletic prowess. But Nena, now in her mid-twenties in San Francisco, probably cared even less. All she saw in him was a soft-hard man, quick and graceful in some ways, but awkward at times. Later on, and above all else, she saw in him a man who did not quite know how to lie.

Kip was not a frequenter of Blanco's. He was not a drinking man to begin with, though he always kept a bottle of Jack Daniel's around. Even in his days of debauchery and squandering, he had never acquired a taste for hard liquor, and beer just made him full after two or three bottles. Crowds often made him uneasy, though he enjoyed people and company. He did not feel comfortable drinking liquor and he did not feel comfortable drinking with a crowd. And the crowd at Blanco's, well . . . it was Rudy that really prompted him to visit Blanco's every now and then. But not this time. This time it was for something else.

He told Rudy everything: that he needed the money for Nena's "going away," that they planned to go to Seattle but he had lost it all at the racetrack. She would rent a place near a relative of Kip's in Seattle. He would go to Alaska and work, then, after a couple of months, return to her in Seattle. And from there, with money in hand, they could make more permanent plans together.

They wouldn't get married even if they could, not right away. For Kip was already married, and his wife's family had paid him two thousand dollars, and were giving him an additional five hundred every three months until their divorce. It had now come to the end of the third year and Kip was going to collect his last five-hundred-dollar installment of the marriage deal. For such an arrangement, he'd had to do some things that inconvenienced him, and probably his wife, too, now that he thought of it. They'd had to see each other a couple of times a month, spend a weekend with each other, and be seen together in public every now and then. But that had not become a chore for Kip until he met Nena again.

"Call me after you get the five hundred from your wife," Rudy told him. "I'll see what I can come up with." And they both headed out of the little room and back into the bar. The tourists were now sitting down at a table, talking and drinking.

Kip sat back down on his stool and said, "Bartender," wiping the counter in front of him, "one more for the road."

When Rudy came with his drink, there were two white men sitting beside Kip. They were drunk and harassing him. Kip had had a few drinks too many, this he knew, but he did not allow the two men to bother him much. His mind was on more important things. He managed to wiggle his way out and leave. He caught Rudy's eye as he did so, and they gestured each other goodbye.

Out in the night and under the garish lights from

streetlamps, Kip stopped by a phone booth near the City Lights Bookstore and called Nena.

"Hello?" Her voice sounded a bit hoarse.

"You still up, *Mahal?*"

"I'm waiting for you."

"Don't wait up for me. How are you feeling?"

"Okay, I guess. Well, not really."

"Okay, I'm coming home now. Want me to get you something to eat?"

"God no. Don't bother. There's food here for you."

"All right. Be right there." He would visit Nena briefly before going to see his wife's people for the five hundred dollars. And he would not tell her about the loss at the racetracks. Yet.

Nena had moved out of her parents' house two weeks before, telling everyone that she was going to Colorado for the stewardess program. Kip had gotten her a room at the International Hotel for forty-two bucks a month, a nice one too, a curtain-partitioned space with a bedroom and a bathroom. "The bridal suite," Manong Freddie had said to Kip. "Espesyal por you two." And for those last two weeks, Kip had been biding his time by going around making and taking bets.

At the hotel, he entered her room and removed his jacket while fumbling for the light switch. He could faintly see Nena through the half-drawn bedroom curtain sitting upright on the bed.

"Don't get up," he said. "I'll be right there." He accidentally kicked one of her shoes as he entered. He picked it up and put it back in place as he put his coat on a hanger by the door. "I thought you might have fallen back to sleep." Through the open window, he felt a slight breeze puff up a fresh tide of mist. "Aren't you cold?" he asked.

"It's good for you," she replied pleasantly.

"You sounded tired over the phone," Kip said as he sat down on the bed. "I was just going to sleep on the floor."

"I'd never let you sleep on the floor. What's the matter with you? What are you talking about?" Then she added flatly, "Not without me."

"Well, I mean, just to rest—for a while. I gotta go get my money from her people," he said without looking at Nena.

"Tonight?"

"Why not? Get it over with and out of the way—so we'll have plenty of time to prepare to leave here Saturday. I got the tickets already," he lied. "Pan Am. 4:50 p.m." He had to cover the lie with two or three more because he didn't know how to lie very well.

"That's good," she said.

"I gotta get everything done before Saturday." They looked at each other for a while, then embraced.

"Ay, I don't know anymore. If things should happen—if things should fall apart, Kip, let's make a pact now. I don't know anymore. Do you?" Then she lapsed into Filipino: "It's such a crazy world out there . . . it's such a fucked up, crazy world. I don't know anymore. We'll have to put some sense, some meaning into it. Let's make a pact." She got up from the bed and walked to the couch in the TV room.

"What do you mean?" he laughed lightly. He tried to re-member the last time he had heard her swear.

"Lovers always make a pact," she said.

"Wow, you're starting to talk like Rudy. What kind of beat-nik shit talk is that?" Kip got up and went to the bathroom cabinet. When he returned, Nena had switched on the little TV in the living room. He poured each of them a double shot of Jack Daniel's. "But I like the idea," he smiled.

"Me too," she said.

238 // San Francisco Noir 2

"Let's do it."

And they drank to that, emptying their glasses.

"Is it okay for you to do this?" he asked, just barely swallowing.

"It's still early on; and that's all I'll be drinking, anyway, so why not? . . . Okay, then, if anything should happen, if things don't work out, we'll contact each other somehow . . . no matter how late it is in our lives. But just once. Because once," she continued, "we were each other's one and only." She raised her drink. "Without any notice?" she asked.

"With or without," said Kip, taking another swig in celebration.

"With or without," echoed Nena. And she took the remainder of Kip's glass and downed it. She looked at him and almost shrugged a shoulder but caught herself, smiled softly, and raised her own drink.

"Even in her silence," said Kip, placing his arms around her shoulders, "she says something."

"*Salamat*," she said.

Nena had a small mole on her left cheek that many people called her beauty spot. But for Kip, her beauty spot was something else. For Kip, her smile was shelter in silence. Her smile was a shelter from both the noise outside and the silence inside him. And she smiled effortlessly, with body and soul.

"I got a right to depend on you; you're the man I love. The others I never took nothing from them, because I didn't love them. But you're the man I love. I expect that from you. It's okay if you help take care of me. But I can take care of myself, too, thank you."

"I know, I know," he stammered. "But only a couple more months. *Babalikan kita*. I'll be back with some cash from Alaska to take care of all this crap. And we can start again." His face flashed a quick glow, then died again when he added, "Just a couple more months. *Pumayag ka na, mahal.*"

"Are you sure?" she asked.

He could tell her anything and she still would be afraid. He offered answers, encouragement, tender touches, anything and everything, and still she would be afraid.

And she asked again, "Are you sure?" She slowly raised her eyes to him. "What kind of life are we going to live?"

"The best," he answered quickly, erasing everything, almost jokingly, with a mystery of casualness. "The best."

"What about the money, Kip? You're still a couple hundred short." She stood, picked up a brush, and started drawing it through her hair.

"I got it all in the bank already," he lied. This time he did not have to worry about whether she was going to believe him or not. She was no dummy, that was one thing. He had to laugh a little.

"You're laughing again, eh? At me?"

"Why the hell do you get up and brush your hair at midnight, just so you can go to sleep and mess it all up again?"

She thought for a while and answered, "I never looked at it that way. You're the weird one. Who would look at it that way?" When she laughed, Kip was already holding her nodding head in his arms. "Happy ending, *tayo*," he said, "*ha?*"

"*Oo*," she answered softly, "yes."

Kip looked at his hands and he thought of all the things they once held—the anvil when he was a boy, leather gloves in a square ring in adolescence and youth, and now, with manhood, the texture of chips and cards, torn tickets from betting on horses and ball games.

\* \* \*

"You're an old soul," Nena told Kip from the couch where they were watching TV.

"Everybody's odd, right?" he retorted quickly.

"I said *old,* darling. Not everyone is an old soul, but you are."

"I like this," he said, touching the top of her forehead.

"That's my widow's peak. You like that?" she replied, getting up from the couch.

"Scary name for it, isn't it?"

"For you, maybe." And they both laughed.

"Maybe I better not divorce my wife, then," he said. And the two laughed some more, but they both quieted down awkwardly as they remembered what Kip had to go do.

"You should go," said Nena. "We all have our obligations."

"I'm going right now."

"Okay. Good, get that over with."

"Get some sleep."

"I will, my happy, married man."

"I am. I truly am," he said in Filipino, and walked out into the city night.

Kip had a small apartment on California Street near his wife's place in Pacific Heights. He decided to stop by his apartment and call them from there. He'd get a chance to pack a little bit and put things away for the upcoming trip.

In his room, looking outside at the delicatessen's neon sign across the street, Kip decided not to ask for an additional loan from his wife. The five hundred dollars that her family owed him would be enough. Rudy would hopefully get about a grand together by Saturday. That would only make him five hundred short and he should be able to raise that before he left.

The phone rang. He looked at it, and after the second

ring, he bet himself five hundred dollars that it would be a woman calling. Then he picked it up.

"Hello?"

"How much did you come up with?" It was Rudy.

"I had five hundred, but I just lost it," he said jokingly. "I thought you were my wife."

"Say what?" Rudy sounded as if he were in a hurry.

Kip looked at his watch; it was 1:30 a.m. How in the hell was he going to call his wife's people at 1:30 in the morning? "Sorry, I was just thinking out loud. I made a bet with myself, and I lost."

"Well, anyway, all I could come up with was a grand."

Kip did not know what to say but, "*Talaga?* All right!" and breathed a sigh of relief. "Thanks, Rudy. You'll get it when I come back from Alaska in the next month or two. You'll get all your money back. *Pare*, that was pretty fast. You could come up with a quick thousand, just like that, you son of a bitch? I thought it would take you till at least tomorrow night."

"I caught them at the right time," said Rudy. "I got 'em running when they should have been fightin', and fightin' when they should have been running. *Walang marupok na baging sa magaling maglambitin*, right? Isn't that what you use to tell me?"

"That's right. There's no brittle vine for the person who knows how to swing."

Rudy's voice suddenly faded away from the receiver. "Good night, gentlemen. And remember, ride her on your way home." Kip could hear some weak laughter in the background.

"Don't tell me you played some cards."

"Yeah, tourists. They wanted to play. So I obliged. I closed the bar right after you left. Slow anyway."

"Same ones you were talking to when I was there, those tourists?"

"I don't remember." After a pause, Rudy asked, "How much did ya get?"

"I'm just going out to get the five hundred from my wife's family right now."

"Pal, I'm holding onto this money till the day you leave."

"But I got to pay for the tickets before that," Kip pleaded.

"Then get your ticket from that five hundred. I'll hang onto this till I drop you off at the airport."

"Thanks, Rudy. You're all right."

"I've spent money on worse things. But right after Alaska—"

"I'll pay the whole thing right here."

"Right *where* is that?"

"I mean right there, at Blanco's."

"Okay."

"Thanks," said Kip again, and hung up.

It was drizzling the next evening when he drove up into the the lamp-lighted hills of Pacific Heights where his wife's people lived, one of their houses, anyway. After parking his car, he crossed the street under a billowing lamp whose beam fought fiercely to ward off the uneven mist surrounding it.

He did not stay long at the house. A few hellos and good-byes and very-good-working-with-you and all that, and by the time he walked out of the house, everybody was happy. He had taken his last five hundred from her.

When he entered Blanco's, he embraced Rudy. "I got the five hundred," he said softly, and discreetly showed his friend the roll of bills.

"Terrific," Rudy replied quickly, covering the wad and pushing it away at the same time. He headed for the back, while Kip moved toward his usual place at the counter. There were two white men near the barstool as Kip sat down. He couldn't remember whether or not they were the same men who had been there the night before. Immediately, however, they started harassing Kip. *Of all the times in the world,* Kip said to himself. *Of all the times in my life, these clowns gotta show up now.* So he tried to ignore them.

There were some people like that, Kip thought, *hasslers,* not necessarily *hustlers,* just *hasslers.* If you ignored them or got aggressive with them, they stopped or moved on to their next victim. But tonight, somehow, it seemed that these two just did not, could not, leave Kip Benito alone. When he couldn't take any more of it, he started to leave. He left his unfinished beer on the counter and walked out the door, signaling Rudy goodbye. The two quickly followed.

Less than ten seconds had passed when the people in Blanco's all heard a violent scream outside. In a flash, Kip Benito came running back into Blanco's, the two white men close on his heels, across the floor, around and behind the counter, and, within seconds, back again into full view, rushing back out into the street. Everyone at Blanco's hurried out after Kip, who now had a wide metal knife tucked along his forearm, blade pointing straight up but mostly hidden. For a moment, the night swallowed the three men. They seemed to have completely disappeared. But only for a moment. The fighters emerged into the blinking neon light as one solid mass of heaving and weaving, with bursts of grunts and groans. The rush of onlookers slowed down when they saw all three slump over and fall to the ground. Then, only one got up. Kip Benito. Rudy dashed forward, but he was too late. The deed was done. *Just a fraction of a moment and people's lives are changed forever.* Yet Rudy didn't have much time to dwell on this thought. He saw Kip Benito leaning against the alley wall, bloody, clothes tattered, disheveled. He was gripping something tightly in his left fist. From his right hand, with a weakening hold, dangled the sharp blade. The other two men lay motionless in a pool of moonlight beneath the streetlamps of the city.

"They tried to rob me, Rudy," Kip explained. "Thought I was drunk and tried to rob me. But this is not just about money, Rudy. You know that." He stuck out his left hand—rolls of bills began to unfold from his grip.

"I know that, champ," Rudy said as he scooped up all the money that sprung from Kip's fist. Rudy felt the crowd gathering behind him.

Kip quickly turned and sliced the blade across his own forearms, shoulders, and thighs. When Rudy looked back to check the crowd, he couldn't tell whether or not they had seen Kip cut himself.

"They tried to rob me!" Kip repeated to the stunned audience. "They tried to kill me!" He looked around slowly and menacingly, seeming to absorb everyone's features. Then he said, as if spitting out a piece of phlegm, "No one saw what happened tonight. No one. I will remember all of you." Then he fled into the night.

Kip Benito was going to Alaska that summer for the salmon canning season in Bristol Bay, anyway. He was just leaving a little sooner than planned.

It was during the afternoon of the next day, just before work, that Rudy decided to go see Nena at the International Hotel. He parked his car in the small employee lot of Blanco's and walked over. The sky was overcast, gray and drizzly, and the news he was about to bring Nena was no different. Rudy was the only person other than Kip who knew about Nena staying in this place.

"He's going to Alaska, and from there to Seattle. Too hot

here, if you know what I mean. He gave me some money for you." Rudy handed her an envelope and a note: *Come to Seattle. After Alaska, I'll meet you there. We will renew our sumpaan there, our vow. Write me. Alaska Packers Assoc., South Naknek, Alaska.*

"You are still my guardian angel, Rudy," Nena said in Filipino. "*Maraming salamat, kuya.* I don't know what else to . . . what we could have done without . . ."

"It's nothin'," Rudy answered casually, and with a white man's accent continued, "*wala yan.*" The strumming of a guitar floated up from the street outside Nena's window. "I'd give my right arm to play guitar like that," Rudy added, turning to go, "but then, of course, what would I play with?"

*The King Butcher always slept with his blade. It was a tradition that went along with the job in Alaska. And during the day he was next to the butchering machines in the Fish House, out in the open, unlike most of the other workers, the regular butchers and the slimers, who were always cooped up in noise and wet and slime and stink. The King Butcher was the only person who worked with the king salmon. And he cut them by hand. They were too big for the machines. The machines catered to the much more numerous and expensive red sockeye. There is always a story about these characters. They say this King Butcher used his own blade to slice the king salmon, instead of using the one that the company supplied. But he got the job done. So no one asked.*

Nena, alone in her room at the International Hotel, looked at the newspaper spread out on her small table. It was the previous week's *Chronicle.* She was wondering if she should go to Seattle and have the baby there, or wait for word from Kip. Maybe if she waited she would hear from him and receive more precise directions. As it was, it had already been a week and she had not heard a word. Kip should be leaving Alaska after a month, so she decided she'd better go there now. She had a Seattle number that Kip had left her, so she was sure his people would take care of her there. She got up and brushed aside the newspaper and scrambled for some pad with numbers, tore off the top piece, and left the rest on the newspaper itself, not far from the small article, a filler:

*July 8, 1966: In a bar called Blanco's on Kearny Street, three men were stabbed by a single butcher knife, two fatally; the surviving man walked away after warning the crowd to keep their silence.*

# INVISIBLE TIME

BY JANET DAWSON

*Union Square*

(Originally published in 1998)


Greta watched the front door of the bakery on Geary Street, choosing her moment. When it came, it was brought by a middle-aged woman who wore a business suit and running shoes.

The woman stopped at the window, eyed the tempting display of cakes, cookies, and breads, then moved toward the door. Greta slipped up behind the woman, a pace back from the leather briefcase that swung from her left hand. The woman pushed open the door, her entry ringing the bell above the door.

The bakery clerk was a gangly young man wearing a silly white paper hat perched on his brown hair. He looked up from his post behind the counter and smiled at the woman. He didn't see Greta.

Fine. That's what she had in mind. Now that she was inside, Greta hovered near the door, keeping one eye on the grown-ups and the other eye on the bakery's wares. Picking a target was tough. The goods were piled alluringly on counters and shelves and stand-alone displays. Finally she spotted her best shot, bags of day-old cookies mounded high in a basket at the edge of a low table, just a few steps from the door that led out to the busy sidewalk.

The bakery clerk's head was down. He was busy boxing up

a cake for a customer, a big man with a fat belly. Looked like he got plenty to eat, Greta told herself as she edged closer to the basket. Unlike some people she could name.

The customer Greta had followed into the bakery stood on the other side of the table, examining the loaves of day-old bread stacked there as she waited her turn at the counter. She hummed to herself and tapped one finger on the edge of the basket that held the cookies. Greta kept her head down, her blue eyes constantly shifting as she observed the bakery's occupants. The woman moved closer. Greta thought she smelled good, like flowers, but she didn't smell as good as the combined perfume of what came out of the bakery's ovens.

Handing the clerk a twenty, the big man put a proprietary hand on top of the box containing his cake. While the clerk looked down at the drawer of the cash register, Greta snaked her hand toward the cookies. She grabbed two bags, whirled, and made for the door.

"Hey, little girl," the woman in running shoes said, sounding surprised and shocked as she moved to stop this theft in progress. The little girl shoved the woman hard, knocking her into the table, and kept going, darting past a trio of teenagers who'd just opened the bakery door wide, giving Greta an open shot to freedom.

Once she was out on the sidewalk, she dodged to the right and ran up Geary Street, against the tide of pedestrians heading down toward Market Street, where BART and the San Francisco Municipal Railway would take them home. Intent on their own destinations, they took no notice of the skinny little girl in baggy blue jeans and a red sweatshirt, her dirty blond hair spilling to her shoulders.

Hank was waiting for her in Union Square, on the side close to the entrance to the Saint Francis Hotel and the cable cars that clanged up and down Powell Street. At his feet was a brown nylon bag with a zipper and a shoulder strap. It contained everything they owned—clothes, a couple of beat-up stuffed animals, and a picture of Mom.

"You get something?" he asked eagerly, brown eyes too big in his pinched face. He looked far more streetwise than a five-year-old boy should.

"Yeah. Cookies. Two bags. Looks like one of 'em is chocolate chip and the other is maybe oatmeal raisin. Did you get anything?"

"Pizza," he said triumphantly, displaying a dented cardboard box. "With pepperoni. Some guy was sitting on that bench over there eating it, and he didn't eat it all. He was gonna throw it in the trash. But he saw me watching him, so he gave it to me. Look, there's two whole pieces left."

"All right!" They high-fived it.

Then they hunkered down on the bench to eat their booty. People hurrying through the square paid no mind to the two children, any more than they did to the pigeons congregating around the statue of Victory atop the column in the center of the square. As she ate, Greta watched shoppers laden with bags scurry from store to store. Hank focused on the food with the single-minded appetite of a little boy who never gets enough to eat.

The store windows in Macy's and Saks were full of glittering decorations, red, green, gold, and silver, signaling the approaching holiday season, and there was a big lighted Christmas tree in the square. But the passage of time meant little to Greta. She only knew that the days were shorter than they had been. The sunshine, what little there was of it, had turned thin and weak. Nights were longer and it was harder for her and her brother to stay warm. Today the wind had turned cold. From what little she could see of the late afternoon sky, it was dark gray.

It was going to rain, she was sure of it. She didn't know what they'd do if it rained. They'd been sleeping in doorways and alleys all over the downtown area, constantly moving so the cops wouldn't find them during their periodic sweeps to rid the streets of human litter.

If it rains we'll have to go inside somewhere, Greta told herself. But it wasn't safe to go down inside the BART station to spend the night. The BART cops would catch them. And there were too many weirdos down there already. Mom had always told Greta to take care of her little brother and to stay away from the weirdos.

She was doing the best she could, but she didn't know how long she could keep it up. She was careful to limit their range to the Union Square area, north of Market Street. That's where the nice stores, restaurants, and hotels were. Greta felt safer where the people were better-dressed. Sometimes those people gave them money, or food, like Hank's pizza benefactor. South of Market and the Tenderloin were different, full of run-down buildings and scary people who would take their stuff, even during the day, though it was more dangerous after dark.

Greta couldn't remember when Mom left. A few weeks, a month, two months, it didn't matter. After a few days, the hours all ran together, like a stream of dirty water chasing debris down the sewer grate. She only remembered that it didn't used to be like this.

Once she'd had a father, though lately it was hard to recall what he'd looked like. They'd lived in a nice apartment, two bedrooms so Greta had a room of her own. She had a baby doll and a crib her dad had made for her, pretty dresses. She remembered all of this. Or maybe she thought she remembered, because Mom had told her.

She knew that one day her father hadn't come home. Although it was a long time ago, she remembered that day and the days afterward quite clearly. Mom crying, people bringing food to the apartment. They talked about God's will and a car crash. Greta didn't understand how or why God could have fixed it so that her father never came home, but no one bothered to explain it to her. She only knew that Mom missed him something terrible.

That was about the time Greta started kindergarten. Mom had a job working a cash register at some store, but it didn't pay much. Not enough to make ends meet, Mom told Greta. At the time Greta wasn't sure what that meant, but now the ends didn't meet at all, she knew. That was when she and Mom went to live with Grandma.

Greta didn't much like Grandma. The old woman seemed as ancient as a dinosaur, and not even half as cuddly as the stuffed stegosaurus her mom had given her. Grandma coughed a lot and smelled bad, puffing on foul-smelling cigarettes even if she did have some sickness with a long name. She had a sharp tongue on her, too, one she used to peel layers off Greta's mom, until Mom didn't have much spirit left.

Then Mom met Hank's dad and got some of the sparkle back in her eyes. Of course, Grandma kicked them out because Mom took up with Hank's dad. He was a different color than Mom, and Grandma said bad things about him, but Greta liked him a lot. He drove a cab and brought her chocolate, her favorite. And when Hank was born, a year or so later, she thought the baby was beautiful. She loved him and swore she'd always take care of him, no matter what. She just didn't think it would be this soon.

Hank didn't remember his dad much. He was not quite three when the cabdriver was shot to death. Greta heard one of the other cabbies at the funeral say Hank's dad should have given the money to the punk who pulled a gun on him late one night. But Greta figured maybe the punk would have shot him anyway.

Hank's dad had left something called life insurance, which was kind of strange to Greta, seeing he was dead. She'd have rather had Hank's dad instead of money. It hadn't been much anyway, and after a while there wasn't any left.

She was nine and in the fourth grade when Hank's dad got killed. She liked school, but the rest of her life was hard. She had to take care of Hank and Mom both. Hank because he was just a toddler, and Mom because she was drinking cheap, sweet-smelling wine in big bottles. Greta would come home from school and find her passed out on the bed of the tiny apartment, Hank roaming around on the floor with soiled pants.

Greta stayed home from school more often, missing classes. No one ever seemed to notice she was gone. Mom got fired from her job at the store and didn't bother to get another job. She said she'd rather die than go back to live with Grandma, but as it turned out, Grandma had died by then and left all her money to some cousin.

They were evicted from that apartment. They moved to a run-down rickety hotel in the Tenderloin, where all three of them shared one room and a bath. Greta stopped going to school altogether, because looking after Mom and Hank was a full-time job. She'd cook their meager meals on a hot plate, put Mom to bed when she drank too much, and read to Hank so he could at least learn his letters. Then she'd put Hank to bed and try to get some sleep herself, which was hard to do. Down on the street, music spilled from the bars, and the hookers called to men cruising by in cars. The hookers worked for a tall man called a pimp, who hung out on the corner and kept an eye on the girls. Sometimes he hit them, and Greta would hear screams and shouts. She'd cover her ears with her hands, trying to keep the sounds out.

Then Mom started bringing men home, men who gave her money. Did that make her a hooker, too? Greta didn't like to think about that. All she knew was that Mom would shut Hank and Greta out of the ugly room. They'd huddle together on the stairs that stank of urine, dodging the other residents of the hotel, those scary-looking weirdos Mom had warned Greta about in those few times when she wasn't giggly and woozy from that stuff she was drinking.

One day Mom left. She said she was going to the store on the corner to get a bottle. But she never came back.

The manager of the hotel told Greta he was going to call social something to come and get the two children. But social something sounded like cops to Greta. She didn't want to go to jail or wherever the cops would take them. She packed what little they had in the nylon bag and they left. Now they lived on the streets and it was getting harder to find food and stay warm.

Hank, his stomach filled by the pepperoni pizza and the cookies Greta had stolen from the bakery, drowsed next to her, leaning on her shoulder. Greta put one arm around him as she savored the last bite of her chocolate chip cookie. Then she felt someone's eyes on her and looked quickly around, her senses honed by weeks of surviving on the urban landscape.

There he was, a man, staring at them across Union Square. She'd seen the man before, staring at them like this. He wore shapeless green coveralls, and stood hunched over the handle of a metal shopping cart. Inside the cart was a black plastic bag that clinked and clattered. Greta knew it was full of cans and bottles. The man had a black beard and a brown knit cap that didn't quite disguise his long black hair.

Greta didn't like the way he was always watching them. Then the man pushed his shopping cart toward them, the wheels squeaking. She jumped to her feet and shook Hank awake.

"Invisible time," she whispered.

That meant it was time for them to disappear into the shadows. She picked up the nylon bag and slung it over her shoulder, then took Hank's hand. The two children darted down the steps that led out of the square, across Geary Street, just as the green "walk" signal changed to a flashing amber "don't walk." As they angled to the left, Greta glanced back. The man in coveralls was following them, pushing his shopping cart into the crosswalk, ambling slowly as though he didn't care that the light had changed to red and the people in the going-home cars were honking at him.

Greta tugged Hank's arm and the two children rushed along Geary, dodging pedestrians. They turned right on Stockton, heading toward Market. Finally they pushed through a pair of big glass double doors and entered the first floor of the Virgin Megastore, sound pulsating around them.

They were in familiar territory now. The store was one of their favorite hangouts. It was brightly lit and full of loud music, where customers bought CDs, tapes, videos, and books. It was open late, and the children frequently spent the evening here, walking the aisles, riding the escalator up and down, and using the restroom on the third floor. Greta figured they'd lost the man with the shopping cart, but even if they hadn't, he wouldn't be able to follow them in here.

"I'm sleepy," Hank told her on their fourth trip up the escalator. "Can we find a place to spend the night soon?"

Greta was tired, too, but she didn't like to admit it. Watching and moving all the time took its toll, but she was afraid to let her guard down. She wished they could find a spot somewhere in this bright, warm store, but she knew that was a bad idea.

"Let's go to the bathroom first," she said. "Then we'll find a place."

They detoured to the third floor, past the videos and into the bookstore. The restrooms were located down a short hallway near the store's café. Greta watched Hank dart into the men's room, then pushed open the door marked with a woman's silhouette. Sometimes, if they didn't know the place, she'd take him with her into the women's side, where they'd barricade themselves into the larger stall usually reserved for handicapped people. But they'd been here before and hadn't had any problems. Greta felt as safe here as she felt anywhere, which wasn't saying much.

When she came out of the restroom Hank was waiting for her, bouncing in time to the music that blared from the overhead speakers. Greta shifted the nylon bag from one shoulder to the other and they walked toward the café.

"You kids okay?"

The speaker was a young woman, wearing thick, clunky shoes and black tights under a short black skirt. Above that she wore a tight black T-shirt with the store's name printed across her tiny round breasts. Her hair was cut short and dyed an odd bright pink. She had little gold rings arrayed up and down both ears, and a glittery jewel in her nose. Greta had seen her before, once working behind a cash register on the second floor and another time waiting tables in the store's café.

Hank stared at her, transfixed. Greta started looking around for the quickest and shortest way out.

"I've seen you before," the young woman said, talking quietly as though she were afraid they would bolt. "You come in and wander around for hours. Don't you have any place to stay?" When neither of the children answered, she continued, her voice low and seductive. "I'll bet you're hungry. Would you like something to eat? Come back to the café. I'll give you some gingerbread."

From the corner of her eye, Greta saw something move, a skinny form in a T-shirt that resolved itself into another store employee, this one a young man with white hair. Trap, she thought. They wouldn't be able to come in here again. If they ever got out.

"Invisible time," she said with a hiss.

She grabbed Hank's arm and ran straight at the young woman, who held out her arms as though to catch them. Greta shoved her hard and the young woman fell back against a bin full of CDs. The young man who'd come to her assistance looked startled as the children darted past him. As they ran toward the down escalator, Greta heard voices behind her, all jumbled as the two sales clerks spoke together.

". . . Almost had them."

". . . Told you . . . bad idea. Shoulda called the cops."

"Poor little things . . . back tomorrow night . . . try again."

Won't be back, Greta told herself as she and Hank hurried down the escalator, heedless of bumping the customers who stood still on the moving stairs. Not safe anymore. Too bad. She hated to lose any shelter, however temporary.

It had started to rain while they were inside the store. Hand-in-hand, Greta and Hank rushed along the wet pavement, until they found themselves heading up Market Street, pushed along with a tide of people. At Sixth they crossed Market, wet and cold, and headed farther away from the bright holiday glitter of the city's main shopping area and into the dingy, neon-pierced blocks where the Tenderloin collided with the area south of Market. Here were lots of people sitting in doorways, bundled up against the rain. Music blared from bars. Hookers, some of them barely older than Greta, called to the passing cars.

These grown-ups scared Greta, and she quickly detoured down a side street where it was much quieter. She found a wide doorway, recessed from the street. It looked like a good place to spend the night. She set the nylon bag down to use as a pillow. But then she spotted the man in green coveralls, back the way they'd come and moving toward them. He was close enough so that she was sure she could hear the clink and clatter of the bottles and cans in his garbage bag, the squeaking wheels of his shopping cart.

They kept moving, Hank stumbling along sleepily at her side. The nylon bag seemed as heavy as lead, and Greta was so tired she thought she couldn't put another foot in front of her. Still she thought she could hear the shopping cart following them, squeaking and rattling as they fled through the wet curtain of rain.

Then she saw something flicker. Was she imagining it? No, it came from inside a big, dark two-story building with broken glass windows. Greta crept closer and peered through the nearest window. But she couldn't see much, just something red and gold glowing farther back in the dark building. She squinted and could just make out some figures nearby.

A fire, she thought. Just the word sounded like a sanctuary, warm and inviting. But there were people, and they could be bad people.

She heard a squeaking noise somewhere back the way they had come, and made her choice. Quickly she boosted Hank up to the window, then followed him through, dragging the nylon bag with her. She held her finger to her mouth and tiptoed forward, trying not to make any noise as she moved closer to the fire.

She saw three grown-ups, two men and a woman. They'd spread big pieces of cardboard on the concrete floor of the empty warehouse to cut the chill. On top of these the grown-ups had constructed their nests of sleeping bags and blankets. In the center they'd built a fire with whatever fuel they could find. Now it danced, red and gold, crackling and popping and hissing. The grown-ups talked in low voices, occasionally laughing as they drank from a bottle, its neck visible at the top of its brown paper bag wrapping. They passed it among themselves, and one of them leaned toward the fire to stir something that was bubbling in a big, shiny kettle, something that smelled rich and savory like the soup Mom used to make.

Greta's foot encountered a piece of broken glass and sent it skittering across the concrete. The resulting tinkle heralded their arrival. The grown-ups grouped around the fire turned, seeking the source of the noise.

"Well, what have we here?" a voice boomed at them. It belonged to a big man with a white beard, bundled up in several layers of clothing, his eyes glittering in the firelight. "A couple of little angels with very dirty faces?"

"More like a couple of pups looking for a teat and a warm place to sleep." The woman who spoke had a hard face and hard eyes, but she reached for a tin mug and the ladle that protruded from the kettle on the fire. She spooned some of the hot liquid into the mug.

"Don't be feeding strays," complained the second man, a

pale, skinny fellow dressed in a dirty gray sweater. He reclined on a gray duffel bag and folded his arms in front of him.

"Don't tell me what to do," she snapped. Then she held out the mug and beckoned at the children. "Come here. It's vegetable soup. We made it ourselves and it's damned good, if I do say so myself."

Hank and Greta stared, mesmerized by the smell and the sight. Then they moved into the warm circle around the fire and sat at the foot of the woman's sleeping bag. Greta reached for the mug, felt the warmth on her hands, smelled the broth. Then she held the mug out to Hank. He drank noisily, hungrily. Yet he was careful to leave half the soup for his sister. He handed her the mug and wiped his mouth on his sleeve.

"You take care of him, don't you," the woman said, as Greta sipped warm soup from the mug. "Bet you do a good job, too. My name's Elva. This here's Wally." She pointed at the big man with the beard. "And this bag of bones is Jake."

Jake snorted, and sank farther into the folds of his sleeping bag. He took a long pull from the bottle, then passed the libation to Wally. "What the hell you kids doing out here all by yourselves?"

"What are any of us doing out here?" Wally boomed, his voice echoing in the dark recesses of the warehouse. "Trying to stay warm, dry, and fed." He tipped back the bottle and grinned at the two children across the glowing heat of the fire. "Look how skinny these little angels are. Stick with us, kids. We'll fatten you up."

Wary as she was after weeks of living on the streets, Greta was also tired. She felt exhaustion creep over her as the warmth of the soup and fire crept over her body. Already Hank was asleep, his little body burrowed into her side, like a puppy pillowed on its mother's belly.

"Look at 'em," Elva said. "Just babies. What you got in that bag, girl?"

"Clothes." Greta's tongue was getting tangled up in the word.

"Not even a sleeping bag, and winter coming on." Elva shook her head. She pulled a raggedy square of cloth that looked like a piece of an old blanket from the depths of her sleeping bag. Then she scooted forward and used it to cover Hank, fussing with the edge as she tucked it around his neck, just the way Mom used to. "Where's your folks?"

"Gone," Greta said, and the word seemed to echo around the warehouse.

Elva frowned and looked at her companions. "All alone? How long you been out here, girl?"

Greta found that she didn't have strength enough to answer. She felt all her caution fall to the onslaught of sleep.

"We can't be baby-sitting a couple of kids."

Greta's eyes were shut, but she identified the voice. It belonged to Jake, the skinny one.

"No one's asking you to look after 'em. They can go with me."

That was Elva, the woman. Greta opened her eyes just a little bit. It was morning, cold gray light filtering into the warehouse. The fire was out, cold gray ashes swirling along the concrete floor. Greta felt warm, though. The children were tucked into Elva's sleeping bag. Hank was next to Greta, curled up in a ball and still asleep.

"Just slow you down," Jake growled as he rolled up his sleeping bag. "Make you a target for the cops. They don't even look like they're yours."

"What the hell do you know?" Elva scowled at him. "All anybody's gonna see is some poor homeless woman with a couple of kids she can't feed. Which ain't far from the truth. With Christmas coming on, people feel generous and guilty. I'll just park the three of us out in front of San Francisco Centre where all those rich people ride that fancy curved escalator up to Nordstrom. You just see how many handouts I get. Take my word, these kids'll be worth their weight in greenbacks."

"More trouble than they're worth, you ask me," Jake grumbled as he tied his sleeping bag with rope.

"Nobody asked you," Elva shot back.

"Now, friends, friends. Let's not come to blows, whether with words or fists." That was Wally, the big guy with the beard. "I agree with Elva. We should care for these little angels. I'm sure we'll be handsomely rewarded. Yes, indeed."

Wally laughed. He was pretending to be nice, Greta decided, but he wasn't. She didn't like the way his eyes glittered when he looked at her and Hank. She abandoned all pretense of sleep and sat up. The nylon bag was no longer beside her, but next to Elva, who had rummaged through its contents. Greta snatched up the picture of Mom and hugged the frame to her chest.

"That your mama?" Elva asked. "She was real pretty." The woman reached over and shook Hank awake. "Let's put another layer of clothes on you, 'cause it's cold out there this morning."

The three grown-ups stashed their sleeping bags in a small room in the bowels of the abandoned warehouse and set out with the two children. In the bleak daylight the south of Market neighborhood didn't look as scary as it had last night, just dirty and down at the heels.

Jake set off on his own, heading up Mission Street, but Wally stayed with Elva and the children until they reached Market. Then he bid them an elaborate and flowery farewell, lingering until Elva told him to get the hell on with it. He bowed, crossed the street, and headed for the Tenderloin.

Then Elva took Hank and Greta another block down Market and did just what she'd said she'd do. She took a position in front of the San Francisco Centre and started cadging handouts from well-heeled shoppers. Soon she had enough money to send the children across Market to the fast-food burger place. Hank ate two cheeseburgers and a big order of French fries all by himself.

"I like Elva," he declared, wiping ketchup from his mouth.

He doesn't know things the way I do, Greta thought. He's just a baby, not experienced, like me. I'm not so sure but what we're better off on our own.

She brooded as she finished her hamburger. Then she cleared off the table and stepped up to the counter to buy another one, for Elva.

But even if Greta had her doubts about staying with the trio from the warehouse, it was easy to slip into the routine, the next day and the day after. They worked the streets with Elva during the day, going from store to store, hotel to hotel, then met Jake and Wally back at the warehouse. Wally found a sleeping bag for the two children to share, and each day the three grown-ups managed to find enough food to put into the kettle. It was so easy to feel comfortable and safe, huddled in the warm circle of the fire on the warehouse's concrete floor. In the morning they'd roll up their sleeping bags and stash their gear in the little room, then head out for a day on the streets.

The two children had been staying at the warehouse for a couple of weeks when Greta saw Wally talking with the tall man from the Tenderloin, the pimp who had all those hookers working for him. She and Hank and Elva were working the Geary Theatre that day. It was a natural, Elva told them. Theater patrons left the comfortable confines where they'd seen a seasonal matinee of *A Christmas Carol*, and stepped onto the dirty city streets and came face-to-face with a couple of contemporary urchins.

"Guilt and generosity," Elva said confidently. "It'll do it every time."

After the matinee Elva led them down Taylor toward Market Street, through the Tenderloin, where Greta saw Wally. He spotted the children and waved. Why was Wally talking to that awful pimp man? Why did Wally's eyes glitter like that, above his white beard? She didn't like it. Especially since Wally came back to the warehouse that night with a big bottle of brandy, evidently the kind Jake and Elva liked a lot, because they drank the whole bottle that night, laughing loudly and acting silly, so drunk they finally passed out and Greta had to finish making dinner under Wally's watchful eyes.

When she woke up the next morning, her head pillowed on the nylon bag, Jake and Elva were still asleep, a couple of lumps in their sleeping bags, snoring like they were sawing logs.

But Wally was gone. So was Hank.

Greta kicked her way out of the sleeping bag and put on her shoes. "Hank?" she called. There was no answer. She darted around the bottom floor of the warehouse, looking for her brother, getting more frantic as she looked in all the shadowy places.

On her third circuit she encountered Wally, who was making his way back into the warehouse with a bag and a large container that smelled like coffee. "What's the matter, little angel?" he asked jovially.

"Hank's gone," she cried.

"I'm sure he's just wandered off." Wally waggled the bag at her. "Doughnuts, little angel. Jelly doughnuts and chocolate bars. I know you like chocolate. Want one?"

"He wouldn't wander off," Greta said stubbornly. "He knows he's supposed to stick close to me."

Greta ran back to where Jake and Elva still lay snoring. She shook Elva, but the woman wouldn't wake up.

"Oh, I wouldn't bother," Wally said, placing a heavy hand on her shoulder. "When those two get a snootful of brandy it would take an earthquake to wake them. Maybe two earthquakes. Have a doughnut. We want to fatten you up."

Fatten me up for what? Greta glared at him. "I don't want a doughnut. I have to look for Hank."

"Have you looked on the second floor? Maybe he went exploring up there."

"How would he get there?" Greta knew there was another floor above this one but she hadn't seen any stairs or an elevator, not that an elevator would work in this place.

"Why, there's some stairs down at the other end, next to what used to be the elevator shaft." Wally laughed and pointed into the dark bowels of the warehouse. "Wait, I'll come with you."

Greta ran ahead, frantic with worry about Hank. She found the stairs and clambered up them, calling for her brother. She heard Wally behind her, chuckling to himself as he climbed the stairs.

Hank wasn't on the second floor of the warehouse. Or if he was, he wasn't answering her. Greta felt tears prickling behind her eyes as she searched the big empty space, skirting the hole near the stairs, where Wally said there used to be an elevator.

"Why, look at this," Wally said. She looked in the direction he was pointing. There was a doorway, open, with blackness beyond. "There's rooms back there. Maybe that's where your brother's gone."

She didn't trust the bearded man, but she had to find Hank. She walked toward the doorway and peered into the dimly lit chamber, her eyes adjusting, picking out shapes. This part of the warehouse had been used as offices, about a quarter of the floor carved up into cubicles by partitions. There was a door on the far side next to a dirty window.

"Hank?" she called, her voice echoing against the walls.

Was that a voice she heard, just a whimper? Maybe he had wandered in here and gotten hurt or something. She moved into the divided-up room, heard Wally step in after her, then whirled in alarm as she heard the door shut. Wally laughed. A few seconds later this portion of the room was brightened by the circular glow from a big flashlight.

In that instant she saw Hank. He was under an old metal desk, his hands tied to one of the legs with a length of rope. He'd been crying, but he stopped when he saw Greta.

She ran to Hank and scrabbled at the rope with her fingers. It wasn't tied very well. If she had enough time, she could get it loose. But did she have enough time?

She turned and shouted at Wally. "What have you done to him?"

Wally laughed, a nasty sound. "Caught me a pair of plump little partridges, that's what. You and him both."

"What are you talking about?" Greta demanded.

"Been talking to a man. The kind of man who'll pay good money for a couple of fat little angels like you. Oh, yes. The kind that likes little boys will have a good time with your little brother. Then there's the kind that likes sweet little virgins like you."

Wally shifted the flashlight from his right hand to his left. Greta saw his right hand go into his pocket and pull out a handful of greenbacks. "This is just seed money. I get the rest when I deliver the goods, when the man comes through that fire escape door in a few minutes."

A few minutes. That's all the time she had. Wally was between her and the door. Greta squatted and tugged at the rope securing Hank's hands, her fingers working the knot. There, it was loosening. Just a little bit more, that's all she needed.

"Look at him," she cried, making her voice teary. "You got it so tight it's cutting his hands. That's why he's been crying."

Hank didn't need to be told twice. He started to wail. Greta joined in, still fumbling with the rope.

"Shut up, both of you," Wally said, shoving the money back into his pocket. "Shut up, I tell you."

Wally walked to the desk and knelt, setting the flashlight aside so he could adjust the rope. Quick as lightning, Greta scooped up the flashlight and brought it down hard on Wally's head. He bellowed and grabbed for her as he tried to get to his feet. She slithered from his grasp, then hit him again, and he went down. She hit him a third time, and he moaned. Then she turned to Hank and helped her little brother pull free of his bonds.

She seized her brother's arm and tugged him toward the door. When they reached it, she jerked it open and they ran for the stairwell. Hank had just reached the top step when Greta was caught from behind. Wally was cursing in her ear as he lifted her off the floor. She wriggled in his arms, almost gagging at the smell of him, and sank her teeth into one of the hands that held her. He screamed as she tasted blood. He dropped her.

She regained her balance and turned to face him as he

came at her again, aiming her fist at the crotch of his baggy pants, at the place Mom said it would hurt if you hit a man. He screamed again when she hit him, falling backward. But he didn't fall onto the floor. He kept going back, and down, into the open elevator shaft.

"He went splat," Hank said when she found him at the bottom of the stairwell.

"Good. I hope he broke his damn neck."

Greta looked dispassionately at the motionless body lying on top of the rusted metal at the bottom of the elevator shaft, about three feet below the first floor of the warehouse. Blood trickled from his mouth. When he didn't move, she climbed down and reached into his pocket, pulling out the folding money he'd been showing off. He wouldn't be needing it anymore.

Greta shoved the money into her own pocket, climbed out of the shaft, and took Hank's arm. They ran through the warehouse, back to where Jake and Elva were still sleeping it off next to the gray ashes of the fire. Greta scooped up the bag of doughnuts and zipped them inside the brown nylon bag. No sense letting food go to waste.

"Where we going now?" Hank asked.

She slung the bag over her shoulder and headed for the street. "Invisible time."

# PART IV

*Desolation Angels*

# STREET COURT

BY SETH MORGAN

*Outer Mission*

(Originally published in 1990)

The state of war with the Wah Ching mandated that the Sing brothers stay constantly on the move. To find them, Joe loitered in Chinatown Park, searching out one of their minions for instructions. There, dozing behind his pulleddown porkpie hat beneath the checker pavilion's snapping pennants, the wizened pigtailed dopepeddler known only as Firecracker.

"Barkersan!" Firecracker cackled once Joe roused him from his stupor. Bright beady eyes laughed from a face like a desiccated apricot. "Doggone no see, long time."

Hastily Joe asked where Joe and Archie Sing were to be found. Firecracker knew the Barker was trusted by the brothers and issued a convoluted set of directions. Thanking him, Joe halfturned to leave, then stopped, flinging back his head and puffing his cheeks disconsolately. Releasing his breath with a curse, he turned back.

"Front me a dime of your gunpowder, Firecracker."

Surprise further wrinkled Firecracker's face. He'd never known Barkersan to use coke. But his next knowing cackle guessed Joe had a good reason for wanting it now. With a motion subtle and fluid as the T'ai Chi performed by nearby youths in martial pajamas, Firecracker swept off his porkpie hat, plucked a plastic pane of white powder from its band, and palmed Joe a quarter gram.

The vast import warehouse near the piers at the foot of Telegraph Hill was owned by one of the brothers' innumerable relatives. A loft that could be reached only through labyrinthine secret passages was on their rotation of hideouts.

"Heard you booked Rooski out of the Troll's just before the cops nailed him," said Joe Sing, the elder of the two almost identical Chinese brothers seated on futons facing Joe in the tan speckled light of bamboo blinds. Their tight facial skin was a luminous saffron not unlike the multitude of ceramic Buddhas sold below.

Joe sat crosslegged, facing them. "News travels."

"Where you got him?" Archie asked.

"Stashed at a chick's crib in the Tenderloin. She's out running credit cards, he's on a nod."

"You figured what to do with him?" Joe Sing asked.

"Book his skinny red ass as far out of Dodge as I can." Joe tipped his head. "You know the Fat Man's porno movie palace on Jones?"

"Yeah, only I thought it shut down with the rest. You know, home videos, new blue laws."

"The Kama Sutra's about the last. The Fat Man only keeps it open for the betting bank he runs out of its basement. I'm gonna rip it."

The elder Sing's obsidian stare narrowed; the Barker wasn't known for daring capers. "You taking down the Fat Man?"

Joe nodded. "Had the idea for months."

"Dangerous dude to fuck with," Archie observed.

"Not as dangerous as the cops if they get their hands on Rooski. I'm dogmeat then."

It was Joe Sing's turn to nod. "What are your drawings?"

The brothers listened with implacable half smiles as Joe outlined his plan. From below arose the sound of the engines and crashing gears of delivery trucks picking up orders. A large ceiling fan stirred the smells of sandalwood and cane, sawdust and varnish, and from somewhere frying fish.

"Right on Front Street," Joe summed up. "Blast in big as Dallas, have Rooski cover the patrons while I throw down on whatever motherfuckers are in the basement."

Joe Sing's brow arched lazily, like a cat stretching. "You're using Rooski?"

"Got to. Cant do it solo. And I need more firepower. I cant use this . . ." Joe withdrew the Browning from the back of his pants. "Rooski's been dropping things lately and I cant risk the cops tracing this through the Troll to us."

Joe Sing's eyes vanished when he laughed. "We thought you might bring along the Troll's piece to barter . . . You must have heard about . . . lunch at the Golden Boar yesterday."

Joe grinned crookedly. He'd counted on the Sing brothers giving him the ordnance used in the restaurant massacre. It was a switch they'd pulled a year earlier. The Sings had knocked off a Republican campaign office fat with cash contributions. The next day Joe and another addict used the same guns and disguises to jack an abortion clinic overstocked with painkillers. Both were alibied for the hour of the others' crime, flummoxing the cops.

Joe dry fired and shot the sliding bolt with a clang, then handed the automatic across. Archie Sing took it behind a screen and emerged with a slideaction, pistolgripped Mossberg Bullpup and a Smith & Wesson Bodyguard, a .38 favored by criminals for its trigger shroud, which prevented snagging on belts and clothing at critical moments.

"Just ditch em close to the scene." Joe Sing's eyes disappeared again.

Archie also handed Joe a paper sack. Peering in, Joe chuckled. He pulled out two rubber masks, the kind that pull down to cover the entire head. One was Ronald Reagan, complete with textured pompadour; the other Donald Duck, blue tasseled cap and all. At the sack's bottom were other essentials: plastic wrist restraints, surgical gloves and tape, extra shotgun shells, wire cutters.

"I owe you guys one," Joe said.

"No," Joe Sing said. "We owe you."

Joe gathered his booty and rose. "You guys figure you can find a party or something to go to around six or seven tonight?"

The Sing brothers nodded in unison.

"Playing against the Fat Man's a dangerous game," Joe Sing warned one last time, "and teaming with Rooski only lengthens the odds."

"Aint no long shot, it's my only shot," Joe said with a peculiar laugh. He halted halfway through the beaded curtain, smiling slyly. He reached in the paper sack and lifted out the Reagan mask like a Medusa head.

"But I'm bettin I can win just this one for the Gipper."

If Nadine Ackley had her druthers, she would have used surgical gloves to collect their money and issue tickets to the Kama Sutra's patrons. No telling where the hands slipping the bills through the cutout glass halfmoon had been. Better yet, Nadine would have preferred the ticket kiosk was fitted like a NASA lunar unit for collecting moon rocks, with robotic arms. That way she wouldn't have to worry about their icky breath either. Breath from strangely breathless mouths which also seemed always, well . . . *wet*. Her ticket booth was a shark cage, and her leaking innocence, the blood drawing the solicitors, slobberers, outright flashers, and—though it hadn't happened yet, she was certain any night—rapists.

This nippy evening a copy of *People* magazine lay open on her lap. With her customary seamless blend of outrage and astonishment, she read between ticket sales the perky paeans to people who feasted at the same groaning boards of life where she starved. From time to time she inadvertently touched the photographs as though feeling for the substance behind the designer sportswear, capped teeth, and flashbulb eyes.

She was feeling up Sylvester Stallone and scowling at the tart towering at his side and thinking as long as Rocky was going to wear elevator shoes, he should at least make sure they made him taller than his bimbos, when there came two taps on her glass. It was growing dark, and her vision was impaired by her own reflection in the glass, and at first she thought someone was furiously squeezing a tube of Finesse Creme Rinse at her, like the kind she used at home. That's what the chubby pink tube and stuff splatting the glass looked like. Only when the tube accordioned back into itself like a giant clam's head did she shriek and grab for the Mace. By then the "perp," as she'd heard TV police call them, was long gone around the corner of Jones to Turk. She replaced the Mace with a jug of 409 and roll of paper towels she kept for just such emergencies. Only she couldn't reach the drippy smear through the small halfmoon aperture. And it was so wet, so . . . *alive*.

"*Tu*-two, please." A pale freckled hand slipped through a ten.

"Help me clean up *that* n you can go in for free," Nadine pleaded, pushing back the ten along with the 409 and a wad of paper towels.

"Help her," said the second man. He stood with his back to the street wearing one of those dimestore rain ponchos. He clutched a big paper sack beneath his arm. Probably obscene ointment and such, Nadine didn't *care*. All depravity paled next to the secretion crusting her window like a squished jellyfish.

"You're so kind, sir," wheedled Nadine, "but you're only spreading it."

"Oh. Sorry." The hand fleeced with pale red hair redid the job somewhat better, although with some difficulty since its owner kept his other hand hiding his face. Nadine didn't wonder why, only why he bothered with her window smeared with that opaque . . . *shudder*.

"Thank you," she said primly and let Joe and Rooski into the Kama Sutra for services rendered.

"Ha . . . Ha . . . Ha," Fabulous Frank honked sarcastically when he saw Ronald Reagan clomping down the concrete steps to the basement office; he hummed a few bars of "Hail to the Chief": "Dum dum dee dum dum . . ."

The bookie was playing gin with Quick Cicero on the metal desk. Quick didn't seem to get the joke. His snaky pale eyes slitted; his lip shivered and curled.

"What's the matter? It's just Lou playin one of his practical jokes." Lou was the bartender down at the Silk'n'Spurs on Geary, Frank's favorite watering hole. "For a guy named Quick, sometimes you aint . . . Hey, Ronnie! What's in the paper sack? Rubber turds? Ha!"

El Fabuloso was still laughing, discarding the deuce of hearts, when the muzzle rose from beneath the poncho.

"Both of you pootbutts. On the floor." Rather than muffle Joe's voice, the latex mask acted like a diaphragm to amplify and resonate it. When the expug made a move for the open drop safe, the Gipper's likeness loudly vibrated: "NOW! Out here, side by side. Face down! And nothing sexy, I'll dust ya, I swear you'll die . . ."

Fabulous Frank had too often heard the selfhypnotic cadences of men desperate enough to kill to lose any time hugging the concrete. Yet Quick lay down slowly and carefully beside him as if worried about his goddam drycleaning bill. Trying to stall. *Now where's the percentage in that?* The gambler in Frank was real curious. He felt something plastic looping and cinching his wrists. Those nifty new disposable cuffs the cops had started using. Seemed every new wrinkle the cops came up with, the crooks turned around and used on registered Republicans like Francis Stutz.

Joe sprang to the open safe. He set the Bullpup on the desk and scooped out several buff envelopes stuffed with cash and betting slips. He didn't have to open them, he could feel they contained only a few hundred. That's why the safe was open, the runners hadn't come in yet.

*Oh shit, Rooski,* howled Joe's heart as his hand searched the safe's bottom—hardly enough cash to get you to Oakland . . . Hold the phone, what's this?

Joe withdrew a velvet pouch. He used his teeth to untie its drawstrings and shook out what resembled a big compass with a blue stone hinge. Joe held it up close to the mask's eye slit, regretting that the Gipper had always to grin, narrowing them. Christ! The hinge stone was a blue diamond bigger than Joe's left nut! Could it save Rooski? . . . No, too hot to hock, raced Joe's mind. Too big to fence. It would have to be hidden for a long time. But there wasn't any time, not with Tarzon breathing down their necks. Time for Joe to defend himself from Rooski was running out where Front Street deadended in a basement on Jones.

"Take the Moon n you're dead n stinkin, punk," Quick Cicero spit.

Ronald Reagan leaped across tromboning a round in the gun and jammed the muzzle in Quick's ear. Fabulous Frank waited for the roar, squeezed his eyes tight so flying skull shard wouldn't poke one out.

Suddenly, commotion above; Ronnie looked at the ceiling, cursed. With wrist flourishes worthy of a rodeo roper Ronnie whipped surgical tape three times around their heads and across their mouths. Then he stuffed the cash envelopes in the paper sack, replaced the diamond necklace in its velvet pouch, stuffing this inside his clothing, and snatched the Bullpup off the desk again.

The next thing heard by Fabulous Frank, Dean of the Daily Double, was the gallop of boots up the concrete steps. The lights went out, the upstairs bolt was shot, and he and Quick Cicero were left in the dark trussed up like Christmas turkeys.

The scene upstairs did what the White House never could, aged Ronald Reagan eight years. He *told* Donald Duck to just wait for him at the top of the basement stairs situated right inside the entrance. Station himself in the back by the projection booth and make sure none of the audience got wise—and *wait*. Nothing too out of place about a jackoff in a Donald Duck suit in *this* theater. When Joe finished robbing the basement bank, they could slip out unnoticed.

But *nooo*, not *this* Donald Duck. The lights were up, the movie still running—looked like the Statue of Liberty blowing a freight train. And beneath the screen it looked as if Donald had organized a summary round pound. Waving the Bodyguard, he had all eleven moviegoers ranked buck-naked before the first row of seats, clothing piled at their feet like guys at an Army physical. Except half these guys had hardons in various stages of tumescence. Nervously they shifted from foot to foot, one eye on the guntoting duck, the other fastened to the Bearded Clam That Ate San Pedro, which was being squeezed down by dirty fingernails the size of steamshovels onto a flesh-toned Washington Monument.

Ronald Reagan ran down the aisle crying, "What is this, a circle jerk?"

Some porno buff *al buffo* was just destined to ask: "Who *are* these masked men?"

"Shut the fuck up!" screamed Ronald. The comic saluted. "Yo, boss."

"Dont get mad," begged Donald. "The projectionist opened the door and asked what I was doin in this . . ." Rooski touched his duckbill.

"Pack that meat in, you cumsuckin bitch!" kibitzed the comic. It was hard not admiring her enthusiasm as, vigorously posting up and down on the monument, she began blowing a shiny black submarine, glans to gonads. The comic was flogging up a big one. Ronald had to slap the Miracle Fibre feathers on the back of Donald's head to retrieve his attention.

"Thu—that's it. Before I could get out the gun, he slammed the projection booth door and locked it. I knew we was made so I did this . . ." Donald swung the two-inch barrel at his prisoners.

"Dont point that thing at me!" one yelled.

"Sorry," Donald mumbled, dropping his bead obligingly.

"*Squish* . . . SLURP . . . *squish*," went the onscreen orifices.

"Phone! Is there a goddam phone in the booth?" cried Ronald.

"I forgot to check. I was just waitin on you to help me clean out these guys."

Ronald snatched the .38 from Donald and slapped the shotgun in his hands. He shouted at him to cover these perverts and ran back up the aisle. Behind him the Clam That Ate San Pedro was going whole hog, wedging the black sub up its companion valve. The screen filled with two pistons chugging in tandem into twin cylinders someone had the practical sense of humor to disguise as human genitalia.

Joe banged on the projection booth door with the Smithy butt and hollered, "Open up or I'll blow the lock off!"

"*I'm comin, OH GOD I'M COMIN!*" the soundtrack answered.

Christ, and that emetic soft rock endemic to department stores and airport lounges. That shlock street characters called shoplifting music. Bad enough alone, but accompanied by the stagey grunting, arty *ooomphing*, and all the other phony phonetics these method players had read some smutty where and were faithfully reproducing for the silver screen—Joe was grateful that the mask was so faithful to the Gipper's physiogomy as to reproduce his partial deafness by stopping the ears with latex.

He decided to skip shooting the doorknob. Probably only worked on TV. Just his luck, it'd ricochet and blow off his foot. He checked for telephone wires. None. Probably just an intercom to the basement.

BOOM! The shotgun blast from below stopped Joe's heart two beats. He stared aghast at the silver screen, where the two Titan missiles had withdrawn their warheads from the Great Divide and were supposed to be geysering like twin Old Faithfuls to the strains of the "Star Spangled Banner" according to Herb Albert and the Tijuana Brass—there instead gaped an enormous ragged hole ringed with smoke.

Rooski had gotten too far into the spirit of the thing and discharged at the same climactic moment.

His neglected fold bolted up the opposite aisle.

Up the ruptured screen rose the pathetic wail: "Jo-WHOA!"

No time to stop the runaway audience. And the zip damn fool just used his real name. Luckily it matched that of the mask's last user. In this instant Joe acknowledged to himself what perhaps he'd known all along he had to do. Had to do before Rooski did the same to him. *It'll hurt me more than you,* ran the old nursery con through his head.

He rushed down the aisle, grabbed Rooski, and hustled him out the fire exit giving onto an alley. There, in an abandoned Pontiac, he ditched the masks, the robbery gear, the Smithy. He wasn't breaking faith with the Sings by keeping the Bullpup. It was enough that it was seen.

In any event, it would be found with Rooski at the end.

While outside, Nadine Ackley was telling herself she always knew it would come to this. A screaming horde of bucknaked smutcrazed rapists banging on her glass ticket kiosk. She crossed herself, and with a single prayer commended her soul to the Lord's Everafter and consigned her flesh to the Devil's own Here and Now.

It was a firegutted Victorian on Treat Street, pooled with black water, where wind through the gashed roof dirged and the homeless and hunted found hospice. In the front parlor Joe shook out the paper sack into the trough of a soggy mattress. Rooski tore open the envelopes, making a paltry pile of betting slips and cash. And nary a dead president could so much as smile; they shared the same look of bemused reproof as the characters staring down at them.

"We would have done better breaking into video games," Joe announced sourly.

"No, it's enough," Rooski wanted him to believe; and began raking the bills together. They rustled like dead leaves.

"Enough for what? Coupla weeks of jailhouse canteen?"

"Cmon, Barker, dontcha *look* so blue." Quickly he counted the money. "Over five hundred. Six, if we down the trombone. Enough to blow town."

"Christ, Rooski. If it werent for bad luck we'd have none at all."

"We gotta make a little good luck of our own," Rooski remonstrated, "cantcha see?"

"Sure," Joe tried shoring up his voice with conviction. Truth was they were trapped like the rats scrabbling behind the charcoaled walls.

"Keep the faith. You always say that, Barker."

Right. Faith. You got to have a little, he always said. But faith in the sidepocket bank shot and that talk walks and money talks; faith in the sucker around each corner and the perennial next score. Not the Faith illumining mean days with grace; not the Faith brimming empty hearts with hope—that faith like a shell game had mocked Joe all his life. Though never so cruelly as now Rooski's fate was subordinated to his biological imperative to defend his own worthless breath.

Nearby mission bells tolled vespers. It was time. Ice twisted along Joe's sinews and lumped under his heart. Now he had to act. He said, "I got one of La Barba's sacks we can split."

"I'll second the fuck outta that emotion!"

Joe always went first. Fumbling and cursing over his ruined blood mains, daggering himself repeatedly. Rooski knew better than to offer help or even talk. Joe liked doing his penance right along with the sin. Taking off his Levi's, he at last struck strong blood high in his groin. With an exhalation mixing weariment and wonder, he handed the works to Rooski the way an officer might hand a blooded sword to his batman after a hard day on the killing field.

"I got it all figgered, Barker," Rooski was saying preparing his shot. "Hook a bus, hook a freight, anything making southward smoke. Sunup day after tomorrow we'll be waking up on the beach at Mazatlan. They got little boys there, Barker, for pesos . . . mere *pennies* . . . they'll catch you a fish and cook it for you right on the beach . . . What you puttin in my cooker?"

"Lil Andes candy . . ."

"I hate coke," Rooski whimpered. "I get the wrong kick." But the glitter was already melted in his heroin solution.

"I need you to fire a bombida, Rooski," Joe said softly.

"Why? With the Edison medicine, shootin speedballs makes me double crazy . . ." But he already had the point poised over a vein.

"I need you a little extra crazy."

"Why?"

"I'm goin out to steal a car to run for the border. A *nice* car, Rooski. We got that comin . . . But while I'm gone I cant have you noddin out n the police come creepin on you. If they do, you gotta hold court in the streets."

Rooski plunged the bombida into his bloodsteam. His angled frame snapped rigid, his brow sprang a halo of sweat; his eyes shot fire like sparklers. Joe asked if he'd heard what he said; Rooski nodded tightly, eyes spinning now like slot machine lemons.

"Down at city prison I seen one of the cons whose cat you got killed," Joe lied. "He said soon as you fell he'd get you. Said whether its firecamp high in the Sierras or the deepest

hole at Folsom, he was going to find you, cut out your heart
. . . and *eat* it, Rooski."

"Hold court in the streets," Rooski repeated the dire oath
with squinch-eyed resolve.

"Got to, my homey. You cant let em take you."

"You know," Rooski said, "even if they caught me I wouldnt
give you up. I'd die first. We all gotta go sometime. Why you
cryin, Barker? It's gonna be all right."

"Aint cryin, Rooski." With the hem of the dragon jacket he
wiped away tears not even heroin could staunch. "It's somethin in the air here. They must have used chemicals to put
out the fire . . ."

"That's good, cuz I dont want you worryin, aint nothin
gonna happen. No one knows we're holed here. What in hell
you doin?"

Joe was trembling so violently he jammed the Bullpup
trying to jack a fresh shell in its breech. Rooski took the
weapon, spit in the breech, and tromboned the shell home
with a clash, saying, "And I thought I was the one who could
fuck up a wetdream."

"Guess I'll be goin," Joe mumbled.

"Guess I'll just pray no police come while you out."

"That's a good idea, Rooski boy . . . So long and good
luck."

"You're all the luck I ever needed, Barker," said that ghost
about to be born.

In the blackened hallway, Joe stopped and pulled the bigass
diamond from beneath his shirt. It burned a depthless blue.
He had to hide it, but where? Its light licked the walls with
tongues of flame, blue wavey shadows reminding Joe . . . Then
he knew where to stash it. Not just in plain sight. On exhibit.

But first the call.

On the corner across the street, a booth stood empty. Its light seemed both to beckon and rebuke—*Come, none will overhear your treachery on my dark corner.* He ran to it, stepped in, and covered his mouth with his jacket sleeve. If 666 was the number of the Beast, then the number he dialed was the Judas code—911. "Gimme Homicide . . . Homicide? Take this address, 183 Treat . . . Chakov's holed there . . . He's hopped up and heavily armed and swears he wont be taken alive . . ."

Oh, that black sump pump in his breast only a doctor would call a heart. Fast, so he needn't further ponder the enormity of the betrayal—steal a car to drive to Golden Gate Park. He couldn't chance a cab. Joe wanted no one to know the watery repository he'd chosen for the diamond Quick Cicero called the Moon.

The valet parking lot attendants at Rossi's Famous Seafood Restaurant hustled hard for tips. Otherwise they wouldn't make it on the minimum wage Mr. Rossi paid. When patrons were preparing to leave, the head waiter called them at their shack at the front of the lot. That way they had the cars waiting at the curb, one hand holding the door open, the other palm up for the dollars Mr. Rossi liked to call gratuities.

Often both were absent from the shack delivering cars at the same time. That night neither saw the Porsche Carrera drive off the rear of the lot or noticed its keys missing from the shack until it was called for in the midst of dinner rush two hours later.

Joe was the day's last paid admittance to Steinhart Aquarium. The usher at the turnstile tore his blue ticket, returning him the half bearing the imprint of a leaping dolphin, and warned him the building would be closing in fifteen minutes. Joe smiled—"Long enough."

He knew the aquarium's corridors as well as the hallways of half the city's flophouses. Times like this when few visitors were around he liked best. When the teeming colors were brightest, the symmetries more fantastic, the liquescent shadows most hallucinative.

Here he was. The plaque introduced the MAKO and TIGER sharks, with a profile of each and world maps showing their ocean ranges. A brief description noted neither was dangerous to man—unless provoked. Joe looked up smiling into the flat black eye of one gray form gliding past, its flexing speckled gills recalling the bamboo blinds in the Sings' loft. Certainly whatever hand brought forth that shape was possessed of the macabre. No more perfect articulation of sudden, silent death was imaginable.

He turned his attention to the tank display. A shipwreck motif. From the Jolly Roger tangled in the helm canted in the sand, a sunken pirate craft. Beside the helm a cutlass, cannonballs, a binnacle, and belaying pin—all arranged around the centerpiece: Davey Jones's locker, an overturned treasure chest spilling its hoard of jeweled dirks and diadems, gold doubloons, and crucifixes; rubies, sapphires, pearls, and diamonds; yes, diamonds, within which galaxy the birth of one more star, a blue one even, would go unnoticed until Joe returned for it.

"We're closing, sir," a guard reminded him politely.

"Yes, I'm coming." He leaned across the railing and peered upward, spotting several gaffs hanging from hooks along the catwalk that crossed over the tank. He'd use one of them to retrieve the Moon when the time was right. He slanted both ways to make sure he wasn't being observed, then used the stolen credit card he kept in his boot to slip the lock on the door marked: NO ADMITTANCE, EMPLOYEES ONLY.

Out went the lights; the aquarium corridors became tunnels of wavery marine light. The colors of the shark tank were cobalt and coral. In a moment, a gasblue scintillance attached to a golden V fell, swinging slowly like a jeweled leaf to land near the treasure chest. The Tiger shark flinched at the puff of sand; then sculled its scythelike tail, gliding on.

"COURT'S IN SESSION!" was Rooski's last scream. The concussion of the first blast blew out the parlor's last remaining window. The second round of Double 0 exploded a door in a maelstrom of cinders. The third rocketed straight through the ceiling from where he lay in puddled black water, the .357 Magnum verdict burrowed deep in his chest.

All Joe had to do now was ditch the Porsche, then get Kitty and maybe they could get shut of this old Life. Go to Galveston, lay low until it was safe to return for the diamond; escape the cooker, crooks, and cops, who had nothing on Joe now if court was adjourned.

But he had to make sure, see for himself. He turned up Divisadero toward Twin Peaks. *You're almost home, you're almost home*, the tires whispered on the fogdamp asphalt . . . *Oh no, Rooski boy. Was it me laid you low? Me?* raved his heart. With an effort he steeled himself. It was selfdefense, pure and simple. More: it was euthanasia. Better to die a man in the streets than an animal behind walls.

He turned onto a side street and parked in its culdesac over the streetcar tunnel. He walked to the railing overlooking the tracks and leaned against a streetlamp that looked, in the swirling mist, like a giant dandelion atop a wrought iron stem. The N Judah car burst out between his legs, rattle-trapping down the cutbacks through the steep backyards, jiggling in its yellow windows like corn in a popper newspapers, crossed legs, a woman applying lipstick. Scanning the gray density of buildings, Joe spotted the house on Treat Street by the police lights. They pulsed in the fog like red amoebas.

He was just in time to see the morgue attendants lug out the stretcher. Coming down the front steps, they lifted it perpendicularly, raising the corpse, and Joe thought he saw Rooski's face splattered once, twice, three times with spinning red . . .

Then, with a suddenness snatching a cry from Joe's throat, the circular chill of steel at his neck, the familiar cold, clipped voice:

"I knew I'd find you close. A rat's never far from its hole. You found him first, saved your ass by setting his up for me to blast. You made him hold court in the streets. You better pray you wont have to pick a jury on a prison yard. Because you're going down for the car. You're penitentiary bound . . . motherfucker."

# THE NUMBERS GAME

BY CRAIG CLEVENGER

*The Sunset*

(Originally published in 2009)

Jimmy Rehab's showing a nine up against my dual eights. The high count is my green light to buck tourist strategy so I split for a hard eighteen-fifteen then stand. Jimmy's ace in the hole gives him a soft twenty which costs me another six thousand milligrams of tetracycline.

Fifteen blocks from here, young mothers push strollers through Golden Gate Park and the electro-poets sip six-dollar coffees at sidewalk tables along Irving. Keep walking west and the bright afternoon grows indecisive at 19th Ave. You hit 25th and take off your shades but can't tell the difference, the light bright enough to see by without throwing any shadows. Come 43rd, you haven't seen another soul for ten blocks and the stores are either empty or closed. The colors vanish along with the shadows, the current drains from the sunlight.

The Outer Sunset, another ghost town trailing another gold rush, the postwar housing boom following the first feeding frenzy a century prior and the dot com locusts forty years later, this is where Jimmy and I play blackjack by the light of a camping lantern, where I'll play two and a half million hands before I see sunlight again.

I'm here because of the Numbers, because this is the one place some very bad people won't know to find me. I'm here because I made a wager and I make good on my bets. I'm here because I keep my word.

Skinner Jones said that would be the death of me and he was half right.

We did a jewelry store together a couple years back. No fireworks, all business. After the dust had settled, the adjusters left the owner with a firm handshake and a fat check. Skinner moved the product, cleaned the cash and handed over my cut. Next day, I'm using the restroom at the doughnut place on Polk. One second I'm holding two bearclaws in a paper bag between my teeth while I take a leak, next thing I've got Smoke and Mirrors on either side of me.

"Johnny Pharaoh."

"Yo. Johnny."

I was shaking off the drops when Smoke slapped the bracelet on my right wrist and gave me to the count of *one* to pack everything up before he cuffed my left. He pat me down way too familiar-like while Mirrors read from his Miranda card. His fingers followed the words as he sounded them out, like he was asking directions with a phrase book.

I was drooling on the doughnut bag in my teeth when Mirrors said, "Do you understand these rights as they've been read to you?"

Yeah.

"Out loud, shithead." Smoke tapped the back of my skull so I dropped breakfast into the hot pool at my feet. Greasy white bag floating with the cigarette butts and that blue chemical puck.

"Not sure I did. Could you run 'em by me one more time?"

Smoke and Mirrors. Bad Cop, Worse Cop. Eleven hours under the light, cuffed to a chair on the business end of their bad day.

"Are those batteries fresh?" I thought the red light on the camera blinked a coupla times.

"Not sure."

"Could be. Or not."

If that camera went dark, I was gonna hit the floor hard, two or three times. All I had to say were two words, *Skinner Jones*, and I'd walk, but I didn't. Taking a job means keeping your mouth shut. Getting stabbed in the back isn't license to likewise shank a brother.

Keeping my word meant keeping quiet which meant doing a year inside, the most they could give me without Skinner.

Jimmy can't shuffle so I do it for him.

"You gonna make me deal for you this time, too?"

He doesn't answer. Jimmy Rehab's silent treatment, day fifty-five.

"You lazy fuck."

His stare is starting to unnerve me.

Jimmy's got a four up and I'm looking at a hard sixteen so I stand. His hole-card is a ten followed by another four, so I push 2,500 more milligrams of tetracycline his way and pray I don't get sick before I can win them back.

I bust three hands in a row and Jimmy doesn't say a word, his expression doesn't change.

I've lost thousands in a single sitting at some big tables and I've always had enough to cover my marker. Most of the time. I can quit any time I want, as long as it's not while I'm playing. If you're anything like me, you tell yourself you've got it under control, but you don't.

One year later I walked through the gates, but my celebration was cut short the same day. Dear Cardholder didn't place and Undisclosed Sum came strong out of the gate but finished dead last. Some old habits die hard and others not at all. That afternoon at the track dumped me twenty grand into Hoyle's pocket. Hoyle knew I was good for it because I keep my word but Hoyle didn't want to look weak. Skinner Jones and his brokering skills were the only things keeping me above the dirt. His driver had been kicked back on a parole violation so Skinner offered me a job.

"Guy blows an early release 'cause he bought his piss from Keith Richards," he said. "He's safer in Folsom."

"I hear that."

Neither one of us said anything for a moment.

"Wasn't me." Skinner slid the car keys toward me.

"Wasn't you, what?"

"The jewelry store. Wasn't me who gave you up."

So there was my chance, served up like a fancy umbrella drink. Call him on it or let it go.

"Forget about it."

"Far as this job goes, you wait and you drive." Skinner let it go faster than I had, went back to talking the job. "Shit hits the fan, Plan Q is still in locked and loaded. We're in, we're out, we hurt nobody and you're off the hook."

"And I won't see a penny of it."

"You won't have pennies over your eyes, either."

True, indeed. His ex-driver's fuck-up and my own were conjoined like circus sideshow babies, two and the same.

A good plan leaves nothing to chance, but a professional knows chance is a long-haul player. Drink enough, gamble enough, sleep around, skydive, hitchhike, or play the lottery and your luck won't run out, but it will change. Skinner and I had been at it for a long time and our luck changed.

Come 10:21 a.m. the next day, I was gunning through red lights down O'Farrell with my back windshield in pieces, my ears ringing and Jimmy Rehab riding shotgun with glass in his hair and blood on his pants. I turned up the police scanner and kept to the speed limit once I was off Lincoln.

The cityscape levels out the same time I stop seeing people, around 14th and Judah. Clapboard craftsman shacks swap rot with crumbling Victorians sandblasted by ocean wind and salt, their bright candy colors dulled to the shade of the surrounding fog. Judah's dead-end disappears along with the horizon, a blur of neither ocean nor sky. Even on a clear day it's like looking at a faded photograph, a plateau of muted roof lines tethered by utility cables at the edge of the world.

Plan Q: a two-bedroom Spanish bungalow on the outside, pure Boy Scout bomb shelter on the inside. Chemical toilet in the bathroom. Floor-to-ceiling warehouse shelving throughout the master bedroom and living room. Bottled water, canned food, foil pouches of freeze-dried field rations with Russian or German labels, two footlockers marked with red crosses, a portable television and a propane-run generator with an exhaust hose that disappeared through a hole in the back door. A briefcase of clay chips with four new card decks and enough liquor to drown the cabin fever. Skinner had shut off the utilities, boarded up the windows and in every respect ensured that a man could wait a long time inside the place. The punch line to it all was the kitchen cabinets labeled *Ralph & George*, every inch packed with tins of smoked oysters, sardines, albacore tuna and Alaskan salmon.

Skinner had a big soft spot for his cats, but they gave me the creeps. The half-Siamese named George had eyes the color of a gas flame and this unwavering, blinkless blue stare, like he could bend metal with his mind. My watch stopped if I pet him too long and I think he tripped my car alarm a couple times, knocked out the street lights when he saw me coming. The other one, Ralph, was a leaden stump of orange fur.

I never saw Ralph move from his spot on Skinner's balcony, not once, but I never saw the same pile of feathers beside him either.

Skinner Jones, secretly sentimental bastard, had planned on spoiling them when the apocalypse came while he lived on protein bars and dried noodles.

"I'm hit." Jimmy sat slumped in a folding chair. His right leg had gone dark and a wet flap of his jeans hung from his bloody thigh.

"You drip anything outside?"

"Fuck you. I'm gonna bleed to death, you don't get me to a hospital."

"You'll bleed to death if you don't relax." I rummaged through the medical trunks, found rubbing alcohol, bandages and everything from basic first aid to field surgery gear and bootleg pharmaceuticals. "Get your jeans off so I can take a look."

"I'm not letting your wannabe-doctor ass play operation on me." Jimmy stood, favoring his good leg. "Where the car keys?"

"By the door."

The dumbshit turned to look. I yanked the cap from a bottle of rubbing alcohol and splashed his wound, but good. Jimmy said *mother*, clenched his teeth and dropped back to his chair.

"If you were hurt serious, you'da bled all over my car."

"It is serious. Fucker shot me."

"Maybe. Looks like a movie bullet to me." Starting with the rip in his thigh, I sliced his jeans open while he called me a choice name or two. "Best you not struggle while my knife's this close to your nutsack."

"The fuck's a movie bullet?"

"One of those statistically mythical rounds, the kind that only hit your shoulder."

"That's my leg."

"Or the leg." I doused the wound with more alcohol and Jimmy twitched, then clamped himself still. "They never hit an artery and they never mushroom or fragment. The kind of shit that only happens to heroes in movies while people in real life drop dead."

"Or a guy drops dead 'cause the quack sewing 'im up decides to make a clever speech while his fucking blood pours down the drain."

Nothing but a few slices in his skin and a wedge of glass that dropped out of his jeans. I decided against going gently with him, poking at his leg with a pair of needle-nosed pliers as I looked for errant shards.

"The guy fired at us from behind, genius. You cut yourself on some glass. Any ideas?"

"Your windshield."

"This is from a mirror. You hit something when they chased you out of there."

"I don't remember. That sawed-off came out and I just ran. Crashed through all kinds of shit."

Once clean, I sealed the cuts with Krazy Glue then wrapped his leg with gauze. Jimmy asked for a hospital again and I said no, that we'd stay out of sight and wait for Skinner.

I cleaned my hands and listened to the police frequencies. Nobody in custody, my car last seen on Van Ness.

"Skinner take anything with him when he split?"

"Big-ass gym bag. Fucker was full, too. Way overdue for pickup," Jimmy said.

"Lotta handjobs."

"And then some. The place is a collection point."

The score was a massage parlor in the Tenderloin. Normally not the most lucrative hit, but I trusted Skinner had his reasons and I was right.

"So they count it and bag it before they kick it up the ladder," I said. "That's gotta be cash from a half dozen hand-towel lube shops."

"At least. After they cut a slice for the cops, the bagmen disappear the rest."

"I don't suppose you know which cops they're friendly with." I tore off a strip of surgical tape with my teeth and sealed his bandages.

"Same ones we all are."

My insides turned to lead. Skinner Jones had pulled a one-eighty on his own plan midway through a job, the job itself both a good score and a calculated burn aimed at the city's two most rancid cops and their double-barreled hard-on for yours truly.

"Skinner didn't fill you in?" Jimmy said.

"He told me nothing."

"Lemme guess. 'No fireworks, all business.'"

"Yeah. Something like that."

"You bein' in the dark with Skinner. I don't like it."

"I like it less."

"How come you know about this place?" Jimmy opened a can of warm PBR. The four-by-four stack of cases between the chairs could double as a card table.

"Belongs to Skinner."

Jimmy took a long pull from his beer, kept his glare fixed on me.

"Chill, Rehab. Anyone tries following the paper trail, they'll starve to death before Skinner's name turns up." I resumed tossing through the medical supplies. "He called this

*Plan Q*, his last resort if anything went thermonuclear, shit-fan wrong. He could wait out the heat, right under their noses. First time I've actually been here. Wasn't sure I'd memorized the right street number until I walked inside."

"Who else knows about it?"

"Nobody."

"You positive?"

"Of course."

"How's that?"

"I gave Skinner my word, Jimmy. You oughtta know me by now."

"I need a shower." Jimmy crushed the can and reached for another. "Wouldn't mind uncovering one of the windows. Place feels cramped."

"Nobody knows this place is occupied. Utilities are cut. We stay inside, keep the windows boarded and doors locked water tight. The full Houdini."

"What if I need some fresh air?"

"We stay inside."

"Because?"

"Because that's the plan." I found a bottle of black market tetracycline amidst the painkillers, aspirin and antihistamines. "Start taking these. Whatever it says on the label."

"I'll be fine," Jimmy said.

"Think about where you got those cuts and whether or not a little rubbing alcohol was enough to clean them."

"I don't like pills."

"You don't like pills."

"Can't swallow 'em. Unnatural."

I wasn't going to ask about his name.

"Learn to make it natural, partner, because I'll gut you in your sleep before I take you to a hospital."

We played Texas Hold'em all afternoon and ate beef stew fired over a camping stove. We kept playing cards into the night. Jimmy killed a case of PBR and I took his every last chip but Skinner never showed.

"Skinner's in the wind." Jimmy moved slowly onto the cot, lifting his leg as though it were made of glass. "I'm outta here tomorrow." He put on a set of headphones and closed his eyes.

Skinner Jones was holding my twenty grand for Hoyle. Alive or dead, anyone found Skinner would tie him to the job and then to me. Smoke and Mirrors would mount his head on their precinct wall and muscle every snitch in the city for the word on Johnny Pharaoh, every day, for the next hundred years unless Hoyle's Numbers found me first.

Nobody met Hoyle. Hoyle was a disembodied name, three degrees removed from the game but still playing the board from a distance. You did business with a guy who worked for a guy who worked for some people. Eventually, the chain of command stopped with Hoyle but nobody made it that far.

Anybody got too close or defaulted on a debt, Hoyle said to handle them by the numbers, as in normal procedure. This often required duct tape. Maybe a trunk or perhaps a body of water. It always demanded discretion and, above all, silence. Hoyle's figure of speech became a running joke among the ranks, who each in turn met with the guy's disapproval for one reason or another. When the last man breathing had forgotten the joke, the joke became rumor, then legend: The Numbers, Thing One and Thing Two. They could reckon the layout of a darkened room from the echo of a dripping tap. Thing One could freeze locks with his breath, Thing Two could walk through glass, and they could measure your sleeping heartbeat with their ears against your door.

A spider clung to the dry lip of the kitchen faucet, a drop

of black oil suspended from eight bent, black needles, its red belly mark like a symbol from a church window. In a blink, it vanished up the pipe. I stuffed a wad of newspaper into the opening and tamped it tight with my thumb.

I didn't sleep. Every itch or stray thread brushing against me in the trapped air of the crumbling house became a drop of black widow oil, poised to plant her cocoon below my skin. Her dark little beads would hatch inside my blood while I waited for Skinner Jones, while I hid from Smoke and Mirrors, Hoyle and the Numbers.


"We can't do shit here." Jimmy coughed, leaned over and hawked into a garbage pail. Two days of poker, canned food, police scanner static, network news and no Skinner Jones. I was restless and Jimmy was sick.

"Too bad. We're gonna stay."

"I need a hospital."

"They're watching the hospitals."

"They?"

"They."

Jimmy argued until a coughing fit seized him and he covered his face with a T-shirt.

"Christ. A few minutes of fresh air, for fuck's sake. There's a coffee place on Ninth, across from the Muni stop. Lemme run out, grab us a couple lattes, maybe some deli sandwiches. On me."

I knew the place. Soon as Jimmy mentioned it, I could almost hear the rumble of the train down Judah and picture the burst of greenery in the park, the shape of crashing waves.

"How long you think we could last in here?" Jimmy said.

"A long time."

"How long?"

"We'd die of boredom before we ran out of food. I'd probably kill you before that happened."

"Come on. Guess. I say six months."

"Both of us."

"Yeah. If we had to."

I surveyed the house, its fallout shelter food and black market drugs, the liquor supply, the plywood window sheets blocking out the sun and trapping in the bad air.

"Sounds about right."

"Like doing time, though." Jimmy shuffled the deck and flaunted his one-handed cut, the only card sleight he knew.

"Then I guess you've never done time."

His fingers slipped and the cards hit the table.

"Maybe I should deal."

"Maybe we should up the stakes." He gave me his idea of a bad-ass stare.

"To what?"

"Time."

I shoulda seen this coming.

"We've got a hundred and eighty days each." Jimmy reassembled the deck. "Five-day ante, two-day raise, ten-day limit."

"Won't work."

"Why not?" He shuffled.

"Suppose I win your whole six months. That mean you walk out of here?"

"Good point." He shuffled a second time. "How 'bout we play for days outside? Each day we lose is a day we stay locked in here."

"But I want to stay locked in here."

"So you can't lose."

Fuck-up though he was, I got why people hired him.

"I've seen you play, remember."

"Like I said, you can't lose." Jimmy shuffled the deck a third time and set it between us.

"Texas Hold'em."

"Draw for the high card."

"Don't bother." I cut the deck and said, "Deal."

Jimmy had been working on his game. He used to be pure shark food. He'd play loose, never check, and he'd see every bet, big or small, to keep chasing some lone longshot card for that mythical winning hand. He was playing tighter now. He checked and folded more frequently, calculating my best possible hand instead of his own.

He might take longer to get eaten, but he was still shark food. He went to sleep three weeks poorer, and the next afternoon he was down a whole month and a half when the news ran a story about another Golden Gate suicide.

"Wonder what makes this guy's high dive worth the airtime." Jimmy checked his cards and tossed a five-day chip onto his two-day ante.

Good question. Unhappy civilians outnumbered the pigeons. Jumpers hit the bay like clockwork.

". . . *won't release the identity of the man found floating* . . ."

I met his five and raised him ten. Jimmy folded and I scooped away another week of his life outside.

". . . *may be linked to several high-profile robberies throughout the Bay Area* . . ."

My vaporous suspicion condensed to certainty.

"Skinner Jones."

"How do you know?"

"One of those things." I stared at my chips, the stack of Jimmy's days together with mine.

"Least we know what happened to the man. You still wanna stay here?"

"Not now, Jimmy."

"Skinner Jones couldn't take the heat, sounds to me like. Let's get out."

"Watch your mouth, Rehab."

He hadn't heard me. He'd stuffed the balled-up shirt to his face to stifle another coughing jag, spat a heavy glob into the garbage pail, then, without warning, shoved his remaining chips into the pot.

"The fuck?"

"All or nothing," he said.

"Jimmy."

"Your homeboy's a floater. And if it wasn't an accident then they know where to find us."

"They?"

"Pharaoh, or whoever took out Skinner Jones."

"Just because you'd start singing at the first whiff of immunity—"

Jimmy hit the television with his fist. The bottle-blonde anchorwoman shattered into pixels and noise.

"You think that was a botched plea bargain? Jesus."

The anchorwoman reappeared. She flashed a smile insured for millions, moved the blank papers around on her desk and nodded at the weatherman.

"All or nothing," he said again. "You lose, I walk. You win, we both stay until provisions run out."

I couldn't figure what angle he was playing. Jimmy didn't know angles. Jimmy did the shit work for the guys who did. So, my angle was win the game and stick to the wager. Jimmy gets drunk, mopes for a day, crawls to the table to win it all back. When I have a plan and decide it's safe to leave, Jimmy's luck will improve.

"Sounds like a bet," I said.

I shuffled. Jimmy cut. I dealt two hands then the flop: ace of spades, ace of clubs and the eight of clubs. The game was Sudden Death Hold'em and we could discard and draw in lieu of each betting round. By the final draw, the six of clubs and the eight of spades were face up with the others.

I called. Jimmy showed. He held a pair of clubs, the king and the two. The odds of drawing a flush in a typical game are five hundred to one. The odds against a king high flush are greater still, and if you're Jimmy Rehab, you start writing zeros until your arms falls off. His game had indeed improved but he was still Jimmy Rehab, shark food.

"Get used to battlefield meals." I dropped my eight of diamonds onto the flop for a full house. "You try sneaking out tonight and I'll gut you."

Jimmy was pale. He stood, cracked open a beer and limped toward the bunk room.

"I'll win it all back tomorrow," he said. That calm of his, again.

First thing, I made coffee, thirty-weight black. Jimmy hadn't moved. I heard the deafening headphone hiss from his CD player eight feet away. Seven hours since he'd crashed and his eardrums were in shreds. I pulled the headphones away and like the spider darting up the dormant faucet, the smell hit my nose, rebounded off my brain and crash landed in my stomach. I'm supposed to say Jimmy, hey man, wake up, but I don't bother. His lids were slack beneath my thumb, the thin skin pliant as an empty rubber glove and his eyes had gone to frost.

I hooked my knife at the cuff of his left leg and sheared his jeans, ankle to thigh. The bandages beneath were damp with something thick and yellow. The veins in his leg had darkened with the trail of infection that had run rampant for the last three days. I dug the antibiotics from the pocket of his coat, the bottle unopened and every capsule accounted for.

I dragged Jimmy to the bathroom, cradled his neck over the toilet and emptied out his blood with a knife stroke. It sounded like the time my father dumped his aquarium but lasted longer. I dropped the carcass into the bathtub and set to tearing Skinner's place apart for the next hour, searching for tools, empty paint cans, anything.

I drew a line above Jimmy's eyebrows and cut around his skull with a hacksaw and pulled at the top of his head until it broke suction with a loud wheezing kiss. His brain held fast to his spine until I dug into both sides with a set of screwdrivers.

"You've never used this thing in your life. Give it up."

It shot loose, bouncing off the shower tile and slipping down to the drain like a lump of gray soap.

Happy Bastille Day, Jimmy.

The guts and brains Jimmy never displayed in his life lay submerged in seven different gut-buckets of paint thinner, rubbing alcohol, or vodka and sealed with duct tape.

Skinner was dead, Ralph and George weren't going to show up. The six hundred cans of gourmet meat were mine, the two hundred fifty pounds of cat litter were Jimmy's. I folded his arms funeral-style, rolled him into a sheet, and returned him to the bathtub, buried in Tidy Cats.

A week passed. I monitored the police and fire frequencies, that godless ocean of misery and chaos beyond the glittery tidepool of evening news. I heard dispatches to investigate suspicious odors but never for this neighborhood. Somebody was always decomposing somewhere else. Thing was, I knew those other addresses, each one. I knew the dead guys and they knew me, but they hadn't known where I'd end up. My word kept me alive while the Numbers kept looking.

I ate canned salmon and drank warm beer. Outside, civilians drank at the Blackthorn, ate pizza by the slice and rode the N Judah through the fog. I breathed bad air and played solitaire and single-deck blackjack, betting painkillers, germ killers, matchsticks, money or cigarettes. I wagered on the closing of the Nasdaq, the next day's weather and sports scores. I lost twenty-five tins of smoked oysters and six candy bars to the house when Foreign Object came in dead last, so I quit the ponies altogether. The civilians on Irving fell in and out of love, in and out of bars, hailed cabs and racked up parking tickets, while I mastered the dart board. I dug damp litter from the bathtub with a gardening trowel and dumped fresh litter in its place. After four fifty-pound bags, it stayed dry.

Jimmy's face could have been cut from a rotting saddle. His lips were pulled back from his teeth for a hardened, loveless smile and his eyes were windows to nothing but the hollow of his head. I don't have a single good reason for having exhumed him from his catbox coffin, though I have many bad ones. A steady diet of boredom and paranoia, spiked with bourbon and painkillers consumed in isolation, has impaired my judgment to such a degree that propping Jimmy in a chair seemed funny during the moment. I'd been wagering against an imaginary and anonymous house and now the house had a name.

I shuffled and cut. Watch and learn, Jimmy Rehab, or at least watch. You can do that much. I burned the top card and dealt the next two and turned them over for the high card. I came up with the two of hearts while Jimmy showed a queen.

"Your deal, Jimmy."

I want to believe I'm still here because of my word. The

truth is, between the law and the Numbers, I'd survive an hour above ground on a good day. I'm safe, and staying here is the only way I'll ever be certain that Skinner Jones didn't hand over a map to Plan Q before they snuffed him, which means Skinner Jones never said *Johnny Pharaoh* so he could walk away from the jewelry store.

Jimmy's expression never changes. He pulls his hands close with his fingers curled inward, clinging to a phantom noose. His fingernails keep growing and I play his hands for him.

I chase my bad run with a big bet, ten thousand milligrams to break even. Jimmy deals me a hard twenty, two kings against his six up. My luck's turning but Jimmy doesn't flinch. I split the kings for a hard twenty and a hard seventeen before I stand.

Jimmy draws a five. Jimmy draws an ace. House rules call it a soft twelve so he hits. The king breaks his winning streak and I drag twenty thousand milligrams into my bottle. My luck is changing but Jimmy Rehab doesn't say a word, doesn't blink. It's unnerving, I tell you. He stares right through me like he's been doing for weeks.

# THE WOMAN WHO LAUGHED

BY WILLIAM T. VOLLMANN

*Tenderloin*

(Originally published in 1989)

T he Zombie had a room in a residential hotel in the Tenderloin, next to a "health club," and on Sundays he sat in Boedekker Park and listened to the whores say, "Wherever *you* be going, *I* be going," and he watched the dark gray pigeons fixed like statues on the roof-ledge of the building adjoining Big Red's Bar-B-Que, while old women sat across from him, combing their hair for hours. Here he whiled away the day, tasting blood as he licked his decaying gums. (The Other did the same.)—"If you ain't got nothin' else, then '*bye*," he heard a whore say. Pigeons gurgled and chuckled and waddled fatly. A man in a black hat leaned against the lamp-post smoking, and the smoke was thick like milk. A woman in a tan coat sat bent over her knees, scuffing her tennis shoes to keep the flies away, and then suddenly raising her graying head, more or less as a jack-in-the-box will pop abruptly out of its gay metal coffin. The Zombie saw that she was weeping. Beside her sat The Woman Who Laughed.

He had found the rooming house when he cane-tapped down Turk Street past The Woman Who Laughed, and a lady on crutches was purring, "I smell *fire*," at which The Zombie swiveled his head up on his long stem of neck to see smoke coming out of one of the barred windows of a black brick building that looked old and dirty and hopeless, and there was a sign saying ROOMS AVAILABLE—LOW MONTHLY RATES, and The Woman Who Laughed came rushing up and sniffed the smoke like an animal, snorting and laughing. The hallway smelled like dead fish and never stopped humming with slow fat flies. There was a security camera in the elevator, under which some knowing soul had scrawled **RAPE BITCHES ANYHOW**. The Zombie lived on the eighth floor, a special place for special people, where the hall lights were burned out and the carpet was charred. The door to his room bore hatchet marks. Inside was a dirty sink which he used as a urinal, a three-legged bed with a greasy mattress, and a window that looked out upon a brick wall. It was very dark and still in that room. The Zombie hid in his bed and looked at the brick wall through the window. Perhaps it was this lack of a view which had impelled him to go wandering in the Blue Yonder. (Oh! Had he lived in a mansion on Russian Hill, then he never would have become The Zombie; is that what I am saying?—Not at all; I do not want to investigate causes and hypothetical has-beens; The Zombie was a *thing* without a cause.)—He did not go out much when he was The Other, either;—for more or less the same reasons that blood in a dead body soon becomes permanently incoagulable, The Other had never been a good mixer. Sometimes The Zombie woke up with a fever headache, the chills racing up and down his fingers like the arpeggios of a concert pianist, and there was a meaningless throbbing in the soft tissues of his buttocks. He lay rubbing his neck and staring up at a brown stain on the ceiling. An ammoniac smell sometimes came to his nostrils then, caustic and clean, as if he had gotten chlorinated water in his nose or sustained a sharp blow to the face. This meant that The Woman Who Laughed was sitting outside on the front steps with her dress hiked up, tapping her toes on the concrete and laughing.

She had a very round pimpled face. She might have been Indian, for her nose was flattish and she had black bangs and high cheekbones. She stank. He did not know where the clean smell came from. Her black eyes were tolerantly knowing, mocking you without malice, as if she had seen every sort of death and found it funny, but if you tried to look into her eyes she would cover herself with her arm and shake with laughter. If you tried to talk to her, she ran away. (She dreaded the warning-pangs of encounters which might poison her laughter, as Carolina had dreaded the defilement of her drinking cup, for we all want to keep something clean, no matter if it is a lump of ice dwindling in our hotly protective hands.) Once a tweed-suited radical woman came marching and smiling down Turk Street, distributing leaflets, and The Woman Who Laughed accepted one politely and read it and started to laugh so hard that her fat legs quivered, and The Zombie heard her laughter up on the eighth floor, so he went downstairs and stared at her through the bars of his golden eyelashes and held a quarter in front of her to draw her inside, and she kept laughing and reaching for the quarter as she followed him step by step, dragging her two black garbage bags behind her through the hallway, and he pulled her and her bags into the elevator in a familiar way, with his hand on her shoulder, and she laughingly suffered his touch because she *knew* him, so he suffered himself to breathe her stench all the way to the eighth floor, while the security camera emitted its death-rattle and a drop of dirty water slunk down the elevator wall, until finally the doors opened and he showed her the quarter again to impel her down the hall, so that then he could unlock his door, sweeping moldy underwear off his one chair and sitting her down on it as he lay back on his bed like a crocodile floating on the surface of some dirty brown river. There he watched her nod her head and spread her hands and wave at the air, and then as her shoulders would sag she'd shake her head and begin to laugh helplessly. She *knew* him! Her feculence aroused his disgust and anger to a degree bordering on sexual pleasure. (How could she smell so bad?) Sitting in his chair, stroking her trash bags tenderly, she unwrapped a lifesaver and ate it. She looked at the wrapping and laughed and laughed. When she laughed on Turk Street or in the brickwork park, passersby smiled slyly behind their hands, thus proving that humor is indeed contagious, especially when joy-wrapped in idiocy and stench; so she contributed some cheer to the world, although of course it was not the reward of the world's scornful merriment which elicited her good deeds; it could not be, because she kept laughing in The Zombie's room even though The Zombie did not laugh or smile or do much of anything. (All he wanted was to know why she smelled so bad, and where the other *clean* smell came from.) What made her so happy? (She smelled like rotten wharves, like tuna-canning factories, like a mass grave on a hot afternoon.) Sometimes the sweet smell of lifesavers on her breath would overpower her odor temporarily, like a soothing cherry coughdrop to put a dead woman to bed. Her hair was washed and done up in a neat mare's-tail; who could have helped her?—She laughed and pointed at the window. For the first time, The Zombie saw something there other than the brick wall next door:—Pigeons were tapping at the window with their wings; they wanted to get in. The Zombie got up and ran his fingers through his hair and opened the squeaking groaning window (he had never done that before), and The Woman Who Laughed peeked over her shoulder to make sure that no one would rob her or hurt her and then took a slice of blue-moldy bread from one of her trash bags and threw it on the floor, and the pigeons rushed down into the room jostling each other in a cloud of feathery dust, dirty-black pigeons and dirty-gray pigeons, and they crowded on the floor around the bread waddling fatly with downcast heads and pecked until all the bread was gone; then they pecked at each other, and the Woman sat there with her black trash bags clutched to her, working her mouth as the pigeons ate, and the smell from her got worse and worse. It was a sweetish rotten smell. Laughing, she opened the other bag to show him. Inside were dead pigeons, so decomposed now as to be squashed fans of feathers stuck together by slime, and flies buzzed out of the bag and landed on The Zombie's underwear and some of them whined and went greedily back inside that dark stinking bag and settled between the feathers and on the sharp black pigeon-heads and walked into the black pits where the pigeons' eyes used to be. Looking at this made the Woman very happy. Oh, how she laughed! (Was she a murderess or just a collector?) The tears rolled down her cheeks. She laughed and laughed and shook her head in smiling humorous disbelief at the ways of the world. Then she sat still for a while, resting her pimpled cheek in her hands. Heat and dust streamed in through The Zombie's window.

# ASH

BY JOHN SHIRLEY

*The Mission*

(Originally published in 1991)

A sh watched the police car pull up to the entrance of the Casa Valencia. The door to the apartment building, on the edge of San Francisco's Mission district, was almost camouflaged by the businesses around it, wedged between the stand-out orange and blue colors of the Any Kind Check Cashing Center and the San Salvador restaurant. Ash made a note on his pad, and sipped his cappuccino as a bus hulked around the corner, blocking his view through the window of the espresso shop. The cops had shown up a good thirteen minutes after he'd called in the anonymous tip on a robbery at the Casa Valencia. Which worked out good. But when it was time to pop the armored car at the Check Cashing Center next door, they might show up more briskly. Especially if a cashier hit a silent alarm.

The bus pulled away. Only a few cars passed, impatiently clogging the corner of 16th and Valencia, then dispersing; pedestrians, with clothes flapping, hurried along in tight groups, as if they were being tumbled by the moist February wind. Blown instead by eagerness to get off the streets before this twilight became dark.

A second cop cruiser arrived, pulling up just around the corner from the first one, which was double-parking with its lights flashing. By now, though, the bruise-eyed hotel manager from New Delhi or Calcutta or wherever was telling the first cop that he hadn't called anyone; it was a false alarm, probably called in by some junkie he'd evicted, just to harass him. The chunky white cop nodded in watery sympathy. The second cop, a black guy, called to the first through the window of his SFPD cruiser. Then they both split, off to Dunkin' Donuts. Ash relaxed, checking his watch. Any minute now the armored car would be showing up for the evening money drop-off. There was a run of check cashing after five o'clock.

Ash sipped the dregs of his cappuccino. He thought about the .45 in the shoebox under his bed. He needed target practice. On the slim chance he had to use the gun. The thought made his heart thud, his mouth go dry, his groin tighten. He wasn't sure if the reaction was fear or anticipation.

This, now, this was being alive. Planning a robbery, executing a robbery. Pushing back at the world. Making a dent in it, this time. For thirty-nine years his responses to the world's bullying and indifference had been measured and careful and more or less passive. He'd played the game, pretending that he didn't know the dealer was stacking the cards. He'd worked faithfully, first for Grenoble Insurance, then for Serenity Insurance, a total of seventeen years. And it had made no difference at all. When the recession came, Ash's middle management job was jettisoned like so much trash.

It shouldn't have surprised him. First at Grenoble, then at Serenity, Ash had watched helplessly as policy-holders had been summarily cut off by the insurance companies at the time of their greatest need. Every year, thousands of people with cancer, with AIDS, with accident paraplegia, cut off from the benefits they'd spent years paying for; shoved through the numerous loopholes that insurance industry lobbyists worked into the laws. That should have told him: if they'd do it to some ten-year-old kid with leukemia—and, God, they did it every damn day—they'd do it to Ash. Come the recession, bang, Ash was out on his ear with the minimum in benefits.

And the minimum flat-out wasn't enough.

Fumbling through the "casing process," Ash made a few more perfunctory notes as he waited for the armored car. His hobbyhorse reading was books about crime and the books had told him that professional criminals cased the place by taking copious notes about the surroundings. Next to Any Kind Check Cashing was Lee Zong, Hairstyling for Men and Women. Next to that, Starshine Video, owned by a Pakistani. On the Valencia side was the Casa Valencia entrance—the hotel rooms were layered above the Salvadoran restaurant, a dry cleaners, a leftist bookstore. Across the street, opposite the espresso place, was Casa Lucas Productos, a Hispanic supermarket, selling fruit and cactus pears and red bananas and plantains and beans by the fifty-pound bag. It was a hardy leftover from the days when this was an entirely Hispanic neighborhood. Now it was as much Korean and Arab and Hindu.

Two doors down from the check-cashing scam, in front of a liquor store, a black guy in a dirty, hooded sweatshirt stationed himself in front of passing pedestrians, blocking them like a linebacker to make it harder to avoid his outstretched hand.

That could be me, soon, Ash thought. I'm doing the right thing. One good hit to pay for a business franchise of some kind, something that'd do well in a recession. Maybe a movie theater. People needed to escape. Or maybe his own check-cashing business—with better security.

Ash glanced to the left, down the street, toward the entrance to the BART station: San Francisco's subway, this entrance only one short block from the check-cashing center. At five-eighteen, give or take a minute, a north-bound subway would hit the platform, pause for a moment, then zip off down the tunnel. Ash would be on it, with the money; escaping more efficiently than he could ever hope to, driving a car in city traffic. And more anonymously.

The only problem would be getting to the subway station handily. He was five-six, and pudgy, his legs a bit short, his wind even shorter. He was going to have to sprint that block and hope no one played hero. If he knew San Francisco, though, no one would.

He looked back at the check-cashing center just in time to see the Armored Transport of California truck pull up. He checked his watch: as with last week, just about five-twelve. There was a picture insignia of a knight's helmet on the side of the truck. The rest of the truck painted half black and half white, which was supposed to suggest police colors, scare thieves. Ash wouldn't be intimidated by a paint job.

He'd heard that on Monday afternoons they brought about fifteen grand into that check-cashing center. Enough for a down payment on a franchise, somewhere, once he'd laundered the money in Reno.

Now, he watched as the old, white-haired black guard, in his black and white uniform, wheezed out the back of the armored car, carrying the canvas sacks of cash. Not looking to the right or left, no one covering him. His gun strapped into its holster.

The old nitwit was as ridiculously overconfident as he was overweight, Ash thought. Probably never had any trouble. First time for everything, Uncle Remus.

He watched intently as the guard waddled into the check-cashing center. Ash checked his watch, timing the pick-up process, though he wasn't sure why he should, since he was planning to rob him on the way in, not on the way out. But he had the impression from the books that you were supposed to time everything. The reasons would come clear later.

A bony, stooped Chicano street eccentric—aging, toothless, with a squiggle of black mustache and sloppily dyed black hair—paraded up the sidewalk to stand directly in front of Ash's window. Crazy old fruit, Ash thought. A familiar figure on the street here. He was wearing a Santa Claus hat tricked out with junk jewelry, a tattered gold lamé jacket, thick mascara and eyeliner, and a rose erupting a penis crudely painted on his weathered cheek. The inevitable trash-brimmed shopping bag in one hand, in the other a cane made into a mystical staff of office with the gold-painted plastic roses duct-taped to the top end.

As usual the crazy old fuck was babbling free-form imprecations, his spittle making whiteheads on the window glass. "Damnfuckya!" came muffled through the glass. "Damnfuckya for ya abandoned city, ya abandoned city and now their gods are taking away, taking like a bend-over boy yes, damnfuckya! Yoruba Orisha! The Orisha, *cabrón!* Holy shit on a wheel! *Hijo de puta!* Ya doot, ya pay, they watch, they pray, they take like a bend-over boy ya! El-Elegba Ishu at your crossroads shithead *pendejo!* LSD not the godblood now praise the days! Damnfuckya be sorry! Orisha them Yoruba *cabrones!*"

Yoruba Orisha. Sounded familiar.

"Godfuckya Orisha sniff 'round, *vamanos! Chinga tu madre!*"

Maybe the old fruit was a Santeria loony. Santeria was the Hispanic equivalent of Yoruba, and now he was foaming at the mouth about the growth of his weird little cult's power. Or maybe he'd done too much acid in the sixties. Or both.

The Lebanese guys who ran the espresso place, trying to

fake it as a chic croissant espresso parlor, went out onto the sidewalk to chase the old shrieker away. But Ash was through here, anyway. It was time to go to the indoor range, to practice with the gun.

On the BART train heading to the East Bay, on his way to the target range, Ash let his mind wander, and his eyes followed his mind. They wandered foggily over the otherwise empty interior of the humming, shivering train car, till they focused on a page of a morning paper someone had left on a plastic seat. It was a back-section page of the *Examiner*, and it was the word *Yoruba* in a headline that focused his eyes. Lurching with the motion of the train, Ash crossed the aisle and sat down next to the paper, read the article without picking it up.

Yoruba, it said, was the growing religion of inner-city blacks—an amalgam of African and Western mysticism. Ancestor worship with African roots. Supposed to be millions of urban blacks into it now. Orisha the name of the spirits. Ishu El-Elegba was some god or other.

So the Chicano street freak had been squeaking about Yoruba out of schizzy paranoia, because the cult was spreading through the barrio. Next week he'd be warning people about some plot by the Vatican.

Ash shrugged, and the train pulled into his station.

Ash had only fired the automatic once before—and before that hadn't fired a gun since his boyhood, when he'd gone hunting with his father. He'd never hit anything in those days. He wasn't sure he could hit anything now.

But he'd been researching gun handling. So after an hour or so—his hand beginning to ache with the recoil of the gun, his head aching from the grip of the ear protectors—he found

318 // SAN FRANCISCO NOIR 2

he could fire a reasonably tight pattern into the black, man-shaped paper target at the end of the gallery. It was a thrill being here, really. The other men along the firing gallery so hawk-eyed and serious as they loaded and fired intently at their targets. The ventilators sucking up the gunsmoke. The flash of the muzzles.

He pressed the button that ran his paper target back to him on the wire that stretched the length of the range, excitement mounting as he saw he'd clustered three of the five shots into the middle two circles.

It wasn't Wild Bill Hickok, but it was good enough. It would stop a man, surely, wouldn't it, if he laid a pattern like that into his chest?

But would it be necessary? It shouldn't be. He didn't want to have to shoot the old waddler. They wouldn't look for him so hard, after the robbery, if he didn't use the gun. Chances were, he wouldn't have to shoot. The old guard would be terrified, paralyzed. Putty. Still . . .

He smiled as with the tips of his fingers he traced the fresh bullet holes in the target.


Ash was glad the week was over; relieved the waiting was nearly done. He'd begun to have second thoughts. The attrition on his nerves had been almost unbearable.

But now it was Monday again. Seven minutes after five p.m. He sat in the espresso shop, sipping, achingly and sensuously aware of the weight of the pistol in the pocket of his trench coat.

The street crazy with the gold roses on his cane was stumping along a little ways up, across the street, as if coming to meet Ash. And then the armored car pulled around the corner.

Legs rubbery, Ash made himself get up. He picked up the

empty, frameless backpack, carried it in his left hand. Went out the door, into the bash of cold wind. The traffic light was with him. He took that as a sign, and crossed with growing alacrity, one hand closing around the grip of the gun in his coat pocket. The ski mask was folded up onto his forehead like a watch cap. As he reached the corner where the fat black security guard was just getting out of the back of the armored car, he pulled the ski mask down over his face. And then he jerked the gun out.

"Give me the bag or you're dead right now!" Ash barked, just as he'd rehearsed it, leveling the gun at the old man's unmissable belly.

For a split second, as the old black guy hesitated, Ash's eyes focused on something anomalous in the guard's uniform; an African charm dangling down the front of his shirt, where a tie should be. A spirit-mask face that seemed to grimace at Ash. Then the rasping plop of the bag dropping to the sidewalk snagged his attention away, and Ash waved the gun; yelling, "Back away and drop your gun! Take it out with thumb and forefinger only!" All according to rehearsal.

The gun clanked on the sidewalk. The old man backed stumblingly away. Ash scooped up the bag, shoved it into the backpack. *Take the old guy's gun, too.* But people were yelling, across the street, for someone to call the cops, and he just wanted away. He sprinted into the street, into a tunnel of panic, hearing shouts and car horns blaring at him, the squeal of tires, but never looking around. His eyes fixed on the down-hill block that was his path to the BART station.

Somehow he was across the street without being run over, was five paces past the wooden, poster-swathed newspaper kiosk on the opposite corner, when the Chicano street crazy with the gold roses on his cane popped into his path from a doorway, shrieking, the whites showing all the way around his eyes, foam spiraling from his mouth, his whole body pirouetting, spinning like a cop car's red light. Ash bellowed something at him and waved the gun, but momentum carried him directly into the crazy fuck and they went down, one skidding atop the other, the stinking, clownishly made-up face howling two inches from his, the loon's cocked knee knocking the wind out of Ash.

He forced himself to take air and rolled aside, wrenched free, gun in one hand and backpack in the other, his heart screaming in time with the throb of approaching sirens. People yelling around him. He got to his feet, the effort making him feel like Atlas lifting the world. Then he heard a deep, black voice. "Drop 'em both or down you go, motherfucker!" And, wheezing, the fat old black guard was there, gun retrieved and shining in his hand, breath steaming from his wide nostrils, dripping sweat, eyes wild. The crazy was up, then, flailing indiscriminately, this time in the fat guard's face. The old guy's gun once more went spinning away from him.

*Now's your chance, Ash. Go.*

But his shaking hands had leveled his own gun.

Thinking: The guy's going to pick up his piece and shoot me in the back unless I gun him down.

*No he won't, he won't chance hitting passersby, just run—*

But the crazy threw himself aside and the black guard was a clear-cut target and something in Ash erupted out through his hands. The gun banged four times and the old man went down. Screams in the background. The black guard clutching his torn-up belly. One hand went to the carved African grimace hanging around his neck. His lips moved.

Ash ran. He ran into another tunnel of perception; and down the hill.

* * *

Ash was on the BART platform, and the train was pulling in. He didn't remember coming here. Where was the gun? Where was the money? The mask? Why was his mouth full of paper?

He took stock. The gun was back in his coat pocket, like a scorpion retreated into its hole. His ski mask was where it was supposed to be, too, with the canvas bag in the backpack. There was no paper in his mouth. It just felt that way, it was so dry.

The train pulled in and, for a moment, it seemed to Ash that it was *feeding* on the people in the platform by taking them into itself. Trains and buses all over the city puffing up, feeding, moving on, stopping to feed again

Strange thought. Just get on the train. He had maybe one minute before the city police would coordinate with the BART police and they'd all come clattering down here looking to shoot him.

He stepped onto the train just as the doors closed.

It took an unusually long time to get to the next station. That was his imagination; the adrenaline affecting him, he supposed. He didn't look at anyone else on the train. No one looked at him. They were all damned quiet.

He got off at the next stop. That was his plan—get out before the transit cops staked out the station. But he half expected them to be there when he got out of the train.

He felt a weight spiral away from him: no cops on the platform, or at the top of the escalator.

Next thing, go to ground and *stay*. They'd expect him to go much farther, maybe the airport.

God it was dark out. The night had come so quickly, in just the few minutes he'd spent on the train. Well, it came fast in the winter.

He didn't recognize the neighborhood. Maybe he was around Hunter's Point somewhere. It looked mostly black and Hispanic here. He'd be conspicuous. No matter, he was committed.

*You killed a man.*

Don't think about it now. Think about shelter.

He moved off down the street, scanning the signs for a cheap hotel. Had to get off the streets fast. With luck, no one would get around to telling the cops he'd ducked into the Mission Street BART station. Street people at 16th and Mission didn't confide in the cops.

It was all open-air discount stores and flyblown bar-b-cue stands and bars. The corners were clumped up, as they always were, with corner drinkers and loafers and hustlers and people on errands stopped to trade gossip with their cousins. Black guys and Hispanic guys, turning to look at Ash as he passed, never pausing in their murmur. All wearing dark glasses; it must be some kind of fad in this neighborhood to wear shades at night. It didn't make much sense. The blacks and Hispanics stood about in mixed groups, which was kind of strange. They communicated at times, especially in the drug trade, but they were usually more segregated. The streetlights seemed a cat-eye yellow here, but gave out no illumination—everything above the street level was pitch black. Below on the street it was dim and increasingly misty. A leprous mist that smudged the neon of the bars, the adult bookstores, the beer signs in the liquor stores. He stared at a beer sign as he passed. *Drink the Piss of Hope*, it said. He must have read that wrong. But farther down he read it again in another window: *Piss of Hope: The Beer that Sweetly Lies.*

Piss of Hope?

Another sign advertised Heartblood Wine Cooler.

*Heartblood,* now. It was so easy to get out of touch with things. But . . .

There was something wrong with the sunglasses people were wearing. Looking close at a black guy and a Hispanic guy standing together, he saw that their glasses weren't sunglasses, exactly. They were the miniatures of house windows, thickly painted over. Dull gray paint, dull red paint.

*Stress. It's stress, and the weird light here and what you've been through.*

He could feel them watching him. All of them. He passed a group of children playing a game. The children had no eyes; they had plucked them out, were casting the eyes, tumbling them along the sidewalk like jacks—

You're really freaked out, Ash thought. It's the shooting. It's natural. It'll pass.

The cars in the street were lit from underneath, with oily yellow light. There were no headlights. None. They didn't have headlights. Their windows were painted out. (That is *not* a pickup truck filled with dirty, stark-naked children vomiting blood.) The crowds on the edges of the sidewalk thickened. It was like a parade day; like people waiting for a procession. (The old wino sleeping in the doorway is *not* made out of dog shit.) In the window of a bar, he saw a hissing, flickering neon sign shaped like a face. A grimacing face of lurid strokes of neon, amalgamated from goat and hyena and man, a mask he'd seen before. He felt the sign's impossible warmth as he walked by.

The open door of the bar smelled like rotten meat and sour beer. Now and then, on the walls above the shop doors, rusty public address speakers, between bursts of static and feedback, gave out filtered announcements that seemed threaded together into one long harangue as he proceeded from block to block.

*"Today we have large pieces available . . . The fever calls from below to offer new bargains, discount prices . . . Prices slashed . . . slashed . . . We're slashing . . . prices are . . . from below, we offer . . ."*

A police car careened by. Ash froze till he saw it was apparently driving at random, weaving drunkenly through the street and then plowing into the crowd on the opposite side of the street, sending bodies flying. No one on Ash's side of the street more than glanced over with their painted-out eyes. The cop car only stopped crushing pedestrians when it plowed into a telephone pole and its front windows shattered, revealing cracked mannequins inside twitching and sparking.

Shooting the old guard has fucked up your head, Ash thought. Just stare at the street, look down, look away, Ash.

He pushed on. A hotel, find a hotel, a hotel. Go in somewhere, ask, get directions, get away from this street. (That is not a whore straddling a smashed man, squatting over the broken bone-end of a man's arm.) Go into this bar advertising *Lifeblood Beer* and *Finehurt Vodka*. (Christ, where did they get these brands? He'd never . . .

Inside the bar. It was a smoky room; the smoke smelled like burnt meat and tasted of iron filings on his tongue. One of those sports bars, photos on the walls of football players . . . smashing open the other players' helmets with sledgehammers. On the TV screen at the end of the bar a blurry hockey game played out. (The hockey players are *not* beating a naked woman bloody with their sticks, blood spattering their inhuman masks, no they're not.) Men and women of all colors at the bar were dead things (no they're not, it's just . . .), and they were smoking something, not drinking. They had crack pipes in their hands and they were using tiny ornate silver spoons to scoop something from the furred buckets on the bar to put in their pipes, and burn with their Bic lighters; when they inhaled, their emaciated faces puffed out: aged, sunken, wrinkled, blue-veined, disease-pocked faces that filled out, briefly healed, became healthy for a few moments, wrinkles blurring away with each hit, eyes clearing, hair darkening as each man and woman applied lighter to the pipe and sucked gray smoke. (Don't look under the bar.) Then the smokers instantly atrophied again, becoming dead, or near-dead; becoming mummies who smoked pipes, shriveled—until the next hit. The bartender was a black man with gold teeth and white-painted eyelids, wearing a sort of gold and black gown. He stood polishing a whimpering skull behind the bar, and said, "Brotherman, you looking for de hotel, it's on de corner, de Crossroads Hotel—You take a hit, too? One money, give me one money and I give you de fine—"

"No, no thanks," Ash said with rubbery lips.

His eyes adjusting so he could see under the bar, in front of the stools—there were people under the bar locked into metal braces, writhing in restraints: their heads were clamped up through holes in the bars and the furry buckets in front of each smoker were the tops of their heads, the crowns of their skulls cut away, brains exposed, gray and pink; the clamped heads were facing the bartender who fed them something that wriggled, from time to time. The smokers used their petite, glimmering spoons to scoop bits of quivering brain tissue from the living skulls and dollop the gelatinous stuff into the bowls of their pipes—basing the brains of the women and men clamped under the bars, taking a hit and filling out with strength and health for a moment. Was the man under the bar a copy of the one smoking him? Ash ran before he knew for sure.

Just get to the hotel and it'll pass, it'll pass.

Out the door and past the shops, a butcher's (those are not skinned children hanging on the hooks), and over the sidewalk which he saw now was imprinted with fossils, fossils of visages, like people pushing their faces against glass till they pressed out of shape and distorted like putty; impressions in concrete of crushed faces underfoot. The PA speakers rattling, echoing.

". . . *prices slashed and bent over sawhorses, every price and every avenue, discounts and bargains, latest in fragrant designer footwear . . .*"

Past a doorway of a boarding house—was this the place? But the door bulged outward, wood going to rubber, then the lock buckling and the door flying open to erupt people, vomiting them onto the sidewalk in a keystone cops heap, but moving only as their limbs flopped with inertia: they were dead, their eyes stamped with hunger and madness, each one clutching a shopping bag of trash, one of them the Chicano street crazy who'd tried to warn him: gold roses clamped in his teeth, he was dead now; some of them crushed into shopping carts; two of them, yes, all curled up and crushed, trash-compacted into a shopping cart so their flesh burst out through the metal gaps. Flies that spoke with the voices of radio DJs cycled over them, yammering in little buzzing parodic voices: "This Wild Bob at KMEL and hey did we tell ya about our super countdown contest, we're buzzing with it, buzzzzzz-ing wizzzz-zzzz—"

A bus at the corner. Maybe get in it and ride the hell out of the neighborhood. But the vehicle's sides were striated like a centipede and when it pulled over at the bus stop its doorway was wet, it fed on the willing people waiting there, and from its underside crushed and sticky-ochre bodies were expelled to spatter the street.

"... *one money sale, the window smoke waits. One money and inside an hour we'll find the paste that lives and chews, prices slashed, three money and we'll throw in a* ..."

He paused on the corner. There: the Crossroads Hotel. A piss-in-the-sink hotel, the sort filled with junkies and pensioned winos. Crammed in between other buildings like the Casa Valencia had been. He was afraid to go in.

Across the street: whores, with crotch-high skirts and bulging, wattled cleavages and missing limbs that waved to him with the squeezed-out, curly ends of the stumps. (It's not true that they have no feet, that their ankles are melded into the sidewalk.)

"*One money will buy you two women whose tongues can reach deeply into a garbage disposal, we also have, for two money* ..."

The whores beckoned; the crowd thickened. He went into the hotel.

A steep, narrow climb up groaning stairs to the half door where the manager waited. The hotel manager was a Hindu, and behind him were three small children with their faces covered in black cloth (the children do not have three disfigured arms apiece), gabbling in Hindi. The Hindu manager smiling broadly. Gold teeth. Identical face to the bartender but long straight hair, Hindu accent as he said: "Hello hello, you want a room, we have one vacancy, I am sorry we have no linen now, no, there are no visitors unless you pay five money extra, no visitors, no—"

"I understand, I don't care about that stuff," Ash babbled. Still carrying the backpack, he noted, taking stock of himself again. *You're okay. Hallucinating but okay. Just get into the room and work out the stress, maybe send for a bottle.*

Then he passed over all the money in his wallet and signed a paper whose print ran like ink in rainwater, and the manager led him down the hall to the room. No number on the door. Something crudely pen-knifed into the old wooden door panel: a face like an African mask, hyena and goat and man. But momentum carried him into the room—the manager didn't even use a key, just opened it—and momentum, too, closed the door behind him. Ash turned and saw that it was a bare room with a single bed and a window and a dangling naked bulb and a sink in one corner, no bathroom. Smelling of urine and mold. The light was on.

There were six people in the room.

"Shit!" Ash turned to the door, wondering where his panic had been till now. "Hey!" He opened the door and the manager came back to it, grinning at him in the hallway. "Hey, there's already people in here—"

"Yes hello yes they live with you, you know, they are the wife and daughter and grandchildren of the man you killed you know—"

"What?"

"The man you killed, you know, yes—"

"*What?*"

"Yes they are in you now at the crossroads and here are more, oh yes—" He gestured, happy as a church usher at a revival, ushering in seven more people, who crowded past Ash to throng the room, shifting aimlessly from foot to foot, gaping sightlessly, whining to themselves, bumping into one another at random. Blocking Ash, without seeming to try, every time he made for the door. Pushing him gently but relentlessly back toward the window.

The manager was no longer speaking in English, nor was he speaking in Hindi; his face was no longer a man's, but something resembling that of a hyena and a goat and a man, and he was speaking in an African tongue—Yoruba?—with a sound that was as strange to Ash as the cry of an animal on the veldt, but he knew, anyway, with a kind of *a priori* knowledge, what the man was saying. Saying . . .

That these people were those disenfranchised by the old man's death: the old armored-car guard's death meant that his wife would not be able to provide the money to help her son-in-law start that business and he goes instead into crime and then to life in prison, and his children, fatherless, slide into drugs, and lose their hope and then their lives and as a direct result they beat and abuse their own children and those children have children which *they* beat and abuse (because they, themselves, were beaten and abused) and they all grow up into psychopaths and aimless, sleepwalking automatons . . . Who shoved, now, into this room, made it more and more crushingly crowded, murmuring and whining as they elbowed Ash back to the window. There were thirty in the little room, and then forty, and then forty-five and fifty, the crowd humid with body heat and sullen and dully urgent as it crowded Ash against the window frame. He looked over his shoulder, peered through the glass. Maybe there was escape, out there.

But outside the window it was a straight drop four floors to a trash heap. It was an air shaft, an enclosed space between buildings to provide air and light for the hotel windows. Air shafts filled up with trash in places like this; bottles and paper sacks and wrappers and wet boxes and shapeless sneakers and bent syringes and mold-carpeted garbage and brittle condoms and crimped cans. The trash was thicker, deeper than in any air shaft he'd ever seen. It was a cauldron of trash, subtly seething, moving in places, wet sections of cardboard shifting, cans scuttling; bottles rattling and strips of tar paper humping up, worming; the wet, stinking motley of the air shaft weaving itself into a glutinous tapestry.

No, he couldn't go out there. But there was no space to breathe now, inside, and no way to the door; they were piling in still, all the victims of his shooting. The ones killed or maimed by the ones abandoned by the ones lost by the one he had killed. How many people now, in this room made for one, people crawling atop people, piling up so that the light was in danger of being crushed out against the ceiling?

One killing can't lead to so much misery, he thought.

*Oh but the gunshot's echoes go on and on,* the happy, mocking Ishu said. *On and on, white devil cocksucker man.*

What is this place? Ash asked, in his head. Is it Hell?

*Oh no, this is the city. Just the city. Where you have always lived. Now you can see it, merely, white demon cocksucker man. Now stay here with us, with your new family, where he called you with his dying breath . . .*

Ash couldn't bear it. The claustrophobia was of infinite weight. He turned again to the window, and looked once more into the air shaft; the trash decomposing and almost cubistically recomposed into a great garbage disposal churn, that chewed and digested itself and everything that fell into it.

The press of people pushed him against the window so that the glass creaked.

And then thirty more, from generations hence, came through the door, and pushed their way in. The window glass protested. The newcomers pushed, vaguely and sullenly, toward the window. The glass cracked—and shrieked once.

Only the glass shrieked. Ash, though, was silent, as he was heaved through the shattering glass and out the window, down into the air shaft, and into the innermost reality of the city.

# ABOUT THE CONTRIBUTORS

**AMBROSE BIERCE** (1842–1914) was a journalist and satirist who contributed to and edited a number of newspapers, including the *San Francisco News Letter,* the *Californian*, and the *Wasp*. His best-known works include the scathing collection *The Devil's Dictionary* and the short story "An Occurrence at Owl Creek Bridge," which has been adapted into film, radio broadcasts, and teleplays.

**CRAIG CLEVENGER** was born in Dallas, Texas and currently lives in San Francisco. He is the author of two novels, *The Contortionist's Handbook* and *Dermaphoria*, and is currently working on his third. He can be found at www.craigclevenger.com.

**JANET DAWSON** created Oakland, California private investigator Jeri Howard, who has sleuthed her way through nine novels. Jeri's first case, *Kindred Crimes,* won the St. Martin's Press/Private Eye Writers of America contest for Best First Private Eye Novel, and earned Shamus, Macavity, and Anthony award nominations as well. Her short story "Voice Mail," in the collection *Scam and Eggs,* won a Macavity Award. Another story, "Slayer Statute," received a Shamus Award nomination. She works at the Institute of Urban and Regional Development at the University of California, Berkeley.

**FLETCHER FLORA** (1914–1968) wrote over sixty mystery and noir stories for major crime publications such as *Alfred Hitchcock Mystery Magazine*. He also wrote sixteen novels and coauthored many more, including *Hildegarde Withers Makes the Scene*, a crime novel about the Haight-Ashbury neighborhood of San Francisco.

**ERNEST J. GAINES** was born January 15, 1933, on a plantation in Pointe Coupee Parish near New Roads, Louisiana. He is writer-in-residence emeritus at the University of Louisiana at Lafayette. In 1993 Gaines received the John D. and Catherine T. MacArthur Foundation Fellowship for his lifetime achievements. In 1996 he was named a Chevalier de l'Ordre des Arts et des Lettres, one of France's highest decorations. His novel *A Lesson Before Dying* won the 1993 National Book Critics Circle Award for fiction, one of numerous prizes that

Gaines has received. His novel *The Autobiography of Miss Jane Pittman* (1971) has become an undisputed classic of twentieth-century American literature and was adapted as the immensely popular, award-winning TV-movie starring Cicely Tyson. He and his wife live in Oscar, Louisiana.

JOE GORES, a former San Francisco–based private investigator, is the author of dozens of screenplays, television scripts, biographies, short stories, and novels, including the acclaimed DKA detective series. A Northern California resident, he has won three Edgar Awards and Japan's Maltese Falcon Award.

DASHIELL HAMMETT (1894–1961) was one of America's greatest mystery writers, the author of over eighty stories, and the namesake of several magazines. He moved to San Francisco in 1922 after marrying a nurse he met during treatments for tuberculosis. It was there that he created Sam Spade, his most popular and enduring character and star of the best-selling hardboiled classic, *The Maltese Falcon*.

DON HERRON is best known for leading the Dashiell Hammett Tour in San Francisco since 1977, giving him a long working acquaintance with the city of the 1920s and hardboiled stories pounded out for publication in the pulp magazine *Black Mask*. He is the author of various books, including *The Literary World of San Francisco & Its Environs* and *Willeford*, a survey of the life and times of cult noir author Charles Willeford.

JACK LONDON (1876–1916), a San Francisco native, is best known today for his adventure novel *The Call of the Wild* and his pro-socialist dystopia *The Iron Heel*. But during his lifetime his greatest successes were his prolific short fiction, many of which are set in the Bay Area.

PETER MARAVELIS has had a lifelong involvement in the world of arts and letters. For over twenty years, he has been a bookseller and events producer. He is currently the events director at City Lights Bookstore. He was born and raised in San Francisco, where he currently lives.

SETH MORGAN (1949–1990) published only one novel, *Homeboy* (1990), which won him high critical praise in many cities including San

Francisco, where the work is set. The novel's preoccupation with heroin addicts and convicts perhaps best captures Morgan's own troubled life of drugs and crime. He won the PEN essay contest for convicts while incarcerated for armed robbery in the mid 1970s.

MARCIA MULLER, a native of the Detroit area, has authored thirty-five novels, three of them in collaboration with her husband Bill Pronzini; seven short story collections; and numerous nonfiction articles. Together she and Pronzini have edited a dozen anthologies and a nonfiction book on the mystery genre. The Mulzinis, as friends call them, live in Sonoma County, California, in a house full of books.

FRANK NORRIS (1870–1902) was born in Chicago and moved to San Francisco at the age of fourteen. After attending Berkeley and Harvard, Norris embarked on an expansive writing career as a news correspondent in South Africa, an editorial assistant for the *San Francisco Wave*, and a war correspondent for *McClure's Magazine* during the Spanish–American War in 1898. Heavily influenced by French naturalism, Norris's most notable work, *McTeague* (1899), explores the life and trials of a dentist at the dawn of twentieth-century America in the city of San Francisco. *McTeague* has also been captured in different film versions and as an opera. His other works include *The Octopus: A Story of California* (1901) and *The Pit* (1903).

OSCAR PEÑARANDA left the Philippines at the age of twelve. He spent his adolescent years in Vancouver, Canada, and then moved to San Francisco at the age of seventeen. His stories, poems, and essays have been anthologized both nationally and internationally. He is the author of *Full Deck (Jokers Playing)*, a collection of poetry, and *Seasons by the Bay*, an award-winning story collection.

BILL PRONZINI has published seventy novels, including three in collaboration with his wife, novelist Marcia Muller, and thirty-three in his popular Nameless Detective Series. He is also the author of four nonfiction books, twenty collections of short stories, and scores of uncollected stories, articles, essays, and book reviews; additionally, he has edited and coedited numerous anthologies. His work has been translated into eighteen languages and published in nearly thirty countries. In 2008 he was named a Mystery Writers of America Grand Master, the organization's highest award. He has also received three Shamus Awards, the Lifetime Achievement Award (presented in 1987) from the Private Eye Writers of America, and six Edgar Award nominations.

**JOHN SHIRLEY** is the author of numerous novels, including *Cellars, Wetbones, City Come A-Walkin', Eclipse, A Splendid Chaos,* and, most recently, *The Other End.* He was coscreenwriter of the film *The Crow,* and his recent novel *Demons* is in development as a movie at the Weinstein Company.

**MARK TWAIN** (1835-1910), born Samuel Langhorne Clemens, is among the finest contributors to the canon of American literature. He began to gain fame when his story "The Celebrated Jumping Frog of Calaveras County" appeared in the *New York Saturday Press* in 1865. His book *The Adventures of Huckleberry Finn* (1884) is widely considered the Great American Novel. Its predecessor, *The Adventures of Tom Sawyer* (1876), is also remarkable for Twain's play with language and his attention to the innocence and imagination of childhood. Twain's literary career evolved when he headed west for San Francisco. There he continued as a journalist, began lecturing and met his wife, Olivia Langdon.

**WILLIAM T. VOLLMANN** was born in Los Angeles in 1959 and attended Deep Springs College and Cornell University. He is the author of various books, including *The Atlas* (winner of the 1997 PEN Center West Award), *You Bright and Risen Angels, The Rainbow Stories,* and a series of novels entitled *Seven Dreams: A Book of North American Landscapes.* In addition, Vollmann's works of nonfiction include *An Afghanistan Picture Show* and *Rising Up and Rising Down,* a seven-volume treatise on violence that was nominated for the National Book Critics Circle Award in 2003. His journalism and fiction have been published in the *New Yorker, Esquire, Spin, Gear,* and *Granta.* In 1999, the *New Yorker* named Vollmann "one of the twenty best writers in America under forty." His most recent work, *Riding Toward Everywhere,* was published in 2008 to great critical acclaim. He lives in California with his wife and daughter.

*Also available from the Akashic Books Noir Series*

## SAN FRANCISCO NOIR
edited by Peter Maravelis
292 pages, trade paperback original, $15.95

*Brand new stories by:* Domenic Stansberry, Barry Gifford, Eddie Muller, Robert Mailer Anderson, Michelle Tea, Peter Plate, Kate Braverman, David Corbett, Alejandro Murguía, Sin Soracco, Alvin Lu, Jon Longhi, Will Christopher Baer, Jim Nesbit, and David Henry Sterry.

"Haunting and often surprisingly poignant, these accounts of death, love, and all things pulp fiction will lead you into unexpected corners of a city known to steal people's hearts." —*7x7* magazine

## MANHATTAN NOIR 2: THE CLASSICS
edited by Lawrence Block
300 pages, trade paperback, $15.95

*Classic reprints from:* Edith Wharton, Stephen Crane, O. Henry, Langston Hughes, Irwin Shaw, Jerome Weidman, Damon Runyon, Edgar Allan Poe, Donald E. Westlake, Joyce Carol Oates, Horace Gregory, Evan Hunter, Cornell Woolrich, Geoffrey Bartholomew, Jerrold Mundis, Barry N. Malzberg, Clark Howard, Jerome Charyn, Susan Isaacs, and, yes, Lawrence Block.

This historically rich collection traces the roots of Manhattan's noir back to Edith Wharton and many others, mixing them with dark contemporary fiction from international best sellers like Joyce Carol Oates and Donald E. Westlake.

## D.C. NOIR 2: THE CLASSICS
edited by George Pelecanos
326 pages, trade paperback original, $15.95

*Classic reprints from:* Edward P. Jones, Langston Hughes, Marita Golden, Paul Laurence Dunbar, Julian Mayfield, Elizabeth Hand, Richard Wright, James Grady, Ward Just, George Pelecanos, Jean Toomer, Rhozier "Roach" Brown, Ross Thomas, Julian Mazor, Larry Neal, and Benjamin M. Schutz.

Pelecanos has established himself as one of the best writers in D.C. literary history, but here he pays tribute to the city's other chroniclers of the darkness, past and present, including Edward P. Jones, Paul Laurence Dunbar, Richard Wright, and others.

## LOS ANGELES NOIR
edited by Denise Hamilton
360 pages, trade paperback original, $15.95
*A *Los Angeles Times* best seller and winner of an Edgar Award.

*Brand new stories by:* Michael Connelly, Janet Fitch, Susan Straight, Héctor Tobar, Patt Morrison, Robert Ferrigno, Neal Pollack, Gary Phillips, Christopher Rice, Naomi Hirahara, Jim Pascoe, and others.

"Akashic is making an argument about the universality of noir; it's sort of flattering, really, and *Los Angeles Noir,* arriving at last, is a kaleidoscopic collection filled with the ethos of noir pioneers Raymond Chandler and James M. Cain."
—*Los Angeles Times Book Review*

## BROOKLYN NOIR
edited by Tim McLoughlin
350 pages, trade paperback original, $15.95
*Winner of Shamus Award, Anthony Award, Robert L. Fish Memorial Award; finalist for Edgar Award, Pushcart Prize.

*Brand new stories by:* Pete Hamill, Arthur Nersesian, Ellen Miller, Nelson George, Nicole Blackman, Sidney Offit, Ken Bruen, and others.

"*Brooklyn Noir* is such a stunningly perfect combination that you can't believe you haven't read an anthology like this before. But trust me— you haven't . . . The writing is flat-out superb, filled with lines that will sing in your head for a long time to come."
—Laura Lippman, winner of the Edgar, Agatha, and Shamus awards

## BROOKLYN NOIR 2: THE CLASSICS
edited by Tim McLoughlin
312 pages, trade paperback, $15.95

*Classic reprints from:* H.P. Lovecraft, Donald E. Westlake, Pete Hamill, Jonathan Lethem, Colson Whitehead, Carolyn Wheat, Maggie Estep, Thomas Wolfe, Hubert Selby Jr., Stanley Ellin, Salvatore La Puma, Gilbert Sorrentino, Lawrence Block, and Irwin Shaw.

"This collection of reprints is packed full of literary treats."
—*Mystery Scene*